DEATH AT THE HIGHLAND LOCH

BOOKS BY LYDIA TRAVERS

THE SCOTTISH LADIES' DETECTIVE AGENCY SERIES

The Scottish Ladies' Detective Agency
Murder in the Scottish Hills
Mystery in the Highlands
Death in a Scottish Castle

DEATH AT THE HIGHLAND LOCH

LYDIA TRAVERS

bookouture

Published by Bookouture in 2025

An imprint of Storyfire Ltd.
Carmelite House
50 Victoria Embankment
London EC4Y 0DZ

www.bookouture.com

The authorised representative in the EEA is Hachette Ireland
8 Castlecourt Centre
Dublin 15 D15 XTP3
Ireland
(email: info@hbgi.ie)

Copyright © Lydia Travers, 2025

Lydia Travers has asserted her right to be identified
as the author of this work.

All rights reserved. No part of this publication may be reproduced, stored in any retrieval system, or transmitted, in any form or by any means, electronic, mechanical, photocopying, recording or otherwise, without the prior written permission of the publishers.

ISBN: 978-1-83525-880-4
eBook ISBN: 978-1-83525-879-8

This is a work of fiction. Names, characters, businesses, organisations and events other than those clearly in the public domain, are either the product of the author's imagination or are used fictitiously. Any resemblance to actual persons, living or dead, events or locales is entirely coincidental.

To Joan
Friend and partner in crime

ONE

*Scotland,
June 1924*

The open-top Bentley hummed along the Scottish country roads under a cloudless blue sky.

In the back seat, behind her chauffeur, her hand resting lightly on the reclining black Labrador by her side, Lady Persephone Proudfoot basked in the summer-scented air. Away in the distance rose the majestic Ochil Hills, while closer the River Forth gleamed in the sunlight.

The motor car passed between the great stone gateposts of Balfour House and up the avenue, which curved to the right to reveal an elegant Georgian country house splendidly positioned on rising ground. Poppy smiled, turned her face up to the sun and felt a thrill of anticipation. A week-long country house party beckoned, and perhaps something exciting would happen.

The only fly in the ointment was the letter Poppy had received earlier that morning from a cousin, who had enquired if a friend could stay with Poppy in Edinburgh on Wednesday night. The young woman had an interview for a nurse position at the Royal Infirmary but nowhere suitable to stay. Of course Poppy had agreed, but it meant she would have to break her stay here in the beautiful historic Kingdom of Fife, ancestral home of Scottish monarchs, to return briefly to the city midway through the house party. She would also drop into Viscountess Shand's evening fundraiser.

Elspeth, Poppy's lady's maid, seated in the front next to the chauffeur and clutching Poppy's jewellery case as if her life depended on it, gave a sniff of grudging approval as the house grew closer. 'Not bad-looking – for New Money.'

Poppy smiled. 'In fact, it is delightful.'

The house was also rather different from Poppy's family seat, Dunearn Castle in Perthshire. The castle had been built in the thirteenth century as a fortified tower. Over the years, the castle had been added to by successive generations of Proudfoots and was now a six-storey granite structure with a wing either side of a central tower, battlements and roofs of various heights. There were also at least two ghosts – what self-respecting castle could not claim a ghost? – that whispered their way along the dark corridors. Assessing the house as the car drew up, Poppy felt Balfour House looked altogether a more *calm* prospect.

The motor car came to a halt at the front door. Poppy drew in a breath of the sweet-scented, lavender-blue wisteria. From the open double door stepped Lady Constance Balfour, a tall, plump and handsome dark-haired woman of middle years. She was dressed in an Edwardian costume of long linen skirt and matching jacket. In her arms she cradled a barking, tan-coloured miniature dachshund. At the sight, Poppy's Labrador leaped out of the Bentley before she could stop him.

'Major, wait!' she called to the dog. He came to a sudden halt, sat and waited, a look of polite enquiry on his face.

A footman hastened out of the house and opened the car door. Poppy alighted from the Bentley and smoothed her rose-pink silk dress, falling at this year's fashionable calf length. She adjusted the red cloche hat pulled low on her neatly bobbed brown hair, and stepped forward.

Constance made her stately way down the front steps. 'Poppy, dear, I'm so glad you could make it.' She advanced towards her and leaned forward to kiss one cheek. 'This' – she indicated the dog in her arms, who had now stopped barking – 'is Ollie.'

'How do you do, Ollie.' Poppy stroked the little dog's head.

A boy came out of the house and stood at the top of the steps. He looked to be about fourteen years old, sturdily built, and bore a striking resemblance to Constance.

'This is my son, Gregor,' she said, leading Poppy up the steps and smiling fondly at him. 'Gregor, this is Lady Persephone.'

'Poppy, please,' Poppy said. 'Persephone is such a mouthful.'

'Pleased to meet you, Lady Poppy,' the boy responded. He bent down to rub Major's ears. 'Can I take your dog for a walk?'

Poppy looked at her dog. 'Well, Major Lewis?'

'Major Lewis?' Gregor laughed. 'That's a topping name for your dog.'

'It's Major for short,' she told him.

He and Major looked hopefully at Poppy. She smiled. 'He might be four years old, but he still thinks he's a puppy. Yes, he would love a walk.'

'That's braw, thanks!' Gregor sped off, the dog running excitedly at his heels, as the chauffeur drove Elspeth and the luggage round to the back of the house.

Constance sighed. 'I'm afraid he picks up these words in the kitchen.' She slipped her free hand through Poppy's arm. 'We are quite a small party at present, but I am expecting a number of people for the midsummer garden party on Saturday.'

'Anyone I know?' Poppy asked as they mounted the wide front steps.

She had met Constance Balfour at a recent cocktail party in Edinburgh and they had got on well, despite their age difference. All she really knew of Constance was that she, like Poppy, was a widow. Poppy's husband had been killed fighting on the Western Front in 1915, while Constance's husband, a wealthy industrialist, had died a little over six months ago.

'My husband's younger brother,' Constance said, lowering her voice as they reached the front door, 'has brought a small group of friends: an American moving picture maker and two of his film stars, as I believe they are called.'

'How thrilling!' Poppy exclaimed. 'Are they making a film here?' She'd read in the newspaper that the world's first moving picture had been shot in 1888 in a garden in Yorkshire. Her eyes sparkled at the thought. 'Is it to feature your garden party?'

'Goodness, no.' Constance looked horrified. 'They are here for what Mr Emmett, the director, calls *atmosphere*. The film is to be produced in a studio in Los Angeles.'

'In a studio?' Poppy could only wonder how a Scottish country estate could be reproduced in a former desert.

As if reading her mind, Constance smiled. 'It seems that nothing is impossible nowadays.'

She addressed the butler who was hovering respectfully in the hall. 'Baird, arrange for some tea to be sent up to Lady Persephone. I'll show her ladyship to her room myself.'

Constance led Poppy through the large and airy entrance hall. Quite different, Poppy thought, from the jumble of the entrance lobby in her own Dunearn Castle, with its gumboots and antlers, umbrellas and ancient mackintoshes. Her father had inherited the earldom and its estates from his unmarried brother four years ago. The death of his brother in the Great Influenza Epidemic and the realisation that one never knew what was around the corner, had prompted Poppy's father to fulfil his lifelong dream of running his own sheep station in Australia. Her parents had immediately moved to the other side of the world and were now happily immersed in sheep, leaving Poppy the mistress of Dunearn.

'Drawing room straight ahead,' Constance said, gesturing to a pair of double doors. 'Dining room to your left and library to the right. You'll soon find your way around.'

One of the delights of a Georgian mansion, Poppy thought, was the spacious rooms laid out in a symmetrical pattern. Dunearn Castle had a large number of small, interconnecting rooms, twisting passages and spiralling staircases, confusing visitors who could find themselves lost for days.

Poppy and Constance turned towards the elegant wooden staircase with beautifully carved spindles. Constance waved a hand at a series of portraits lining the staircase as they walked. 'Late seventeenth century.' She caught Poppy's surprised look and laughed. 'They're not *our* ancestors. My husband bought them in an auction at Lyon & Turnbull. Bruce made his fortune in manufacturing mining equipment. His ennoblement is recent.' At the mention of her husband, Constance's face grew serious.

'You must miss him,' Poppy said softly.

'I do, my dear.' Constance sighed. 'But you must also miss your husband.'

Poppy glanced down at the rings on the third finger of her left hand. The wedding band was plain gold, the engagement ring an opal surrounded by diamonds.

'Our marriage was of such a short duration,' she sighed. 'Barely three months, so I never really had time to get to know Stuart.'

In her last year at the University of Glasgow, she had fallen in love with Stuart. They married in July 1915, when she was just twenty-one and newly graduated, and his life had ended that October.

'I sometimes wonder if I dreamed the whole thing,' Poppy added with a smile.

Constance reached out, squeezed her hand and gave a sympathetic smile. 'Bruce's younger brother, Nick,' she went on, changing the subject, 'insisted on the house party taking place as usual. He means well, thinking it will distract me. But the gathering will, of course, be a smaller affair this year.'

At the top of the stairs, she turned right and led Poppy to the end of the passage. 'Here we are,' she said, throwing open a panelled door.

Poppy entered and gazed around, admiring the large sash window which allowed plenty of light to fall onto the half-tester bed hung with a delicately patterned chintz. 'What a beautiful room.'

'I'll leave you to settle in.'

'Thank you, Constance.'

As Constance departed, Poppy went over to the window. The room overlooked a sunny garden with borders filled with a flurry of colourful flowers. A lush green lawn, dotted with a few great elms, swept down to where, in the distance, gleamed the waters of a loch, partially hidden by a shrubbery which grew round it. To the east lay woodland and, not far beyond that, a church tower. To the west was a tennis court, a small orchard and further away pasture land and farm buildings.

She turned away and pushed open the door in the corner of her room, which revealed – *oh joy!* – a complete set of indoor sanitation.

A soft knock on the bedroom door heralded the arrival of a housemaid, dressed in black with a white apron. She carried in a tray laden with afternoon tea things, which she placed on the table standing against the wall. 'Will there be anything else, my lady?'

'No, thank you.'

No sooner had the girl bobbed a curtsy and gone than the door opened again and Poppy's lady's maid arrived, followed by two footmen with the luggage.

'Put the trunk there,' Elspeth directed the footmen sharply. 'And mind you put it down carefully.' She pressed her thin lips together and watched them with eagle eyes.

Elspeth might be of slight build, Poppy thought removing her cloche hat, but her character was considerably more robust. Her long, sharp nose and the grey curls pinned close to her head showed she was made of sterling stuff. And at five feet five, a full three inches taller than Poppy, Elspeth made good use of those extra inches.

Poppy sat on the stool at the dressing table and sipped her tea, as her maid dismissed the footmen and started to unpack her luggage.

'Those Americans,' Elspeth began, with the familiarity of a trusted servant. She placed Poppy's jewellery case neatly on the dressing table. 'With their strange words and accents, the housekeeper tells me no one can make out a word they are saying.' She bent to open the trunk, removed Poppy's black evening dress with bold splashes of orange, shook it out and slid it onto a hanger. 'Just as well these motion pictures don't allow for speaking. Can you imagine if they did!' Elspeth continued to unpack the trunk. 'As for the clothes worn by that forward young *actress*... And not a valet or lady's maid in sight, so the household servants have to do for them.'

Poppy smiled. 'I expect we will get used to them.' She put her teacup on its saucer, opened the inlaid walnut jewellery case and idly poked her finger around the jewels nestling in the purple velvet interior.

She glanced up and caught sight of herself in the mirror. A woman – perhaps not so young at almost thirty – a little under medium height, slim, with glossy chestnut-brown bobbed hair, stared back. She tilted her head a little as she gazed into the glass. She saw candid hazel eyes, a scarlet-lipsticked mouth and a chin that some had described as determined.

Elspeth held up a purple-blue silk scarf in the reflection.

'Must you really wear this, my lady?' She frowned, her long nose twitching.

Poppy turned from the mirror. 'As a bandeau? Yes.'

Since the wonderful discovery of King Tutankhamun's tomb less than two years earlier, tying a scarf around the head with the ends hanging over one shoulder, as worn by the rulers of ancient Egypt, was the height of fashion.

'I really think, my lady, that you should send it back. It's four years since your father inherited his title, time enough for you to realise that such a garment isn't suitable for a Lady.'

'Well, I disagree, Elspeth,' Poppy told her firmly. 'We must move with the times.'

'I'm sure you know best, my lady,' said Elspeth, in a tone which suggested otherwise.

Goodness, a lady, with or without a capital L, must be allowed to wear what she chooses, Poppy thought. 'What tales from below stairs?' she asked, changing the subject.

Elspeth paused in the act of folding the scarf away in a drawer. 'Naught but gossip,' she said coldly, clearly still smarting from the business with the scarf.

Poppy waited. Elspeth liked to imply she was above such coarseness as below-stairs gossip, but she was a mine of information, which Poppy could draw from her with only a little patience.

Elspeth huffed as she closed the drawer, but she gave in. 'It seems there's no love lost between one of the footmen and the other servants.'

'Oh?'

'The footman, the good-looking young fellow who was just in here, walks Lady Balfour's dog each forenoon and afternoon.' She lowered her voice. 'The other servants see Freddy as a favourite with her ladyship, complaining that it allows him to get out of work.'

'I can see that wouldn't make him popular with the rest of the household,' Poppy agreed.

'They might not have felt so aggrieved, but he was tight with his lordship as well.' The maid opened another drawer and began to pack away Poppy's lingerie.

'I see,' said Poppy, fixing a thoughtful look on her face as if the information were an important part of a puzzle. It always made Elspeth say just a little more.

'Mrs Oakley, that's the housekeeper, told me the Americans have no breeding. Might as well have a bunch of teuchters staying for the week.'

Poppy turned back to the dressing table, head bent to riffle in her jewellery box to hide a smile. She doubted very much that the film people were unsophisticated peasants.

After two cups of tea and a number of cucumber sandwiches in her room, Poppy washed and dressed in her green country tweeds and sturdy brogues, then made her way downstairs.

Much as she looked forward to meeting the infamous Americans, she'd sought out Constance and excused herself for now because she needed to stretch her legs – and there was new territory to explore. Goodness, she thought with a laugh, I am like my Labrador. Don't they say that dog owners develop the same characteristics as their pets? Or was it the other way round?

Pondering this question, Poppy fetched her dog from the kennels next to the stables and, carrying Major's leash in one hand, strolled back along the path. Major, delighted to have two walks in one afternoon, bounded joyfully around her. At that moment, a tall young man in a footman's dark green livery came walking from the direction of the servants' door. By his side on a leash trotted Constance's miniature dachshund, its little tail wagging at the sight of a fellow canine.

This must be Freddy the favoured footman, Poppy thought, having not really taken all that much notice when he was in her room. 'Good afternoon!' she called.

'Good afternoon, my lady.'

As they drew nearer, she noted that Elspeth was right; he was indeed handsome. Tall and lean, with wavy brown hair and an intelligent, agreeable face.

'How fortunate,' she said. 'I am just about to exercise my dog and was unsure which direction to take.'

'There is a very pleasant walk by the side of the loch, my lady.' He indicated to where the smooth green lawn of the house sloped down to the expanse of glittering water.

'It looks delightful, but I thought I might walk to the village. Is it far?'

He looked doubtful. 'Culross is about a mile along the road, my lady, which you might find tiring.'

'Not at all! There's nothing I, and Major here, like better than a walk.'

'Then, my lady, if you turn left at the end of the driveway, you will be on the road that leads direct to the village.'

Poppy thanked him and strode off down the avenue. The rhododendrons which lined the driveway looked glorious with their masses of crimson blooms. Here and there were viburnums, their clusters of white flowers like spicy-scented snowballs. A blackbird sang and the afternoon sun bathed everything in a glorious gold.

'Major, heel,' she instructed, reaching the road that led towards the village, still carrying the dog's leash in one hand. With Major trotting nicely by her side, they walked for some fifteen minutes along the side of the River Forth. A couple of cars passed, and an elderly lady on a bicycle, but otherwise the warm air was quiet and Poppy breathed in the faint smell of brine from the Forth.

They reached the village. Its cobbled streets were busy with folk engaged on last-minute errands before the shops closed for the day.

There stood Culross Palace, glowing with its yellow-ochre walls and orange pantiled roof. A town hall, with a clock tower showing half past five and an impressive double staircase beneath, stood overlooking the village green on one side and the Red Lion Inn on the other.

Charmed by it all, Poppy chose a narrow lane with the intriguing name of Stinking Wynd and wandered up the cobbled hill, to where it widened into a small square. This was bordered by a few shops and several large, old houses – one of which was the old tan-house, which explained the name of the street – and in the centre of the square stood the Mercat Cross. Further up the twisting hill, she could see the ruins of an abbey and the tower of the parish kirk.

Poppy decided she'd do that walk another day. Being late to dinner on her first night would be unpardonable. She'd spotted a post office and general stores and would buy a picture postcard for her parents.

She was surprised to see further along the pavement the handsome young footman who had given her directions to the village. He looked splendid in his dark green uniform, walking in her direction with his small canine charge happily cradled in his arms. He didn't appear to have noticed Poppy.

As she advanced towards him, a middle-aged man in a dark brown tweed jacket and cap came out of the post office and almost collided with the footman. The brief exchange of words that followed didn't appear to be of the friendly kind.

Before Poppy had time to observe the two men further, Major made a break for it and darted through the open door of the butcher's shop. Too late Poppy remembered the Labrador's penchant for raw sausages. From inside came a man's angry bellow.

'*Major!*' she cried.

She dashed into the butcher's, just in time to prevent Major from snatching a link of sausages off the counter. Grabbing hold of the Labrador by his collar, she clipped on his leash. The scowl on the face of the butcher, his cheeks stained as red as the blood on his apron, said it all.

'I'm most awfully sorry,' she said.

The butcher glared. 'You need to keep your dog under control.'

'Absolutely! Frightfully sorry. Bad dog!' she admonished Major Lewis, who didn't look the slightest degree abashed. She quickly led him outside. Looking along the main street, she saw Constance's footman follow the tweed-jacketed man into the saloon bar of the inn. How mysterious.

Poppy smiled to herself. They were probably just going to settle their disagreement over a beer, and she was making something out of nothing. She'd always enjoyed puzzles; not the carefully written puzzle of the detective story, but the real life case studies that had been part of her law degree.

But she was letting her imagination run away with her. After all, at present there wasn't a puzzle to be solved.

TWO

Later that afternoon, with Elspeth fussing over her, Poppy changed into a dropped-waist evening gown in pastel blue crêpe georgette with a bow at the side, and slipped a silver bracelet in an intricate Celtic design over her slim wrist. At the appointed time of half past six, she joined the rest of the house party in the drawing room for drinks before dinner.

A gracious, elegant apartment, it had large, comfortable settees and chairs, and a finely woven silk carpet in pink and cream, the two colours echoed in the wallpaper and fabrics. Dresden vases were arranged on the mantelpiece, with bowls of flowers dotted around the room. Very tasteful, she thought, before turning her attention to the assembled guests.

An older man stood deep in conversation with a stocky young fellow with a broad jaw at the far end of the room. Short and thin, with a pair of gold-rimmed spectacles and a receding hairline, the left side of his jacket held back by a hand casually stuffed into his trouser pocket, the older man was presumably the motion picture director, Poppy thought. Both he and the younger man were dressed in classically tailored wool suits, after the style of the Prince of Wales.

Next, there was an exceedingly pretty young woman, her blonde hair fashionably Marcelled-waved. Standing beside the two men, she was taking in the splendour of the room. The young woman's heavily beaded pink cloche hat was smart, Poppy thought, but not as striking as her own bandeau in the purple-blue silk. She made a mental note to mention this later to Elspeth. She would not, however, mention to her maid that the hemline of the girl's yellow silk dress hovered scandalously close to her knees.

Constance approached Poppy, bringing with her a couple who appeared to be in their forties.

'Poppy,' she said, 'this is my brother-in-law, Nick Balfour, and his wife, Morag.'

Nick was a good-looking man with fair hair, blue eyes and a full-lipped mouth. Nature had been less kind to the bony woman by his side. Morag wore a plain silk jersey dress of the type made fashionable by the French designer Gabrielle Chanel, expensive but ill-fitting, as if it had expanded in the wash. Her greying hair was coiled into buns over her ears and was already beginning to escape from its pins.

'Nick and Morag,' went on Constance, completing the introductions, 'this is a friend of mine, Lady Poppy.'

'How d'you do, Lady Poppy,' Nick said warmly.

Morag merely nodded at Poppy. As Poppy looked at her more closely, she realised the other woman's pale eyes seemed unfocused.

The usual brief pleasantries were exchanged, then Constance led Poppy over to where the three Americans stood, each sipping a dark red cocktail garnished with a large orange peel twist.

The extremely pretty young woman with the short dress smiled at Poppy and raised her glass. 'Nothing beats some Hanky Panky, honey.'

Poppy's eyebrows rose. 'I beg your pardon?'

'A sweet gin martini. I showed Connie here how to make them.'

Constance winced at the abbreviation of her name. 'Poppy, dear, let me introduce Mr J. Franklyn Emmett, the film director' – she indicated the older man, who bowed – 'actress Miss Beth Cornett, and this is Mr Eddie Peavey—'

'Actor.' The young man stuck out his hand.

Poppy shook his hand. 'I'm Poppy Proudfoot.'

'I'm pleased to make your acquaintance, Miss Proudfoot.' He flashed her a white-toothed smile.

'It's *Lady* Poppy,' Constance corrected.

'Another real-life Lady!' Beth's smile widened. 'This country sure is full of them.'

Poppy took a sip of the red drink Constance had placed in her hand. This was a new cocktail to her and the strength of the alcohol in its spiced fruity sweetness was unmistakable. She quickly resolved not to drink too many.

Constance was returning to her brother-in-law and his wife when her son, Gregor, burst into the room and went straight over to where Poppy and the Americans stood.

'Have you been in any decent pictures, Miss Cornett?' he asked eagerly. 'I don't mean glaikit stuff about love and all that sort of thing.'

'Well, honey, I've no idea what glaikit means,' Miss Cornett said with a smile, 'but I'm sure as hell your momma wouldn't like you to see my films.'

His face dropped, then his eye lit on the cocktails. 'Can I have one of those?'

'Now then, young fella,' put in J. Franklyn Emmett, 'your mama wouldn't like you to drink a cocktail.'

'She sure as hell wouldn't.' Gregor's face brightened. 'But I would.'

His voice carried across the room and, alarmed, Constance hastened over to them. 'Gregor, darling, do mind your manners.'

The boy opened his mouth, no doubt to tell his mother where he had learned this new expression, but decided against it.

'Dinner is served, my lady,' announced the butler from the doorway.

Mr Emmett offered his arm to Constance. Behind them, in couples, the rest of the guests walked in to dinner, Gregor almost beside himself to be escorting the glamorous Miss Cornett. In the dining room, Poppy found herself seated at the large mahogany table with Nick Balfour on one side and Eddie Peavey on the other.

She eyed the guests discreetly as they all settled themselves at the table. Eddie Peavey was a good-looking but quiet young man, unsure of himself, while Nick was already proving amusing company, with Beth Cornett laughing heartily at all his comments. Morag Balfour was concentrating on pushing the Finnan haddock *au gratin* around her plate, while Constance and Mr Emmett conversed in a stilted sort of way.

'Oh, shucks!' said Beth Cornett loudly, administering a gratified slap to Gregor's arm. 'Anyone can act.'

In the soft glow of the candlelight, Poppy's eye was caught by the sparkle of a diamond and emerald bracelet, partially hidden by Beth's yellow silk sleeve. Poppy had a good idea of jewellery; the actress must make a great deal of money, she thought, to be able to afford such an exquisite piece.

'I bet no one's as good as you at acting, though,' Gregor was saying, a faint blush on his cheek.

Constance turned from Mr Emmett to address her son. 'Gregor,' she said in a low, warning voice.

'The way I figure it—' the boy began.

'Talk English!' interrupted Nick.

'I was only trying to make our American friends feel at home,' Gregor complained to his mother. 'You're always saying how important it is to set guests at ease.'

Beth burst out laughing. 'You really are the cat's whiskers!' she said affectionately.

'Do tell us about the picture you intend to make, Mr Emmett,' Poppy said with a smile, tactfully moving the conversation on.

'Well, now.' The director set down his wine glass, the candlelight reflecting off his spectacles as he spoke. 'It's about a murder—'

'A murder!' breathed Gregor.

'In *Scotland*?' said Constance faintly.

'How extraordinary,' Morag said, her pale eyes staring straight at Beth.

'Such things don't happen here, Mr Emmett.' Constance's voice was firm now.

Poppy felt that this was going to be an entertaining little party. She swiftly resolved to see one of Mr Emmett's moving pictures as soon as it came to Edinburgh.

At the breakfast table the following day, the guests all discussed what they intended to do with their morning.

Poppy, dressed in white blouse, riding breeches and jacket, and leather boots, was in the middle of explaining to Eddie that the 'skirt' he would be wearing as the laird in Mr Emmett's film was actually called a kilt, when the dining room door burst open.

Startled, everyone turned towards the white-faced footman on the threshold.

'My lady,' Freddy panted. 'There's a... a dead man by the loch!'

There was a stunned silence in the room.

'What do you mean?' said Constance.

'Good Lord!' exclaimed Poppy, hastily putting down her

coffee cup. She had wanted some excitement, but hadn't expected *this*.

'Crivvens!' said Gregor, a slice of toast halfway to his mouth.

Major pushed past the shaking footman and into the dining room, followed by the excitedly barking dachshund. The Labrador went to sit by Poppy's chair as Constance scooped up her little dog.

'What do you mean, Freddy: a dead man?' Constance repeated sternly.

The footman was visibly shaking. 'Just that, my lady. I was walking the dogs near the loch when Lady Persephone's Labrador suddenly shot forward and disappeared through the bushes. He wouldn't come when I called him, so I went to investigate and I saw the body lying there.'

Eddie stood and guided the footman to his vacated chair. The butler, in the act of pouring coffee and shocked at seeing the footman seated with the family, missed Mr Emmett's cup and the brown liquid pooled onto the polished wood surface of the table.

'You clever thing, Major,' Poppy murmured. But she'd have expected nothing less. If there was a dead body to find, Major was the dog to find it. His tail thumped the parquet floor. She bent to scratch the animal's silky ears and pat the smooth head. 'Good dog!'

'It's not a dead body but a sleeping vagabond, is my guess,' put in Nick Balfour, cutting into his eggs and bacon.

'No, sir.' Freddy had regained his breath and composure. 'The man is definitely dead—'

'You should have poked him in the ribs,' Nick went on. 'That would have woken him up.' He put a forkful of the breakfast into his mouth.

'I didn't need to, sir,' Freddy said respectfully. 'Ollie licked his face and the man didn't move. I had a closer look at him and that's when I saw his eyes were wide open.' The footman paused, then blurted, 'He's been dunted on the back of his heid.'

'Good God!' Nick exclaimed, dropping his cutlery and starting up from his chair, knocking it backwards.

'*Dunted?*' Mr Emmett frowned. 'What do you mean by that word?'

Freddy gazed around the room, now apparently enjoying being seated in the family dining room and the centre of everyone's attention. 'I mean, there's blood on the back of his head where he's been hit hard with something.'

Mr Emmett had pulled a notebook from his pocket. '*Dunted means coshed...*' he murmured as he wrote.

'He would have been hit with a blunt instrument,' Gregor said knowingly. 'I've read books where that happens.'

'But why should anyone do that?' asked Morag Balfour coolly.

Why, indeed? Poppy wondered. A flutter of expectancy immediately ran through her thoughts. Perhaps her years reading for a law degree had not been wasted and here was an opportunity to put it to some use! After all, as part of her degree she'd studied criminal law, and the law of evidence, and had helped a fellow student at the University of Glasgow trace a stolen textbook...

'Gee,' said Beth Cornett, leaning back in her chair. 'This'll be something to tell the folks back home. I just knew this would be the sort of quaint Scotch place where funny business can happen.'

'Don't worry your pretty head, Beth,' Eddie said with fervour, sticking out his manly jaw. 'I'll protect you.' He put his hand over hers on the table.

'Cheese it,' she told him, removing his hand. 'I don't need protecting.'

'A real-life murder mystery,' Mr Emmett observed with satisfaction. 'We're plumb lucky to have landed here.'

'Is the man anyone we know, Freddy?' Constance asked.

The footman shook his head. 'I don't think so, my lady.'

'That's a comfort, at least,' she said.

Poppy glanced around the room. Was no one going to take any action? She threw her napkin onto the table and got to her feet as she addressed the butler. 'Baird, please telephone for the doctor. Freddy, show me where you found the man. We should examine the situation, as the man may have simply fallen and cut his head. If it looks suspicious, we will have to notify the police.'

'The police!' Constance looked startled. She breathed in deeply through her nostrils. 'I had better come too, before that decision is made.'

Freddy reluctantly relinquished the dining chair and stood. 'This way, my ladies.' He turned and walked out of the room.

Poppy set off after him, with Constance on her heels and still carrying Ollie, followed by Major and the rest of the party.

'Isn't this swell?' Gregor said cheerfully as they hurried across the hall to catch up.

'Don't let your mother hear you use that film talk,' cautioned Nick.

Gregor sighed. 'She doesna like me to use *ony* kind of talk, Uncle Nick.'

'A real-life murder, Ed,' Beth was saying as they went out the main door. 'Can you credit it?'

With the footman leading the little group and Poppy close behind, they hastened across the lawn and down to the loch. As everyone followed the footman through a gap in the shrubbery, Poppy told Major to stay. The dog sat and gave a little whine of displeasure at being left out.

'There, my lady.' Freddy pointed to the sandy bank.

Poppy could see a shape... it looked like a pile of clothing.

She had seen dead men before, but this was different. She pushed aside the image of the vaulted great hall of Dunearn Castle, with its rows of beds and the anguished cries of the occupants – soldiers wounded during the Great War. She and the women she'd employed had done their best to nurse them, but sadly some of the men's injuries were so severe that they could not be saved. Here in this idyllic setting, where the loch sparkled in the sunlight and dragonflies hovered over the blue water, the obviously violent demise of the man lying at their feet somehow felt more obscene. She moved forward to examine the body.

The man lay sprawled on the bank, turned sideways as though asleep save for his wide-open eyes. His head rested on his flung-up right arm. A heavily built fellow, near fifty, she judged, for his hair was turning grey. He was clad in a brown tweed jacket, trousers of some serviceable fabric, Argyll-patterned socks and heavy boots. A tweed cap lay nearby, and the matted hair and blood were visible on the back of his head. Poppy felt the nausea rise in her throat. She knelt beside the body and felt his neck for a pulse. There was nothing.

'I fear Freddy is correct,' Constance murmured as she watched Poppy.

'Oh dear,' said Morag. She held a handkerchief to her nose.

'Shouldn't one of the ladies tear off a piece of their petticoat or something to bandage his head?' asked Mr Emmett, frowning.

Constance sent him a withering glance. 'To what purpose, Mr Emmett? This is not one of your moving pictures.'

'He's dead,' Poppy confirmed. She removed her fingers from the dead man's neck and closed his eyes. What should she do? *Leave everything to the police*, said one part of her brain. *But there must be something I can do to help, now that I'm here*, said the other part.

His pockets, she thought; they might at the very least

contain information as to his identity. The police would naturally be annoyed if she disturbed any evidence, but patting his pockets could surely do no harm...

'Perhaps he's had a stroke,' suggested Eddie.

'No, he hasn't, you dolt,' Beth said. 'Look at the blood on the back of his head. He's been murdered.'

'He might have had a brain attack,' Eddie persevered, 'and fallen and hit his head on a rock.'

They all scanned the surrounding area for the guilty rock.

'Then where is it?' Beth demanded.

Dash it, thought Poppy, as she patted the man's pockets; she could feel a few small items, but no obvious wallet.

On the wrist of the man's left arm was a cheap nickel watch. Carefully, not touching his wrist, she angled her head to peer at it. The glass had broken, presumably in the fall, and the hands stopped at six o'clock. Was that six yesterday afternoon, or six this morning?

She considered the ground around the body, looking for any objects that might give a clue as to what had happened. Beth was right, there was no stone, or anything that could have been used as a weapon. How perplexing! What about footprints? And now she noticed the sand around the corpse was a confused mass of shoe, boot and paw prints. *Oh dear.*

Poppy rose from her knees and looked about the scene. The sandy edge of the loch was confined to the small area where they stood. The rest of the bank as it bordered the water was grass. Where the edge curved away, she caught the glimpse of a footpath. That needed investigation.

She looked up, her gaze going beyond the gently rising lawn to where Balfour House sat in the morning sunshine. She gazed at the upper windows of the house under the flawless sky. She could see the loch and the shrubbery from her window, which meant that others with rooms on the same side of the house must have the same view.

Poppy brushed her jodhpur-clad knees. 'Doesn't *anyone* know who this man is?' she asked.

Everyone shook their heads.

She stared down at the man lying on the ground. It was difficult to be sure, but now she thought he looked vaguely familiar. Why? Her gaze travelled from the man's face down to the jacket he wore and the memory popped into her head. Surely, though, there must be any number of men with dark brown tweed jackets... She couldn't be certain – the encounter had been only brief – but he bore a very strong resemblance to the fellow who had bumped into the footman in the village yesterday afternoon. And whom Freddy had followed into the Red Lion.

Poppy looked up quickly at the footman, who was staring at the corpse, his face as pale as milk. If it was the same man, why hadn't Freddy said he knew him? But then, she had no proof that the two had actually known each other. The fact that they had entered the inn at the same time could be mere coincidence.

Regardless, here was a murdered man and there were procedures to follow. 'We need to send for the police,' she said.

'Surely there is no need,' said Nick. 'He looks so peaceful. It must have been an accident—'

'Some accident that kills a man with a dunt to the back of the head,' put in Gregor, 'and with nothing he could have bashed himself on!'

Constance now became aware of her son's presence. 'Gregor! What are you doing here? Run back to the house immediately,' she said, 'and tell Baird to telephone the police office.'

'The police!' he said with relish, his eyes round. 'Sure thing!' The boy shot off towards the house, his cardigan open and flapping.

'And fasten your cardigan!' she called crossly after him.

He took no notice but sped across the lawn to the house.

'Constance,' Poppy said, 'I suggest that we all go back inside. I'm afraid we've already muddled the evidence around the body.'

Constance nodded her agreement, as the gathering looked at the myriad of prints.

'Apart from Freddy.' Poppy turned to address the footman. She waited for him to look at her, but he kept his eyes averted. 'Stay here and look after – oh, that's not really the right term – but take care that no further harm comes to the poor fellow. Nothing else must be disturbed before the police arrive.'

Poppy called for Major to follow her as the rest of the little party retraced their steps across the lawn, shocked into silence or murmuring quietly to one another.

She glanced back once to see the footman standing by the body and smoking a cigarette. Even if he did know the fellow, she reasoned, surely it couldn't do any harm to leave Freddy with him? After all, he'd already been alone with the body. If he had wanted to tamper with the evidence, he'd already had the opportunity to do so.

Yet the footman clearly had *something* to hide. Poppy tried to keep an open mind – but Freddy had to be a key suspect.

THREE

Back at the house, everyone gathered again in the drawing room, talking in low, tense voices.

Constance, Morag and Beth were seated in armchairs, while the gentlemen stood at the opposite end of the room and smoked. Poppy stood by the hearth, considering the matter of the view from the house. It would be easy enough to establish whose bedrooms faced the loch, although if the occupants state they saw nothing – as she hadn't – that wouldn't provide any answers.

The next thing she had to consider was exactly where the man was murdered. Had he been killed there or moved to that spot afterwards? She should have examined the grassy bank of the water for possible signs of the body having been dragged there.

Gregor, kneeling on the window seat and staring out of the window, suddenly cried, 'They're here! Two of them, in a two-seater Chummy. The one in plain clothes might be a detective!' He scrambled off the seat and the room fell silent.

The guests glanced at each other, before turning their attention towards the door.

A few minutes later, there was the sound of approaching footsteps. Ollie rose from his basket and started to bark. Constance hushed the little dog, as the door opened and Baird brought in the two men.

The butler cleared his throat. 'The *police*, my lady,' he said to Lady Balfour, with a note of distaste. 'Inspector MacKenzie from Edinburgh's Detective Branch,' he said, before discreetly withdrawing.

From her position by the fireplace, Poppy looked at the inspector with interest. He was almost how she expected a police inspector to look: tall and with coal-black curls, large and splendidly proportioned. He was perhaps in his mid-thirties, and was wearing a belted mackintosh and holding a fedora at his side. *Almost* as she expected one to look. She certainly hadn't imagined those bold, black eyes and long eyelashes, or the sullen sensuality of his mouth.

The sensual mouth opened. 'Good morning, Lady Balfour,' the inspector said in the melodious voice of a man from the Western Isles. 'This is Constable Watt.' He gestured towards the uniformed officer beside him, his cap tucked under one arm. The young man, fair-haired and with a rosy face, smiled at them.

'You came all the way from Edinburgh?' Constance rose from her chair and addressed the inspector. 'Then you have arrived in record time.'

'I did not come direct from Edinburgh. It is fortunate that I happened to be visiting a friend not too far away,' Inspector MacKenzie told her in a soft, solemn voice. 'Constable Watt is from the local police office and requested my presence.'

'I'm relieved to see you both here, gentlemen,' went on Constance. 'You know what has happened, of course, Inspector?'

'Yes, my lady. The details were conveyed to the police office by your butler.'

'Such a terrible thing to have happened.' Constance fingered the gold locket at her throat. 'One hardly knows what to do...'

Gregor was gazing with admiration at the inspector. 'Have you got a gun?' he suddenly asked.

Inspector MacKenzie looked down at the boy from under his heavy lids. 'Not on me, young sir.'

'Gregor, don't plague the inspector,' hushed Constance.

'I'm nae *plaguing* him,' muttered the boy, throwing himself into a chair. 'I bet if he were an *American* cop, he'd have a shooter.'

'You must forgive my son, Inspector,' Constance went on. 'He's rather taken with American novels and moving pictures. I suppose I'd better show you where the body is.' She faltered. 'Oh dear, I don't know if I can bear to see the poor man again.'

Aha, here was her opportunity to be involved in the case! Poppy stepped forward. 'I can take them, Constance.'

Inspector MacKenzie's gaze landed on her, his dark eyes intense. He was a man not to be trifled with, she thought, but he did not intimidate *her*. She met his look boldly.

'Would you mind, my dear?' Constance said.

Poppy turned back towards her. 'Not at all.'

Gregor leaped up. 'I'll come too.'

'You will stay here,' Constance said in a firm voice.

Gregor dropped back disconsolately into the armchair.

'I'll take the officer, Constance,' Nick Balfour said, stubbing out his cigarette. 'It's not a suitable job for a lady.'

'You seem to have forgotten that it was I who examined the man's wound and closed his eyes less than an hour ago, Mr Balfour,' Poppy told him. 'I'm sorry to say I'm very well acquainted with death, from when I nursed wounded and dying soldiers under the roof of my home during the war.'

Nick shot her a surprised look. Had Constance told him, Poppy wondered, that her own husband had died nine years ago in France, leaving her a young widow? After that tragic event, she'd had no difficulty persuading her parents to volunteer part of Dunearn Castle as a hospital.

'The body has not been touched?' the inspector asked, gazing around the room.

Poppy decided to interpret his question literally. Patting the man's pockets was not *actually* touching the body, she reasoned. She shook her head.

'No, *sir*,' Mr Emmett said. 'I know the rules.'

'Oh?' Inspector MacKenzie was instantly alert. 'You're a police officer in America?'

Mr Emmett beamed. 'I direct the cops.'

The inspector frowned. 'You work for some sort of detective agency?'

Beth laughed. 'He makes *moving pictures* of them, honey.'

The inspector drew back sharply. Poppy smiled inwardly at the slight flush on his cheek. Was it his mistake about the moving pictures or being called 'honey' by an astonishingly pretty young woman?

MacKenzie turned to the constable next to him. 'Watt, take everyone's details. And when the doctor arrives, bring him down to the loch.'

'Aye, sir.' The constable saluted, then took out his pocket-book and pencil.

'This way, Inspector.' Poppy led him out of the drawing room, through the hall and the open front door. She paused on the steps and pointed to the glimpse of shimmering blue water. 'You can just about see the loch from here, between the trees. I've left a footman with the body.'

The inspector replaced his fedora. 'Who found the body, miss?' he asked, looking at her as they crossed the lawn.

Another time would do to correct his mistake as to her title. 'It was Freddy, the same footman who is waiting with the dead man.'

Inspector MacKenzie nodded. Would he approve, Poppy wondered, if he knew the footman might have had something to do with the murdered man but wasn't saying so?

'And no one knows who the man is?' he went on.

How much should she tell the inspector at this stage? 'Apparently not,' she said, deciding to keep it simple for now. 'Freddy dashed into the dining room during breakfast and said he'd found the body when he was exercising the dogs.'

They walked in silence until they reached the scene. Freddy was sitting on the grassy bank, smoking. He hastily stubbed out the cigarette on his tobacco tin and jumped to his feet when he saw Poppy and the inspector approaching.

Inspector MacKenzie nodded at Freddy and went quickly up to the body. He lowered himself carefully to his knees beside it. A brief glance was enough to show him that the man was indeed dead.

'Watch stopped at six o'clock,' he observed.

'Broken in the attack, no doubt,' Poppy remarked.

'Or he had forgotten to wind it,' the inspector commented. 'Or it didn't keep correct time.'

Good point, she thought. The man had beauty *and* brains.

'Yes, there is that too. Or,' she added helpfully, 'he may have kept it deliberately fast. Like the clock on the North British Hotel running three minutes early, so that Waverley passengers don't miss their trains.'

The inspector felt in the man's jacket pockets and from one withdrew a box of matches and a crumpled packet of Woodbines.

'Whatever the man's job, he must have been doing all right, buying ready-made,' MacKenzie muttered.

From his own mackintosh pocket, he removed a brown envelope and slipped the match box and cigarette carton into it. He continued his search, but the dead man's trouser pockets revealed only a small amount of change, a door key, a pencil and a handkerchief.

'A pencil, but no notebook,' Poppy said.

The inspector made no comment on this as he put the other items into the envelope. 'A pity; no form of identification.'

'Perhaps it was removed by the killer,' she said thoughtfully. 'Although I believe it's not usual for working men to carry identification.'

Inspector MacKenzie, his eyes dark under their brows, looked up at her. 'I'm aware of that.'

She gave him a bright smile. 'Just trying to be of help, Inspector.'

'Miss,' he said sternly, 'it would be wiser if you left it to the police to do their job efficiently.'

The insolence of the man! Poppy tapped a booted foot on the grass. 'As you will no doubt have noticed,' she went on as if she hadn't heard him, 'the man's jacket is not finely tailored, but off-the-peg. His shoes are not handmade. As for his hat, it could not have come from the sort of establishment where customers are preferred to have titles. From this it can be concluded that he was *not* well-to-do.'

The inspector sighed and rose from his knees with surprising grace. He picked up the cap lying near the body and examined it. Poppy could see from the maker's label that her observation was correct. The inspector folded the cap and put it in his pocket. On the grassy bank a partially smoked cigarette had been trodden on. Possibly the first one Freddy had smoked, she thought, but said nothing. The inspector lifted the squashed cigarette end, added it to the envelope and placed it in his pocket.

Turning to the footman, he said, 'I'm hearing that it was you who found the body.'

'Strictly speaking, Inspector,' Poppy intervened, 'it was Major Lewis who did so.'

'Major Lewis?' Inspector MacKenzie's dark eyebrows came together as he looked at her. 'Why was I not told about this gentleman?'

'Because Major is not a gentleman, but my dog.'

The inspector shot Poppy a smouldering look. 'I'll thank you not to waste my time, miss. Please be more precise with your answers in future.'

Enough is enough! Smarting at being addressed in this way by the police officer, Poppy retorted, 'I am not *Miss*, Inspector, but Lady Persephone Proudfoot. The daughter of the Earl of Crieff of Dunearn Castle, Perthshire.'

MacKenzie flushed. 'Begging your pardon, your ladyship.' He doffed his hat. 'I was not aware...'

Poppy smiled sweetly at him and held his gaze. 'How could you be, Inspector, when your mind is so bent on the task of clue finding?'

As he replaced his fedora, the sound of a motor car drew their attention and the three of them turned to see it drive slowly up to the house.

'The car belongs to the doctor, I imagine,' Poppy said. She returned her attention to the inspector and saw him noting the footpath. He looked back at the raised position of Balfour House.

'The house overlooks the loch,' he said slowly, 'but the bushes obscure the footpath. Where does this path lead?'

'I have no idea, Inspector. I arrived here for the first time yesterday. I expect Freddy will know.' She glanced at the footman.

'It runs around the edge of the loch,' he told the inspector.

'I can see that,' observed Inspector MacKenzie, 'but is it going anywhere else?'

Freddy shrugged. 'It joins a rough track that leads to the village, but it's overgrown.'

That could be relevant, Poppy thought.

'That could be relevant,' said Inspector MacKenzie.

Poppy tried not to smirk.

'It might have been used by the killer,' the inspector continued. His gaze travelled from the path back to where the body lay. 'Unless someone unconnected to the crime happened to be wandering about down here around six o'clock either yesterday afternoon or this forenoon, the murderer would have been able to work unseen behind this hedge. Now, the question is,' he murmured, 'was the man murdered here, or elsewhere and then moved here?'

'I've considered that, Inspector,' Poppy said brightly. 'The body would have been a dead weight, so it's unlikely it was carried here. And if he were dragged to the spot, there would be some sign of that on the ground. Unfortunately, of course, the sandy area was disturbed by the feet of everyone who came to look—'

'Not to mention paw prints,' he added dryly.

'To my mind, the man was killed here,' she told him firmly.

'Is that so, my lady – to your mind?'

'It seems the most logical explanation,' she went on, unabashed. 'As you say, the blow was probably struck under cover of the shrubbery. The murderer must have been waiting for him. The question is, what was the victim doing here? Did he have any business with the estate?'

Inspector MacKenzie raised an impressed eyebrow. 'And what is your thinking on this matter, my lady?'

'Only that the servants are more likely to know him than are Lady Balfour or any of her guests, don't you think, Inspector?'

'It's a valid point,' he conceded.

'Also,' she went on, in full swing now, 'did the murderer call out to him as the victim was strolling by the water's edge? Or was the fellow decoyed to the loch?'

'And why leave the body here,' he mused, 'when it could

easily have been tipped into the water where it might have been some time before it was found?'

'A good question, Inspector MacKenzie,' Poppy said, pleased. 'We are already making progress.'

He shot her a terse look. 'And what would be your answer to the question, your ladyship?'

She frowned. 'The murderer must have been disturbed.'

'You are certain it was murder?'

'I'll explain it in the words of young Gregor, as he so eloquently put to his uncle the reason why it couldn't be an accident. "*Some accident that kills a man with a dunt to the back of the head, and with nothing he could have bashed himself on.*"'

A ghost of a smile appeared on the inspector's face. He was really quite attractive when he smiled, she thought. He cleared his throat. 'I can't argue with the young fellow's reasoning, considering the evidence.'

'In order to find the next clue, I expect we need to find out whom he was meeting.'

'Not who committed the crime?' Inspector MacKenzie raised his eyebrows.

'When we know whom he was meeting, Inspector, I suspect we will know who did it.' Poppy smiled at him, before glancing out at the loch. 'I wonder what the reason was for meeting here?'

At that moment, the young constable, accompanied by a middle-aged man in a suit, a bowler hat and carrying a medical bag, came hurrying across the grass towards them. A plump man, carrying a camera, followed in their wake.

'Dr Hardie.' The doctor introduced himself to the inspector with an outstretched hand and an enquiring look. 'I came as fast as I could.' He sent a curious glance and a polite nod towards Poppy.

'Detective Inspector MacKenzie, out of Culross police

office.' MacKenzie introduced himself, before turning to the body.

Poppy seethed. The inspector had deliberately ignored her in the introductions! Despite all the help she was giving him...

'This is Mr Kerr, the local photographer, sir,' said Constable Watt, indicating to the inspector the young man waiting behind him.

Inspector MacKenzie nodded his thanks and explained to the other man the photographs he required. They watched Mr Kerr work quickly and efficiently. As soon as the photographer left, MacKenzie stepped back to allow the doctor to examine the body.

Dr Hardie put down his bag, knelt and looked keenly at the dead man. 'Let's see what we have here.'

'A sharp contusion just below the crown,' Poppy supplied.

Dr Hardie gazed up at her. 'Yes... that is true. A severe blow to the bone above the medulla oblongata, which controls the heart and breathing, will cause death.' He bent again to the body and felt the bone of the skull. 'As far as I'm able to judge by a superficial examination, death was caused by a heavy blow to the back of the head resulting in a fracture to the skull, no doubt producing internal haemorrhage and possibly paralysis of the brain.' He paused to raise one arm of the corpse, but it refused to move. 'Rigor mortis well established, so I'd say that it's safe to assume he is very dead indeed.' The doctor wiped the congealed blood from his fingers on the grassy bank and stood up.

MacKenzie nodded. 'What is your thinking as to how long he's been dead, Doctor?'

'Taking into account that the deceased appears to be an otherwise normally nourished man of about fifty years of age, and given the warm night and the state of rigor, I would say between six and eighteen hours.'

Poppy lifted her left arm to check her wristwatch. As she

did so, the opal and diamonds in her engagement ring flashed in the sunlight. She saw the inspector glance at her ring as she pressed on, making a quick calculation. 'It's now half past ten. That would mean the man was killed between half past four yesterday afternoon and half past four this morning.'

'I'm thinking that's verra broad. Could you be narrowing the time down at all?' Inspector MacKenzie asked the doctor.

'I can't be certain,' Dr Hardie said carefully, 'but death probably occurred closer to some fifteen to seventeen hours ago.'

'That would make it between half past five and half past seven yesterday evening,' Poppy remarked. 'So he could have been killed around six o'clock? That's the time the man's watch stopped,' she added.

The doctor nodded.

'In your opinion,' she continued, addressing the doctor, 'could the blow have been self-inflicted?'

'Certainly not. It has been made from behind with a heavy, blunt instrument, perhaps an iron bar of some sort, using some force,' he replied. 'It is quite impossible that it was self-inflicted.'

'Could it be the result of an accident?' Poppy asked, just to be sure.

'I am asking the questions, my lady,' Inspector MacKenzie said testily.

'If the man had fainted, perhaps,' went on Poppy, undeterred, 'and had fallen onto a rock or large stone?'

'It's possible.' Automatically he looked at the sand near the man's head. 'Although there seems to be no rock or stone here that could cause such an injury. But, of course, that's a matter for the police.'

'Can we say he was murdered here?' Poppy raised a questioning eyebrow at Dr Hardie.

Inspector MacKenzie impatiently moved his hat to the back of his head. 'Your ladyship, that is police business.'

Poppy frowned and gestured towards the body. 'This man's

position, given the stiffening of the body muscles as demonstrated by the doctor, suggests he has not been moved since death.' Seeing the inspector's frown, she added, 'I believe I mentioned earlier that I have some experience of nursing. During the Great War, I ran a hospital for wounded soldiers.'

The doctor sent her an approving glance. 'Our very own Lady with the Lamp.'

'I cannot claim to have set any standards in nursing, as Florence Nightingale did during the Crimean War, but we all did our best for our brave lads.'

'In answer to your earlier question,' Dr Hardie said, 'the victim can't have known anything about it. I would say he probably died almost immediately after sustaining the blow.'

Poppy sent the inspector a victorious glance, before adding, 'At least he didn't suffer.'

'Inspector,' said Dr Hardie, 'do you have any idea who the unfortunate fellow was?'

'You have not seen him before?' Inspector MacKenzie asked.

'No, I'm afraid he's not one of my patients.'

I might know something. But Poppy kept silent. Since the inspector thought he was so clever, she should give him the chance to find out for himself.

He turned sharply to Poppy. 'I'm sorry, did you say something?'

'No, Inspector,' she said. 'I was merely thinking very hard.'

FOUR

'I'll arrange for the wagon to take the body.' Dr Hardie picked up his bag and shook his head. 'This is quite shocking. Such a thing has never happened in all the years I've been in practice here. A nasty business indeed. I'd best inform Lady Balfour.'

'That is my job,' said Inspector MacKenzie, shaking the doctor's hand, 'but thank you for your help. I'll be in touch if I have any further questions.'

'Of course.' Dr Hardie took his leave.

The inspector turned to address the young constable. 'Watt, stay here with the body. I notified the Procurator Fiscal Depute from the police office, and when he arrives, I will speak to him. Once the ambulance has taken the dead man, return to the house and question the servants.'

'Aye, sir.' Constable Watt touched his cap.

Inspector MacKenzie turned next to Freddy. 'Footman, I'll have questions for you later. And my lady, if you would return with me to the house, there are some questions I'd like to ask you as well.'

With a final glance at the dead man, Poppy set off back to

Balfour House, Inspector MacKenzie and Freddy following close behind.

In the hall the footman disappeared through the green baize door to below stairs, where Poppy was certain he would enjoy regaling the events to the rest of the servants.

She and Inspector MacKenzie entered the drawing room, to find everyone still there and talking in animated voices. All looked apprehensive, apart from Gregor, who roamed about the room, his hands stuffed in the pockets of his cardigan.

'I should jolly well have been allowed to see the body again,' he said bitterly to no one in particular. 'I might have been able to make some useful comments.'

'There was no need. Lady Persephone has filled that position more than adequately,' Inspector MacKenzie murmured, placing his fedora on a side table.

Poppy, standing next to him, heard this. As she was no doubt meant to. She tilted her determined chin. *We shall see who wins this battle of wits.*

'Gregor,' Constance said sharply, 'take your hands out of your pockets and stop grumbling. The inspector can make all the proper enquiries without the need of any advice from you.'

The boy snorted, but did as his mother instructed.

Inspector MacKenzie cast a swift glance round the assembled company and pulled a police pocketbook from his mackintosh. 'I will start by asking if anyone has any knowledge of the name of the victim. Lady Balfour, may I start with you?'

'I really can't tell you anything, Inspector,' she said, a note of apology in her voice. 'I've never seen the man before.'

He turned next to Nick Balfour. 'Your name, sir?'

'Nick Balfour, Lady Balfour's brother-in-law.'

The inspector noted it down. 'And had you seen the man before, sir?'

Nick Balfour shook his head.

'Nor me,' put in Beth. 'That's *Miss* Beth Cornett.' She

smiled at the inspector. 'You could of knocked me down with a feather when that tall, good-looking young fellow in the snappy outfit—'

'The footman,' put in Constance for the inspector's benefit.

'—dashed in at breakfast and said there was a stiff by the loch.'

'And then we all went out to have a look,' went on Mr Emmett. 'I'm J. Franklyn Emmett, director of moving pictures and a guest of Constance here. None of us had seen the man before.'

'That is true, Inspector,' Poppy said. 'Not one of us claims to know the man.'

The inspector's dark gaze lit on her and, with an almost imperceptible dip of his head, let her know he'd caught the meaning of her words. He turned back to the assembly and in his pocketbook completed the list of the adults' names.

He looked up. 'According to the doctor, the man met his death yesterday, some time between half past five and half past seven in the evening. Could each of you in turn tell me where you were at that time?'

'That's easy to answer,' said Nick. 'We were all here in the house.'

'Just so.' Inspector MacKenzie nodded. 'But where precisely in the house? One at a time, if you please.'

'We all gathered in this room for drinks at half past six and then dined at seven,' Constance said. 'During the previous hour, I was in my room dressing.'

Nick had drawn a tortoiseshell cigarette case from his jacket pocket and was turning it over in his hands. 'I think you'll find that's true of all of us, Inspector.'

'It's not quite true for me,' put in Poppy. 'I walked to the village and didn't get back here until a little after six o'clock.'

Inspector MacKenzie sent her a sharp glance and scribbled in his pocketbook.

Now perhaps he would ask her a relevant question, she thought.

He glanced around the room. 'Is this everyone?'

'My wife is reading in the library,' Nick told him. 'This morning's events have been rather trying for her nerves. But look here, is this questioning of us all really necessary? I would have thought you'd do better grilling the servants.'

'Constable Watt will be interviewing below stairs, sir.'

Nick gave a dramatic sigh. 'Well, then, after dinner we were all together in the drawing room for a while. I played the piano, sang a few songs. I think one of them was "Ain't We Got Fun".'

'And you tell me to speak properly,' muttered Gregor.

'Then Mr Peavey' – Nick gestured to Eddie – 'and I played a couple of games of billiards.'

'And you, Miss Cornett?' asked the inspector.

'I was watching them play,' the young woman said, flashing him a smile.

'That's right,' added Eddie, gazing at her devotedly.

'What about you, sonny?' Inspector MacKenzie turned to Gregor.

'I'm not your sonny,' the boy said crossly. 'I'm the Honourable Gregor Bruce Balfour.'

A flush of embarrassment crossed the inspector's usually taciturn face. Oh dear, thought Poppy with pleasure, he *is* putting his foot in it this morning.

'My apologies, young sir. Can you tell me where you were yesterday evening?'

'Before dinner I was in my room reading *The Murder on the Links*, which was topping, then we had dinner which was chicken *à la* king with rice and peas. And then Uncle Nick had to spoil it all and send me to bed. And that's where I was until I came down for breakfast this morning.'

'Thank you, young sir. Now—'

'But' – Gregor hadn't yet finished – 'I bet if I'd been allowed outside like *some* people, I would have seen something suspicious down by the water.'

'Who was outside?' The inspector's sharp glance went from Gregor to the others in the room.

A flash of annoyance crossed Nick's face. He shrugged. 'Miss Cornett, Eddie Peavey and myself smoked on the terrace for a short while after dinner.'

So Gregor had been looking out of his bedroom window, for part of the evening at least, thought Poppy. What a pity he hadn't been doing so before dinner instead of reading Agatha Christie's latest novel...

'Did any of you notice anything suspicious at all – in the grounds or down by the loch?' Inspector MacKenzie asked.

'Not a bird,' Beth said.

'Same as she said,' put in Eddie.

'I saw no one,' confirmed Nick.

'Were you together the entire time?' the inspector asked.

'I came indoors first,' Nick told him.

'And Eddie and me schmoozed for a while,' Beth said.

Inspector MacKenzie looked up and frowned. 'Schmoozed?'

'We hung about shooting the breeze, chewing the fat...'

Constance sighed and addressed MacKenzie. 'They mean talking, Inspector. We all retired for the night about eleven—'

'They hit the hay early up in this part of the world,' explained Beth.

'And then the butler locked the doors to the house,' Constance finished smoothly.

'There would have been nothing to stop one of you coming downstairs after that,' Inspector MacKenzie said, 'letting yourself out and going down to the loch?'

'That would have been some hours after the doctor's estimated time of death,' Poppy put in.

'You said it yourself, my lady: estimated.'

'But this all seems far-fetched, wouldn't you say, Inspector?' Poppy raised an eyebrow. 'Surely none of us had a motive to kill a complete stranger?'

'If he *was* a complete stranger,' muttered Gregor darkly.

The inspector fixed his eyes on Gregor and brooded for a moment. 'That will be all the questions for now, Lady Balfour, but I must stress that none of you leave the estate in the near future. I may verra well need to question you again. Now, I will see Mrs Balfour in the library before I speak to the Procurator Fiscal Depute.' Inspector MacKenzie looked at his wristwatch. 'He will probably have arrived by now. And then I'll be joining Constable Watt below stairs.'

'Can't we even go into the village?' Beth looked dismayed.

'The village is *on* the estate,' Constance pointed out.

'No kidding! A country house with its own village. Say, that's something else to tell the folks back home, wouldn't you say?'

'Come, Inspector,' Poppy offered with a smile, 'I'll show you the way to the library.'

The inspector's jet-black eyes smouldered at her. 'There's no need to trouble yourself, my lady.' He turned towards the doorway, as Constance pressed the bell by the hearth.

Dash it, thought Poppy, as she felt the opportunity to be a part of the murder investigation slipping away. And she needed to speak to the inspector about a possible connection between the footman and the murdered man. There was also the matter of what or who had disturbed the killer down by the loch, not to mention the pencil – but no notebook – in the dead man's pocket. Well, if MacKenzie wasn't going to investigate these important clues, then she would have to.

The butler appeared in response to Constance's summons. He was given his instructions and withdrew with the inspector.

'Now you must all excuse me,' Constance said to her guests. 'I need to see the housekeeper to discuss the day's business.'

She drew Poppy to one side on her way out of the room. 'I will be finished with Mrs Oakley in about half an hour. Would you then come and see me in the study?'

'Of course, Constance. This is an upsetting thing to have happened, and in your own house...'

'It's not the murder I want to talk to you about, my dear, but... another matter.'

'Oh?' Poppy waited for further explanation, but Constance simply patted Poppy's arm and left the room.

'What do we do now?' Beth, from her position on the settee, looked around the room. She removed a cigarette from the silver case she carried in her clutch bag and waited for a reply. None came.

Poppy considered creeping along the corridor and listening in at the door of the library while the inspector interviewed Morag Balfour.

'I don't know what's customary here,' Beth went on, tapping one end of the cigarette on the back of the closed case. She inserted the other end in a cigarette holder.

'I doubt that any of us know the etiquette in such a situation,' Poppy said.

Gregor began to sidle out of the door.

'Where are you off to?' Nick called to him. He leaned towards the actress, lighter in his outstretched hand.

The boy paused. 'I'm going to see if Major wants a walk.'

'Stay away from the loch,' Nick warned. He lit Beth's cigarette for her and straightened, as Gregor disappeared through the open door.

'Say, let's go downtown,' suggested Eddie, getting to his feet. 'See what there is to see in Cul-ross.'

'It's pronounced Coo-ross,' Poppy put in distractedly.

He frowned. 'No, really?'

Beth stood and linked her arm through his. 'That's a peachy idea. Are you coming, Mr Emmett?'

'Why not? There's going to be little else to do here for a day or two, I guess. And it will add to the local colour of our research.' He pushed his spectacles up the bridge of his nose. 'So long.'

The three left the room and silence fell.

'This is dashed awkward,' Nick said, lighting a cigarette of his own as he lowered himself into the spot newly vacated by Beth Cornett. 'It seems wrong to do anything, but one can't just sit and stare at the furniture.'

Poppy, still in her riding attire and with a mind buzzing with questions, felt frustration twitching the tiny muscle in her determined jaw. She took a seat opposite Nick. If nothing else, she could interview him after a fashion.

'What is your opinion of what's happened?' she asked him.

'I don't know that I have an opinion. A stranger murdered here, yesterday, on my late brother's land. It's hard to believe.'

'I find myself wondering who might have been in the gardens between half past five and half past seven,' she said carefully. 'Not the servants, of course, as they'd be too busy at those times.'

Nick teased a small flake of tobacco from his lower lip and flicked it into the ashtray. 'They're not permitted in the gardens.'

Apart from Freddy, to walk Constance's dog, Poppy thought.

'As to the grounds, the poacher, I suppose...' Nick pulled on the cigarette, its tip glowing red in the morning light streaming in through the window.

Ah, that possibility hasn't been mentioned before. 'Is poaching a problem here?' she asked.

'My sister-in-law doesn't see it as a problem, as long as the only thing the fellow takes is rabbits. They are vermin, after all.'

'Anyone else?'

'A courting couple?' Nick took another pull on his cigarette.

'Or perhaps the chap's lady friend did him in, as the Americans say.'

'It's possible,' Poppy said doubtfully. 'I suppose it depends on the weapon used. A degree of strength would have been needed to inflict that blow on a man who looked to be otherwise fit and healthy.'

'Some females are strong,' Nick informed her.

As if she were a wee girl and not a full-grown woman who'd helped lift many a sick man into his hospital bed! 'We won't rule out a woman with a cosh hidden in her petticoat, then.'

'I don't intend to be the one to rule anybody in or out.' Nick looked shocked. 'It's up to the police, not us, to find the man's killer.'

Poppy leaned back against the settee. *We shall see.*

FIVE

The thirty minutes Poppy had to wait before visiting Constance in the study threatened to pass slowly.

Nick had left the room and Poppy was left with nothing to do but pace up and down. She needed to discuss the case with someone – and that someone *had* to be Elspeth.

She ran up the stairs, burst into her bedroom and rang for her maid. Then she flung herself into the chair at the little writing table, took a sheet of headed notepaper from the stand, placed it on the blotting pad and uncapped the fountain pen provided for the guest's use.

At the very least, Poppy decided, drawing a line down the centre of the page, she should make a list of the timings in the case.

Time she wrote in a confident hand at the top of the left hand column, and *Event* at the top of the right hand column. As she paused to put her thoughts into order, Elspeth entered the room.

'Oh, my lady! I've been hearing from the footman about the dreadful thing that's happened down by the loch. *Murder...*'

Elspeth now saw that Poppy was seated at the writing desk with pen and paper at the ready, and she brightened. 'Oh, you are writing to your parents. Such a *suitable* thing for a lady to do. When I was Lady MacCorkindale's personal maid...'

Poppy had been compared to the conveniently deceased Lady MacCorkindale rather too often by Elspeth. 'The murder is dreadful, as you say, Elspeth, and so I thought I might give the police inspector a hand in solving the crime.'

'My lady! Whatever are you thinking of? You can't do that!'

'Why not?' Poppy turned to face her maid. 'I am a witness, after all.'

'A witness? You saw the man being murdered?' Elspeth paled.

'No, of course not. I meant that I saw the young footman Freddy in the village with the man who was murdered shortly afterwards.' The stuffy inspector didn't know *that*, of course, so she had a head start on him.

'My goodness.' Elspeth put her hand on her chest and staggered a little.

'Sit down, do,' Poppy said kindly, 'before you fall down.'

'Thank you, my lady. I think I will have a wee rest.' Elspeth sank into an armchair.

'Now, then,' went on Poppy, 'would you mind if I ran through what I know and reviewed the evidence? It would help to clarify my thoughts.'

'Won't Lady Balfour wonder where you are, your ladyship?'

Elspeth was trying vainly to distract her. 'Not at all.' Poppy turned back to the page and her pen hovered above the clean sheet of paper, eager to begin. 'I have some time to spare.'

'Och, well, what else would a lady do when she finds she has nothing better to do,' Elspeth said in a prim voice.

'I think you might have put it a little better than that,' Poppy said with reproach. 'However! We will make a start. Let me see.

I bumped into Freddy outside the house yesterday at quarter past five.' Although she hadn't checked her watch at that point, she was fairly certain of the time because the walk into Culross couldn't have taken her more than fifteen minutes – she would need to check that – and when she'd arrived, the town hall clock showed half past five.

'In the *Time* column I shall write 5.15 *p.m.* and, in the *Event* column, *Spoke to Freddy the footman outside the house.*' Poppy did so.

'What did the footman say to you, my lady?' Elspeth asked.

'He gave me directions to the village,' Poppy replied as she wrote.

'And that is an *event*?' Elspeth asked, astonished.

'Not in itself, no. But it's part of the bigger picture.'

Elspeth gave a disparaging sniff.

Poppy was not to be deterred. 'Pay attention, Elspeth. This is a serious matter.' She returned to her writing. 'A short time later, I spotted Freddy in Culross. I know it was after half past five and it must have been before, say, five minutes to six, which is when I left the village to return here. I had to make a wee detour into the butcher's shop—'

'The butcher's?' Elspeth exclaimed. 'Isn't Lady Balfour feeding you properly upstairs?'

'She is. The detour wasn't my idea,' Poppy admitted, 'but—'

'Major's.' Elspeth tutted. 'That dog and his raw sausages.' She rose, clearly feeling better, and began to straighten pictures that didn't need straightening.

'Please sit down, Elspeth. I haven't finished laying out the evidence yet and your moving about is distracting me.'

Elspeth returned to the armchair, perched on the edge and picked an imaginary piece of lint from her navy blue lady's maid dress.

'I'll put that I saw Freddy in Culross at 5.45 p.m.' Poppy made the next entry. 'And then that I returned here at 6.10.'

Elspeth raised a respectfully critical eyebrow. 'That doesn't sound like very much evidence so far, my lady.'

'Let me get to the end of my account and we will see,' Poppy went on in a firm voice. '*Then*, when the doctor arrived this morning, he said death probably took place between half past five and half past seven the previous evening. The dead man's watch had stopped at six o'clock, so it's very likely that was when he was murdered.'

'If his watch had been properly wound up,' said Elspeth.

'Yes, I have already thought of that,' Poppy told her untruthfully. It had been the inspector's suggestion, although she was sure she would have thought of it herself eventually. 'But we have to assume some things, and a watch that was cracked in a fall is as good as anything.'

She wrote *Around 6 p.m.* in the left-hand column and *Unknown man murdered by the loch* in the right-hand column. 'Then *5.30–6.30 p.m.: All – apart from me, see above – in their rooms, dressing*,' Poppy said as she continued to write. 'And finally, *6.30 p.m.: Drinks in the drawing room* and *7 p.m.: Dinner.*' She finished writing and set down the pen with a flourish.

'What about below stairs, your ladyship? Surely all the servants must be equally under suspicion?'

'Absolutely, Elspeth.' Poppy looked eagerly at her maid. 'Now, tell me, is there something you've discovered in the servants' hall?'

'Not really, my lady. Apart from supper at six, everyone is busy about their various tasks during the time you mention. Freddy, of course, was out walking Lady Balfour's wee dog.'

'Did you notice what time he returned from the village?'

'I could hardly be expected to have noticed that, your ladyship. I came up to your room a wee while before half past five, expecting to find you here so that I could help you dress for dinner.' Elspeth sent her a reproachful look.

'Still, least said, soonest mended, as my late mother used to say.'

'A wise woman,' Poppy replied, wondering if Elspeth's mother had been as annoying as her daughter.

'However,' Elspeth went on, 'there is something, my lady...'

'Go on.' Poppy's exasperation with her maid was immediately forgotten.

'You mentioned you saw the footman in the village with the other man shortly before he was murdered. Well, when Freddy got back to the kitchens this morning, he was full of his finding the dead man by the loch.' Elspeth shook her head in puzzlement. 'But he didn't say anything about having seen the man before.'

Poppy frowned. Of all those currently residing in the house, she thought, only she and Freddy had been outside at the relevant time.

She knew *she* hadn't killed the man by the loch. Had Freddy murdered him between walking Lady Balfour's Ollie and tucking into his supper?

When exactly thirty minutes had passed, Poppy, full of curiosity, presented herself at Constance's study.

'Come in, dear, do.' Constance rose from behind the desk.

Poppy felt it must have been Lord Balfour's study once, with its dark panelling and stale cigar smell. The masculine ambience of the room probably gave some comfort to his widow.

Constance gestured to the settee. Poppy paused to pet Ollie, who, having given a few barks as she entered the room, was now too occupied in chewing a soft toy on the Turkish carpet to take any further notice. She joined her hostess on the Chesterfield.

'The rest of the house guests will arrive in time for dinner this evening,' Constance said. 'Goodness knows what they will make of recent events.' She hesitated for a moment. 'Oh dear, I suppose I should cancel the weekend party.'

'Isn't it too late, Constance?' Poppy remarked, settling herself.

'It's only Tuesday. Letters would arrive in time, I'm sure. Or I could telephone, but not all my guests are on the telephone communication system.' She sounded doubtful. 'It would be difficult to put off people at such short notice.'

'I suppose I really meant that so much preparation has gone into the weekend.'

'There is that, my dear, and I don't like to let others down.'

'I believe one of the new guests will be your brother-in-law's son?'

'That's right. Innes.' Constance smiled. 'He's a delightful young man, although he can be a trifle frivolous at times. Innes will bring some sunshine into this awful situation. He is coming with his lady friend, Miss Rosalind Hall. Although I should say his betrothed, as they announced their engagement two months ago.'

Poppy smiled and waited for Constance to reveal her true purpose in arranging this private conversation.

There was a pause.

'I have a problem, Poppy.' Constance said at last, staring down at her hands folded in her lap.

'Is there anything I can do to help?' Poppy asked, her curiosity piqued.

'I'm not certain.' Constance looked up. 'But I must tell someone and I think you might be the right person.'

Intrigued, Poppy gave Constance an encouraging smile.

Constance began again. 'It's rather a delicate matter.'

Poppy nodded and waited. A man, she thought; it's always a man.

'My husband...'

A man, just as she had thought. But surely not, because Lord Balfour had recently passed away.

'His death must have been a shock for you,' Poppy said softly.

'Yes, it was. But he was some years older than me, and perhaps his heart attack wasn't quite the bolt from the blue it would have been in a younger man.' She sent Poppy a sympathetic glance. 'I'm sorry, my dear. It must have been so much harder for you.'

'It was difficult at the time.' After so long – nine years – she found she could think about Stuart quite honestly. She'd fallen in love with his looks, and could admit to herself now that he had neither brains nor character; not a recipe for a successful marriage. 'But you were telling me about your husband,' Poppy added.

'Well,' Constance said, 'the matter concerns a bracelet – a diamond and emerald bracelet to be precise... I'm afraid I can't find it.'

'You've lost a bracelet?' Poppy asked, frowning.

'Not so much *lost* as... not found in the first place.'

Poppy was intrigued. 'It must be somewhere, surely?'

'Exactly.' Constance took a breath and began again. 'A fortnight after my dear husband passed away, I received an invoice from an Edinburgh jeweller for the bracelet. It was rather an expensive item, as you might imagine. Our twentieth wedding anniversary was approaching, so naturally I thought the bracelet was for me. The problem is I can't find it – in our Edinburgh house or here at Balfour House.'

'Do you trust your servants? In both houses?' It had to be asked.

'Most definitely.' Constance was adamant. 'And nothing has ever gone missing before.'

'Then...' The thought came to Poppy that the husband had kept a mistress, but she couldn't say this. A look flashed between the two women and she knew that the same notion weighed on Constance's mind.

'I can't believe that Bruce was having a relationship with another woman, but I fear it must be the only explanation.' Constance flushed, but kept her gaze firmly on Poppy's face.

Something sparked in Poppy's mind, but then was gone. She wanted to help Constance, but how? She remembered a conversation she'd had some years ago with Lady Duddingston. 'I believe there's a detective agency in Edinburgh, run by two women who pride themselves on their discretion. Perhaps you could ask them to investigate?'

Constance drew back. 'Oh no, dear. I couldn't possibly involve private investigators.'

'I was told of the McIntyre Agency by an elderly lady I've known since I was a girl. She praised the female detectives,' Poppy continued. 'They solved the theft of a priceless necklace *and* a murder at her country house.'

Constance shook her head. 'If you feel you cannot help me, Poppy dear, then let us just forget this. It's just some silly idea of mine. It's of no real importance.' She began to rise from the settee. 'I will settle the invoice. I've recently received a reminder, and I fear I have delayed long enough.'

Poppy's next words were out before she knew what she was going to say. 'Would you like me to visit the jeweller and see what I can find out?'

Constance sank back on the settee. 'Would you?' Relief was evident in her voice. 'I didn't know who else to ask. I've heard that you studied law. And I saw how efficiently you dealt with the situation earlier of that poor murdered man by the loch. I feel I can trust you.'

Asking questions of a jewellery shop owner was not the same as working for a law degree – but how hard could it be? At least he could answer her questions, and it would be interesting.

Not to mention that solving this mystery would be a poke in the eye for that unpleasant inspector.

'I have to return briefly to the city tomorrow, so I could visit the shop then,' Poppy told her.

Constance nodded. 'Of course, you said your cousin's friend has an interview at the hospital, and there's the viscountess's fundraiser. But oh, my dear,' she said, suddenly remembering, 'the inspector expressly stated we should not leave the estate at this time.'

'Yes, I know, but this arrangement was already made and I can't abandon a young woman away from home for the first time. Besides, I'll be away for only one night.' Poppy wasn't sure the inspector would agree with her action or reasoning, but she continued, nonetheless. 'May I leave my maid and my dog? If they are here, the inspector will assume I am too. Elspeth can look after Major, and I'll tell her she must show herself if the inspector appears. That way, he'll be sure to think I'm in another room or out riding.'

And, Poppy thought, Elspeth can keep an eye on matters for her in the servants' hall regarding the investigation, and on the inspector.

Constance smiled. 'Major will be company for Ollie on their walks.' She sent a fond glance at her little dog.

At the mention of his name, Ollie looked up, raising quizzical eyebrows. Poppy laughed at his comical face.

'If you could let me have the original invoice,' she said to Constance. 'I should like to take it with me as proof of your permission.'

'Certainly.' Constance rose, went round to the front of the desk and pulled open a drawer. 'Here we are.' She returned and handed the sheet of paper to Poppy. 'This is so kind of you.'

'Not at all.' Poppy glanced down at the invoice on the jeweller's headed paper. *A three-row bracelet, set with alternating diamonds and emeralds*, she read. *15th November 1923.*

'You husband purchased it last November?' she said. That was seven months ago.

'Bruce passed away four weeks later, on 15th December, but I didn't receive the bill until after Christmas,' Constance explained. 'Our anniversary would have been in January.'

'I see.'

And then the image that had flashed through Poppy's mind returned. Beth Cornett at dinner last night, playfully slapping young Gregor's arm, a flash on her wrist of diamonds and emeralds sparkling in the candlelight. Poppy's view of it had been too brief to be sure, and it might not have had three rows, but still...

Constance couldn't have noticed the young woman wearing it, or she would not have asked Poppy to find the bracelet. She needed to think this through before saying anything to Constance. Was it possible in practical terms for the now deceased Lord Balfour to have given it to Beth? He had died six months ago. Constance told Poppy yesterday the Americans had arrived at the house that morning. Over dinner last night, Beth had mentioned meeting Nick Balfour at a party in Edinburgh, but she hadn't said when. Was this Beth's first visit to Scotland? If she had become close to Lord Balfour on a previous visit, had it given her a thrill to wear the jewellery in her late lover's house?

Oh dear, thought Poppy. She very much hoped that Constance was not nourishing a viper in her bosom...

She needed to know more about the young woman. When Beth returned from her morning's excursion to the village, she would question her.

After all, that smug Inspector MacKenzie was not the only one who could interview suspects.

While the American party were out at Culross, Poppy decided she'd see if Elspeth had finished pressing her dress for this evening and, more importantly, if she had learned anything of interest in the servants' hall.

Poppy was in luck. Her maid had returned to the bedroom and was carefully hanging in the wardrobe the sleeveless gown in emerald chiffon with its scarf in the same fabric.

Poppy dropped into an armchair. 'What news from below stairs, Elspeth?'

Elspeth closed the wardrobe door. 'I don't think you should be concerning yourself with the talk in the kitchens, my lady.' She gave a small sniff.

Poppy laughed. 'Don't be so disapproving! I am naturally curious as to what anyone has to say about the murdered man. Come, now, I'm sure you are interested too.'

'Perhaps a wee bit,' her maid admitted reluctantly. 'But it's not a suitable topic for a Lady...'

What would Elspeth think, Poppy wondered, if she knew that Her Ladyship was about to begin a second, this one her very own, investigation? Admittedly only into a missing bracelet, but it would be a real piece of detection.

'I won't disgrace you, Elspeth,' she said with a smile. 'And now, please sit down and tell me of the talk in the servants' hall.'

Elspeth perched on the dressing table stool. 'The inspector,' she began, 'was asking if any of the servants had seen anyone by the loch yesterday afternoon or evening. And someone said they had.' Elspeth paused.

'Really?' Poppy sat forward in her seat. 'Who? Who said that?'

'It was Charlie, Lady Balfour's chauffeur.'

'Good Lord!' She sank back in her chair. This investigation could be over before she'd had a real chance to get involved. 'The chauffeur? Did he see the killer?'

'No, my lady, Charlie didn't say that. He told the inspector he'd been washing Lady Balfour's landaulette outside the garage – the old coach house – and had seen the footman, Freddy, by the loch in the late afternoon.'

Poppy frowned. 'I don't think that can be correct. I was in the village then and I saw the footman there.' A thought occurred to her. 'Was Lady Balfour's dog with him at the loch?'

'He didn't mention that.'

Did that mean Ollie was present or not? How frustrating! But surely no murderer would be so *low* as to take a dog with them? Dismissing that as a ridiculous thought, Poppy moved on.

'Did the chauffeur say what time he saw the footman by the water?'

'I wasn't listening *that* closely, my lady,' Elspeth demurred.

'Just tell me what you *think* you heard.' Poppy could feel her frustration rising.

'Well, then, Charlie told the inspector that he couldn't be certain as he'd removed his wristwatch to wash the motor car, but that it must have been about six o'clock.'

The town hall clock was showing half past five, Poppy remembered, when she arrived in Culross. She'd walked a little way before spotting Freddy with Ollie, then there had been the sausages episode, and after that she'd seen the footman enter the Red Lion. Would he have had time for a conversation with the mystery man, then to return to the house, possibly to deposit the dachshund, and finally walk down to the loch, all by six o'clock?

But, wait! What about the rough track that Freddy said led to the village? He'd added that it was overgrown, but not that it was unused. Presumably it was a shortcut between the house and Culross village. She'd investigate the track for herself as soon as she could.

Another thought occurred to her. Had the chauffeur lied to the police?

'Elspeth, you told me yesterday that the other servants are envious of Freddy. I wonder if Charlie pointed the finger at him in a fit of pique?'

Elspeth bristled. 'I couldn't possibly say, my lady. And your ladyship should not become involved. Let the police chase the criminals.'

How frustrating to keep being told that! 'Really, Elspeth,' Poppy exclaimed, 'you are my lady's maid, not my nanny.'

Elspeth rose from the stool and spoke in an aloof tone. 'If that is all you require at present, my lady.'

'Yes, carry on, Elspeth.' Poppy could see that was all she would get from the woman for now.

But there were other avenues to explore. Firstly, though, she needed to add to her timings list. Pulling open the drawer of the little writing desk, she took out the sheet and added 6 *p.m.* to the *Time* column and opposite it in the *Event* column *Charlie the chauffeur sees Freddy by the loch?* The question mark was necessary because she had only the chauffeur's word for it.

Poppy got to her feet. 'Is Inspector MacKenzie still in the kitchens?'

'He was when I left.' Elspeth picked up the cushion from the chair vacated by Poppy and pummelled it.

'I'm going down to speak to him.'

'Very good, my lady.' Elspeth gave the cushion one more thump before dropping it back in the chair.

Poppy threw open the bedroom door, strode along the corridor and down the carpeted staircase. The heels of her riding boots made a sharp clicking sound as she marched across the large, tiled hall, through the green baize door and descended the stone steps. Here she came to a passage and paused. *Which way to the servants' hall?* Turning left, she set off along the passage and round the corner into another flagged corridor. Now she could hear the sound of voices from further along the passage.

She reached a window set in an interior wall and through it saw the inspector and the constable, pocketbooks in hand, standing in the kitchen. The servants were seated around a long, scrubbed table. The door was ajar and Poppy pushed it open. Conversation immediately ceased, a newspaper and one or two teacups were hurriedly put down, and all got to their feet.

'Your ladyship,' said Baird.

'Is there anything you require, my lady?' asked the flustered housekeeper.

From the threshold, Poppy smiled sweetly at Inspector MacKenzie. 'Merely a word with the inspector.'

Inspector MacKenzie looked at her steadily. 'Is it important, your ladyship?'

'Obviously. Or I wouldn't have sought you out.'

He took a breath and turned to the constable. 'Watt, carry on here.'

'Aye, sir.'

'*J'en ai marre!*' A dapper little man in a long apron got to his feet. 'I 'ave 'ad enough! I 'ave food to prepare and to cook.' He lifted a saucepan from its hook on the wall and clattered it onto the range.

Inspector MacKenzie gestured for Poppy to leave, and he followed her into the stone passage. He closed the door behind them. 'What is it this time? Something your dog wishes me to know?'

Ignoring his comment, Poppy led him a short distance along the passage, away from the eyes and ears of the servants, and launched into her statement.

'I have reason to believe that Lady Balfour's chauffeur might not be telling the truth.' She tilted her chin.

'Very well. Then tell me why you think that.'

'My maid told me he'd informed you—'

He raised an eyebrow. 'You have a spy in the camp, so to speak?'

'A jolly useful thing to have, don't you think?' she replied pertly.

The inspector gestured for Poppy to carry on.

'She said the chauffeur had informed you he'd spotted the footman by the loch yesterday afternoon about six o'clock. I'm not sure that is possible, because I saw him, the footman, in the village not long before that.'

'Can you be more specific, my lady?'

'I went out with Major—'

'Your dog?' He smiled. 'Just to clarify.'

Poppy drew a breath and continued. 'I decided to take him for a walk. As we left the kennels, I met and spoke briefly to the footman. When I reached Culross, the clock on the town hall showed half past five—'

'Can you be certain that the clock keeps good time?'

Dash it! 'Well, no…' What an amateur mistake she'd made, not considering that, especially as she had commented to the inspector only a short while ago on the timing of the North British clock.

'No matter, I can find that out. Please continue.'

'I walked on a bit further and I saw the footman with Ollie. That's Lady Balfour's dog,' she added.

Inspector MacKenzie frowned. 'The footman had reached the village before you?'

'Well, yes.'

'And yet you left before the footman and didn't see him on your walk there?' Inspector MacKenzie looked at her steadily.

Poppy shook her head. 'He must have taken the track, the one he said was overgrown,' she conceded reluctantly. She couldn't believe Freddy was a murderer. 'Anyway,' she went on, 'my maid also tells me that the rest of the servants don't like Freddy because they see him as a favourite of Lady Balfour's.'

'Freddy, is it? It sounds like the young man is a favourite with more than just Lady Balfour.'

'Inspector!' Poppy retorted hotly. 'Remember to whom you are speaking.'

There was a small smile about his mouth. What right did he have to be so attractive and at the same time so annoying! Feeling her cheeks burning, she took a steadying breath.

'For your *further* information, I believe I saw not only the footman but also the murdered man in the village yesterday afternoon, some time after half past five.'

And with that, Poppy turned smartly on her heel and marched off, leaving the policeman standing in the passage.

How *dare* he speak to her like that! If Inspector MacKenzie wanted to know more, he would have to find her.

SIX

Having no plan of where she was going, Poppy marched up the servants' staircase, strode through the baize door, across the hall, through the main door of the house and out into the sunshine.

She stopped at the top of the steps and breathed deeply. *That's better!*

Wondering what to do next, she gazed about her. A brightly coloured butterfly, orange and yellow and black, sunned itself on the terrace's balustrade, spreading its wings flat in the heat. The idea of returning to the house on such a beautiful day was not appealing. Besides, she wanted to avoid that irritating inspector. Let him search for her without success!

She tapped the sole of her riding boot on the step and looked at her watch: shortly after midday. There was time for a ride as she'd originally intended, but it would have to be a short one. She could return via the loch and examine the scene of the crime again for any clues.

Poppy entered the stables and breathed in the familiar smell of horses and straw. The place was neat and orderly, with stalls lining one long wall. Sunlight streamed in through the high windows on the opposite wall. A stable boy was working there and he touched his forelock respectfully.

'Good morning,' she said to him. 'I believe Lady Balfour has asked for a horse to be made ready for me.'

The boy stepped along the row of occupied stalls, with Poppy following, and indicated a beautiful bay gelding. 'Aye, it's that one, my lady. His name is Arthur.'

'And he's happy around dogs?'

'He's the best.' The lad beamed and opened the stable door for Poppy to enter.

'Hello, Arthur.' She stroked the animal's muzzle and whispered to him. The gelding dropped his nose and snuffled into Poppy's hand. 'What a well-behaved horse you are.'

She waited while the stable boy saddled up the bay. He made sure the tack was properly buckled, before leading the horse to the wooden mounting block. He held the animal as Poppy placed one foot in the stirrup and rose into the saddle. The boy checked Arthur's girth and adjusted the stirrups. Poppy settled herself and gathered up the reins. Thanking the stable boy, she pressed her heels into the gelding's flanks, guided the horse out of the stables, under the archway and into the sweet-smelling morning.

She heard her dog bark in the adjoining kennels as she and Arthur approached him. Poppy leaned over to slide the bolt and free the Labrador.

'Major, we are going for a ride.'

He gave a little jump of happiness. Labradors were always so pleased with life, she thought fondly.

Turning onto the gravelled drive, Poppy urged her mount on, Major running beside them, his ears flapping in the breeze. And then they were off, riding across fields, jumping over low stone dykes; the warm air rushing past, the horse below her, and above the bright blue sky. A roe deer and her fawn cropping the grass, startled, looked up in perfect synchronisation, before bounding away into the trees.

Poppy slowed the horse to a walk as they splashed through the clear cold water of a burn and ascended a wooded hill. The sun was climbing high, and she was grateful for the shade of the beech trees.

They came out of the trees and onto the brow of the hill. From this vantage point, she could see for miles in all directions. A patchwork of sun-dappled fields, with tiny farmhouses dotted about and a single motor car like a child's toy travelling along a distant ribbon of road. The prosperous Balfour estate stretched out below her, with its tailored lawns and gardens and the blue loch gleaming in the midday sunshine. And there sat Balfour House, its windows glinting in the sun. What might be transpiring above or below stairs at this very moment? Was it really possible that someone in the house was a murderer?

Had the killer been seen from the house? Poppy reminded herself that she must find out whose bedrooms overlooked the loch.

The breeze ruffled her bobbed hair, and she tucked a thick lock behind one ear and turned Arthur homewards. As they drew closer to the water, its surface like a shimmering mirror, she reined in the horse to an easy trot. Major scampered ahead. He reached the bushes and pushed through.

She heard muffled exclamations and then saw two figures rise from the other side of the bushes. *Good heavens! The actress and the footman!* It sounded like an Edwardian novelty act.

It was too late now to pretend she hadn't seen them. Drawing to a halt, she slid from her horse. Major came back though the low shrubbery, sat on the grass and wagged his tail furiously.

'Good afternoon, Miss Cornett. And Freddy too, I see.' Poppy nodded civilly.

Beth came out from behind the shrubbery and tidied the

double frilled hem of her tangerine-coloured dress. 'Freddy has been showing me where he found the body.' She straightened her cloche hat.

'That's very kind of him.' Although Poppy knew that Beth had been one of those who had followed Freddy to this very spot yesterday morning.

Freddy stepped out from the other side of the bushes and hastily brushed down his uniform. 'I'd best get back to my duties now, my lady.' He nodded to Poppy and then to Beth, 'Miss Cornett,' before hastening away across the grass in the direction of the house.

Beth smiled at Poppy. 'So useful to get the low-down from an insider, don't you think?'

'For the local colour?' Poppy said, using Mr Emmett's expression.

Beth looked at her admiringly. 'Say, you're good.'

Poppy laughed. It was impossible not to like the young woman.

'This is some pile, huh?' Beth gestured back towards the house, its stone glowing in the sunshine.

'It will be difficult to recreate in a studio,' Poppy agreed.

'Oh, we won't bother with the whole house, honey. Just the front of the building – what you call a façade – painted on wood and held up behind with props. As for the rooms, some of them will be made up in the studios.'

'Really? How... interesting.' She needed to put the question, in a natural manner, as to when Beth had arrived in Scotland, to work out if the actress had time to become Lord Balfour's lover. 'Where else have you visited since you arrived in the country, Miss Cornett?'

'Oh, heaps of places!' Beth smiled. 'Well, I'll get back to Eddie. The poor boy frets if he thinks I'm away for too long. Now, if he knew I was out and about with that handsome footman...' She winked at Poppy before setting off back to the house.

Dash it, thought Poppy; she'd have to find an opportunity to ask Beth later. Now, though, she was at the loch and would concentrate on looking for clues.

Telling Major to stay, she threw the reins of her horse over the hedge and went through the gap in the shrubbery. All the activities of the house party as they'd gone hither and yon, the police, the removal of the body and whatever Beth and the footman had been up to, meant that the sandy area where the man had been found was a churned-up mess.

Footprints were completely out of the question, but what other clues might there be? No murder weapon had been found near the body. What about fragments of clothing caught on the bushes? Had the constable, while he waited for the ambulance to take away the body, searched in the shrubbery? She felt sure he must have, but there was no harm in looking anyway.

Poppy worked her way along the hedging, parting branches and peering in. All she achieved was a tear in the cuff of her blouse. *Drat!* She pictured Elspeth looking down her long nose and sniffily asking what her ladyship had been up to.

Poppy looked around. There didn't seem to be anything else here to investigate. Her thoughts turned to the conversation she'd had with the doctor at the murder scene. It had seemed unlikely to both of them that the man had been killed elsewhere and brought here, but she needed to be sure.

She considered again the murdered man's frame. Not particularly tall, but stout, so he would have been heavy to carry. Could a killer acting alone have carried him any distance? No, unless they were looking for a pair of killers, it was much more likely that the victim had been struck down here...

Her eye fell on the path, which Freddy had said led to a track and in turn to the village. It was close to one o'clock and it would be impolite to be late for lunch. There was nothing else for it; she'd have to come back later to investigate the track.

'So, Major Lewis,' she said, returning through the gap in the shrubbery and addressing the dog reclining on the grass, his chin on his front paws. He looked up. 'Had the murderer come from the house or the village?' Poppy was determined to keep an open mind as to who the killer might be. 'And had he been hanging about in the bushes on the chance that the victim – or perhaps *any* victim – would come along, or did he know the man's habits, or had the two men arranged to meet here? What do you think?'

Major sat up and sneezed.

'I agree. The murderer must at least have known that his victim would be here at that time. Which means that either it was the victim's custom to walk by the loch at that time of day – in which case, surely Constance or one of the servants would know, or, much more likely, the victim had agreed to meet the man here, who then murdered him.'

Poppy felt a moment of satisfaction, before realising that this took her no further forward. If only the identity of the dead man was known. She sighed. Perhaps it wasn't so easy being a detective, after all.

But *nil desperandum*, she told herself, straightening her spine. Never despair. 'Ready, Major?'

The dog got to his feet, disappeared through the hedge and she heard a loud splash. A pair of mallards rose in fright, the male with feathers in iridescent green, the mottled brown female quacking loudly. Peering over the top of the shrubbery, Poppy watched Major swim in a large circle. He returned to the grass where she stood and shook himself, sending droplets of cool water flying.

'That wasn't quite what I meant when I asked if you were ready,' she told him, brushing off the droplets.

He gave her a look to indicate *he* was perfectly satisfied.

Her horse was growing restless. 'You're ready to go, Arthur, I think?'

Poppy placed one foot in the stirrup, sprang up into the saddle and made her way back.

Arthur was trotting up the avenue leading to the house, Major gambolling happily alongside, when a tall, dark figure emerged from the main door and began to stride in her direction.

Inspector MacKenzie...

She slowed the horse to a walk as the policeman drew near.

'Were you looking for me, Inspector?' she asked brightly, enjoying the experience of looking down at him from the saddle. His tousled black hair was level with her knee.

He looked up at her. 'Do you have something to tell me, my lady?'

'Not at present.' She pressed her knees into the horse's flanks and urged the animal into a trot.

Startled, the inspector took a step back, out of her way.

Poppy guided Arthur round to the side of the house and towards the stables. That was ill-mannered, she chided herself. And foolish. Even if she had nothing she wished to tell him at present, he might have some information she could use. The reliability of the town hall clock, for example. A small matter, but one that could be important.

What *were* the things policemen look for in a crime? She had been concentrating on the scene of the crime, and the footman and the chauffeur, but she needed to be more focused. Method, motive and opportunity. They were the things the police considered.

The method had been the blow to the head, but the weapon was yet to be found. Motive was also as yet unknown, but the rough track suggested opportunity.

This she would investigate after lunch.

. . .

'How did you find Culross?' Poppy asked the Americans over lunch, wondering if she should avoid Beth's eye.

Beth, however, was unabashed. 'It's the prettiest little place. It was a real pity we had to come back early, but Mr Emmett was feeling a bit off colour. I'd say it must have been the heat, but California is much hotter than little old Scotland.'

'Oh dear,' Constance said. 'I hope you're feeling better now, Mr Emmett?'

'Much better, thanks.' He speared a piece of roast pigeon on his fork.

'And that you, Miss Cornett, found something else to amuse you before lunch,' Constance added.

Beth smiled broadly. 'Yes, I did, Connie.' She winked at Poppy.

Poppy had to admire the girl's audaciousness. 'You were saying about Culross,' she prompted.

'So many old buildings! There's a palace and a market cross, a church with a tower and a ruined abbey. *And*,' Beth shuddered theatrically, 'a town hall where they used to jail and torture witches.'

'After their trial, the witches were strangled and their bodies burned, so there was no record of them,' Gregor said with a fourteen-year-old boy's relish.

'Don't you mean after a guilty verdict at their trial?' put in Poppy.

'Oh, they were always found guilty,' Gregor went on cheerfully. 'In fact,' he added darkly as the thought came to him, 'I wouldn't be at all surprised if a witch had killed that man by the loch by putting a spell on him.'

'Don't be foolish, Gregor,' said Constance, clattering her cutlery down. 'The poor man was hit on the back of the head.'

'And those unfortunate women were not actually witches,' Poppy pointed out.

Gregor sent her a disgruntled look. 'Says you,' he muttered, taking care that his mother, picking up her cutlery again, didn't hear him.

Poppy looked around the table at the diners and her eyes settled on Beth. How she would love to get a better look at the bracelet the young woman had worn, now that she had read the description on the jeweller's invoice.

'You mentioned earlier that you've visited a number of places since you arrived in the country, Miss Cornett,' Poppy said, steering the conversation in that direction in the hope that she might uncover a previous link between Beth and Lord Balfour.

'I sure have. Now let me think.' Beth sat with a small frown. 'First there was Edinburgh, where we met Nick, of course.' She smiled warmly at him.

So the party Beth had mentioned when they'd met Nick had been only a short time ago. Certainly after Lord Balfour's death, which meant she couldn't have got to know him then. Had she met him *before*, somehow?

'Then we went to some other cute villages,' Beth went on, 'and then we came here. Yes, that's about it.'

'What did you think of our capital city?' Constance asked.

'It was swell,' put in Mr Emmett, lowering his fork. 'All that history.' He returned his fork to his mouth.

'I trust you had enough time to see all the sights?' Poppy said politely.

Eddie replied. 'We sure did. Edinburgh is only a small town, so we did it in a couple of days.'

Poppy drew in an affronted breath. Edinburgh was a small *city*, as cities go, but there was a lot to see: the castle, Holyrood Palace, the museum and art galleries, Camera Obscura, the Scott Monument, Calton Hill, Arthur's Seat... Forget Arthur's Seat, she told herself, as Beth didn't seem the type to go hiking, even on sunny days. Poppy couldn't imagine Miss Cornett climbing the steep rough ground in her high heels and short shimmery dresses.

She still had questions to ask. Picking up her glass of wine, Poppy said casually, 'So how long have you been in Scotland?'

'Only a few weeks,' Beth added, before glancing at Nick, 'but it feels like we've known Nick for much longer.'

'Our acquaintance does seem to have gone on somewhat,' Morag interjected. She gazed mildly round the table, before returning to the food on her plate.

Poppy stifled a gasp at the woman's subtle rudeness, but Beth didn't seem to have noticed the put-down.

So Beth and the others had been in Scotland for only a few weeks, Poppy reasoned. Thank goodness. That meant that Lord Balfour could not possibly have given the bracelet to Beth. Relief flooded over Poppy for Constance's sake.

'Although,' Mr Emmett said, 'this is not our first trip to the United Kingdom.'

Poppy started. 'Really?'

'The three of us were in London in early November.'

'Dad was down then too!' put in Gregor. 'I wanted to go with him, but he said he had business to see to and besides I was too young.'

Poppy caught her breath. The Americans – more particularly, Beth Cornett – and Lord Balfour were both in London towards the end of last year?

'Your father was correct,' said his mother sternly. 'Sixteen will be quite old enough for you to visit London.'

'Are you going to take me when I'm sixteen?' he demanded of his mother.

'Your uncle will,' Constance said evasively.

'I won't,' stated Nick. 'Not unless your behaviour has improved by then.'

'Well, I call that absolutely rotten of you!' Gregor fell to glaring at his uncle.

None of the Americans had volunteered they'd met Lord Balfour in London, Poppy observed. Even if he and Beth had grown close in London, there would hardly have been enough time for him to purchase the bracelet in Edinburgh and then present it to her before he died.

Poppy let out her breath. Another admirer might have given Beth the jewellery. Poppy's glance fell on Eddie. He was not a famous actor, so it was unlikely he could afford to buy an expensive bracelet. Eddie was casting a dark look at Beth. Now, what was that about?

'I am sure I would be very uncomfortable so far from home,' Morag announced placidly. 'But then I am not at all fond of foreign travel or foreign food.'

Mr Emmett coughed on the wine he was drinking, before wiping his mouth with the napkin and asking, 'Has that cop finished here now?'

'I wouldn't have thought so.' Constance's voice was grim. 'The inspector has gone into the village for what he called his dinner, but I imagine he will return again.'

So that's where he was going, thought Poppy. Why couldn't he simply have told her? Because she hadn't given him a chance, muttered a voice in her head. Anyway, why wasn't he eating in the kitchen with the servants?

She blushed. Had she actually thought his place was in the kitchens? Poppy shook her head and, as her face cooled, returned to the task of gathering information.

'Such a delightful view, Constance.' Poppy gestured towards the large sash window where sunlight streamed in. 'How fortunate I am to have a room overlooking the gardens.'

'Beautiful, isn't it? The house has been very well designed, to ensure a number of the bedrooms look out over that view.'

Yes, but whose? She prepared to try again, but Mr Emmett spoke first.

'Constance here has done us proud,' he said with a smile. 'The three of us can also see the backyard.'

Constance paled at the description of her splendid gardens as a backyard.

Nick and his wife said nothing about their rooms. But then, why would they? Whatever the view from their respective rooms, it would be normal for them as presumably frequent visitors, hence not worth a comment.

She now knew the Americans could see the loch, but they had said earlier they'd noticed nothing untoward during the evening of the murder. Had one of them lied? But why would they, unless they had something to hide? Then again, what were the chances they'd be looking out of the window at the exact time someone bludgeoned the man to death? Very low. Poppy sighed inwardly as the chatter around the table grew louder, and decided this line of her murder investigation could be dispensed with.

Until she returned to the city tomorrow and questioned the jeweller about Constance's bracelet, there was nothing to do about the hunt for the missing piece. Her thoughts turned to the murdered man and she wondered if the inspector had yet wrung a name out of Freddy. Whether he had or not, she was determined that the next thing she must do was speak to the footman about the identity of the murdered man.

She glanced across to where the butler and Freddy stood by the sideboard, ready to pour more wine, or clear the dishes and serve the next course. When lunch was over, she would find a way to speak to the footman without attracting unwanted attention.

Poppy was growing increasingly certain he had something to hide.

SEVEN

As soon as the rest of the party had left the table, and the butler taken himself off for a short rest in his pantry, Poppy slipped back into the dining room.

Startled, Freddy looked up from clearing the lunch dishes. 'My lady,' he said, putting a china serving dish hastily onto the silver tray. 'Is there something I can do for your ladyship?'

'There jolly well is, Freddy.' Poppy stood opposite and fixed him with her gaze. 'I saw you with the murdered man yesterday afternoon in the village. Why did you tell the police inspector you'd never seen him before?'

The footman flushed. 'I don't know what you mean.'

'Oh yes, you do,' she said firmly. 'The man bumped into you in the street and a short while later you followed him into the Red Lion.'

'Can't a fellow have a drink?' he muttered, moving a second used dish onto the tray.

'Freddy, look at me.'

He did so reluctantly.

'Well?'

Poppy waited. It was her experience that a long enough

wait usually produced an honest answer. Freddy's shoulders sagged and he took his hands from the tray. 'I don't know his real name, your ladyship.'

Aha! Her instinct had been correct. She folded her arms. 'What name *do* you know him by?'

'Honest Harry,' Freddy said quietly.

'Honest Harry!' She dropped her arms. 'What sort of a name is that?'

'It's a very good name – for a bookie's runner.'

'A bookie's runner!'

'Please, your ladyship.' Freddy cast an anxious glance at the open door behind her.

Poppy stared at the footman. She knew that taking bets, and running with them to the officially registered bookie, was illegal. Quickly she closed the dining room door.

'If Lady Balfour found out you were placing bets, you'd lose your job.' It was a statement, not a question.

'Yes, my lady.' Freddy hung his head.

One of the many rules in large houses was often that servants were not to engage in gambling of any description. Such a servant was open to being blackmailed into telling their employers' secrets. Had this already happened to Freddy?

Poppy again waited, certain there was something more, and she was right.

'Lord Balfour liked a flutter on the horses,' Freddy said eventually. 'He got me the job of walking her ladyship's dog, so I could go to the village to meet Honest Harry and place his lordship's bets for him.'

Lord Balfour! So *he* was the person gambling. 'But betting on horses is not illegal. Lord Balfour could have placed his bets at the racecourse, or by post or telephone.'

Poppy suddenly realised that she had never seen Constance play any form of cards. Nor was it suggested by her hostess they have a game yesterday evening, despite whist being popular at house parties. 'Lady Balfour disapproves of gambling,' Poppy said. Another statement.

Freddy nodded unhappily. 'His lordship didn't want Lady Balfour to know.'

'Did he lose often?'

'Let's just say the horse didn't always come in first.' Freddy's voice was rueful.

Oh dear, Poppy thought.

'Once he dropped five hundred pounds,' Freddy added quietly.

She gasped. 'Five hundred pounds! Good Lord. How did he choose the horses?'

'I'd suggest two or three and he made the final choice.' Freddy looked worried. 'You won't tell Lady Balfour, will you?'

'Can it matter any longer, now that Lord Balfour has passed away?'

The footman straightened his back. 'Perhaps not, my lady, but I promised his lordship I would always keep it under my hat.'

So Freddy was a man of principle, in this at least. 'You said you placed the bets with Honest Harry in the village. Was that at the Red Lion Inn where I spotted you yesterday?' she asked.

Freddy nodded.

'This doesn't quite make sense,' Poppy went on slowly. 'Lord Balfour died six months ago. Why are you continuing to meet the runner?'

Freddy gazed down at the table, covered in the dirty dishes. She had a fleeting memory of that morning when she'd entered the servants' hall to speak to the inspector and had seen the footman seated at the table, eyes down as he read a salmon-coloured newspaper.

'*The Pink 'Un!*' she exclaimed.

He looked up quickly. 'You know it?'

'I know *of* it. *The Sporting Times* is *the* newspaper for horse racing.' It was known popularly as *The Pink 'Un*.

'That's correct, my lady. I would go through it, choose the most likely-looking horses for, say, the two thirty race at Musselburgh, tell his lordship and place bets on his behalf.'

Poppy took a guess. 'And at the same time, you placed your own bets with Honest Harry?'

Freddy gave a slight shrug. 'I was trying to build up a nice little nest egg. I don't want to be in service all my days. But Honest Harry told me yesterday that he wasn't coming here any longer. He said my bets weren't big enough to make it worth his while coming out from Musselburgh.'

No, they wouldn't be, Poppy thought. Poor Freddy; the end of his dream to set himself up in some business, perhaps. But would the runner's decision to end the arrangement have been enough for Freddy to have killed the man? She didn't think so, but once this came out, and it would, Freddy would be at the top of the suspect list.

'He had no other customers in this area?' she asked.

Freddy shook his head. 'I don't think so. Or if he had, they would be small punters like me.'

The footman appeared to be telling the truth, but how could she be sure? 'Why did you not tell the inspector this?'

'Our bets – Lord Balfour's and mine – have nothing to do with Honest Harry's murder.' Freddy's hands curled into fists. 'The police don't need to know.'

The inspector should probably be the judge of that, Poppy thought. On the other hand, she had tried to help Inspector MacKenzie with his investigation and he'd brushed her off, telling her to leave policing to the proper authorities. She was inclined to let him discover the information for himself.

'One last question, Freddy. Did you meet Honest Harry by the loch yesterday, after you'd walked Ollie?'

He flushed deeply. 'Who told you that?'

'Never mind who said it—'

'I can guess!' Two pink spots appeared on his cheeks. 'It'll be that chauffeur, Charlie Lamont. He's always looking for a way to get rid of me.' Freddy gathered up a handful of cutlery and it clattered onto the tray.

'But did you meet this man, Honest Harry, yesterday afternoon by the loch?' she persevered.

'No, my lady,' Freddy answered, his voice sullen.

'And the track you said was overgrown: did you use that to get to the village and back?'

'It *is* overgrown; I didn't say it was never used. Aye, my lady, I've always taken it when meeting Harry in the village, so that I'm not away from the house for too long,' he reluctantly admitted.

'What time did you get back from Culross?'

Freddy shook his head. 'I don't know for certain, as I don't possess a watch, but it must have been not long before six o'clock.'

'And you saw no one by the loch on your return from Culross – not Honest Harry or anyone else?'

Freddy's cheeks were still flushed. 'No, my lady.'

Could she believe him? He'd not exactly told a lie but had been economical with the truth when asked this morning about the track to the village.

'I'll let you get on with your work, Freddy,' Poppy told him.

Now it was time for her to move onto the next step and investigate the rough path into Culross. Her instincts were turning out to be right. She would show that inspector a thing or two about crime puzzles.

And may the best girl win!

With Major running ahead and sniffing for rabbits, Poppy walked down to the loch and followed the path that went around the edge of the water. Before long, Major found the start of the track leading off the path and he hesitated, sending a questioning look back at Poppy.

'Good boy!' she called, hastening her steps to reach him.

She glanced down at the track. It was like one of those paths in *Peter Pan* that have made themselves: wide at one spot, and at another so narrow that you can stand astride them. It was certainly narrow at this end and she wasn't sure she would have found it without Major. She nodded at him and he bounded forward, the tall bracken swaying at his boisterous progress. She followed.

The track was formed of dry, beaten earth and it was impossible for Poppy to tell if it had been used recently or not. The bracken brushed aside as they pushed through and closed again behind them.

The rough path ran around the edge of a potato field, the neat rows of green leaves shining under the blue sky. She strode on, Major disappearing from sight every now and again as he investigated some new scent.

Her conversation with Freddy troubled her. What the footman had told her about the bookie's runner being no longer interested in Freddy's small bets could certainly be true. But what if it was something else? What if Honest Harry hadn't lived up to his name and, thinking the horse had no chance, had not placed Freddy's bet with the bookmaker, but instead had kept the money and then been unable to pay out Freddy's winnings?

She'd heard such things sometimes happened. If so, had Freddy killed Harry in a fit of rage? Poppy had noticed the way the footman's hands had curled into fists when she was talking to him in the dining room. But if the runner had done such a thing – not paid Freddy – why would he have met Freddy by the loch? Surely it would be easier just to... well, *run*.

The track took her into the outskirts of a wood. The sweet

resin smell of the Scots pine, released by the heat, was pleasant, but the tall, dense trees in the plantation cast a dark and unwelcoming gloom. She quickened her steps.

Some distance through the trees, Poppy caught sight of a single-storey cottage, surely uninhabited with such a sagging thatch roof. She started at a mournful, high-pitched mew and a large, brown buzzard soared out of the tree tops, up and away into the cloudless sky. She laughed softly at herself and walked on.

Now the track skirted round a second field. Cheviot sheep, with the breed's famous wee smiles on their white faces, chewed as they gazed about them.

'Major, heel,' she called and the Labrador returned, walking along beside her.

Before long, she could see the village ahead. 'Almost there,' she told Major. He glanced up at Poppy, a look of enquiry on his face which could well have been about the opening hours of the butcher's shop.

She glanced back down the track. It was an excellent way of arriving at Balfour House unseen, for it passed no dwellings, save the forlorn-looking cottage. If the killer had come this way, he was most unlikely to have been seen by anyone.

No sooner had Poppy thought this than Inspector MacKenzie's unmistakable figure appeared walking towards her from the direction of the village. He had shed the ridiculous raincoat, but his clothing still looked too hot for the weather. Although, she had to admit, he did look good in the dark suit...

Major, his tail wagging, ran towards him.

'Major Lewis, you traitor,' she muttered between her teeth. 'We meet again, Inspector!' she called.

He raised his hat. 'Just so, my lady.'

Major bounded up and nudged the policeman's long legs, who obliged with a pat on the dog's head. Major sat and looked hopefully between Poppy and the inspector.

'He seems to like you,' she said at length.

'And I like him.' Inspector MacKenzie smiled.

She waited; she couldn't get past the inspector without stepping into the long grass and she had no intention of doing that.

He cleared his throat. 'I'm thinking that, after what you said this morning, the footman might be involved in this business in some way.'

'Bravo, Inspector!' Poppy clapped her hands. Instantly she regretted her childish outburst on seeing a dark flush warm his face. 'But tell me, Inspector, what brings you out here on this glorious afternoon? Surely you didn't come just to tell me that I have been even a little helpful to your case?'

He began again. 'Don't be taking this the wrong way, your ladyship, but are you certain that you saw the footman in the village yesterday afternoon? Because the chauffeur is insistent that he'd seen him by the loch. If you are certain, the chauffeur must no' be telling the truth.'

'I certainly saw the footman in Culross. What exactly did the chauffeur say?'

'He told me he'd been outside the garage and had just finished washing Lady Balfour's car, at about six o'clock, when he spotted Freddy coming away from the loch.'

'He could hardly have been certain of identity at that distance, surely?'

'The man was in footman's livery and he was walking towards the house.'

'With Lady Balfour's dog?'

'He had no dog with him.'

'And he was *sure* it was Freddy? Did he wait and watch the footman enter the house?'

'No, my lady, he did not watch him go into the house because his tea was ready, but he is certain it was Freddy.'

'It does seem rather conclusive... *if* Charlie is telling the truth.'

'Just so.'

Poppy frowned. She'd seen Freddy in the village between half past five and six o'clock. He could have run all the way back to the house, presumably with Ollie tucked under his arm, using this very shortcut that Inspector MacKenzie was now blocking. 'Was there anything else you wanted to speak to me about, Inspector?'

'No, I just needed to have your confirmation that you had seen Freddy in the village yesterday afternoon and that it could have been no one else.' He bent to give Major a gentle scratch behind one ear.

'I am certain it was he,' she said firmly.

'Very well. Thank you.'

'Inspector, can I ask a question?'

'You can, but I cannot guarantee to answer it.'

'The cigarette end found by the body. Could it have been the murderer's?' Freddy had been smoking when he was left with the body, which would be a good way for him to cover any cigarette ends he'd dropped while waiting for Honest Harry to appear.

'It could have been, but it was the same make as those in the dead man's pocket, so it's just as likely that the victim was smoking it when he was attacked.' Inspector MacKenzie doffed his hat and prepared to stand aside.

'Inspector.'

He turned back. 'Aye, my lady?'

'Can I do anything to help?'

'Such as?'

'I don't know... chat to any suspects. Oh, I suppose we are all suspects...' *Of course we are!* She smiled at him, but he made no response. 'Nevertheless, I'm sure I can find out things that a police officer can't.' Poppy warmed to her theme. 'The house guests, for example, won't be on their guard with me.'

He was not to be drawn. 'Real detective work involves questioning people, finding out who's lying and piecing things together.'

'I can do that!'

'And then arresting the culprit? I think not. Do you believe they'll come along politely for you because you're a lady? This is a hanging offence, your ladyship. No one comes along nicely for one of those. Besides, it takes a trained eye to spot a culprit and it's rarely the least likely person. It's almost always the most likely person who's done it.'

'Then it should be easy,' Poppy said brightly.

Inspector MacKenzie sighed. 'I feel I must caution you in the strongest possible terms to leave policing to trained officers, my lady.'

Poppy gritted her teeth at his tone. *Then you can find out for yourself the name and occupation of the deceased.* And, she suddenly realised, the connection between Freddy and Harry. Good relations between the police and the public are necessary if the police have any chance of catching criminals... and so it really was Inspector MacKenzie's own fault that he didn't know what she knew.

'I am on my way to speak to Lady Balfour,' he went on, 'and to remind everyone that I require none of the party leave the area until further notice.'

Well, that's just too bad, Poppy thought, channelling her inner American. She gave Inspector MacKenzie a warm smile, while thinking she was going to Edinburgh first thing in the morning as planned and didn't give a fig for what he thought of that. She had a case to solve for Lady Balfour.

'Delightful as it is to see you, Inspector,' she said, indicating her wish to continue along the track, 'I must get on.'

'For a path that isn't used, it's busy this afternoon,' he observed, gently scratching Major behind one ear and not moving out of her way.

She smiled. 'Yes. Isn't it marvellous? For once we agree on something.'

'You are not on this track with the intention of investigating, are you?'

Good Lord, she thought, he sounded like Elspeth.

He removed his hat and ran his fingers through his thick, dark curls.

But he was definitely better-looking than Elspeth.

'I am simply exercising my dog, Inspector,' Poppy said with a smile.

'That's good to hear.'

She suddenly remembered the village clock. 'Oh, Inspector, have you discovered if the clock on the town hall keeps good time?'

'That question sounds verra much as though you are investigating,' he said slowly, replacing his hat.

'It's always useful to know if the time on a clock is correct.'

He didn't look convinced, but he answered her question. 'I have checked and yes, it does keep good time.'

He tipped his hat and stood aside to let her pass. She nodded her thanks and stepped forward. The track was so narrow at this point that she couldn't prevent her hand brushing against his warm thigh.

'Apologies, my lady,' he said, his voice deep. He took a further step back into the bracken.

'No apologies needed, Inspector,' she told him as she passed. It had been rather a pleasant experience.

'No doubt we will meet again,' she heard him say behind her.

'No doubt,' she replied over her shoulder. But not tomorrow, Poppy thought. She had a young lady to meet off the train at Waverley station and a jeweller to question.

But first, she was going to see if there was information to be obtained from the Culross postmistress.

EIGHT

Poppy strode on, trying to banish thoughts of the inspector.

At the end of the track stood a wooden stile. Taking care not to catch and tear her pale green pleated skirt, she climbed over and stepped down onto the road. A few yards further on stood Culross.

She looked at her wristwatch. Her guess had been correct when drawing up the timings sheet: the track had taken around fifteen minutes to walk. Deducting time for the conversation with Inspector MacKenzie, this route between Balfour House and the village would probably take only ten minutes, making it five minutes shorter than walking along the main road. She would check the timing on her way back to be certain. It was also, bar meeting the inspector who was no doubt on the path for the same reason, considerably more private.

Poppy headed to the general stores and post office. She was convinced the postmistress was something of a gossip. They often were and, judging by the length of time it had taken to be served the previous afternoon when queuing to buy the picture postcard, she was right.

As she made her way down the street, women peeped

round curtains or came to the doors of their cottages to watch her. One put on her hat and grabbed a shopping basket to follow Poppy, presumably in the hope of learning what was happening up at the big house. The news of the murder by the loch would have reached the village.

Poppy held tightly onto Major's collar as they passed the butcher's shop. The dog's nose twitched and his eyes brightened, but he controlled himself today.

She had almost reached the post office when a bookshop caught her eye, and more particularly a book in the window. She stopped and gazed at the bright red cover printed with the words *The M. McIntyre Detective Agency's Casebook*. This must be the same agency Lady Duddingston had spoken of. Instructing Major to follow her, Poppy turned the door handle and entered the shop.

'I'd like to see a book you have in the window,' she told the elderly man who looked up from dusting the shelves.

He put the duster down. 'Which one, madam?'

'*The M. McIntyre Detective Agency's Casebook*,' she informed him.

'Certainly, madam.' He reached into the window display and removed it. 'Our last copy. It's been very popular.' He smiled as he handed it to her.

Poppy flicked through the pages. It was a fairly slim volume, but exactly what she needed now that she was detecting on her own.

'Thank you.' She realised she had brought no bag, and therefore no money, with her. 'I will take the book with me – Lady Persephone Proudfoot, staying at Balfour House – and my maid will come to pay for it tomorrow.'

'Very good, your ladyship.'

A thought struck her. 'Do you also have a notebook?'

'I do, indeed.' He indicated two neat piles on a table. She examined them both, decided against the kind with a paper cover and lined pages – her handwriting was too much of a scrawl for that – and handed the man a notebook with plain pages and a stiff black cover.

She waited while he wrapped both books in brown paper and tied the little parcel with string. He handed it to her, she thanked him, bid him good day, and she and Major left the shop.

Swinging her parcel by the string, she continued along the street and came to the post office and general stores. The window held a display of tins of fruit and clothes pegs, packets of sugar and cleaning products. Instructing Major to sit and stay outside, she pushed open the door. The scents of tea, cheese, bacon and biscuits permeated the place, and would have been too much for her dog's quivering black nose. Today there were no other customers present, but the postmistress, a large woman, with untidy grey hair and a small mouth, was weighing raisins at the counter.

'Good afternoon, madam,' she said to Poppy. 'I will be with you in just a moment.'

'Good afternoon.' Poppy waited while the woman tipped the contents of the scales onto a sheet of thick blue paper and expertly folded the dried fruit into a neat package. She placed it to one side on the counter.

'How can I help you?'

'I'm staying at Balfour House, where you may have heard there's been an unfortunate incident.'

'Most unfortunate,' murmured the woman, her grey eyes lighting up.

'I'm helping Inspector MacKenzie to investigate the crime.' Well, that was only a little white lie – she *was* helping him. That he didn't want her help was by the by. He'd be grateful, soon enough, if it led to an arrest. 'My name is Lady Persephone Proudfoot.'

The postmistress audibly sucked in a deep breath, her eyes widening.

'It would be very helpful if you could tell me anything about the man who was in here yesterday afternoon. He wore a dark brown tweed jacket.' That was very little to go on, Poppy realised, but if he lived in the area, the postmistress would know him, and if he didn't, she would remember him for that reason alone.

The postmistress hesitated, clearly caught between her professional duty and the desire to know more. 'What sort of information are you looking for, my lady?'

'His name would be helpful,' Poppy began.

The woman shook her head. 'I can't tell you that, your ladyship. As a civil servant, I'm sworn to secrecy, you understand.'

'Quite,' Poppy said, realising she needed to take a different tack. 'Then I wonder if you can tell me what the gentleman came in for? In purely general terms, that is.' If it had been for tobacco, say, that didn't take her any further forward. But if he had put money into a savings account, for example, that suggested he might have lived locally. The footman had told her the man came out from Musselburgh, but there was no harm in checking for herself.

'I do mind that, your ladyship,' the postmistress said hesitantly, 'but...'

Poppy smiled her most engaging smile. The one that had loosened the purse strings of many a society lady to help fund her hospital for wounded soldiers.

'He had been paying in a muckle amount of money on a regular basis.' The words flew out of the postmistress's mouth.

Poppy nodded. That was most helpful.

'Can you give me an idea of how muckle?' After all, she thought, they may well have differing ideas as to what amounts to large.

The woman looked shocked. 'I couldna possibly reveal that,

your ladyship.' She began to rearrange the jars of gobstoppers and aniseed balls on the counter.

'Of course not,' Poppy said quickly. 'Please continue.'

The postmistress returned her attention to Poppy and lowered her voice, despite there being no one else in the shop. 'As I was saying, he was paying in large sums, until about six months ago, when the payments became... much less.'

'I see,' Poppy said. 'So was he a local man?'

She frowned, her head drawing back. 'Michty me, no.'

It fitted in with what Freddy had told her. She heard the shop door open behind her and close again.

'I won't be long, Mrs Anderson.' The postmistress resumed a business-like manner as she peered over Poppy's shoulder to address the new customer.

'That's all right, my dear,' came the reply. 'I'll only be wanting half a yard of knicker elastic.'

Poppy could see the postmistress wasn't going to tell her anything else, not with a customer in the shop to overhear her, so feeling disappointed, she thanked the woman and left.

'Good boy,' she said to Major waiting outside. His tail wagged as she patted him absent-mindedly on the head.

So the dead man had been paying money into an account, but whose? Surely the job of a runner was to take the bets he collected to the licenced bookmaker and not pay the cash into the post office? And where was the paying-in book now? No such thing had been found on his dead body.

She had to think what exactly her next steps should be in the murder investigation. And there was the missing bracelet case to solve too.

A little shiver of anticipation went through her. A detective's work is never done!

. . .

In her room later, Poppy slipped out of her blouse and threw it onto the bed as she dressed for dinner.

Elspeth immediately pounced on the garment. 'How did you get this tear in the cuff, my lady?' she asked, turning the white sleeve over in her hands.

'Oh, I went riding this morning,' Poppy said casually as she wriggled out of the jodhpurs.

Her maid looked concerned. 'Did you fall from the horse?'

'It was more of a *scramble*,' Poppy told her.

Elspeth frowned and gave one of her disparaging sniffs. 'Investigating again, my lady?'

It was dashed difficult trying to hide anything from her maid. 'I paid a brief visit to the loch,' Poppy admitted, 'and the shrubbery got in the way.'

'Indeed, your ladyship. The assault on this blouse is quite severe. Perhaps you should make another of those columned pages and call it *The Case of the Violent Shrubbery*.'

Poppy looked at her maid in astonishment. 'Elspeth, you have made a joke!'

Elspeth put the torn shirt carefully aside and gave a small smile. 'I have been known to do such a thing from time to time, my lady.'

Poppy grinned. While Elspeth was in such a good mood, she would tell her what she'd learned today. 'I also had a chat with Freddy and found out the name of the murdered man, and I followed the footpath that the killer probably used, and—'

Elspeth's face fell. Oh dear, thought Poppy. Too much, too soon.

'Does the inspector know about this, your ladyship?' Elspeth had recovered her chilly tone.

'Some of it,' Poppy conceded. 'I met MacKenzie on the footpath.' She moved into the bathroom.

'Don't you think you should tell him all of it?' Elspeth said through the door.

Poppy turned the taps on full and ran water into the basin. 'I'm sorry, I didn't hear what you said,' she called back.

By the time Poppy had washed and come out of the bathroom, Elspeth had laid out her emerald chiffon evening gown and her white stockings.

'I think the pearl necklace, the short one, and the matching drop earrings for this evening,' Poppy said as she sat on the edge of the bed and rolled each stocking in turn over her foot, smoothing the sheer silk up her leg.

'I bought a book in the village today,' she went on, clipping the stockings to her suspenders.

'Very good, my lady.' Elspeth set out the jewellery on a velvet cloth on the dressing table. 'I trust it is of a self-improving nature.'

'Oh, it is, absolutely!'

Elspeth was clearly still displeased by her investigative work and wasn't going to ask the title.

Poppy stood and submitted to Elspeth sliding the chiffon dress over her head. She attempted not to move while her maid did up the buttons on the back.

'Try to keep still, my lady,' Elspeth said. 'These wee pearl fastenings are footery enough as it is.'

'Sorry, Elspeth. They must be fiddly. It's just that there are so many thoughts in my head...'

Elspeth only response was a heavy silence.

'By the way,' Poppy said casually, 'I am going to Edinburgh tomorrow and will be away for the night. Pack a bag for me, please.' She felt her maid's fingers pause on a pearl button.

'Edinburgh, my lady? I thought the inspector said no one was to leave the estate.'

'I wouldn't be going if it weren't important, you know.'

Elspeth's hands continued with their work. 'And what will happen when the inspector discovers you are not here?' she asked.

'That is where you come in, dear Elspeth! You and Major. Your presence here will mislead Inspector MacKenzie into thinking I am also present.'

'I'm sure I have no wish to mislead a police officer.'

'You won't need to *do* anything; simply be here.'

Another heavy silence. The woman could be so stubborn!

'The book I mentioned earlier,' Poppy went on. 'Can you go into Culross tomorrow and pay for it?' she continued, keeping very still.

'Yes, my lady.'

'Thank you, Elspeth. Oh, and I also bought a notebook.'

Elspeth finished the buttoning and came round to face Poppy. She raised her eyebrows. 'A notebook, my lady?'

'Yes, one of those books for making notes.'

After all, the sheet of paper she'd started to use wasn't going to be enough for all the clues she was gathering.

After dinner, a warm evening breeze filtered in through the open windows as the house party gathered in the drawing room. The butler and Freddy had been dismissed and a tray of after-dinner drinks stood on the sideboard for people to help themselves.

Conversation over dinner had strayed little from the events of the day, despite Constance repeatedly attempting to change the subject. But Gregor had been relentless in quizzing the adults for information on how a murder investigation was conducted.

'That fellow!' Nick said, in a tone of disgust, when Poppy told the assembled group of Inspector MacKenzie's reminder that none of them leave the area. 'A requirement, indeed! I think he meant a request. I despair of the working man these days. Since the war, these fellows seem to think they are allowed to voice their opinions any time they jolly well please and to whomever they jolly well please.'

Constance sighed. 'In the circumstances, we must do as we're asked, Nick.' She sent Poppy an agitated look. In response, Poppy shot her a warning glance not to mention her trip to Edinburgh in the morning.

'Still, I do hope the inspector will now leave us in peace while he goes about solving this awful business,' Constance went on. She turned to the Americans. 'I'm so sorry this should have happened during your visit.'

'Say, no need to apologise, Constance,' said Mr Emmett cheerfully as the telephone in the hall trilled out. 'It's given me some swell ideas for my next picture.'

'I did wonder if I should cancel the weekend party,' Constance went on.

'Shucks, no!' exclaimed Beth. 'We wouldn't want to miss it for the world.'

'They are right, Constance,' added Nick. 'It's better that the midsummer party goes ahead. I'm sure that's what Bruce would have wanted.' Seeing his sister-in-law's frown, he went on, 'And it will take your mind off what happened by the loch.'

'The inspector didn't say that no additional people should arrive,' Poppy pointed out, guessing that he had not thought to add that requirement.

The butler entered the drawing room. 'Beg your pardon, my lady, but the Marquess of Bannockburn is on the telephone and wishes to speak to you.'

'I suppose the news must be all over the neighbourhood,' Constance said. 'Tell him I've taken to my room with a headache, Baird. I have no wish to engage in gossip.'

The butler withdrew.

'Don't worry, Constance,' said Nick in a soothing tone, 'by the weekend this will all be forgotten.'

Poppy doubted it very much. She turned her thoughts to

tomorrow's trip to Edinburgh and the telling-off she would receive from Inspector MacKenzie when she returned – if he should realise she was absent, that is.

'I wonder what has happened to Innes,' Constance said, not for the first time.

'Don't bother fretting about him,' Nick said. 'I'm sure he'll arrive soon.'

'But he said they would be here in time for dinner. I do hope he's not met with an accident.'

'Like as not' – Nick paused to light a cigarette – 'like as not, he and his fiancée decided to stop for dinner somewhere en route. That's the sort of thoughtless behaviour I'd expect from my son.'

'I'm beginning to wonder which one of us did it,' said Morag, taking a sip of her whisky.

The drawing room fell silent.

'Did what?' Nick turned slowly to look at his wife.

'Murdered that man,' Morag said.

'For heaven's sake, Morag, why would you say something like that?'

She turned her vacant gaze around the room. 'But don't you all wonder that?'

Poppy cast her more focused eye around the room. Everyone looked uncomfortable to some degree at Morag's words, but did anyone look *furtive*? Could she be sure no one here had committed the crime?

'No, of course we don't wonder that,' Constance said crossly. 'Now can we please talk about something else?' She rose hastily at a series of loud, impatient thuds on the main door, echoing through the entrance hall. 'Oh dear, it sounds urgent. It might be the police.'

Nick sighed. 'It's probably just my good-for-nothing son's idea of a jape.'

As if in confirmation, footsteps and muffled laughter

sounded in the hall. The drawing room door flew open and a fair-haired man with a neat moustache, dressed in a driving coat, stood on the threshold. Major and a barking Ollie came running in with the new arrivals.

'Good evening, Aunt Constance. Mater and Pater. Americans, I believe. Young scallywag Gregor.' Innes nodded at each in turn, a beaming smile on his attractive face. 'That leaves only this delightful creature, who can be no other than Lady Persephone Proudfoot.' He stripped off his motoring gloves as he advanced towards Poppy, fixing her with a pair of grey eyes. A man with a smooth self-confidence, she decided, and not unattractive for that, although her preference these days leaned towards more studious men.

She extended a hand. 'Good evening, Mr Balfour. And to your fiancée.'

A young woman with a small, sharp nose and a jutting little chin stepped to Innes's side. Rosie removed her green cloche hat to reveal red hair cut in the very latest shingle style, shorter than a bob with the back of her neck exposed. She smiled confidently round the room at everyone.

Her gaze stopped at Beth Cornett. 'Are you the actress?'

'I sure am, honey.' Beth fluttered her eyelashes in a theatrical manner.

'Then you must know Rudolph Valentino?'

Beth's smile became fixed. 'Not yet.'

'How utterly grim for you. He's a frightfully good actor. I simply adored him in *The Sheik*.'

The butler had followed the couple into the room and stood by waiting for their outer garments. Rosie put her hat on Baird's head and draped her mink stole over his impassive shoulder, before opening her coat to reveal an impressive bust just about contained in a low-necked violet and pink dress.

'Rosie and I stopped for a spot of dinner along the way. I knew you wouldn't mind,' Innes said, unbuttoning his coat. He caught sight of his father's scowl and grinned. 'I say, Aunt, I hope you didn't hold the meal for us?' He went over to where Constance had resumed her seat on the settee and planted a kiss on her cheek.

'I persuaded Constance not to.' Nick took a step towards his offspring. 'But, dash it all, Innes, can't you think of anyone but yourself for a change?'

'I'll get you a drink, Rosie,' Innes addressed his fiancée, shooting an *as you see, I can think of others* smile at Nick as he strolled to the sideboard.

'We hear there's been a murder,' said Rosie, slipping off her coat and handing it to Baird. 'How simply thrilling.'

'Not thrilling, Rosie. Damned inconvenient, if you want the truth.' Nick stubbed out his cigarette in a nearby ashtray.

'Have a seat, dear.' Constance patted the space on the settee next to her.

'Do the police have any idea who killed the fellow?' Rosie asked, sitting down and keeping an eye on the little dachshund sniffing round her silk-clad ankles.

'No.' Constance bent forward to pick up Ollie and put him in her lap.

'Here, Major,' Poppy called to her dog, seated by Innes at the sideboard and looking up hopefully at him. 'None of us know,' she added as she instructed the Labrador to sit by her side. With a soulful expression, he rested his head on Poppy's knee.

'I had just been saying, one of us could be the murderer,' announced Morag, her tone matter-of-fact.

Poppy watched the others for a reaction. But what motive could anyone in the room possibly have? If Honest Harry's murder was related to his job, as she felt it must be, then his decision not to return to the village because of the lack of large bets must mean that no one above stairs used him. Or did they?

'I've always imagined that a murderer wouldn't be a normal

person,' Rosie said, accepting a lurid-coloured cocktail from Innes and lifting her glass. '*Slàinte.*' She took a sip of her drink. 'The killer must be someone who isn't in this house.'

'Of course he isn't, old girl.' Innes shrugged off his coat and tossed it to the waiting Baird, who caught it with an inscrutable look and silently withdrew.

Eddie produced a cigarette packet from his jacket pocket and moved from Beth's side to Rosie. 'Will you smoke, Miss...?'

'Hall, but do call me Rosie.' She looked at the packet in his hand. 'Would you think me very rude if I have one of my own?'

He flushed. 'Not at all.'

Rosie downed the remainder of her drink and held out the glass towards Innes, who went back to the sideboard for a refill. She extracted an enamelled case from her handbag and took from it a cigarette with a gold tip. Holding it to her lips, she waited for Eddie.

The young man took a lighter from his pocket, flicked it into life and leaned forward to light her cigarette. Rosie drew in the vapour and expelled it through her nostrils, narrowing her eyes at Beth as she did so.

'And now, Father dear,' said Innes cheerfully as he scooped up two full cocktail glasses and turned to face the rest of the gathering, 'tell us more about this grisly murder.'

By the time the new arrivals had been told as much as was known of the murder, Rosie was looking less composed and Innes considerably intrigued.

'Well, well, well,' Innes said with a grin. 'And who do you suspect did the foul deed, Aunt?'

'I'm sure that none of us had anything to do with it,' Constance stated.

'Of course not,' Nick said, scowling at his son. 'What an idea.'

'It's a case of waiting to see what the police find,' Poppy said quite untruthfully.

'Gosh-dingit,' exclaimed Beth, 'this party needs cheering up. What say you we have some music and a bit of a dance?'

'Gregor, it's time for your bed,' Constance told her son.

'That's nae fair,' Gregor grumbled. 'Just as the evening is getting going.'

'Do as you're told,' said Nick crossly.

'I'd rather stay. There might even be another murder.'

'Scram!' said Innes with a wink.

'Whose house is this, anyway?' demanded Gregor.

Constance flushed. 'Darling, don't be impertinent.'

'It's not your house,' Nick said sharply to his nephew.

'I never said it was. It belongs to my mother now, anyway, so it's all the same.' Gregor sent a beseeching look at his mother. 'Can I stay up, Mother? I won't get in the way, honestly.'

'Not tonight, dear. Go down to the kitchens and someone will make you a nice cup of Ovaltine.'

'Ovaltine!' he muttered.

'Bad luck, honey.' Beth gave him a sympathetic smile.

'All right, I'm going!' He directed a glare of veiled menace at his uncle as he left the room.

'Now, let's have that tune on the piano,' said Eddie.

Poppy glanced at Constance. Did their hostess think this appropriate, given a man had only yesterday been found murdered on the estate?

Seeing Poppy's surprised look, Constance said, 'I do feel dreadfully sorry for that poor dead man, of course, but, well, he's not one of us.'

Poppy bit back a retort. As she did so, a terrible thought came to her. Could Constance have been aware of her husband's gambling and of Honest Harry? Knowing Constance's view on betting, had Honest Harry been threatening to make the situation public? That would put Constance to shame, but surely the disgrace wouldn't be enough for her to murder the runner? And even if it were, Poppy couldn't see Constance herself killing the man, although she knew it was not impossible. Might she have persuaded Freddy to do the deed? After all, thought Poppy, she didn't know her hostess very well.

'Say, Innes,' Beth was saying, 'do you play?'

'Not the piano,' Innes replied with a wink.

Beth smiled coyly. 'Now you behave.'

Nick rose from the arm of the chair where his wife sat and strode over to the grand piano. He flicked up his coat-tails and took his seat on the stool. Constance moved to the sideboard and set about refreshing everyone's drinks, Ollie still under her arm.

'Say, honey, give us a five-chord ragtime progression. Do you know "Ja-Da"?' Beth sang, 'Ja-da, ja-da, jing... Along those lines.'

Nick played the opening bars.

'You're a peach!' she cried, jumping to her feet. 'Now everyone watch this. It's a new dance called the Charleston.' She held her hands out in front of her, pointed the toes on her left foot as she swayed her hands to the left, then swayed her hands to the right as she tapped her left foot to her right.

They all watched, mesmerised, while she went on to perform a further set of foot pointing and hand swaying, before starting all over again. As Nick got used to the tempo and played faster, Beth's dance grew ever more lively. She laughed at Nick as she danced, the fringed hem of her silver sequined dress flapping and revealing her knees, and he laughed back.

Poppy saw Eddie glowering at Beth, and noticed that Innes's gaze of admiration at the dancing girl was not lost on Rosie, while Morag watched Nick with a puzzled expression. No, not puzzled, thought Poppy. The strange faraway look in the woman's eyes and her distracted behaviour could mean something else: that Morag was addicted to drugs.

This realisation was followed by a further unpleasant thought. The 1920 Dangerous Drugs Act had changed drug addiction from a disease to an offence. Someone had to be supplying drugs to Morag, and her husband could hardly be unaware of it.

If Nick was procuring them, perhaps to keep her subdued for reasons of his own, what else might he be capable of? Poppy had a sudden mental image of this morning in the drawing room when they were quizzed by Inspector MacKenzie: Nick nervously turning his tortoiseshell cigarette case in his hands, and his rebuke to the inspector that the police would do better questioning the servants. And, now she came to think of it, Nick was insistent that the man by the loch had not been murdered but had met with an accident.

Poppy realised that it wasn't just Constance she didn't know as well as she thought.

Everyone in this room was almost a stranger to her.

And one of them could well be the murderer...

NINE

Poppy left Fife early the following morning, with Elspeth's admonition to *Remember you are a Lady!* ringing in her ear. The look in Major Lewis's dark brown eyes, when she called in to the kennels to bid him farewell, suggested he'd already planned some mischief.

Fergusson her chauffeur made good time to her house in Edinburgh. The warm yellow sandstone, bathed in the morning sunshine, the Georgian sash windows perfectly spaced and the imposing cream front door exactly in the middle of the house never failed to please her.

By half past ten, having washed, changed and breakfasted, she stepped out onto her doorstep in Ann Street and glanced around. Taking in a breath of the city air, she realised that, as much as she liked Edinburgh, the countryside at this time of year was much more pleasant. But she was a girl of action, eager to be doing something practical and helpful, and she had the mystery of the missing bracelet to solve. The case of the murder of Honest Harry would simply have to wait.

Poppy touched the cloche hat of black satin – very fetching with its white stitching and a large, white button ornament – to ensure it was sitting low on her brow. She fastened the buttons on her lightweight coat, black with white stitching, stepped down onto the garden path and turned into the leafy street. A walk of less than twenty minutes would bring her to George Street, housing Campbell's jeweller's shop.

Poppy turned jauntily into Dean Terrace, swinging her small, beaded bag on its chain. Taking a shortcut down quiet and charming Gloucester Lane, the low heel of her bar shoes tapping on the cobbles, she emerged into Queen Street, thronged with shoppers and sightseers. She dashed across the street, dodging the horse and carts, motor cars and buses, down North Castle Street, past the former marital home of Sir Walter Scott, and onto George Street.

Making her way along the crowded pavement, Poppy reached the jeweller's. She stood under the awning and gazed in the window at the displays of necklaces and bracelets, and rings slotted into black velvet trays. She considered what story to tell the proprietor and decided that honesty was the best policy: the bracelet could not be found and could he tell her when and where it had been delivered.

Poppy turned the highly polished brass handle. The bell above the door jangled as she entered. It was dim inside the shop after the sunshine outside, and it took her a moment to see the young assistant standing behind the counter with a welcoming smile.

'Can I help you, madam?'

Poppy peeled off her gloves and put them with her beaded bag on the glass counter. 'I'd like to speak to the owner.'

'I'm awfully sorry, but Mr Campbell is away pricing a jewellery collection.'

'That is disappointing.' Poppy went to retrieve her gloves and bag. 'Tell me when he is expected and I will return.' In the meantime, she could visit a dress shop or take tea in Jenners.

'Mr Campbell is often out of the establishment, madam,

doing valuations, and I'm not at all sure he'll be back before we close,' the shop assistant responded in her efficient voice. 'Are you sure I can't help?' She had clearly noted Poppy's well-cut coat.

Poppy decided to dispense with honesty and take a different approach. 'I'm looking for a bracelet.'

The assistant smiled. 'Then you have come to the right place. My name is Miss Strachan. If you could let me know your particular taste in jewellery...'

Poppy appeared to consider. 'Something elegant, obviously.'

'Obviously,' murmured the young woman.

'With diamonds.'

Miss Strachan inclined her head in agreement.

'And emeralds.'

Now Miss Strachan shook her head regretfully. 'Alas, we did have a piece I believe you would have liked, but it was sold some months ago. We do, however, have a particularly fine diamond and emerald necklace.'

'Oh, what a shame. I particularly wanted a bracelet. May I ask who was the lucky lady?'

The assistant simpered. 'I'm afraid I can't reveal that information, Miss...'

'Lady Persephone Proudfoot,' said Poppy. Using her title did have its merits, she thought.

Poppy glanced around the shop. 'There is no one else present. As you cannot name names, perhaps you could give me some information about the lady. It's quite possible I know her and might be able to persuade her to part with the bracelet for a suitable sum of money.'

Miss Strachan at once lowered her voice. 'It was a gentleman who bought it, my lady. He has a most discerning eye and has purchased a number of exquisite items from us in the past.'

'A fortunate lady indeed, to have such a devoted husband!'

Poppy said with a smile. Now she was getting somewhere. 'He came in alone, then, and not with his wife?'

'The gentleman did come in alone, but on this occasion the piece was not for his wife. He said the bracelet was a gift for his niece's eighteenth birthday.'

His niece! Thank goodness, Poppy thought; Constance will be relieved to learn this. She gave a soft sigh for the benefit of Miss Strachan. 'Ah, well. I shall have to continue looking.'

'Are you sure I cannot interest you in the necklace?' The assistant looked hopeful.

Poppy shook her head. 'I had my heart set on a bracelet. But we must bear these disappointments as best we can.' She took up her gloves and handbag from the counter. 'Good day, Miss Strachan.'

The assistant hastened round the counter and towards the door. 'Good day, my lady.' She held the door open. 'Please call again if we can help you at all. Perhaps you would like to commission a bracelet to your own design?'

'Perhaps. I will consider it.' Poppy gave a nod and a smile, and sailed out of the shop.

She turned back in the direction of her town house, excitement and satisfaction coursing through her. She wanted nothing more than to telephone Constance with the good news.

As she crossed the road, she spotted a short, straight, heavily tasselled gold dress in the window of *Magasin de Vêtements de Lux* opposite. Suddenly she was aware that she wanted something a little more modern for the weekend party, something... more like Beth's attire. Poppy reached the dress shop and stood looking in the window, wondering if she dared. After all, she might be a widow, but she wasn't very much older than the actress.

She was about to go in and examine the garment when a small brass plaque set to the side of a stationer's shop doorway seemed to wink at her. She paused for a moment to read it.

M. MCINTYRE DETECTIVE AGENCY
DISCREET AND RELIABLE FEMALE DETECTIVES
TOP FLOOR

Poppy's smile widened. The very McIntyre Agency of the *Casebook* she had devoured in bed at Balfour House last night!

For a brief, heady moment she was tempted to go up the stairs to the McIntyre office and ask if they had any openings for a private detective. After all, wasn't she also a detective? Hadn't she just solved her first, and very own, investigation? She laughed out loud, picturing Inspector MacKenzie's face if she were to do just that.

But she could call into the agency's office to see if they had any tips for a new investigator. She could and she would! She opened the door and climbed the stairs.

The sounds of lively chatter and a typewriter clacking grew louder as she reached the door. It stood ajar and she read the sign M. MCINTYRE DETECTIVE AGENCY, before pushing open the door and walking in.

The noise stopped as two inquisitive female faces turned towards her, one topped with bobbed red hair and the other with dark waves tight to her head.

'Good morning,' said the red-haired woman politely, getting to her feet. 'I am Miss Daisy Cameron and this is my assistant, Kirsty. How can we help you?'

Poppy gazed about the office. Small, but painted in a soothing sage green. Desk with telephone and typewriter, notepad with fountain pen and red leather diary, all carefully positioned; a small bookshelf on the wall. The sash window stood open to the warm day.

'The room is just as I imagined it to be.' Poppy smiled. And Daisy Cameron looked just as cheerful and alert as she had imagined her to be.

'Och, you've read the book Maud and I wrote?' Daisy grinned.

'Absolutely!'

'Have a seat, Miss...?'

'Just call me Poppy.' She took the chair at the desk, facing Daisy, who resumed her seat.

Kirsty, seated in front of the typewriter at the end of the desk, reached for the pad and pen. 'I'll take notes,' she said.

'There's no need, ladies. I won't stay long,' Poppy said with a smile. 'I simply wanted to say how much I admire what you are doing and, well, to ask if you have any tips for a new detective.'

'A *new* detective?' Daisy's grin widened. 'We were all at that stage once. What can I say, but be canny and follow your instincts. It's what I've always done and it's not worked out badly.'

Poppy laughed. 'I can see that. But you must have more advice than just follow your instincts?'

Daisy wrinkled her brow. 'You've read the *Casebook*, so you know all the important things.' She looked over at her assistant. 'You've been doing this job for more than a few years now, Kirsty. Would you like to add anything to what's in the book?'

'Only to mind to keep your eyes open and your wits about you. The first thing the boss' – Kirsty nodded towards Daisy – 'taught me was that it's better nae to get into an awkward situation than to try to get out of one. That's why we work in pairs. Daisy says women are better thinkers than men, but in a tight spot a bit of muscle can come in handy. So for dangerous occasions we take along one of our trusted male employees.'

'Really?' So they now employed men?

'Aye,' Kirsty said. 'Of course, it used to be Daisy who waded in whenever there was a stushie. You just ask Maud—'

'That's enough, lass,' Daisy warned.

'Daisy wouldna tell you herself, but she saved Maud—'

'Wheesht!'

Kirsty gazed down at her typewriter, a smile about her lips.

Daisy glared at her unrepentant assistant. 'I'm sorry about that. Kirsty does like to exaggerate about me and Maud's early escapades.' She turned her attention back to Poppy. 'So, you're thinking of setting up your own detective agency?'

'I'm just helping a friend who didn't feel comfortable talking about her problem to people she didn't know.'

Daisy pushed a business card over the polished desk towards Poppy. 'In case you, or your friend, ever want to speak to us, here's our details.'

'Thank you.' Poppy beamed as she rose. 'I mustn't take up any more of your time, but I'm so pleased to have met you both.'

Daisy got to her feet and followed her to the office door. 'I'll tell Maud you dropped in, Poppy. And,' she called out as Poppy began to descend the stairs, 'dinna put up with nae nonsense, just because you're a woman!'

'I'll remember.' Poppy gave her a friendly wave, continued down the stairs and out into the street.

Telling herself the flapper dress was somehow an essential part of her investigation, Poppy pushed open the door to the dress shop.

As soon as she returned to Ann Street, Poppy carefully placed the large white box containing her new dress on the hall chair, and dropped her bag and gloves after it. The telephone stood on the hall table and she removed the earpiece, briskly turning the handle to ring the exchange. She asked the operator for the number of Balfour House.

'Lady Balfour please, Baird,' she said, on hearing the butler's voice. 'It's Lady Poppy.'

His voice came down the line. 'One moment, if you please, your ladyship.'

Poppy waited, humming softly as she glanced at the smart dress box tied with a pink ribbon. Her pulse gave a little skip at the thrill of buying something so daring. When she had asked the assistant if a special girdle was required under the dress, she'd been told that no girdle was worn at all. It was her first ready-to-wear garment too. Not that a flapper dress, with its flatter bustline and loose, dropped waist, needed to be custom made.

'Hello? Poppy?' came Constance's voice through the earpiece. She lowered her tone. 'Have you news from the errand you kindly undertook for me?'

'Yes, I have, and you need not be concerned, Constance.' Poppy smiled proudly. 'The bracelet was for the birthday of Lord Balfour's niece.'

There was a pause at the other end of the telephone line.

'Oh, but, my dear,' said Constance, 'Bruce has only a nephew.'

Poppy's mouth was suddenly dry. She thought she'd been getting on so well with the investigation and now to hear this was crushing.

'Then the assistant must be mistaken,' Poppy said, trying to keep her voice firm. She hoped that the young woman was. 'I'll return to the shop straight away.' She glanced at her wristwatch; it was shortly after midday. 'Isla's train – the young woman who's to stay with me – doesn't arrive for another two hours.'

'I'm afraid I'm putting you to so much trouble...' Constance's voice was strained.

'Not at all!' she reassured the older woman. Another idea came to Poppy. 'By the way, Constance, could you let me have the name and address of your husband's business partner?'

'Robert Todd?' Constance said sharply. 'Why would you want to visit him?'

'It may not be necessary, but he still runs the business, I take it?'

'If you do go to see him, don't expect him to be very helpful.' She sighed. 'You will find him in Hanover Street.'

Did Constance dislike the man because he was now running the business, Poppy wondered, or did she dislike him for another reason?

'I will telephone again when I have something to report,' she said.

'Thank you so much, my dear. Goodbye.'

Poppy replaced the mouthpiece on the stand, set the telephone on the hall table and stared at it. This detective business was turning out to be more difficult than she'd thought. She wasn't like Maud and Daisy at all – she was a fraud!

The letter box rattled, shaking her out of her humiliating thoughts, and an envelope dropped onto the doormat. Not waiting for her butler to appear, pick it up and place it on the silver salver lying next to the telephone for that particular purpose, she swooped on the letter.

Straightening, Poppy saw that it was addressed to her in a neat hand. 'Who can this be from, Major?' she asked, before realising the dog was still enjoying life in Fife.

'There's only one way to find out,' she told herself, picking up the mother-of-pearl letter opener placed neatly on the tray and slitting open the envelope.

As she pulled out the letter, a picture cut from a newspaper fell out. Poppy bent to pick it up. It showed her and Lady Balfour at a charity event – the occasion when she'd met Constance for the first time – smiling for the photographer.

Puzzled, she turned to the letter. It was written on inexpensive paper in the same small script as on the envelope.

Dear Lady Persephone Proudfoot,

I saw a photo of you in the society pages of The Lady *and thought I should write to you, to let you know that the woman you are standing next to is a murderous hussy. She was known then as Mary Murray, but I recognised her face as soon as I saw it.*

Poppy stared at the single sheet. What could the writer possibly mean? Constance a *murderous hussy*? For a moment, Poppy was tempted to throw it away. A letter such as this could surely only contain malicious gossip. But then she paused.

Once again, she was forced to acknowledge that she knew very little about her new friend. And over the last few days, she had been made very aware that all sorts of emotions and actions bubbled under the surface of everyday life. What if this was somehow a clue to the runner's murder?

Poppy took the letter into the drawing room, sank onto the settee and read on.

Mary was a nursery maid at Achavarasdal House by Thurso. She became a favourite of the mistress, Mrs Abbott, who used to say that one day Mary would make the perfect lady's maid for her young daughter. Before the girl was old enough to have her own maid, Mary Murray was with child. She hid it as best she could, but we knew. When it came close to her time, she wasn't seen for almost a day, and when she came back, there was no bairn. We were certain she'd killed the wee bairn.

Poppy realised she'd been holding her breath. She let it out. 'Oh dear Lord. Poor Constance,' she murmured. Or should that be Mary? But was the story of her pregnancy, and the killing of her newborn, true? *Murderous hussy* was a serious allegation...

Poppy suddenly remembered Constance's hatred of gambling. What had taken place in Constance's young life? Had the lives of her family been blighted by a father's gambling, perhaps, forcing her into service at a young age?

Poppy looked again at the sheet of paper. There was no

signature and she hadn't expected one. No one should be condemned by the word of an anonymous writer. She slowly folded the letter and the newspaper cutting and put them back into the envelope. Where had it been posted? The postmark showed Thurso, the most northerly town in mainland Britain.

What should she do? If the story was true, then there was the horrifying possibility that, having killed once, Constance could kill again. Of course, there was a difference between a defenceless baby and a healthy man, but it wouldn't take a lot of strength to deal the adult a mortal blow with the right weapon. It was all too unbelievable.

She would write to Mrs Abbott at Achavarasdal House, to see if there was any element of truth in the story. Poppy had no wish to cause trouble for her new friend, so she would have to tread carefully.

She ran up the stairs to her bedroom, closed the door and crossed to her small desk. She took out a sheet of notepaper headed with her Edinburgh address and uncapped the fountain pen.

After gazing at the clean white paper for a while as she gathered her thoughts, Poppy began to write.

Dear Madam,

Forgive my writing to you unannounced, but I wonder if you could give me your opinion on the character of Mary Murray, whom I believe worked as a nursery maid in your house.

Poppy broke off. She didn't know when Mary Murray had worked there, but it would have been quite some time ago. Constance looked to be about forty years of age and she could have gone to the house as soon as she left school aged fourteen. That would make it some twenty-six years ago. The letter hadn't made it clear how long Mary had worked at the house, or if she had continued in her employment there after the birth. It said only *when she came back.*

Poppy felt a deep wave of sympathy for whoever this young woman was. Had she given birth on her own, dealt with the pain and shock all alone, in goodness knows what sort of condition, and then... what? The child had been stillborn, or died shortly afterwards, or...

Poppy shivered. The letter called her *murderous*. Had Mary – Constance? – murdered her newborn? Poppy could imagine the shame and sheer terror that might drive a young woman to commit such an act.

She thought again about the wording in the letter. *We were certain she'd killed the wee bairn.* Who were the *we* referred to in the letter? A nursery maid had direct contact with the master and mistress of the house because of the importance of her role, but it seems she managed to conceal the pregnancy from them. A day's absence would be noticed by the children's nurse, though, and could be covered by her. Which of the other servants in the house would have noticed the girl was missing? The governess and the housekeeper, as the meals of the nursery servants and the governess were taken in the housekeeper's room.

Reluctantly, Poppy again removed the letter and the cutting from the envelope. The small, neat handwriting could be that of a governess or housekeeper. Her gaze went to the photograph from *The Lady* magazine. The caption read *Lady Balfour at her first public occasion since the death of her husband, the industrialist Lord Bruce Balfour. She is pictured here next to Lady Persephone Proudfoot.*

Poppy bent to her letter again and looked at what she had written. Why would she, a widow for nine years, want a nanny? Heaven forbid that rumours began to circulate about her supposed condition!

I am writing on behalf of a friend in India, where her husband is posted.

Did that sound plausible?

Your earliest reply would be much appreciated.

Yours respectfully.

Poppy quickly signed the letter, blotted it and folded the sheet of paper into a new envelope before she could change her mind about the advisability of her action. She addressed the envelope and capped her pen. There – it was done.

Picking up the letter, she returned to the hall, just as her butler appeared. He saw the envelope in her hand. 'I was about to check if the post had been delivered, my lady.'

'It has. Can you get this posted, Fleming?' She handed him the letter. 'I'm expecting an early reply, so if it hasn't arrived by the time I leave tomorrow morning, please send it on to Balfour House as soon as it does.' And until she received a response, she must put it out of her mind. The missing bracelet was her priority now and that involved a return visit to the jeweller's shop.

'I'm going out again,' she said, gathering up her gloves and her bag, 'and won't be back for lunch.'

'Yes, my lady.' Fleming moved to open the front door, and she set off once more for George Street.

Onward and upward, Poppy told herself, thinking for some reason of the Onward and Upward Association founded some years ago by Lady Aberdeen for the Material, Mental and Moral Elevation of Women. What a lot women had to aspire to!

She was determined to get to the bottom of all these mysteries by whatever means she could.

TEN

The assistant gazed at Poppy in surprise as she pushed open the shop door and entered the jeweller's premises for the second time in as many hours. Poppy was relieved to see there were no other customers present.

'Your ladyship! Back so soon. What a pleasant surprise.' The professional smile returned to the young woman's face. 'Have you decided you would like to see the necklace I mentioned?'

'No, thank you, Miss Strachan. Just a few more questions about the bracelet, if you don't mind.'

'Not at all.' But the woman's face showed that she did mind. Her attractive features were marred by a sullen look.

Poppy launched straight into her question. 'Is it possible you might have made a mistake in recalling the customer who bought the bracelet?'

Miss Strachan frowned. 'I'm not certain what you mean.'

'You told me earlier that a gentleman bought the bracelet for his niece's birthday,' Poppy said.

'Yes, my lady.' The young woman looked happier now, back on more secure ground.

'Are you sure that it was the same gentleman who bought the bracelet and made that comment?'

'Oh, yes.' She smiled again. 'I'm sure.'

'How can you be certain?' Poppy persisted.

'The purchase stuck in my mind because the gentleman had looked at two pieces, the diamond and emerald bracelet, and another set with rubies,' Miss Strachan added helpfully. 'He couldn't decide which to buy. He telephoned from his office later that day with his choice and said he would call to collect it before we closed, which he did.' She paused. 'Is there a problem?'

'You might say that. I'm afraid the bracelet can't be found.'

Miss Strachan gazed at Poppy and gave a little laugh. 'Are you a detective?'

'In a manner of speaking.' Such a pity, Poppy thought, that she didn't have a police identity card. All she had were her own visiting cards. She took one from her bag, handed it to the young woman and showed her the invoice Constance had given her. 'I am investigating the missing item on behalf of Lady Balfour, the gentleman's widow.'

Miss Strachan took a moment to study the card and the invoice. 'Oh dear,' she said sadly. 'I am very sorry to hear that the gentleman is no longer with us. Such a charming man.'

Poppy pushed on. 'When did Lord Balfour come into the shop and look at the bracelet?'

'Would you excuse me a moment, as I would need to consult the purchase book?'

'Of course.'

Miss Strachan disappeared through a door behind the counter, closing it behind her. Poppy gazed around the shop. They certainly did have some exquisite pieces of jewellery. She'd had a fascination with jewels since she was a child, and would play with her mother's jewellery while her mother dressed for dinner.

The choicest pieces were in the display case under the counter. A pair of emerald and diamond drop earrings by Cartier; hadn't she seen a photograph of the American actress Gloria Swanson wearing something similar? A Tiffany cocktail ring, the round aquamarine surrounded by a double row of shimmering diamonds. Her eye was caught by a pretty little blue topaz pendant and she bent her head to look more closely at it. She would have to come back and try that on for herself. Once she'd solved the case, of course...

The door opened and the assistant returned, carrying a large, leather-bound book. 'The invoice is dated 15th November last year.' She placed the purchase book on the counter, opened it and began to turn back the pages. 'Let me see... yes, here we are. Thursday 15th November. *Lord Balfour. A three-row bracelet, set with alternating diamonds and emeralds.*'

'Exactly as described on the invoice,' Poppy murmured.

The assistant looked up. 'Of course, my lady.'

'Very well. Thank you.' Poppy picked up the invoice, put it in her handbag and closed the bag with a sharp click. 'If you think of anything, anything at all' – *isn't that what detectives are supposed to say?* – 'then please let me know.'

Lord Balfour was turning out to be an enigma, and she was no closer to solving this case. Her next port of call would be to his office, where she had high hopes of learning something of interest to the case of the missing bracelet.

Five minutes later, Poppy reached the premises of Balfour and Todd in Hanover Street and mounted the stone steps up to a black painted front door. A neat, elderly woman with grey hair showed Poppy into a large, stuffy office on the ground floor.

Mr Todd rose from behind his desk as Poppy entered. He was short, dapper and rather stout, his brown hair parted in the middle and plastered to his head with a generous amount of

Brylcreem. He leaned across his desk, shook hands with Poppy, indicated a wooden chair and resumed his own upholstered seat. Silhouetted against the closed sash window, his expression was difficult to read, while her own face was deliberately exposed to the glare of the sun. What an unpleasant wee man. No wonder Constance didn't like him.

Poppy's opinion of him was strengthened when he spoke.

'Now, madam.' He pulled a gold watch from his pocket and consulted it. 'You told my secretary your business with me was important. I can give you ten minutes. I am a busy man.'

Poppy wordlessly handed him one of her visiting cards. He replaced his watch and looked at the card. '*Lady* Persephone Proudfoot?' He looked up, startled, and blinked a couple of times. 'What can I do for your ladyship?'

Poppy moved her chair out of the direct sunlight. 'I have no wish to waste your valuable time...'

'I beg your ladyship's pardon. A misunderstanding.' He produced a large handkerchief from his pocket and mopped his sweating forehead. 'Sorry about the heat, but I have to keep the window closed because of the noise from the traffic.' He gave her a sickly smile, and in the silence Poppy could hear the click-clack of the secretary's typewriter in a room next door.

'The fact is I have been asked by Lady Balfour to trace a bracelet bought by her husband for his niece about a week before he died,' she explained.

'I was saddened by his passing,' said Mr Todd in a sorrowful voice. 'We had been partners for a good long while.' Then he frowned. 'But what has this bracelet to do with me?'

She noted the man had not commented on the question of a niece. 'I wondered if he might possibly have placed it in the office safe.'

Mr Todd's frown deepened. 'I can tell you categorically that Lord Balfour did not place the item in the safe. I have had cause to open the safe on many an occasion in the last six months and can assure you there is no bracelet there.'

'I'm sure you are right,' she said in a soothing voice, 'but I do need to reassure Lady Balfour that I have examined every avenue. Would you object if I looked in there? And also in the drawers and cupboards in his office.'

Mr Todd's face assumed a sour expression. 'Most irregular. If any of our customers knew... But to aid Lady Balfour, I'll allow you. This is in strictest confidence, of course.'

'Thank you.'

'Come this way.'

He got to his feet and came round the desk, revealing his very correct attire of morning coat and striped trousers, patent leather boots and spats. He led her along the passage and ushered her into a small room.

It contained only a small, black safe standing on the floor. A tiny, barred window let in a little light. As they approached the safe, Mr Todd pulled a pair of wire-rimmed spectacles from his breast pocket. He put them on carefully and bent down, his back to her and obscuring her view of the safe's combination. She heard him rotate the dial four times. He turned the handle and the steel door swung open.

He rose and stepped back to allow Poppy to peer inside. The safe contained only papers; nothing even vaguely resembling a bracelet.

'Who else would know the combination,' she asked, straightening, 'besides Lord Balfour and yourself?'

Mr Todd's eyes were wary. 'No one.'

'Is it possible for someone to have broken into the safe?'

'Certainly not.' He looked astonished at such a thought. 'This is an S&G 6730 lock, you know.' When she didn't reply, he closed the door of the safe and spun the dial, before clearing his throat. 'I'm afraid I must bring this to a close now, your ladyship. I really do have another appointment.'

'Of course.' Poppy made to move towards the door.

He looked relieved.

She paused and turned back towards him. 'Oh, I wonder if I might have a quick word with Lord Balfour's secretary?'

'Miss Menzies? Whatever for?' he said sharply.

'Lord Balfour may have spoken to her about the bracelet.'

'To the secretary! I doubt it.'

Silence fell. He looked at Poppy. She looked back at him.

'Very well,' he sighed. 'She can help you search the office too, if you are so certain you need to waste precious time for no gain.'

Mr Todd marched out of the small, dark room, Poppy following, and back along the passage to his office.

He tugged at a bell pull by the empty fireplace. The sound of swift heels clicking on the parquet floor brought the elderly lady who had shown Poppy into Mr Todd's room. If Lord Balfour had been involved with another woman, Poppy thought, it seemed unlikely it was his secretary. Although she wouldn't rule it out; people's tastes can be surprising. Her mind wandered back to a particularly well-preserved friend of her mother's, who flirted outrageously with men of all ages, and not without success if three marriage proposals in her sixties were anything to go by.

'Miss Menzies,' Mr Todd said, 'Lady Persephone Proudfoot would like to ask you a few questions.'

'Me?' the woman squeaked.

'Yes, you, woman. You needn't look so scared. Her ladyship isn't going to eat you.' He laughed at his own witticism. 'Oh, and she wishes to make a search of Lord Balfour's office.'

'Yes, Mr Todd.'

'And now if you'll forgive me, my lady.' He resumed his seat in the swivel chair behind his desk and steepled his fingers.

'You have been most obliging, sir,' Poppy said dryly.

Mr Todd nodded his acceptance of her praise, as she turned and followed the secretary out of his office.

As soon as they had stepped from the room and Miss Menzies had closed the door behind her, Poppy said, 'What an unpleasant man. I wonder you can bear to work for him.'

Miss Menzies flushed. 'I don't have much choice, my lady.' She spoke softly. 'There are not many positions for women of my age.'

It was Poppy's turn to colour. 'Oh, forgive me...'

Miss Menzies led Poppy up a flight of stairs. 'Lord Balfour's office is just up here. He was a lovely man,' she said with genuine sadness.

'You worked for both Lord Balfour and Mr Todd?'

The secretary nodded. 'Now the company is jointly owned by Mr Todd and Lady Balfour, but she hasn't been into the office yet. I expect becoming a widow so suddenly is taking its toll.'

They reached Lord Balfour's room on the first floor. Like Mr Todd's, its window overlooked the bustling Hanover Street, but it seemed lighter in here, somehow. Perhaps it was simply because the desk's surface had been cleared.

Poppy turned to face the secretary. 'I won't take long, Miss Menzies. I'm sure Mr Todd keeps you busy.'

'He does, miss... my lady.'

'I wanted to know if you knew anything about a bracelet Lord Balfour bought for his niece's birthday about a week before he died.'

'His niece?' Miss Menzies frowned. 'But he doesn't have a niece, only a nephew.'

No niece by marriage either, Poppy thought, or even impending marriage. Constance had said that Innes's engagement to Miss Hall had taken place only a couple of months ago, which meant after the death of Lord Balfour.

Interesting, Poppy thought: Mr Todd hadn't questioned the

existence of a niece when she had mentioned it to him. Miss Menzies appeared to know more about Lord Balfour's personal life than did his business partner. But why should that surprise her? Men rarely bother to know about other men's lives, whereas women are a mine of information.

'Lord Balfour never mentioned a bracelet to me,' the secretary went on, 'although he usually asked for my advice when he bought jewellery. Not that I know anything about precious stones, of course,' she hurriedly added, 'but I used to tell him what I thought was especially pretty.'

Poppy smiled. 'I'm sure you have an excellent eye.'

'What is the problem with the bracelet, my lady, if you don't mind my asking?'

'I'm afraid it seems to have gone missing.'

'Oh dear!' Miss Menzies's hand flew to her cheek. 'How worrying for Lady Balfour.' She dropped her hand. 'But I don't understand why Lord Balfour said it was for his niece.'

'I'm not sure that he did,' Poppy told her. 'The important thing now is to find it for Lady Balfour, as she has asked me to do.'

What else could she ask Miss Menzies? She didn't have much to go on. Perhaps... Poppy thought hard. Perhaps he wasn't at work on the day he bought it and so he hadn't asked the secretary for her opinion.

'Was Lord Balfour in the office on 15th November last year?'

'I would need to consult his diary, my lady.'

Poppy nodded.

Miss Menzies stepped round to the desk, pulled open the top drawer and withdrew a large diary in handsome dark brown leather. 'It didn't seem right to throw this out,' she explained, a note of sadness in her voice.

'I'm very glad that you didn't.'

The secretary sent her a grateful smile, placed the diary on the desk and began to turn the pages.

'Yes, here it is.' She looked up at Poppy. 'Thursday 15th November. He was in the office that day and busy with a number of appointments.'

'But he would have gone out for his lunch?'

'Well, yes... But I can see from the diary he had only an hour free.'

An hour would be long enough to walk to the jeweller's. But Miss Menzies had said he always consulted her on such purchases. Did he not do that on this occasion because it was for his paramour?

The jeweller's assistant had said Lord Balfour couldn't immediately make up his mind between two items and so he'd gone away to think about it and later telephoned with his decision.

'Do you know what telephone calls he made that day?' Poppy asked Miss Menzies.

'None at all, my lady.'

'You sound very certain.'

'I am, my lady.'

Poppy frowned. 'How can you be so sure?'

'Because,' the secretary said, 'he never used the telephone. A childhood illness had left him profoundly deaf.'

ELEVEN

Poppy stared at Miss Menzies.

'Good heavens! Lord Balfour was profoundly deaf? I had no idea.'

'Lord Balfour didn't like people to be aware of it. But he was an excellent lip reader, so it wasn't widely known.'

'Which meant that he never used the telephone?'

'That's right. I made all his calls for him,' the secretary explained. 'If he needed to have a discussion with a client, he went to great lengths to meet them in person. Visiting them at home after office hours and the like. This sometimes encouraged gossip surrounding his nights away from home, but I can assure you that Lord Balfour cared deeply for his wife. This matter of the missing bracelet must be a source of great distress to her ladyship.'

Poppy nodded, then glanced around the room. 'Would you mind if I do a quick search of the office?' she asked.

'Not at all, my lady, but, apart from his diary, the desk and cupboard were emptied of their contents months ago.'

'And no bracelet found?' Poppy knew the answer.

'No bracelet found,' Miss Menzies confirmed sadly.

Poppy went over to the desk and opened each drawer; she moved across to the cupboard and flung open the doors. All empty.

She put her hands on her hips and thought. If the jeweller's assistant was lying about the phone call, then what else was she lying about?

Miss Menzies was gazing at her, looking worried. 'I hope Lord Balfour's reputation isn't in any sort of trouble.'

Poppy dropped her hands. 'Not at all. Quite the opposite.' The secretary had saved her employer's reputation. 'Thank you for your help, Miss Menzies.'

'I don't think I can have been of much assistance,' the elderly woman said doubtfully.

'Oh, but you have been,' Poppy assured her.

Back on George Street, as Poppy approached the jeweller's, she saw a young woman who bore a remarkable resemblance to Beth Cornett come out of the shop and turn in the opposite direction along the street.

It *was* Beth, Poppy was certain! She couldn't mistake the blonde hair waved close to the head, the high heels and the short skirt swaying with Beth's unmistakable jaunty walk.

Poppy resisted her immediate impulse to hasten after the girl and express surprise at seeing her. Inspector MacKenzie had told them all to stay in the area of Balfour House. *She*, Poppy, had a very good reason for being in Edinburgh, but what excuse did Beth have?

Walking slowly towards the shop, Poppy wondered what would a lady detective of the M. McIntyre Detective Agency do in this situation? Daisy Cameron would undoubtedly don a disguise and follow Beth, but Maud McIntyre would go into the shop and question the assistant. Poppy like the idea of a disguise, but there was no time for that. She entered the shop.

Miss Strachan was once again behind the counter. On

recognising Poppy, a wary look flashed across her face, to be quickly changed to one of polite greeting.

'Good afternoon again, your ladyship.'

The young woman was an asset to the business, Poppy thought, to remember her. Although perhaps it was because of the questions Poppy was asking. And she wasn't finished yet.

She walked up to the counter. 'Good afternoon, Miss Strachan. Your previous customer... I caught only a glimpse of her, but it looked like an acquaintance of mine, Miss Cornett.'

Miss Strachan inclined her head and the wary look returned. 'The young lady wished to buy a string of pearls for a garden party.'

That could well be true, Poppy thought, but she needed to concentrate on the reason for returning to the shop. Her gaze dropped to the items in the display cabinet under the counter as she mused how to begin. *Good Lord!* There, glinting on a dark velvet cloth, lay an exquisite diamond and emerald bracelet. Had Beth, fearing the item was not safe to wear, sold it back to the jeweller?

Seeing her interest, the assistant said quickly, 'The bracelet is a recent purchase. Very much in the style of what you were hoping to purchase earlier today, but I'm afraid an order has already been taken for it.'

'Already? So, the young lady whom I saw leaving just now was not the person who sold the bracelet to you?'

'My lady?'

'And why is it displayed as if for sale?' Poppy demanded.

'The purchaser isn't able to collect it yet. Mr Campbell likes to keep a full cabinet,' the assistant told her without blinking.

That was an unlikely excuse. For whatever reason, the woman simply didn't want her to have anything to do with the bracelet. She was never going to tell her the truth. Poppy stared out of the window in the direction Beth had gone.

Miss Strachan broke into her thoughts. 'Your ladyship, I

wondered if, just out of curiosity, you understand, you are any nearer finding out what had happened to the bracelet bought by Lord Balfour?'

Poppy met the young woman's interested gaze. Not wanting to admit defeat, she said, 'Yes. Yes, I am.'

'I see. So you still wish to chase down that particular piece of jewellery, rather than commission another, similar item?'

'Yes,' Poppy said shortly.

She glanced at her wristwatch. It was almost time to meet Isla off the two o'clock train. Bidding the assistant a curt good day, she left the shop.

Poppy hastened her steps and reached Waverley station with a few minutes to spare, still bristling at being lied to by the jeweller's assistant. Hurriedly she bought a platform ticket from the machine on the forecourt. And then *The Scotsman* on the newspaper stand caught her eye.

Beneath the announcement of *Paris Olympics Latest* was a smaller heading: *Murdered Man Named*. A grainy photograph appeared in the column on the front page. Her heart gave a leap. It was a small image but unmistakably Honest Harry. She plucked the newspaper from the stand, paid the newsagent and stepped away to read the piece. It was very short.

Inspector MacKenzie of Edinburgh's Detective Branch has named the man found murdered in the grounds of Lady Balfour's residence in Fife yesterday as Henry Harvey from Musselburgh.

Before Poppy could think further, the arrival of the train from Dunfermline was being announced. She folded the newspaper, tucked it under her arm and moved towards the platform, clouds of steam already billowing.

Pausing to show her ticket to the inspector at the gate, she walked onto the platform as the train pulled into the station.

With a hiss of brakes, it drew slowly to a halt. The train doors were thrown open and passengers tumbled out.

Further along the platform, Poppy saw a young woman step down from the train. She wore a fawn-coloured skirt, matching long jacket and a brown velvet hat, her dark hair pinned into a low pompadour. Holding a small valise in one hand, she looked about hopefully. Poppy set off towards her.

Catching sight of Poppy weaving purposely through the crowd, an expression of relief crossed the girl's face and she raised her free hand.

'Miss Isla Macgregor?' Poppy said, when she reached her.

'And you must be Lady Persephone Proudfoot. I'm so pleased to meet you.'

'Poppy will do nicely.' Poppy returned her smile and shook the girl's outstretched hand.

'Thanks so much for letting me stay with you.' Isla's smile grew wider as she gazed around. 'I've never been in Edinburgh before! The journey seemed to take an age, and I was afraid it would arrive late and you would've gone away.' She finished on a breathless note.

Poppy smiled at the girl's excitement. 'I would have waited for your train, Isla. I've been looking forward to your visit.'

They were beginning to be jostled by impatient passengers manoeuvring around them and the piles of boxes, mail bags and porters with trolleys cluttering the platform. A young man bumped into Poppy, tendered his apologies with a raised hat and hurried on.

'Shall we move away?' she said. 'It'll be safer.'

'Och, aye, of course. We dinna want to end up on the tracks in front of the train.' The girl's bright eyes drank in every detail of the station as they left the platform. 'Or get run over by a taxi,' she added as they left the platform and dodged the motor taxis manoeuvring on the station forecourt.

They climbed the steep steps out of the station and emerged

onto Princes Street, where people bustled to and fro, motor cars spluttered past and trams clanged.

'It's *hoatching* out here,' Isla breathed.

'It must be a shock when you first arrive,' Poppy said, steering her through the crowds and along the street in the direction of her Ann Street residence. Isla was the same height as Poppy, which made their progress easier.

'Och, I'm nae complaining.' Isla gazed at Poppy's stylish black and white outfit and sighed. 'I love your modern clothes and hairstyle. Can we go somewhere I can buy a coat like yours?' She flushed. 'I'm sorry, Lady Poppy. I don't mean *exactly* the same, of course.'

'Just Poppy, please,' she corrected the girl. 'Would you like to have a cup of tea first, or some lunch?'

'I had lunch on the train and I'm much too excited to manage a cup of tea. I'd like to visit the shops first.' She touched her own brown hat with its wide brim and grimaced. 'I look like a teuchter.'

'You look charming,' Poppy said quite truthfully.

Isla spotted a ladies' clothing shop across Princes Street. 'Can we try there?' she asked eagerly.

'Their costumes are really very expensive,' Poppy told her. She feared Isla would not be able to afford anything like the money required to buy something from that shop and she had no wish to see the girl embarrassed. Seeing Isla's face drop, Poppy took her arm. 'But we can at least look in the window.'

They crossed the busy road, dodging trams travelling down its centre, stopped outside the shop and gazed in the window.

'They're all so bonnie,' Isla murmured. She turned to Poppy. 'I'd like to buy a hat too and have my hair cut.'

Poppy knew that at Madame Dubois's shop, Isla would at least be able to purchase a cloche hat. 'Let me take you to a shop I know you will like.'

'Would you, Poppy?' Isla's face lit up.

'It would be my pleasure.' Poppy smiled.

'Och, but I'll need my hair cut first,' Isla faltered. 'I want to be up to date and modern for my interview.'

Poppy considered the girl's beautiful dark hair pinned in its neat chignon. 'Are you sure you want to cut it? You look very fetching as you are.'

Isla sent Poppy a determined look. 'I'm sure. I've been thinking about it all the way here on the train.'

Poppy nodded. 'Very well. Next stop, Jenners.'

As they continued along Princes Street, Isla's attention was caught by the tall, thin, gloriously Gothic structure in the Gardens opposite.

'What is that?' she asked in awe.

They stopped and Isla gazed up at it.

'It's a monument to the writer Sir Walter Scott,' Poppy told her.

'It looks awfa tall.'

'Over two hundred feet high, with almost three hundred steps to the top,' Poppy stated.

'And all those folk carved into the stone!'

'There's some dispute as to the number. It's known to be at least sixty-four, but some say ninety-three people are there, plus two dogs and a pig.'

Isla gave a small frown. 'Who are they all?'

'Well, that's Scott and his dog at the foot of the monument. The people are Robbie Burns, Lord Byron, Queen Mary, King James, Robert the Bruce, characters from Scott's novels...'

Isla quirked an eyebrow. 'And the pig?'

'From *Ivanhoe*.'

Isla smiled. 'One day I will count them to see the exact number.'

The doorman held open the door of Jenners department store for Poppy and Isla. They were greeted by the scents of perfume and cosmetics. A female shop assistant in a bright sash immediately approached them and asked if they would like to try the new fragrance by Caron.

'We most certainly would,' Poppy said.

The assistant drew them towards her counter. 'It's an amber floral fragrance for ladies and is called Narcisse Blanc.'

Poppy went to peel back her white cotton glove from her wrist. 'Good heavens!' She gazed at the material with a puzzled frown. 'My fingers are black.'

Isla looked at Poppy's gloves and then the newspaper tucked under her arm. 'That's because your butler hasna ironed the pages to set the ink.'

'Oh. I see. Well, it can't be helped now.' Poppy held out her upturned bare wrist and the assistant placed a little of the scent on her skin. 'Madam will notice the tones of jasmine and linden blossom.'

Madam did, Poppy thought.

Isla held out her wrist for a dab of the perfume. She lifted her wrist and sniffed tentatively. 'It's nae bad. How much is it?'

The assistant recoiled, before hastily regaining her poise. She lowered her voice and named the price.

Isla, learning quickly, affected nonchalance. 'It's perhaps a bit too fruity for someone as young as me.'

Poppy nodded her thanks at the woman, and she guided Isla towards a grey metal door, where she pressed a button set to the side in the wall. After a degree of clanking, the door opened to reveal a small, enclosed space.

Isla stepped back. 'What's this?'

'It's an hydraulic lift. I'll take us up to the hairdressing salon.'

Isla shook her head. 'I don't like the look or the sound of it. I'm nae getting in.'

'It's a very simple device,' Poppy told her. 'A pump pushes oil from the reservoir into the cylinder, which pushes the piston – and us – up. To go down, the valve open and the oil flows back into the reservoir. It was installed when I was a very young girl, so it's been here for a number of years.'

Isla shook her head. 'I still dinna trust it.'

Poppy smiled. 'Others feel the same. Don't worry, we can walk.'

'Edinburgh is so exciting,' breathed Isla as they mounted the stairs to the next floor. 'When I left home this morning, I never really thought this would happen – being in a famous shop with you!'

'One never knows what the future will bring,' Poppy observed. She could solve the cases of the missing bracelet, the murdered man... who knows what else? She smiled at Isla. 'Do you know, the first policewomen in Scotland were attested as constables in Glasgow only four days ago? Admittedly only to deal with cases where females are involved, but it's a start. One day women will be employed as detectives.'

'The world is our lobster?' ventured Isla.

Poppy laughed. 'Something like that.'

TWELVE

Poppy and Isla reached the hairdresser's salon in Jenners, where Poppy asked for her hairdresser, Benoît.

'I'm sorry, my lady,' said the middle-aged woman at the desk, 'but he has clients all afternoon.'

'*Non, non.* What is it you are telling Lady Poppy?' An elderly Frenchman came hastening towards them. 'I can see you now, my lady. I am, as you say, between customers.' He beamed.

'We are not disturbing your afternoon cup of tea?'

He shook his head. '*De rien.* Not at all. Please to come this way.' He gestured to an empty armchair in front of a dressing table with a mirror.

'It's not actually for me, Benoît,' Poppy told him, 'but for my young friend here.'

He wrinkled his brow as he looked at Isla. '*Oui*, I can see something needs to be done.' Cocking his head to one side, his gaze fixed on Isla's hair and face, he went on, 'Marcelling, I think.'

'Oh no,' put in Isla quickly, with a smile at Poppy, 'not waves. I want a bob cut, like Poppy's.'

Benoît clapped his hands. '*Alors!* It will be done. Tea,' he added to the woman at the counter, 'for both ladies, if you please.'

He led Isla to the empty chair and made her comfortable, while Poppy was given an armchair and the latest copy of *Vogue*. Ignoring the magazine for now, and pushing aside the thought of her maid's displeasure at the condition of her gloves, she turned to the piece in *The Scotsman* on Henry Harvey and read it again. It still revealed no information other than that Inspector MacKenzie had named the man found murdered in the grounds of Balfour House.

Poppy sighed. She now knew the real name of Honest Harry, but the only other thing she'd learned from the news item was that the inspector was ahead of her in the investigation – which would make him even more condescending about her detective skills.

She put the newspaper on the table by her side, accepted the cup of tea and turned to the copy of *Vogue*. Sipping her tea, she turned the pages, considering the latest creations of Gabrielle Chanel and Georges Lepape. Premet's *La Garçonne* boyish look, with silhouettes that draped over the curves, was rather attractive. Jeanne Lanvin's *Robe de Style*, by contrast, with a wide, gathered skirt was highly feminine, but not at all practical.

Poppy looked up from her magazine to see Benoît putting the finishing touches to Isla's glossy bob. The girl turned her head and grinned at Poppy.

Poppy set down *Vogue* and walked across to Isla. 'You have made a beautiful job, Benoît.'

'Aye, it's bonnie,' said Isla, turning her head this way and that, admiring herself in the mirror.

'But it is easy with a *belle fille* such as she!' Benoît exclaimed.

Isla blushed with delight.

The hairdresser removed the cape around the girl's neck,

and she thanked him, got to her feet and made her way to the reception desk.

'Thank you so much, Benoît,' Poppy murmured, slipping a bank note into his hand.

'You are too kind, my lady,' he replied.

She joined Isla at the desk, where the girl opened her purse and carefully counted out the payment. Poppy could see the haircut had taken rather a lot of her money, and decided she would pay for the new hat Isla wanted.

'The milliner's next?' Poppy asked brightly. 'And you must let this be my treat.'

'I canna let you to pay,' Isla protested. 'You've been so kind already, taking me around the shops and letting me stay with you for my interview in the morning.'

'I insist.' Poppy smiled. 'It isn't often I have the pleasure of shopping with a young friend.'

'Well, if you're sure.' Isla said, an element of doubt in her voice.

'I am, and let that be an end to it.' Poppy took Isla's arm and they descended the wide staircase to the street outside.

Isla tried on what seemed to Poppy to be every hat in the shop, exclaiming over each and every one.

Poppy told herself that as delightful as it was to watch Isla's face light up when she donned each new hat, she herself ought to be more usefully occupied in something other than gazing at headwear. Once again finding herself settled in a chair and waiting, she turned her thoughts to more serious matters.

Despite her buoyant spirits earlier this morning, the investigation into the missing bracelet had come to a dead end. And she had no idea where to go from here. All the evidence, such as it was, suggested that no servant had stolen the bracelet because it had never reached the house. The shop assistant was clearly not to be trusted as she had made at least one false statement to Poppy, when she said Lord Balfour had telephoned with his choice of jewellery.

On the other hand, Beth Cornett had certainly been wearing a similar item at dinner on the first evening at Balfour House. She may have met Constance's husband in London in early November and charmed him sufficiently to be made a present of the bracelet he'd bought a week or two afterwards. Poppy couldn't imagine this, somehow. And yet, it looked very much as though the actress had disposed of the item at the jeweller's this afternoon.

Frustrated, Poppy moved on to consider the murder. Honest Harry had been killed at some point on Monday, between late afternoon and early evening, by a blow to the back of the head with a heavy instrument. At the time of Harry's murder, there had been six guests, including Poppy herself, plus their hostess and her son, at Balfour House. She already had reason to consider Constance as a possible suspect, but could Gregor, a boy of fourteen, have done such a thing? He was probably both tall and strong enough. Poppy shook her head. It was impossible. For all Gregor's glee at the macabre, she didn't think there was any harm in him. He was at that age when boys like to shock their elders, nothing more.

She thought about his uncle Nick and his aunt Morag. They had each exhibited behaviour which could be described as suspicious, in Nick's case, and strange, in Morag's case. Were either of them the murdering type? But what did the murdering type look like? No, she was letting her thoughts run away with her, like a Victorian penny dreadful. What had Inspector MacKenzie said? *It's almost always the most likely person* who's the culprit. So did that mean Mr Emmett, Beth Cornett and Eddie Peavey should be discounted?

Motive, Poppy reminded herself. She needed to consider motive. What possible motive could the Americans have?

Constance or Gregor *might* have known about Lord Balfour's gambling and wanted to silence his runner if he was threatening to reveal all. As to Nick and Morag, she could well have a drug addiction, and Nick could be buying them for her, but what could that have to do with Honest Harry? Unless Harry was the supplier?

The more Poppy examined the case, the more she felt confident that the killer had to be someone in the house, else why would Harry have been murdered in the grounds? No other line of thought made sense. Inspector MacKenzie had interviewed all the servants but didn't seem to be concerned with any of them, apart from Freddy, and only then because the chauffeur had said he'd seen the footman by the loch at the relevant time. Poppy pursed her lips.

It irked her that her own eyewitness statement seemed to have been quickly discounted by Inspector MacKenzie. He might have taken her evidence more seriously if she'd told him that a man of such good looks as Freddy was as hard for a woman to forget, just as a beautiful woman was for a man.

She frowned. Freddy had admitted to her he'd known the bookie's runner for some time, had been placing his own bets with him, and on the day of the murder had had a disagreement with Harry in the Red Lion. Had he told the inspector all this? She doubted it. Taking these facts into account, it didn't look good for the footman. But if it wasn't him – and she believed the young man when he swore he wasn't the killer – then who was it?

Poppy was brought back to the present by Isla, who was modelling a black cloche hat with an ornamental twist of white lace.

'I think this is the one. Do you like it?'

'It's very attractive and looks perfect on you,' Poppy told her. 'Let's get it boxed up.'

'Oh no,' Isla said, 'I'm going to wear it. My old hat can go in the box.'

Poppy paid and they made their way back out into the street. 'Dinner will be served at seven,' she told Isla. 'And after dinner I will need to leave for the evening fundraiser. Are you sure that you won't come with me?'

Isla shook her head. 'No, I won't ken a soul there.'

'You'll know me.' Poppy smiled.

'I ken, but... well, I'd just feel out of place. And besides, I can easily entertain myself. I'll probably go for a wee stravaig to get to know the city.' It was Isla's turn to smile. 'Maybe I'll even count the number of figures on that Scott memorial!'

Poppy looked at the suit Isla was wearing. 'It'll be cooler by this evening and you'll need more than that. We're of a similar height and build. You can borrow this coat.' She indicated the one she wore.

Isla frowned. 'But you'll need it.'

'I have a new coat I intend to wear this evening,' Poppy said. 'And this black and white coat will go nicely with your new hat. There, that's settled.'

Later that evening, dinner eaten, Poppy left her house.

She strode along in her new burgundy coat, pleased she'd given her chauffeur the evening off. She liked to walk in the city whenever possible and it was a pleasant evening. Isla would be glad of a coat, though, by the time the girl set out for her stroll.

Poppy crossed Princes Street, walked up The Mound, which divided Princes Street Gardens into two, and on to the south side of the city. She had so much to write in her new notebook and would make the entries this evening when she returned.

At Shand House yellow lights streamed from all the windows. She walked up the wide, shallow steps and rang the bell. The door opened to show the spacious marble-floored hall, graceful circular stairs, lamps burning bright and vases of fragrant flowers everywhere.

Her coat was taken at the door by a manservant as Viscountess Shand came towards her. From a downstairs room came loud chatter.

'Poppy! My dear girl, let me look at you!' Her admiring gaze travelled from Poppy's beaded cloche, down her black and silver dress with its tasselled hem around her calf, to her silver shoes with a strap and button. 'I swear you look more delightful than ever!' She kissed Poppy's cheek. 'Now then, Poppy, do you know Miss Taft, the famous romance novelist?' she went on, gesturing politely to another guest who had stepped in through the open front door.

'How do you do,' Poppy said to the middle-aged woman, who was wearing an extraordinary bright green jersey dress which stretched tightly across her enormous bosom.

'I'm so glad you have both come to my little do,' continued the viscountess. 'Miss Taft, I hear you have a new book out shortly. You must tell me all about it presently. If you'd like to place your donation to the charity in there, the dear little orphans would be so grateful.' She indicated the upturned top hat positioned on the marble-topped hall table.

Poppy took bank notes from her small evening bag and dropped them into the hat, while Miss Taft rummaged around inside her copious bag. The exclamations and laughter spilling out from one of the rooms grew louder.

'Now, come along, do!' called Viscountess Shand gaily as she shepherded them through the hall and towards the good-natured hubbub. The large and lofty drawing room was filled with men and women, cigarette smoke and conversation.

'*Poppy!*' the cheerful voice of her cousin rose effortlessly above the din as Agnes, in a red sequinned dress, pushed through the crowd, her cigarette in its long ebony holder held aloft. 'So glad you could make it. I thought you were at Balfour House for the week. I heard there were American film people staying there. Was it simply too awful for words?' She lowered her voice. 'Mind you, looking round this crowd, a few film people might be entertaining. There are some frightfully dull people here tonight.'

Poppy gazed around the room. There was Lady Argyll with her daughter, one of the Bright Young Things; a dowager duchess with a particularly sharp tongue; and wasn't that Percy Fearon, the satirist?

'You must have something to drink,' Agnes was saying. 'A cocktail!' She gestured towards a long side table covered with a display of colourful bottles. A deep laugh caught Agnes's attention and her gaze went to a group of men, the younger ones in dinner jackets and the older ones in tailcoats. 'I thought so. There's Fergus. I must have a word with him. You don't mind, do you, darling? I'm trying to cultivate a Right Honourable with a view to influencing legislation on women's rights.'

Poppy watched Agnes threading her way through the crowded room, her cigarette swaying in its long holder held high above the Brylcreemed heads of the men and the bobbed and Marcel-waved hair of the women.

Women's rights, she reflected. Some steps had been taken, but there was still a long way to go. The suffragettes had fought a hard battle for the right of women to vote, but that wasn't granted until six years ago. Even so, she didn't qualify, having not yet reached the age of thirty. At least then she would be able to vote, but only because she was fortunate enough to own property. As to her own would-be career... When she had graduated with a degree in law, women weren't allowed to practice. That legislation was repealed five years ago; but in the intervening years her life had changed. She'd married, been widowed...

'I say, have you got a light?'

Poppy turned sharply to find the question wasn't addressed

to her. A passing man stopped and struck a match for the middle-aged woman who had spoken. The woman, of stocky build, with thick grey hair and a weather-beaten complexion, lit her cigar from the match and tilted up her head to inhale a deep breath of smoke. She stood, her stoutly shod feet well apart, her free hand thrust into the pocket of her crumpled tweed jacket.

'Pretty beastly, isn't it?' the woman said to Poppy, catching her eye.

Did she mean the smoking or the gathering? Before Poppy could formulate a suitable answer, the woman went on, 'There's no room to swing a cat.'

Poppy immediately had a mental picture of the woman, eyes screwed up against her own cigar smoke, attempting to swing a plump black and white feline by its tail, and laughed.

'I'm Dahlia Dalrymple.' The woman pulled her hand from her pocket and extended it to Poppy.

Poppy found her hand being shaken vigorously. 'How do you do. I'm Persephone Proudfoot, but do call me Poppy.'

'Poppy Proudfoot?' Dahlia Dalrymple frowned in concentration. 'That name is familiar.' She waved a hand to waft away the smoke from her face. 'Aren't you supposed to be at Constance Balfour's country house this week?'

'Yes, I am,' Poppy said with surprise. 'You're a friend of hers?'

'Och, we met as boarders at St George's. We go way back, Connie and me. Long before she married that fool Bruce Balfour, but she's free of him now.'

Fool? Free of him? That wasn't quite the story Poppy had picked up from Constance.

Dahlia laughed at the look on her face. 'My dear girl, don't look so shocked. Connie never called him a fool and nor has she said she's free of him. They're my words. But the careless fellow dropped a lot of money on the horses, you know. Poor Connie, she loathes gambling.' Dahlia puffed on her cigar and shrugged.

'Anyway, he made his own money, and I suppose he had a right to do with it what he liked.'

'Why does Constance disapprove so much of gambling?' Poppy asked, genuinely curious. 'It's not considered a vice – in moderation.'

'Exactly, my dear girl: in moderation. Bruce never knew when to stop. You know Connie's father lost her to Bruce in a card game?' Dahlia let out a roar of laughter, which ended in a bout of coughing.

Poppy's eyes widened. 'I thought she and her husband were very fond of each other.'

'Och, they came to be. It took a year or two for Connie to realise he loved her, despite how their marriage had come about.' Dahlia wiped her eyes with the back of her hand. 'Stands to reason – he wouldn't have played for her hand if he wasn't interested in her, would he? But as you can imagine, it made poor old Connie see all forms of gambling with a jaundiced eye.'

Poor Constance indeed, thought Poppy; both her father and her husband gamblers. 'I wonder she agreed to marry Bruce Balfour, in the circumstances. We're not living in the seventeen hundreds, after all.'

Dahlia suddenly became serious and looked away. 'I suppose it shows how grim her life must have been, to accept such a proposal.'

She knows! Dahlia knew about the baby, Poppy realised with a shock.

But what exactly did Dahlia know?

THIRTEEN

Poppy looked at Dahlia carefully. Did she know only that Constance had given birth, or that afterwards the new mother had done the unthinkable? How on earth could she broach such a sensitive subject with a woman she had only just met?

Poppy became aware that a young woman in a floaty dress was waving at Dahlia from across the crowded room, her slim arm sheathed in a large number of bangles.

'There's Irene,' announced Dahlia. 'I must go and have a word with her, but I look forward to seeing you again at Connie's on the weekend.'

'You'll be there for the midsummer party?' Poppy didn't disguise her delight.

'Try and keep me away. But first, dear girl, tell me: what are the Americans like?'

Poppy smiled. 'They're rather—'

'*Dahlia!*' shrieked Irene from across the room.

'Sorry, have to go. See you on Saturday!' And with that, Dahlia shouldered her way through the throng and was quickly lost to Poppy's sight. Poppy stood lost in her thoughts for a moment. So Constance's marriage had come about thanks to her father's gambling habits? How she must have hated her parents... and her husband in the early days. And if Dahlia Dalrymple knew that Lord Balfour gambled – and gambled heavily – then surely others knew this? Dahlia wasn't exactly the reticent sort. More importantly, had Constance been aware of his regular bets on horse racing? Poppy needed a drink. She made her way over to the cocktails. A loud blast of music suddenly erupted to a chorus of cheers. Someone had wound up the gramophone and put on a record, and 'I'm Just Wild About Harry' filled the room. Almost immediately couples were dancing the foxtrot on the crowded floor.

Poppy raised her voice to the footman standing in attendance at the side table. 'An Angel Face, please.'

She watched while he poured gin and two different types of fruit brandy into a cocktail shaker with ice. He shook it, strained the drink into an ice-filled glass, garnished it with a large orange peel twist and handed her the glass.

As Poppy thanked him and turned back towards the room, Agnes returned. 'That was a waste of time. The Right Honourable is so set in his ways.' She tapped the ash from her cigarette into a potted plant. 'Do you see that woman over there?'

Poppy looked to where her cousin indicated. 'Miss Taft?' she asked.

'Oh, you've met her.'

'Not really. We happened to arrive at the same time.'

'Well, she's been having an affair with a certain peer for some years. His wife turns a blind eye, of course,' Agnes said in a conspiratorial tone. 'Anyway, the Taft woman has written a new book that is sure to be delightfully scandalous. She's passing it off as fiction, but we all know it's based on her relationship with the Earl of Swinton.'

Poppy opened her mouth to ask her how she could possibly know, but Agnes was claimed by an acquaintance in gold lace and jewelled turban, who screamed, 'Agnes!' above the din and dragged her away. The gramophone was wound again and the record changed, as more couples took to the floor to dance and bump into each other, screaming with laughter.

'Would you care to dance?' A tall, thin young man stood in front of Poppy, his eyes having difficulty focusing.

'No, thank you,' she replied politely, already beginning to tire of this noisy gathering.

Poppy watched Miss Taft standing alone by the drinks table, as the young man wandered off in search of someone more willing to partner him. She thought the older woman looked a little lost and decided to make her way over. 'Hello, again.'

Miss Taft stopped her slightly out-of-tune humming and turned to Poppy with a frown. 'Are you anyone important?'

Good Lord! 'I like to think I am.'

Her frown deepened. 'But I don't seem to know you.'

The woman was insufferable. 'I am a friend of Viscountess Shand.'

Miss Taft gave Poppy a condescending smile. 'Isn't everyone here?'

Not necessarily, Poppy thought. But if Miss Taft wanted more names, she could have them. 'I am also a friend of Lady Constance Balfour.'

The woman looked interested. 'Constance Balfour? Has she invited you to her summer garden party on the weekend?' Miss Taft didn't exactly sneer, but she might as well have done. 'I hear that this year there will be American film stars there.'

'Yes, that is true. I'm already a guest at Balfour House.'

'Oh.' There was a pause. She started again, in a lower voice. 'I expect you know all about that husband of hers.'

'What about him?'

'Don't quote me on this, but they say—' Miss Taft glanced about her. At that moment the drawing room door opened and her attention was taken by the distinguished-looking gentleman who entered. He was perhaps in his mid-forties, his dark hair greying at the temples.

The man smiled and nodded at Miss Taft. Her enormous bosom swelled. 'The Earl of Swinton,' she murmured, and without further ado, she turned from Poppy and sailed towards the new arrival.

How frustrating! What had the dreadful woman been about to say?

Poppy felt a sudden need for some air. She had made her financial contribution to the charity evening and had done her bit. It wasn't late, only a little after ten o'clock, but still. She wouldn't take a taxi home, but instead would walk. It would give her a chance to reflect on what she had – and hadn't – learned this evening. She put down the cocktail and set off to make her excuses to Viscountess Shand.

She thanked her hostess and bid good night to the manservant who helped her on with her coat at the front door, then went down the steps and out into the street. The sun had not long set and the gloaming would remain for another hour. As she strolled along, Dahlia Dalrymple's words rang in her head. *Connie loathes gambling. You know Bruce won her in a card game? How grim her life must have been...* And what had the frightful Miss Taft been about to tell her?

Poppy's investigation was becoming ever more muddied – but it looked as though Constance must now be towards the top of the suspect list.

Poppy turned down The Mound, admiring on one side the dark, centuries-old castle perched on its high rock and on the other the National Monument, a replica of the Parthenon in Athens, on top of Calton Hill. Her mind jerked uncomfortably to the gruesome Calton Jail, built in the shadow of the hill. There had been an execution only last year when Philip Murray, who had pushed his wife's lover from their bedroom window to his death, was hanged inside the prison. She remembered seeing the solitary black flag flying to signal that it was over. Poppy shivered at the thought that Constance might be the next person to suffer that fate, and she determined to do all she could to find Honest Harry's *real* killer.

As she drew near Princes Street Gardens, Poppy heard a small dog's frenzied barking. Some sort of commotion was taking place in the East Gardens. She entered and saw ahead of her a huge, lively crowd and a wire-haired fox terrier, its leash trailing, running around and barking.

A scream came from someone in the gathering. Poppy's pulse quickened as she approached.

'The fellow's getting away!' someone yelled. 'This way!'

A handful of men detached themselves from the crowd and set off in hot pursuit of a man wearing a long, hooded evening cloak and running like the dickens. Before she knew what she was doing, Poppy had seized a bicycle propped against a bench, hitched up her dress with its tasselled hem, put one foot on the pedal, thrown her other leg over the saddle and had set off in pursuit, pedalling furiously after him.

'Excuse me!' she screamed, furiously ringing the bell on the bike. 'So sorry!' she shouted as people strolling on the footpath jumped out of her way.

The cloaked figure glanced behind as he pounded along the path and saw her gaining on him. He was fast approaching a moustachioed young man seated on his bike and chatting to a young lady. With one hard shove from the fugitive, the surprised young man was off his machine and sprawled on the ground. His young lady screamed as the cloaked assailant fumbled a little in his haste to climb on the bike, then sped away, his cloak streaming behind him.

The stumble with the bike had cost him time; Poppy was gaining on her quarry. The posse of running men had been left far behind. Along the footpath in the gardens the fugitive raced, with Poppy following, past the Scott Monument, passers-by stopping to stare at the spectacle.

The man whizzed past a startled policeman. Recovering his senses, the officer pulled out the whistle from his breast pocket and blew on it sharply. Poppy sped past him, her stocking tops flashing as she rode. The path sloped upwards out of the gardens and onto Princes Street. Travelling on the wrong side of the road, the fleeing cyclist, followed by Poppy, narrowly avoided another cyclist, a horse and cart, and a motor bus travelling towards them.

The man glanced behind him, the electric streetlamps throwing an uncanny light over the scene, casting his face under the hood into shadow. Poppy pedalled on determinedly.

He suddenly turned right onto Waverley Bridge. Pressing her calf against the side of the bike as if she were on a horse, Poppy turned after him, cycling furiously down the hill, her dress filling up like a parachute. It billowed out behind her, slowing her down. And then the road began to climb steeply towards the Royal Mile. She peddled faster, but couldn't catch him. Her legs screaming at her to stop and her heart pounding fiercely, Poppy came to a halt.

She could see the cloaked figure ahead struggling with the ascent, but she could cycle no longer. The fellow cycled away up twisting Cockburn Street and disappeared from view into the gloomy gas-lit streets beyond.

Poppy took in gulps of air. *Darn it, I almost caught him!*

She heard an ambulance bell in the near distance and now realised she'd joined the chase after the man with no idea what he was supposed to have done. A thief, she had vaguely assumed. Now it came to her that someone must be badly hurt. Perhaps she should count herself lucky not to have caught him. What had Inspector MacKenzie said to her only yesterday? *Do you believe they'll come along politely for you because you're a lady?* Dash it, there she was, quoting the inspector again.

She dismounted, turned the bike and pushed it back up Waverley Bridge. When she reached the top of the hill, Poppy climbed back on the cycle, pedalled round the corner and finally back into Princes Street Gardens.

By this time there was no sign of the ambulance, but ahead of her groups of people were standing around, talking in shocked voices. Poppy returned the bike to the bench, straightened her slightly skewed beaded cloche and apologised to the bemused owner who stepped forward from one of the little gatherings to hastily reclaim his property.

'What has happened?' Poppy asked the others in the small crowd.

A short, thickset woman turned to her. 'A young couple have been stabbed,' she said, her eyes wide.

'Good Lord!' Poppy said. 'How awful.'

'Aye,' said a grey-haired man standing next to the woman. 'It wasna as if there was even a rammle. A man just came running out of nowhere, someone said, and stabbed the laddie and then the lassie.'

'I heard it was the other way round,' put in a young woman, her orange cloche slightly askew. 'The man attacked the lass first and then the lad.'

'Did anyone here see the assault?' Poppy asked.

The first woman spoke again. 'Not me.'

'Nae me either,' the man chimed in.

'Do you know if the young couple were very badly hurt?'

'I dinna ken,' he replied. 'There seemed to be a fair bit of blood, though. They've been taken away to the Royal Infirmary.'

'I think the policeman looked for the knife, but he couldn't find it,' added the young woman.

As Poppy glanced around for the police officer, she spotted the fox terrier no longer emitting its high-pitched bark but sitting quietly with a worried look on its face. She went over to the dog, introduced herself and picked up the leash, before making her way to the officer who stood talking to another little group of people.

'Excuse me, officer—'

'Just a minute, miss,' the policeman replied, glancing up from his pocketbook, 'I'm getting details from these people.'

'I just wanted to say—'

'I said *just a minute*, miss,' he repeated testily, still writing.

'This is important, officer.' Poppy's voice brooked no argument.

He looked up in surprise, his pencil poised over the page.

'The assailant stole a bike and has made off onto the Royal Mile.'

The policeman stared at her. 'And how do you know this, miss?'

'Because I... *borrowed*' – she held the officer's gaze, despite her lie – 'a bicycle and gave chase.'

There were gasps from the little group around him.

He frowned. 'That was a very dangerous thing to do, young lady.'

'Just doing my best to help the Edinburgh constabulary,' she said airily.

He eyed her suspiciously, as if uncertain as to whether or not she was making fun of him.

'He will be long gone by now,' she added with a sigh. The Royal Mile, connecting Edinburgh Castle at one end and Holyrood Palace at the other, was thronged day and night with tourists and other pleasure-seekers. It was also a maze of alleyways and closes, where a wanted man might easily hide.

'You had better give me your details,' the policeman said.

'Certainly, officer. Lady Persephone Proudfoot.'

'And your address, please, my lady.'

'My Edinburgh residence or my Perthshire residence?'

'Your city one, if you please.'

'Ann Street.'

He finished writing, closed his book and looked up. 'I will ask for an officer to call round in the morning and take a statement.'

'I will be leaving Edinburgh some time tomorrow. After that, I can be found at Balfour House, Fife.'

He opened his book again, made a note and snapped it shut.

'Oh, and officer, I think this dog belongs to the young couple.' Poppy handed him the leash.

She turned and made her way home.

Upon Poppy's return to Ann Street, her butler opened the door.

'Good evening, Fleming.' She stepped into the hall.

'Good evening, my lady.' He took her coat and folded it smoothly over his arm.

She handed him her gloves and hat. 'Has Miss Macgregor gone to bed?'

He cleared his throat. 'I'm afraid the young lady has not yet returned.'

Poppy glanced at the long case clock in the hall. A quarter to eleven. 'What time did she go out?'

'Sometime after dinner, my lady. I would say about half past eight.'

Good Lord, Isla had been out for over two hours. She was young and didn't know the city. 'Thank you, Fleming.'

'Will you be requiring anything else this evening, my lady?'

'Could you bring me a glass of warm milk in the library and then take yourself to bed. I will wait up for Miss Macgregor.' She couldn't possibly go to bed with Isla not yet safely home. She was responsible for the young woman, for goodness' sake.

Poppy crossed the hall and went into the library. She picked up *The Scotsman* from the desk and sat in an armchair to wait anxiously for Isla's return. Fleming brought her milk and wished her good night.

She took a sip and gazed at the newspaper. There it was, on the front page, the words *Murdered Man Named* and underneath the grainy photograph of Henry Harvey. Thoughts of Honest Harry and now Isla swirled in her head. Of course there was no connection between the two of them, but that didn't stop her from dwelling on the body by the loch and being worried about her young friend.

She took another sip of the milk, looked at the mantel clock. Barely ten minutes had passed. Poppy returned distractedly to the newspaper, turning the pages but reading nothing. The time seemed to crawl by.

She jumped as the clock began its Westminster chime, and although she could see very well where the hands pointed, she started to count the strikes... nine, ten, eleven. Eleven o'clock. Isla couldn't possibly still be walking around the streets at this hour. Something must have happened to her.

Poppy threw down *The Scotsman* and got to her feet. What to do? She had never been in this position before. Should she wake Fleming and get him to scour the streets for Isla? Or should she telephone the police? But wouldn't they say Miss Macgregor was a grown woman and it was not a matter for them? At least, not unless... She began to pace.

The hospital! Could Isla have decided to pay a visit to the Royal Infirmary on Lauriston Place and lost track of time? Surely she would not have called there at this time of night? No, it was unlikely the girl had done that.

But the hospital now had another association for Poppy. The young couple who had been stabbed this evening in the gardens. A chill ran through her. What if the girl was Isla? But she could have had no time to form an acquaintance with a man in the city.

Poppy came to a halt as another unwelcome thought struck

her. Had Isla's true purpose in coming to Edinburgh involved a sweetheart? She didn't believe the young woman would be so deceitful.

A loud knock on the front door startled her, before a wave of relief washed over her. Her heart still thudding, she hastened to the door and threw it open.

'Isla, thank goodness you're back—'

The rest of the sentence died on her lips when she saw who was standing there.

FOURTEEN

'Inspector MacKenzie?' Poppy stood there, staring at him.

'Your ladyship.'

'What are you doing here?' To have followed her from Balfour House, simply to complain that she had left when under instructions not to do so, was a bit thick. She was in no mood to put up with him. 'Dash it all, Inspector, isn't it a bit late in the evening to be calling to tear a strip off me?'

'I have not returned to Edinburgh to reprimand you, my lady.' He removed his hat. 'I'm not here about that matter but, I am afraid, another.'

Poppy's heart jumped and stuck in her throat. 'Has something happened to Isla?'

'May I come in?' the inspector said grimly.

'Of course.' Poppy stepped back to allow him to enter.

The butler appeared at the top of the stairs leading up from the semi-basement. 'I do hope nothing is wrong, my lady?' He had pulled a dark overcoat on over his nightshirt and his usually impassive countenance held a look of concern.

'I'm... I'm not certain, Fleming, but please go back to bed.

This gentleman is from the police office, so I will be quite safe. I will call you if I need you.'

'Very good, my lady.' The butler nodded and disappeared quietly back down the stairs.

Poppy closed the front door. 'Come into the library,' she told the inspector, leading the way.

She gestured to an armchair.

'I'd rather stand, if you don't mind,' he said.

'What has happened?' Poppy fought to keep her voice steady.

His voice softened. 'It's about your young friend, Miss Isla Macgregor—'

'Yes, yes, just get on and tell me!' Poppy cried.

'It appears that the young lady was walking in Princes Street Gardens this evening when someone attacked her with a knife...'

'Dear Lord,' whispered Poppy, sinking into an armchair. It *had* been Isla.

'Can I get you a drink of water?' Inspector MacKenzie asked, stepping forward.

She waved a hand. 'No, thank you. Is Isla badly injured?'

'She has a wound to her left shoulder.'

'The knife missed her neck? Her lung? Her heart?'

'Yes, my lady.'

'Thank goodness.' Poppy shook her head. 'But I don't understand why anyone would want to attack Isla. She's never been in Edinburgh before today. She can't have made any enemies!'

'I wish I knew the answer to that.'

'And the young man who was with her?' Poppy asked.

'He was walking his dog and came to her aid.'

Questions buzzed in Poppy's brain. 'How did you know Miss Macgregor was staying with me?' Of all the ridiculous questions to start with, but she needed to know.

'Miss Macgregor was conscious and able to give the police officer your address.'

Thank goodness, Poppy thought with relief. That meant she couldn't be too badly hurt. 'And the fellow who rushed to help her?' she asked. 'How is he?'

'The good Samaritan tried to drag the attacker off your friend and in consequence his injuries are more serious.'

'I'm so sorry,' Poppy murmured. She looked up at the inspector. 'They are both in hospital?'

'Aye,' he replied, his face grim.

Her heart pounding, Poppy jumped to her feet. 'Then I must go at once. To see Isla and to thank the young man for saving her life.'

Inspector MacKenzie held up a hand. 'There is no visiting at night, my lady. You'll do best to wait until tomorrow. They should both be better able to talk to you then.'

He was right, Poppy realised. 'Thank you, Inspector, for bringing me the news.' She suddenly felt weary and a headache threatened.

'When I saw the address Miss Macgregor had given, I suspected it was yours.'

'You looked me up in *Who's Who*?'

'It's in the nature of a policeman.' He gave a quick smile. 'I had noticed the rings on your left hand – that's also in the nature of a policeman.' His voice became deeper, softer. 'I was sorry to read of your husband's death on the Western Front.'

Poppy saw the genuine sympathy on his face. 'Thank you,' she said, touched by his concern. 'The British Army suffered over fifty thousand casualties at Loos. You must also have seen action during the Great War.'

He nodded. 'I was one of those in Kitchener's New Army. Although we were keen to do our bit, we had very little training and weren't prepared for trench warfare. Germany had already used gas on the battlefield, of course, but our use of chlorine gas for the first time proved a problem, to say the least...'

'A terrible time for everyone,' she murmured, meeting his gaze, her face growing warm.

He seemed to recall his position, hastily straightened and took a step back. 'Regarding the murder on the Balfour estate and the attack on your own young house guest, your ladyship, I thought I should at least be warning you to be on your guard.'

'You can't think the two incidents are connected?'

'At this stage of an investigation, your ladyship, I can rule out nothing.'

Poppy felt the colour drain from her face. 'I was in Princes Street Gardens tonight, you know. I chased the assailant, thinking he was a thief.'

He said, his voice low, 'I thought you understood the danger—'

'But that was to do with the murder case.'

'It's to do with putting yourself in danger, my lady. You don't come from a world with villains in it.'

'Oh, trust me, Inspector, there are villains enough in high circles.'

'Perhaps, but you'll not be left for dead in some close off the Royal Mile unless you go looking for trouble.' His voice came out as a soft growl.

Poppy gazed at him. 'What do you mean?'

'I've seen Miss Macgregor in the hospital, and it struck me how remarkably similar you both are. It might have been that the young lady was in the wrong place at the wrong time, but there seems no obvious motive for the attack. Unless the assailant had not been after your friend, but you.'

Poppy's eyes widened. Now the inspector had commented on it, she had to admit that Isla could have been mistaken for her. The girl's newly bobbed brown hair, her black and white cloche not unlike the one Poppy had worn yesterday and, perhaps most damning of all, Poppy's coat. And if the assailant had followed her from Poppy's house...

But Poppy had no intention of cowering. 'It's possible that you are correct, Inspector, but let me remind you that I'm a grown woman and I'll please myself where I go and what I do!' Seeing the look on his troubled face, she softened. 'I will give your words my consideration for future exploits.'

He sighed, then spoke again. 'There is one other thing, my lady.'

'Yes?'

'I mind telling you to stay in the area of the Balfour estate and yet here you are.' He gestured around the room. 'Would you like to enlighten me as to how that came about?'

She raised her eyebrows. 'I had Miss Macgregor to meet off the train.'

His eyebrows went up. 'Something is telling me it was more than that.'

'Well, yes,' Poppy admitted. 'I also had an errand to perform for Lady Balfour – a delicate matter. You know the sort of thing I'm alluding to.'

'No, I don't think I do.'

And I will not tell you. 'I had intended to return to Balfour House tomorrow, but now that depends on Isla's condition.'

'I see,' he said gruffly. 'Kindly let me know when you do leave Edinburgh, so that I have some hope of keeping track of you.'

'I will, Inspector,' she assured him. She was almost at the front door when a question came to her. 'What brought you to Edinburgh? Is it anything to do with the murder case?'

He nodded. 'I am following a lead.'

Could she ask him? 'What is the lead?'

'I'm sorry, my lady, but I'm not at liberty to say.'

She drew in a deep breath. 'Very well.'

As she wished him good night, she saw a flicker of unease in his dark eyes and she hastily looked away, closing and locking the front door behind him.

Poppy leaned against the door, her thoughts in turmoil. Could the attack on Isla really have been meant for her, as Inspector MacKenzie suggested? He now knew the name of the murdered man, but was he also aware of Honest Harry's job as bookie's runner? Where was Harry's Post Office book? And a pencil had been found in the man's pocket, but not the book he must have kept with a list of punters' names and bets taken. What was the murder weapon, and could Constance have administered the fatal blow? And was MacKenzie's anxiety about her safety simply that of a police officer for his witness – or something more? Poppy's head thumped.

Then she realised in all the worry about Isla, she had forgotten to begin making entries in her new notebook. It was late now and she was very tired.

Poppy went to bed and slept fitfully, her dreams of Beth and bracelets, Isla and hooded assailants, and Inspector MacKenzie... and clues that wouldn't be pinned down.

The following morning Poppy was up early, desperate to see Isla and check the young woman was okay.

Wondering how Elspeth was getting on at Balfour House, Poppy stepped into a blue dress with a dropped waist, short sleeves and white collar and cuffs. The clock on St Stephen's Church struck nine as she pulled on her royal blue beret with its amusing bee brooch, adjusted it to sit over one ear, and climbed into the Bentley. Fergusson drove the car out of Ann Street and south to the city hospital.

Bidding her chauffeur to return to Ann Street for the time being, Poppy took the basket of grapes he handed her. She mounted the steps to the Royal Infirmary and pushed open the tall double doors. The outside of the building was impressive with its Gothic clock tower; as was the inside with its marble entrance hall and panelled walls.

Poppy knew the hospital had six hundred beds and so she needed to inquire where to find Isla. She approached a thickset, bespectacled woman seated at a desk on which stood a rack of coloured forms and a large pewter inkpot.

'Good morning. I'm looking for Miss Isla Macgregor, brought in last night.'

'The stabbing victim?' The woman pushed her spectacles back up her nose. 'Can I ask what is your relationship to the girl?'

'She's a friend of my people.'

The woman nodded and consulted a sheaf of papers on the desk. 'Up the stairs to the second floor and she's in the first ward you come to.'

'Thank you. Do you have any idea how she is getting on?'

The woman shook her head and readjusted her spectacles. 'We're not given that sort of information down here.'

Poppy climbed two flights of stairs, wrinkling her nose a little at the smell of antiseptic, floor polish and stewing fish, and emerged on the second floor.

She entered Isla's ward to see rows of occupied beds, and tall windows opposite each other flooding the room with light. The Royal Infirmary lived up to its reputation as the best planned hospital in Britain, she thought, with its design based on Florence Nightingale's model of large wards. A doctor in a white coat tended to a patient, while nurses in long white aprons and little caps moved about briskly.

To her huge relief, Poppy saw Isla sitting up in bed. She hurried over.

'My dear, how are you?' Poppy put the basket of grapes on the side table, leaned over and carefully gave the girl a kiss on the cheek. Drawing the chair up to the bed, she sat down and studied her closely. Isla's face was pale and her left arm was in a sling.

'How are you?' asked Poppy again. 'What happened? Tell me everything. That is, if you're not too tired.'

Isla gave a cheerful smile. 'I feel well, thanks. All I have is a cut on my shoulder. Not a deep one, but they want me to stay in for observation.' Her face dropped. 'Oh, but Poppy, I feel beastly about this. I got blood on your lovely coat.'

'My coat! Good heavens, Isla, a coat can be replaced, but a person cannot. I'm the one to feel beastly. You were in my care and I've not looked after you properly.'

'You couldna have known this would happen. It was just one of those things.'

Poppy gazed at her. Was it really *just one of those things*? With Isla's hair styled similarly to her own, Poppy could see how alike they might appear. She'd had the long night to consider what Inspector MacKenzie had said and was forced to conclude that he could be right. The attack on Isla might have been meant for her.

'I don't know what to think,' she told the girl truthfully. 'But tell me exactly what took place.'

'It's difficult to remember,' Isla began. 'It all seemed to happen so quickly. One minute I was strolling along the path in the gardens – I wanted to count the number of figures on the Scott Monument, like I said – and the next thing I knew this person in a cloak came running towards me. I saw the knife raised and felt a sort of blow on my shoulder.' She shuddered as she remembered it.

'Here, let me make you more comfortable.' Poppy rose and indicated to Isla to lean forward to allow the pillows behind her to be plumped up. That done, the girl leaned back again.

'I think it would have been much worse,' she went on, 'if the young man with his dog hadna come to my rescue. He leaped behind the attacker and pulled him away from me. I think the blade might have otherwise killed me.' Her voice trembled. 'How is he, do you know? I haven't had a chance to thank him.'

Poppy shook her head. 'I don't know, but I will visit him next.'

'Oh, please do!' Isla's glance fell on the grapes. 'Thank you so much, Poppy. I love grapes. But can you take some of them to the man who saved me, please, and give him my very best wishes?'

'Of course. You know,' Poppy went on, 'I can't help wondering what prompted the attack.'

'There is one thing...' Isla's voice was doubtful.

'Yes?' Poppy asked quickly.

'It sounds silly, but when I left your house, I noticed a man standing at the end of the road, reading a newspaper. As I turned into the next street, he no longer had the paper and was walking behind me.'

It might not be as ridiculous a thought as Isla imagined. 'What was he wearing?'

'Just ordinary clothes – a suit and a hat. I didn't really pay that much attention. Oh, and he was carrying a brown-paper parcel under his arm.'

Poppy nodded, encouraging the girl to continue.

'Since then, I've been thinking about everything that happened, and it seemed a strange thing to do.' Isla frowned. 'I suppose he might have followed me, although I dinna ken why.'

Poppy took her hand; she had to tell her. 'I'm so sorry, Isla, but it's possible he mistook you for me. You were wearing my coat and your new hat is quite similar to mine.'

The girl's eyes widened. 'Someone wanted to harm you?' she whispered. 'But why?'

'I could be wrong. There was a murder in the grounds of the house where I'm staying in Fife and I've been trying to track down the killer—'

'Poppy! You never have?' Isla breathed.

'Clearly not a very clever thing to do, if it's put your life at risk.' Poppy squeezed Isla's hand and released it, her voice grim.

'Did they catch the man who attacked me?'

'Not yet, Isla. But they will, I'm sure. Inspector MacKenzie is working on the case.'

Isla looked relieved. 'I'd hate to think the person might do the same thing to someone else – to *you*.'

'Did you get a look at your attacker?'

'Nae really. That is, nothing of any use. He was wearing a long evening cloak and had the hood up and covering most of his face. But it can't be the man who followed me before that, because he was wearing a suit. Oh!' Isla's eyes grew wide. 'The cloak was in the parcel?'

'It's possible. I wonder why he waited so long before the attack. Fleming said you left the house about half past eight yesterday evening and yet he didn't strike until something like an hour and a half later.'

'I've thought about that. He might have wanted the place to be busy, so that he could slip away in the crowd. In a quiet street he would have easily been spotted running off.' Isla's voice wobbled.

'Did he say anything to you?' Poppy asked. 'If he had a particular accent or way of speaking, that might help to find him.'

'No, he didna say anything. Just rushed at me with the knife...' Tears ran down Isla's pale cheeks.

'Please don't distress yourself, my dear. I'll go now, so you can rest, but I'll visit again.'

'I'd really like to leave the hospital.' Isla rubbed at her tears with her hands. 'I feel well enough and I want to go home. Do you think you could arrange that?'

The doctor, a short, chubby man with a pair of gold pince-nez on his nose, was making his way towards Isla's bed.

'I'll see what I can do,' Poppy reassured her.

'And oh, Poppy, there's something else,' Isla whispered, her eyes downcast. 'I won't be able to pay the hospital bill.'

'Don't concern yourself with that,' Poppy said firmly. 'I'll take care of everything. And,' she added quickly, 'please don't thank me. I feel responsible for what has happened.'

The doctor reached them. 'Good morning, young lady. Young *ladies*, I should say.' He beamed. 'And how is the patient today?'

'How *is* the patient today, doctor?' Poppy asked him.

He peered more closely at Poppy. 'Bless my soul, if it isn't young Persephone!' Seeing her startled face, he went on, 'You don't remember me, do you? Your dear father and I were old friends. I used to visit Dunearn Castle when I stayed in Perthshire. Och, happy days.' He sighed. 'But then I moved to Edinburgh to take up this post and, well, one loses touch. How is the old chap?'

'Living with my mother on a sheep station in Australia,' she told him.

'Is he, by Jove? Isn't that just the sort of thing he would do! I seem to remember hearing that he's now the Earl of Crieff.'

'Yes, after his elder brother died in the Great Influenza Epidemic.'

'Terrible, terrible.' He shook his head. 'Well now, remember me to him when you next see him.' The doctor prepared to move on.

'Doctor, one moment, if you please. Miss Macgregor feels well enough to go home. Can she be discharged?'

'I don't see why not,' he said cheerfully, looking at Isla. 'You were very lucky, young lady. But you're young and healthy, and will be right as rain in no time.'

'Thank you,' Poppy said. 'I will arrange for her to be taken to her mother's house.'

'Very good, very good.' The doctor wandered off.

'Poppy,' Isla began, 'there is one other thing I must ask...'

'Ask away.' Poppy smiled.

'The interview I was supposed to have this morning.' Isla's voice wobbled.

Good Lord! In all the turmoil of the last few hours, Poppy had completely forgotten Isla's interview. 'Goodness, yes, we must do something about that. I will speak to the lady superintendent of nurses. What is her name?'

'Miss Annie Warren Gill,' Isla whispered fearfully. 'I hope she's not too cross I missed my appointment.'

'I'm sure she won't be when I explain what has happened to you. And perhaps we can arrange another date.' In fact, Poppy had a better idea. Isla was already in the hospital. Perhaps Miss Gill could pop along to the ward and have a wee chat with Isla...

'Just concentrate on getting better,' she told the girl. 'I'll speak to Miss Gill and to your young knight, while the nurse helps you get ready to leave. I'll telephone Fleming and tell him to arrange for our belongings to be packed up and brought round with the car. We can stop for lunch wherever you like and I'll have you home in time for tea.'

'Aren't you going back to Lady Balfour's today?'

'I am. But not before I deliver you safely to your mother.'

'But Dunfermline isn't on the way to Culross!' Isla protested.

'It's barely six miles from the North Queensferry crossing. That's hardly out of the way at all. I'll take these to the young man, as you ask.' Plucking a small bunch of grapes from the larger one on Isla's bedside table, Poppy bid the girl goodbye for the present.

A nurse directed her to the office of the lady superintendent of nurses, which turned out to be a small room at the end of the corridor on the lower floor. Poppy tapped on the door, which stood ajar, heard the call, 'Come,' and entered.

A short, wiry-looking woman in a dark dress and a large

white cap, perhaps in her early sixties, with deeply scored lines between her brows, looked up from the desk where she had been writing.

'Miss Gill, I am Lady Persephone Proudfoot, here on behalf of Miss Isla Macgregor.'

'Oh yes, the young woman who didn't appear for her interview this morning.' Miss Gill slowly put down her pen and the creases between her eyebrows deepened. 'She sent your ladyship to ask for another appointment, I take it?'

'In a manner of speaking.' Poppy slid onto the chair opposite the desk.

'Well, I do not feel inclined—'

'If I can stop you there, madam. Miss Macgregor was the victim of a serious knife attack yesterday evening in Princes Street Gardens and her life was saved only by the intervention of a brave young man, a total stranger.'

'Dear me!' Miss Gill's eyebrows rose. 'I heard of the incident, of course, but had no idea that the young lady in question was Miss Macgregor. Then, of course, she must be given another appointment.'

'I have a better idea, Miss Gill, if you are agreeable. Isla is very disappointed to have missed this morning, and I wondered if you might possibly be able to speak to her at her bedside?'

The superintendent again frowned. 'It is most irregular...'

Poppy gave an encouraging smile.

Miss Gill let out a sigh. 'Oh well, I'm sure I can do that. After all, we need all the nurses we can get, and Miss Macgregor has gained first-hand experience of being in a hospital – albeit on the other side of the bed.' She rose. 'No time like the present.'

Poppy got to her feet. 'I couldn't agree more. May I use your telephone? I need to speak to my butler to arrange for the car and so forth.'

Miss Gill gestured to the instrument on her desk. 'Help yourself.'

As the superintendent left the room, Poppy picked up the receiver. The sooner she made this call, the sooner she could get Isla home safely.

And then Poppy could return to the case of the body by the loch.

FIFTEEN

Next on Poppy's list was the young knight. Returning to the woman in the entrance hall, she enquired after the young man brought in with Isla.

'Mr Fraser?' the receptionist said. 'You'll find him on the first floor in the men's surgical ward.'

Poppy made her way to the other building and climbed the stairs. Mr Fraser looked to be in much worse shape than Isla. His arms and hands were heavily bandaged, his face pale under a shock of red hair. He lay listless in the white sheets. His eyes opened as Poppy took the seat by his bed.

'Mr Fraser?' she said softly.

'Aye.' His voice came out as a croak.

'I am Poppy Proudfoot, a friend of Miss Isla Macgregor, whose life you saved last night.'

He moistened his dry lips with his tongue. 'How is she?' he managed to ask.

'Let me get you some water.' Poppy laid the grapes on his bedside table and poured a glass of water from the jug set there. She eased an arm behind his head to help him take a couple of sips, as she had done many times for the injured soldiers.

'Thank you.'

'Miss Macgregor is doing well, thanks to you. She sends these grapes and her best wishes.' Poppy replaced the glass. 'Would you mind if I asked you a few questions, Mr Fraser?'

He shook his head and winced.

'I'm so sorry. Are you badly hurt?'

'The doctor says I've lost quite a lot of blood. I wrapped my arms round the attacker's shoulders to pull him off the young lady and he turned the knife on me; slashed the back of my forearms and hands.' He gave a faint smile. 'But I'll live.'

'Isla Macgregor will be pleased to hear that.' Poppy smiled back.

'My dog,' the young man asked. 'Is Bella all right?'

'She is. The police are looking after her for the time being. Mr Fraser, do you think you could describe the attacker?'

'His head was covered by the hood of his cloak, and it all happened so quickly, but I saw a wee bit of his face when he turned and ran.'

Poppy had an idea. 'If you describe what you did see, no matter how little, I could draw the face. That might help the police find him. Would you be prepared to do that?'

'Aye.' The young man nodded.

From her bag she took out her new notebook and a pencil. In their *Casebook*, Maud McIntyre and Daisy Cameron recommended carrying these items at all times, as it was never known when they might be needed. How right they were!

Poppy positioned the notebook on her lap. 'Ready when you are.'

'A thin-ish sort of face...'

Poppy drew an oval on the blank page.

'Thin, arched eyebrows...'

She sketched these in.

'Evil eyes...'

Poppy glanced at Mr Fraser. 'I'm not sure how to draw evil eyes.'

'That's just how they looked to me when he used the knife.' Mr Fraser gave a slight, obviously painful shrug. 'They probably don't look like that in everyday life.'

Poppy reminded herself that the assailant probably lived a normal life, not standing out from his neighbours in any way.

'Nose?' she asked.

'Aye, he had one.' The young man gave a faint smile.

'A joke,' said Poppy. 'That's good. It sounds like you might be on the mend.'

'Normal nose, as far as I can say. And normal mouth.' His voice was growing tired.

'Just two more questions, if you can manage them,' Poppy said quickly. 'What colour hair did he have?'

'Couldna see,' he murmured.

'And a moustache or a beard?'

'Clean-shaven.'

Poppy finished her sketch as best she could. 'There.' She showed him. 'A likeness?'

'Aye.'

She studied the drawing. To her disappointment, it showed a bland face with no distinguishing features.

'I'll leave you now, Mr Fraser. Thank you for your help.'

'I'm sorry I've nae been much help with the description.'

Poppy disagreed and wished him a speedy recovery.

Her drawing might not be much, but it was at least a start.

She returned to Isla's ward and found the young woman dressed and ready to leave, and in a state of great excitement.

'Thank you so much for arranging the interview with Miss Gill!' Isla beamed. 'She came to see me a wee while ago and I've got the nurse position. I can hardly believe it! I start in September, when I'll be completely recovered.'

'I'm very pleased to hear that, Isla.' Poppy returned the beaming smile. 'You'll make a wonderful nurse.'

'I intend to be just like Nurse Cross here, who's not cross at all! She explained everything she was doing when she changed the dressing on my wound after Miss Gill had left,' Isla chatted excitedly. 'I have stitches but will heal in no time if I rest until they come out. She said my local doctor can do that for me.'

With Nurse Cross praised and enthusiastically thanked, Poppy helped Isla, her arm held to her body by a sling, down the stairs and out of the building, to where her chauffeur waited at the front door with the open-top Bentley. The day was already warm and threatening to become uncomfortably humid before much longer. Sunshine bathed the streets of the city and glinted cheerfully off the car's paintwork. Fergusson touched his cap as Poppy approached.

'I have one visit to make before we leave Edinburgh,' Poppy told Isla as she and Fergusson assisted the young woman into the back seat of the car. 'The Police Chambers in Parliament Square. Your young man from yesterday—'

Isla blushed. 'He's not *my* young man.'

Poppy smiled. 'He was able to give me some idea of what your attacker looked like and I've drawn a tolerable likeness. I will give the sketch to the police.' She climbed into the seat next to Isla.

Fergusson eased his way along Lauriston Place, turned into Forrest Road and was approaching George IV Bridge, when an impressive French Renaissance-style building came into view. The library! An idea came to Poppy. She would see if the attacker had consulted the library's copy of *Who's Who* to find her address. If he had, the librarian might be able to give her a more detailed description of the man.

'Isla,' she said hastily, 'would you mind very much if I called into the library for just a moment? I'll be as quick as I can, I promise.'

'That's fine, Poppy,' Isla told her. 'I don't mind waiting in the car.'

'Thank you, my dear. Fergusson! Pull over outside the library, will you?'

Her chauffeur did as requested and, without waiting for him to open the door, Poppy jumped out of the car, ran up the path and into the library. Reverting to a hurried walk, she made her way to the reference section.

'Can you tell me,' she asked the tall, grave man behind the desk, 'if anyone has borrowed the library's copy of *Who's Who* in the last day or two?'

He pressed his thin lips together. 'That is an unusual question, madam.'

'But one you can give me the answer to?' Poppy offered him her most persuasive smile.

'I don't see why not. It can hardly be against the law to do so.'

'No, it's not.'

He stared at her, but this was not the time to go into lengthy explanations. 'At least, I feel sure it isn't.'

He nodded. 'No one has borrowed that volume in over a week.'

'Are you absolutely certain?'

'My dear young lady, are you suggesting that I don't know my job?' he said, his voice rising, to the visible consternation of the other library users. He lowered it again to just above a whisper. 'I am in charge of the reference library and I can assure you that volume has not moved from its shelf for at least the past week.'

She thanked him politely and strode out of the building, before running back down the path and jumping into the Bentley.

'Thank you, Fergusson,' she said to her chauffeur. 'Please proceed.'

As he pulled out with a blast of the horn into the stream of traffic, Isla turned to Poppy. 'Did you find what you wanted?'

'Yes and no.' Poppy smiled at Isla, seeing her puzzled expression. 'Nothing for you to worry about.'

But it was something for Poppy to ponder. The attacker hadn't got her address from the library. The book itself was expensive to buy, so that meant he was someone who already knew where she lived. A small shiver went down her back.

The chauffeur manoeuvred the Bentley onto the Royal Mile and into Parliament Square.

'Will you be all right waiting here again with Fergusson?' Poppy asked Isla, climbing out as the chauffeur held the door for her. 'I won't be long.'

'I'm very comfortable, thank you,' Isla assured her.

Inside the police office, a young officer stood behind the desk.

'I'd like to see Inspector MacKenzie,' Poppy said.

He shook his head. 'You canna do that, lassie. He's busy at present.'

'Kindly give him my card.' Poppy pulled one from her handbag and slid it over the counter.

The officer picked it up, read her name and gave a low whistle. 'I'll see what I can do, your ladyship.'

'I'd be obliged. My young charge, just collected from the hospital, is waiting outside in my motor car and I don't want to leave her for long.' Poppy sat down in one of the uncomfortable seats, as the flustered young officer made his telephone call.

He replaced the receiver on its stand. 'The inspector will be with you shortly, my lady.'

She nodded and waited.

Before long, Inspector MacKenzie appeared from a door at the back of the hall. He strode towards her, looking less than pleased at her visit. Really, she thought, would a smile be too much to ask for? He was so much better-looking when he didn't scowl. But perhaps it wasn't a scowl; more of a frown. And a detective would naturally wear a solemn expression, she supposed...

He stood in front of her. 'My lady, what can I do for you?'

Having him looming over her was not good for morale. Her morale, that is; no doubt it was doing wonders for his, Mr Delicious Detective Inspector MacKenzie. She put the nickname from her head.

Uncrossing her silk-clad legs, she stood and from her bag withdrew her notebook. Turning to the page containing her sketch, she held it out to him. 'This, Inspector, is a fair likeness of the assailant in Princes Street Gardens.'

Inspector MacKenzie didn't even take it from her. He looked at the drawing and gave a soft laugh. 'Aye, verra fair. '

Stung, Poppy snatched her hand back. 'Mr Fraser thought it a reasonable likeness.'

'Mr Fraser has been seriously injured and canna think too clearly at the moment.'

'I doubt he would agree with you,' she retorted.

'Which is exactly my point.' Inspector MacKenzie fixed Poppy with his steady gaze. 'Now, is there anything else, my lady, you are wishing to tell me?'

Many things, she seethed, but nothing that should be said by a lady. Poppy stuffed her notebook back into her bag, controlled her tongue and began again.

'I think you were right about Miss Macgregor being mistaken for me last night,' she said sternly.

He raised a dark eyebrow. 'What makes you say that?'

'Because there is a certain similarity between us, as you pointed out. And because she was wearing a hat very similar to mine and I had lent her my coat.'

The inspector studied her closely. 'How would the attacker

have kent where you – that is, Miss Macgregor – would be last night?'

'Miss Macgregor believes he followed her from my house.'

'And how would he have kent your address?'

How much should she tell him? The bare truth. 'Well, of course I am in *Who's Who*, Inspector, as you know.'

He fell silent and thought for a moment. 'There could be something in what you say.' He drew his dark brows together. 'I will look into it. You can return to your parties.'

Poppy sent him a sharp look of her own. Did he really think her life was one of parties and such like? She had to admit that it might look like that. What else did she have to do with herself in the eyes of the world except find a second suitable man to marry? The thought gave rise to anger.

He continued to stand there, studying her, while she glared at him. She would not allow him to make her feel foolish. After a minute or two, the silence became uncomfortable. Poppy broke it.

'Mr Fraser was asking about his dog.'

'She's being well looked after in the Home for Lost and Starving Dogs.'

Poppy opened her mouth, but the inspector got there first. 'Aye, I'll send a constable to the hospital to let the young gentleman know,' he said wearily.

'Thank you. I'm sure that will aid Mr Fraser's recovery. Just one last thing, Inspector.'

The young officer at the desk was staring wide-eyed at them. He caught Poppy's gaze, blushed and hurriedly began to rearrange the papers on the desk in front of him.

Inspector MacKenzie gave a sigh of resignation. 'Aye?'

'Miss Macgregor has been quite shaken by her ordeal and wishes to return to her parents' house in Dunfermline. I'm sure being at home and under her mother's care will be a tremendous boost to her. I'm taking her there now, on my way back to

Balfour House. If the police need to speak further to her, kindly arrange for an officer to interview her at her home.'

MacKenzie gave a resigned nod.

'Good day to you, Inspector MacKenzie.'

'Good day to you, my lady.' He followed her to the door and held it open for her. 'Before you go,' he added quietly.

Surprised at the tone of his voice, she turned. 'Yes?'

'Don't take any risks. Please.' He fixed her with his dark, unfathomable gaze. 'The attacker could strike again.'

SIXTEEN

Fergusson started the Bentley as soon as he saw Poppy emerge from the police office. Once Poppy was settled in the back seat with Isla, he slid behind the steering wheel and the car set off again. Soon Edinburgh's impressive Georgian buildings were left behind and the Bentley cruised along the country road under a blue sky.

Poppy was not surprised to find Isla fatigued after her recent brush with death and their conversation was naturally light, but they both marvelled at the view. Poppy never tired of it. On one side, as far as the horizon, the Firth of Forth glittered. On the other, ripening maize swayed in the slight breeze like the waves of a golden sea. They reached Queensferry, where the steamer *Dundee* waited to take them across the Forth.

'The town was named in the eleventh century when the Queen of Scotland, Margaret, founded a free ferry to take pilgrims north,' the young man issuing their tickets told them proudly.

'Aye, and she's buried in Dunfermline Abbey,' Isla responded equally proudly.

They stopped for lunch at some charming refreshment

rooms and made good progress to Dunfermline. With Isla delivered safely to her parents, and the girl promising to let Poppy know how her recovery progressed, Poppy continued her journey.

She relaxed against the Bentley's leather seat and her thoughts returned to the events at Balfour House. Poppy resolved to put aside any suspicion about Constance's past until she received a reply from Mrs Abbott about Mary Murray.

They reached Culross, drove past the row of cottages, public buildings and palace, in through the pillars of Balfour House and drew to a halt in front of the house.

As Fergusson handed Poppy out of the car, an anxious Constance waited for her at the front door. Poppy wasted no time in suggesting that they go somewhere private where she could tell her hostess all that had happened in Edinburgh.

'But first, have you eaten lunch?' Constance asked.

'Yes, thanks. We stopped at a pleasant little restaurant on the way to Dunfermline.'

'Dunfermline?' Constance looked bemused.

Poppy handed her coat, hat and gloves to the butler hovering in the hall. 'I will tell you shortly. But first a cup of tea would be welcome.'

'Tea in the study, Baird,' Constance instructed him.

No sooner than they had seated themselves on the Chesterfield, with Constance's wee dachshund settling himself on the settee between them, than Poppy began to tell her tale. She broke off briefly when a footman brought a tray of tea things and began again when he had departed.

'Good heavens, Poppy!' Constance stared at her when Poppy had finished her account. 'What an exciting time you have had.'

'I'm not sure about exciting, although I must say chasing the assailant was rather thrilling,' Poppy said with a smile.

'And your young house guest is doing well? An attack like

that can have more than physical consequences.' Constance's brow was creased with concern.

'She's in good hands. Her mother will be a great support, and I'm sure Miss Gill, the superintendent of nurses at the Royal Infirmary, will keep an eye on her when she moves to Edinburgh.'

Constance set down her cup and saucer and frowned. 'So, the jeweller's that Miss Cornett visited was the same one that sold the bracelet to Bruce?'

'No doubt about it.' Poppy was adamant.

'And you say she may have sold a diamond and emerald bracelet to the shop?' Constance continued.

'I can't be sure it's the same bracelet. The question is, did she choose that shop because she knew the bracelet had come from there, or was it just coincidence?'

'I mentioned to her over dinner the other evening that Scottish freshwater pearls feature in the Crown Jewels, and may have told her they had a fine selection in Campbell's. I should have realised she would be determined to buy a rope of the pearls for herself. She took a train to Edinburgh yesterday morning, defying the inspector's instructions to stay in the area.' Constance shook her head.

'I think I must have played my part in that, leaving as I did.'

'Your defying the inspector is hardly a reason for Miss Cornett to do so as well. Her standing doesn't afford her the same protection as we enjoy, does it?'

Feeling uncomfortable, Poppy went quickly on. 'Has she returned?'

'Yes, yesterday evening—'

Ollie suddenly barked, jumped down from the settee, nosed open the door and shot from the room as muffled voices and thuds in the hall filtered through to the study.

Constance smiled fondly. 'The little fellow thinks he's a big guard dog and I don't like to tell him otherwise.'

The noises in the hall were growing louder.

'Constance,' Poppy said quickly, before the activity could erupt into the room, 'was Lord Balfour deaf?'

'Yes, he was, dear. Why do you ask?'

'It was just something that came up in conversation with his secretary...'

'*Halloo!*' A woman's deep voice, calling as if she had seen a fox break cover, came from outside the study and almost immediately the door was thrust wide open.

'Dahlia!' exclaimed Constance and Poppy.

Dahlia Dalrymple stood there, dressed in the same crumpled tweed jacket and skirt as Poppy had seen her wear the previous evening. Now a crushed felt hat sat rakishly over her crop of thick grey hair. Dahlia beamed at the two women. 'How spiffing to see you both again.'

'You've met?' Constance looked between Dahlia and Poppy.

'Only briefly, at the fundraising event last night,' Poppy said.

'And I thought what a delightful girl,' Dahlia said briskly, stepping into the room, 'and why not go to dear Constance's today instead of waiting until the garden party. I knew you wouldn't mind.'

'This is an unexpected pleasure, Dahlia. And is Irene with you?'

'Certainly not! The woman is impossible! No doubt she will still turn up at your garden party on Saturday. But never mind about her. My taxi is at the front door.' Dahlia drew in a deep breath and charged on. 'I've instructed your butler to pay him. I've packed my damn purse somewhere in my luggage. Speaking of which, your man will get a footman to deal with my bags, won't he? The taxi driver just dumped them in the hall.'

Ollie barked again and Constance hurried out to him, muttering, 'Whatever can be the matter with him?'

Poppy followed, Dahlia behind, arriving in the hall in time to see the little dachshund staring fixedly as he barked at luggage on the floor, which consisted of a small, battered suitcase and a large handbag.

'Foolish little creature,' boomed Dahlia. 'Give me a large, sensible dog any day.'

Like Major, Poppy thought proudly. After all, it was sensible to go into a butcher's shop for sausages.

'A good deal has gone into Ollie's breeding!' Constance protested, gathering him up. 'He's highly intelligent and was only protecting me.'

Dahlia snorted. 'From assault by a suitcase and a handbag?'

Ollie sent Constance a shamefaced look from the corner of his eye.

Poppy felt this an appropriate time to liberate her own dog from the kennels. 'I'll go and say hello to Major.'

She excused herself to Constance and Dahlia, made her way past the butler, footman and taxi driver engaged in various remonstrations, and with a sense of relief stepped out of the open main door.

She found herself looking down the drive for Inspector MacKenzie and was disappointed there was no sign of him. But why should there be? He must still be in Edinburgh. No doubt there was a suspicious death or two there to keep him occupied.

And she was busy with two crimes to solve here: the missing bracelet and the murder at the loch. She'd leave the attack on Isla to the inspector. It wouldn't do any harm to take his advice on that one since he might be right. His suspicion that she could have been the target played on Poppy's mind. But who would want to kill her? Wrack her brain as she might, she could think of nothing she'd done to draw such attention to herself.

She reached the kennels. Major dropped the bone he was chewing and bounded to his feet, his tail wagging furiously. Poppy smiled as she unlatched his door.

'Hello, old thing.' He turned to pick up the bone again and brought it to her. 'Thank you.' Accepting the bone from him, she laughed and stroked the dog's warm, solid flank.

'Come on, let's stretch our legs.' Poppy dropped the bone into the straw of his bedding, discreetly so as not to hurt his feelings, lifted his leash from the hook by the side of the door and strode out, Major frolicking beside her.

She wasn't surprised when her feet took her towards the glittering loch. Not only was the shining water a magnet for its beauty, but also it drew her back with thoughts of the dead man.

'Lady Poppy!'

Poppy jumped, startled by the cry coming from the lochside shrubbery as she drew near. A boy's head poked through the greenery. Major gave a delighted woof and shot forward to say hello.

'Gregor!' she exclaimed. 'What are you doing in the hedge?'

'Oh, just *stuff*. Actually,' he added, poking an arm through the bushes to stroke the Labrador, 'I saw that awful Dalrymple woman arrive—'

Poppy interrupted him. 'Do you think your mother would approve of your describing her guest in that way?'

'Probably not,' he admitted. 'But, anyway, I decided to make myself scarce.' He gave her a sly look. 'Didn't you want to stay and have tea with Mrs Dalrymple either?'

Poppy laughed. 'Time enough for that. I gather she's here to stay until the midsummer party.'

Gregor pulled a face.

Feeling she shouldn't encourage the boy, Poppy went on sternly, 'So, what *are* you doing in the shrubbery? You didn't need to go to that length to hide from Mrs Dalrymple.'

'Oh.' He emerged fully from the bushes. 'I say, if I tell you, you won't let on to my mother?' He flushed.

'Not unless I have to.'

Gregor seemed to think that an acceptable answer. 'I was waiting for Miss Cornett.'

'Miss Cornett arranged to meet you here?' Poppy couldn't hide her astonishment.

'Well, not exactly,' he admitted. 'It's more a case of I hoped to see her here.'

'Miss Cornett is in the habit of walking by the loch at this time of day?'

Gregor shrugged. 'She does sometimes.'

Poppy glanced at her wristwatch. It was almost four o'clock, which was only a little earlier than the doctor's original assessment of death between half past four in the evening and half past four in the morning.

Had *Beth* murdered Honest Harry? She didn't look as though she could lift a heavy weapon, much less bring it down with any force. But why would she want the man dead? Or had Gregor, in the absence of Beth Cornett, done the deed? Again, why? Poppy considered him as he removed twigs from his cardigan. He was of sturdy build, and his temperament, though apparently amiable, could occasionally turn belligerent.

No, she told herself. He was a fourteen-year-old child – admittedly on the verge of adulthood. But, whispered a small voice inside her, if Constance knew of the extent of her husband's betting – and losses – on horse races, did that mean Gregor was also aware?

And was it possible that he had acted to silence the bookie's runner in order to protect the family name?

As she walked back to the house, Major at her heels and a chattering Gregor by her side, Poppy remembered that she had still to speak to Constance's chauffeur, Charlie, and the poacher, who both seemed to have a part to play in this drama.

Perhaps only a small, walk-on part, but she wouldn't know until she'd talked to each of them.

'Have you ever seen the poacher near the loch?' she asked Gregor as they walked across the lawn.

'Jack Finnie? He catches rabbits there and in other parts of the estate. Mother doesn't mind.' Gregor looked at Poppy. 'He's all right, you know. He's going to show me how he does it when I'm older. He's got nothing to do with the murder.'

'How can you be sure?' she asked. After all, a poacher kills his quarry.

'Well, I can't be *absolutely* sure... but I jolly well bet he isn't a murderer.'

'Your mother wouldn't object, though, if I speak to him?'

'Of course not! But you'd better not take Major with you, because Jack Finnie's collie is aggressive with other dogs.'

She nodded. 'Where does Mr Finnie stay?'

'In a cottage in the woods, over there.' Gregor pointed in the direction of the tumbledown place she'd spotted when she'd walked to the village along the track. 'He lived there with his parents until they died. Mother says it's not fit to live in anymore, but he won't move. I expect he'll do the repairs on it one day when he has time,' the boy added wisely.

'I think I know the cottage.' Poppy was shocked to learn that someone lived there.

'Actually, when you come to think about it, it's just the sort of old cottage in the woods where there might be a killer lurking.' Gregor pulled what he assumed to be the face of a murderer, his blue eyes sparkling with excitement.

Poppy suppressed a smile. 'You said yourself Jack Finnie isn't a murderer.'

'But you have to change your ideas when fresh evidence comes to light, don't you, if you're going to solve the case?' Gregor said cheerfully.

'You've been listening at doors again.'

Gregor sent her a wide-eyed grin.

'There is no fresh evidence,' she reminded him gently.

Gregor's smile disappeared. 'Well, what should we do now?'

'We?' she asked, in her most matronly voice. '*We* are not going to do anything.'

'But—'

'*I* am going to speak to your mother's chauffeur.'

'That's not going to be much use. Charlie won't know anything as he never goes down to the loch.'

'Never?'

'Well, I've never seen him there.'

'He might have noticed something, so I'll still have a word with him. I imagine he has a flat above the old coach house?'

Gregor nodded. 'It must be almost tea time,' he said, following a different train of thought as they reached the house. 'I'm starving.'

'You go ahead,' said Poppy. 'I need to take Major back to the kennels.'

Gregor rubbed the dog behind both ears, before disappearing into the house.

And then I'll see if Charlie is in, she added to herself. Constance hadn't said she needed the chauffeur to take her anywhere, so it was reasonable to assume he was at home.

And Poppy had questions that needed answering.

With Major returned to the kennels, Poppy walked round to the coach house and knocked on the downstairs door at the side of the building.

She heard the sound of heavy footsteps descending the stairs. A heavily built man with dark hair, tanned skin and broad features opened the door.

'Mr Lamont?'

'Yes,' the man said with a bemused look.

'My name is Lady Persephone Proudfoot and I'm one of her ladyship's guests at the house. I wonder if I might ask you a few questions?'

The confused look deepened, but he held the door wider and stepped back. 'Please come in, your ladyship.'

He led her up the wooden staircase, opened the door at the top and ushered her into what appeared to be both sitting room and dining room. Another door stood ajar and through it came the smell of frying sausages. Two chairs were placed at the small table under the window, which framed a view of the loch and the woods beyond. On the table stood a brown teapot and in the centre a plate with piled up with cut bread.

'I'm sorry,' Poppy said, 'I am disturbing your tea.'

'It's all right,' he said gruffly.

The room looked clean and homely. A pair of armchairs arranged with lace cushions, a framed photograph on the heavy sideboard showing a young couple in wedding clothes, and a few books arranged in orderly piles on a side table added to this impression. On the mantelpiece sat a china dog each side of a clock, a collection of little jugs and a glass snowstorm globe containing a church. The décor had a woman's touch; his wife's, she supposed.

The chauffeur indicated one of the armchairs. 'Pray, be seated.'

Poppy did so and he took the other easy chair.

'That is you and Mrs Lamont?' she inquired politely, indicating the photograph, to ease her way into the conversation she wanted to have.

His hands were tense on his knees. 'What exactly can I do for you, my lady? I'm sure you haven't come here to talk about my wife.'

That approach hadn't worked, Poppy thought. She would get straight to the point instead. 'You are right. It's about the death of the man by the loch.'

Charlie relaxed a little. 'Aye, it's a tragic business. You may rely on my co-operation, as far as is possible, in catching the person who did it.'

'I understand that you told Inspector MacKenzie you saw the footman Freddy by the loch late on Monday afternoon.' She could see that Charlie was again on his guard.

'I don't wish to sound impertinent, my lady, but why are you asking me this?'

'I thought you might prefer to speak to me, rather than to the police. You see, I saw Freddy in the village at about the same time that afternoon.'

A flash of anger crossed the chauffeur's face. 'Aye, well, it's like this, my lady. That footman is a bad 'un. I'm sure I saw him down by the loch on Monday, but if you say otherwise, then maybe it was someone else. Even so, Lady Balfour would best be rid of him.'

'Why do you say that?' Poppy asked, her eyebrows rising.

He looked keenly at Poppy. 'He's always shirking his duties. Men like him get into all sorts of rough company. I wouldna be surprised if he turned out to be the murderer.'

'But what makes you say that?'

'He gambles and he owed money to the runner. At least, so I've heard. He owed a lot of money to him afore his lordship passed away and I expect he owes a tidy bundle of it still.'

'And that is the reason you believe that the footman is the murderer?'

'It's a good reason,' Charlie retorted. 'What better way to write off a debt that you couldna pay?'

'It was quite a lot of money, then?'

'One hundred pounds. A year's wages for him. I'd say that was quite a lot.'

'*One hundred pounds!*' Poppy was astonished.

That might be enough to kill for.

SEVENTEEN

'How was Freddy allowed to run up such a debt with Harry?' Poppy asked the chauffeur.

'Because he worked for Lord Balfour, and Lord Balfour was Harry's biggest customer and Harry wouldna want to upset Lord Balfour. Och, and Freddy is Lady Balfour's favourite and his lordship wouldna have wanted to upset his lady.' Charlie shrugged his heavy shoulders. 'Maybe his lordship said he'd vouch for Freddy, which Harry took to mean he'd pay off the fellow's debt if need be. I couldna say.'

'It doesn't seem likely that his lordship left a direction in his will to pay Harry,' Poppy said thoughtfully.

'If he did, I'd nae heard of it!' The chauffeur's face assumed a belligerent expression. 'I *did* see Freddy walking away from the loch that afternoon, I'm sure of it.'

'From the window?' Poppy glanced towards it.

'No, I was outside, washing her ladyship's motor car.'

'And the footman was with Lady Balfour's dog, Ollie?'

He gave a nod. 'He was carrying it.'

Poppy could see that Ollie's little legs wouldn't be able to cope with the overgrown track – after all, her Labrador had frequently disappeared from sight when they'd walked along it. She wondered how many others took this rough path.

'Are you aware of the track between the loch and the village?' she asked.

'Of course, my lady. Everyone is,' Charlie replied gruffly.

'Is it much used?'

She could see that Charlie knew precisely why she was asking this question, but he answered with apparent honesty. 'I couldna say, my lady. Most of us steer clear of it because of all the bracken, but it must be used occasionally.'

Charlie glanced towards the kitchen. 'If there's nothing else I can do for you.'

Poppy sensed he was eager to have his dinner, and wondered why his wife hadn't appeared from the kitchen. Perhaps she was shy. Poppy quickly moved on to the missing bracelet.

'I won't keep you much longer, but I would like to ask you about one other thing. Are you aware that Lady Balfour has misplaced a bracelet, a present to her from her late husband?'

'I heard something about it in the servants' hall some months ago,' he admitted. 'She'd asked her personal maid if she'd seen it, and the word got around.' He flushed. 'I didna steal it, if that's what your ladyship thinks!'

'Certainly not, Mr Lamont. But, I wondered, do you think Freddy might have taken it, given the debt he's in?'

'He's nae in debt anymore – at least, not to the bookie's runner, now the man's dead. Whether Freddy would be capable of helping himself to a bracelet, I couldna say. But I'm not sure how he would have laid his hands on it,' Charlie admitted. 'A footman would never have cause to go into Lady Balfour's bedroom.'

'Or into Lord Balfour's bedroom?'

'Not usually, as that would be the job of his lordship's valet.'

'Where is his valet working now?'

'With his lordship's passing, he got a job with his lordship's brother.'

'Mr Nick Balfour?' That meant the man was again below stairs at Balfour House, albeit on a temporary basis.

'Aye. But thinking on it, I suppose it's possible Freddy might have needed to go into his lordship's room for some reason. Perhaps they wanted to discuss what horse to waste their money on without being overheard by young Gregor's flapping ears.'

Poppy flashed the chauffeur a disapproving glance and stayed seated. He could wait for a moment while she took time to think. If the valet had stolen the bracelet, would he risk returning here? Yet Constance had said she trusted her servants, and presumably she'd given the man a reference. Poppy would see what Elspeth could find out in the servants' hall about the valet.

'Thank you for talking to me, Mr Lamont.' Poppy's tone was a little too curt to be polite as she rose to go. Then she added, 'You dislike the footman a great deal, I think?'

Taken off guard, Charlie burst out, 'I *hate* him. The way he goes about as if he's Lady Balfour's treasured servant. I've worked here for over twenty years and served Lord and Lady Balfour faithfully. If that preening footman worms his way in any further and I have to teach him how to drive, then he'll take my job. A chauffeur is paid more than twice the wages of a footman. And if I lose my job, I'll lose my home. And then there's my wife. She... He turned away.

'I hope your wife wouldn't leave you if you suffered such misfortune,' she told him quite truthfully.

He didn't reply.

If the chauffeur wanted to murder anyone, Poppy thought as she made her way back to the house, there was little doubt in her mind that it would be Freddy.

. . .

Poppy was the last person to arrive in the drawing room for afternoon tea.

Beth had been speaking, and the young woman paused long enough for Poppy to take a seat on the settee.

'What do you think of these?' Beth raised the long string of pearls hanging down her chest. 'Aren't they just dandy?'

Poppy observed Freddy's calm demeanour as she accepted a cup of tea from him. 'They are beautiful,' she agreed.

Beth looked pleased. 'I just had to treat myself for the little party on Saturday. I didn't want to put Connie here to shame.'

'You would hardly have done that,' Constance told her.

'I suppose the weather will improve for the party,' said Morag, glancing idly out of the window at a single grey cloud moving across the sun.

'Lady B is right, Beth.' Admiration shone in Eddie's eyes. 'You are beautiful with or without the pearls.'

'Now don't you interrupt.' Beth beamed. 'I just love these colours.' She fingered the pearls. 'Pink, cream, white and purple. The store had brown too, but that's not really my colour.'

'Where did you buy them?' Poppy asked casually.

'In Edinburgh; at a jeweller's in George Street.'

'That's where you were yesterday, Poppy,' said Constance, before realising her mistake.

Beth studied Poppy. 'You were in the city yesterday too?' She laughed. 'Say, that's two of us that cute police inspector has to tear off a strip.'

Cute? Were there no men the girl wasn't interested in? Not that it mattered, Poppy chided herself. She had important work to do.

'The assistant told me Scottish pearls are highly sought-after around the world.' Beth tied a loose knot in the long necklace. 'This is how pearls are worn in New York City. It's so they don't get in the way when you're dancing.' Beth swung the string of pearls in a circular motion.

Gregor's eyes grew wide. 'They must have cost a bomb.'

'*Gregor!*' his mother remonstrated.

'I meant they must have been jolly expensive.' Gregor said, looking sullen.

'We know what you meant, you little ass,' growled Nick. 'A gentleman should never mention money in front of a lady!'

Gregor coloured and sent a look of agony towards Beth.

To have been spoken to like this, by his uncle in front of the object of his affection, had embarrassed him. The boy was right, though, Poppy thought: the pearls *would* have been jolly expensive. She thought it was unlikely Beth earned that sort of money... unless the actress had first sold a diamond and emerald bracelet.

As she sipped her tea, Poppy wondered if perhaps Beth and the shop assistant were somehow acting in collusion?

'Your ladyship should have come up to your room first, instead of gadding about with that dog of yours.' Elspeth fussed over Poppy as she helped her out of her blue dress.

'I was hardly gadding about, as you put it, Elspeth. Lady Balfour drew me into her study as soon as I arrived. And I was in dire need of a cup of tea.' Poppy kicked off her low-heeled shoes, wrapped herself in her red and cream silk kimono and tied the belt. 'Then I simply had to say hello to Major and take him for a walk by the loch. You know how much he likes water.'

Elspeth tutted as she shook out Poppy's dress and hung it in the wardrobe. 'Aye, I know that – to my cost.'

'Did you walk him yourself while I was away?' Poppy smiled. Elspeth generally had as little as possible to do with the large and boisterous Labrador. Could it be that, despite the protestations, her maid had a soft spot for him? 'I thought you would order one of the footmen to do it.'

'The idea! Me ordering anyone about.' Elspeth turned back to Poppy with a look of offended dignity on her face. 'Now take off that hat. I keep thinking the bee is real.'

Poppy hid a grin as she removed her beret decorated with its bee brooch in sapphires and diamonds.

'Thank you for taking care of Major, Elspeth.' Her ruse to deceive the inspector hadn't worked, but that was not her maid's fault. She stretched out on the bed, wriggling her stockinged toes and resting her hands behind her head. 'Did you remember to pay for the books?'

'Of course I did, my lady. And while I was in the village, I took the liberty of buying you a nice new pencil.'

Poppy smiled. Elspeth wasn't such a bad old thing. 'Have you met Mr Balfour's valet?' she went on.'

'The fellow who used to work for Lord Balfour? Yes.'

Poppy propped herself up on the pillows. 'What is he like?'

Elspeth brushed a speck of dust off Poppy's beret and set it on the top shelf in the wardrobe. 'He seems a pleasant fellow, and he and the other servants get on well.' She picked up Poppy's patent leather shoes. 'And look at the state of these!' She tutted. 'Grass on the heels. I'll take them downstairs and get them cleaned with a wee drop of soap and water.'

Poppy remembered the coat Isla had been wearing last night, which she'd picked up from the hospital along with the young woman that morning. 'I'm afraid there's something else that needs cleaning, although it might not be possible given its condition.'

'Its condition, my lady?' Elspeth raised an eyebrow.

'My black and white coat...'

'Aye?'

'It has rather a lot of blood on it.'

Poppy's shoes fell from Elspeth's hand. '*Blood*, my lady?' she whispered as she stared at Poppy.

'It's not mine...'

Elspeth's face grew even whiter. 'Whose is it?'

'Isla's.'

Elspeth sank onto the dressing table stool. 'You mean she's ... dead?'

'Thankfully, no.' Although she might very well have been. 'Poor Isla has a knife wound to her shoulder. She spent last night in hospital, where she had to have it stitched up. She's now safely home in the care of her parents, where I'm sure she will make a good recovery.'

Elspeth straightened her back. 'And she was wearing my lady's coat?'

'It'll need mending too, I'm afraid. The knife went right through the fabric.'

Elspeth gave a little gasp. 'This criminal activity you are engaging in, my lady—'

'It's not criminal activity, Elspeth. I'm *investigating* a crime.' *Or two.*

Her maid took a deep breath. 'Whatever you call it, it's not a suitable occupation for a lady. And now you're telling me it's dangerous. What would your dear mother say?'

'As she and my father are sheep farming more than nine thousand miles away, she doesn't need to know. In fact, she might think I'm putting my law degree to *some* use.' Poppy wasn't entirely sure how that worked, but it suited her to say so.

Elspeth sniffed. 'Very well, my lady.' She got to her feet.

'The coat is in the top of my luggage.'

'A baking soda paste will deal with the blood stain.'

'That can wait, Elspeth. First, tell me if anything of interest happened below stairs during my absence.'

Her maid removed the coat and folded it distastefully over her arm. 'Cook's daughter has had a baby'

'Elspeth,' Poppy fixed her with a stare, 'don't do this. You know that is not the sort of news I mean.'

Elspeth sighed. 'I'm not keen on gossiping...'

'And nor am I,' Poppy lied. After all, gossip was a wonderful source of information. 'Anything new on the murder of Honest Harry?'

'Honest Harry? Who's that?' Elspeth caught her breath. 'Don't tell me there's been another murder?'

'No, I meant the man by the loch.'

'Oh, Henry Harvey. I don't know why you called him by that ridiculous name.' She shook her head. 'It makes it seem worse, somehow, when a murdered man is named.'

'Tell me, Elspeth,' Poppy pressed, 'has the inspector returned to ask any more questions or provide any further details?'

Elspeth shook her head. 'We've not had sight or sound of him since you left.'

Of course not, Poppy thought. Inspector MacKenzie appeared in Ann Street yesterday evening and must now be very busy in Edinburgh. And he had still been in the city when she'd left it this morning.

'I don't suppose we'll hear from him again – not unless he comes to tell us when he's caught the villain.' Poppy sighed.

Elspeth picked up Poppy's shoes again. 'There was one thing, my lady, but I'm sure it's not of any importance. Thomas, the footman who is looking after Mr Emmett during his stay, him having no valet of his own, told us all at supper that the American gentleman had said something about what a jolly time they had had with his lordship in November in London.'

Poppy sat up on the bed. She had considered that possibility earlier, but dismissed it. 'Mr Emmett definitely said that they'd had a jolly time with Lord Balfour in London in November?'

Elspeth frowned. 'He used another word. I think it was *swell*...'

'Very likely. Well, thank you, Elspeth.'

Poppy wondered why Mr Emmett, or Beth or Eddie, hadn't admitted they'd spent time with Lord Balfour, when the subject of the Americans being in London had come up two days ago? Was the clue in the word *admitted*? Perhaps Constance didn't know they had met and so the conversation had been tactfully steered in another direction. Had Lord Balfour been the person at the Edinburgh party who had introduced the Americans to his brother Nick?

What Thomas had reported didn't necessarily mean that Lord Balfour indulged in fast living away from home, but a different picture was beginning to emerge of the industrialist. The notion of his having a fancy woman, or two, no longer seemed far-fetched, especially after learning that he had acquired his wife as the result of a game of cards...

'Until it is time to dress for dinner, will there be anything else your ladyship requires?' The maid looked pointedly at the coat over her arm and the shoes in her hand.

'No, thank you, Elspeth. Perhaps if you could just listen out for anything that seems at all important when you're in the servants' hall?'

Elspeth sniffed audibly. 'I cannot promise to do any such thing, my lady.'

Poppy waited until her maid had left the room, before swinging her legs over the side of the bed. She would not be told what to do by Elspeth! She glanced at her wristwatch. It was five o'clock. There was still time to talk to one other person whose name had come up in the Honest Harry murder investigation: the poacher, Jack Finnie. Poachers must work in the evenings; if she hurried, she could catch him at home.

Dressed in her green tweeds, Poppy pulled on the matching cloche and slipped on her brogues. Quickly, she went down the stairs and nodded briskly at Constance's butler, who'd appeared at the sound of her light footstep in the hall. The man must have the ears of a bat, Poppy thought.

She set off at a smart pace across the lawn. She'd decided against taking Major with her in case Gregor was correct about Mr Finnie's collie. Her Labrador was easy-going, but if the collie took an immediate dislike to Major, it wouldn't help Poppy get answers to her questions.

She reached the loch, the water dull under a sky which now contained rather more grey clouds than earlier. Poppy hastened along the loch-side path until she reached the start of the rough track.

It all looked different in the gloomy late afternoon. Reminding herself that she was a country lass and there was nothing to be concerned about, she plunged into the bracken.

The earthen track was deserted. It took her round the edge of the potato field, where the tall plants stood in rows looking like sentinels. Wild things scuffled in the hedgerows as she passed. She jumped at the sudden beating of wings as a surprised owl rose from the woods ahead.

Poppy hurried on and wished she had brought Major, after all, and risked the collie's temper. Major Lewis could handle himself when it came to it. She knew her own estate like the back of her hand, but this place, only two days after the body had been found, felt very threatening. Both the owl and the poacher were night hunters, and she began almost to feel like the hunted...

The wood loomed closer, the trees appearing more thickly planted than they had when she'd last walked this way. Peering through them, she caught a glimpse again of the dilapidated cottage. No light or sound came from it. She wondered uneasily if the bird had been disturbed by another person, someone who didn't want to reveal themselves.

How easy it would have been for Jack Finnie to steal along

the track to the loch, there to dispose of, for whatever reason, Henry Harvey...

She crept forward cautiously, further into the wood, the carpet of pine needles under her feet making her progress almost silent. All was still around her. She went on for another fifty yards or so, her heartbeat loud in her ears, and reached the cottage. The thatch was in an even more ruinous condition than she had earlier thought. In front of the cottage was a small, neglected garden. The wooden gate, with one hinge missing, stood wedged open on the path and she went through it. The panes of the small windows were grimy, the windows curtainless and dark.

With a hand more shaky than she would have liked, Poppy tapped at the door. There was no reply. She thought she heard a cough from inside, so she tapped louder, her pulse racing. After a short pause, she tried the handle, found the door wasn't locked and, gathering her courage, pushed it open.

'Hello?' Poppy called into the silence. 'Is anyone there?'

There was no reply. 'Hello!' she said more loudly. 'Mr Finnie?'

She hadn't come here simply to turn around and go away again, so she entered. The front door led immediately into a gloomy parlour, smelling of wood smoke, although the hearth contained only the ashes of a long-dead fire. Inside, the dwelling was in as poor a condition as the outside. The single, frayed rocking chair had been recently vacated, for it still rocked a little by the grate. An upright chair stood with its seat pushed roughly under a kitchen table, on which stood a loaf of bread, partially eaten, and an almost-empty bottle of whisky.

There was the sudden sound of movement. A man appeared in the doorway, a collie by his side and a poker in his hand.

EIGHTEEN

Poppy stared at the poker. Her pulse leaped.

Is that the weapon that killed Harry?

'Who are you?' the man snarled.

'Are you Mr Jack Finnie?' she asked, trying to sound confident.

He gave a suspicious nod.

'I'm Lady Persephone Proudfoot, a house guest of Lady Balfour.' She found her voice wasn't quite steady.

'You've come from the big house? What do you want?' he growled. 'Lady Balfour kens I only take a coney every now and again. She no' minds.' The collie gave a low growl. The man put his free hand on the dog's head and she sat, silently watching Poppy.

Finnie's face was ruddy, broken veins covered his cheeks and nose, sweat glistened on his forehead.

'It's not about rabbits, Mr Finnie. I'd like to ask you a question.' Poppy was suddenly aware of how ridiculous that sounded.

'You're no' the police,' he said.

'You are quite right, I'm not. May I sit?' She glanced at the upright chair by the table.

'Get away from here,' he hissed. 'It isna safe.'

Shocked for the moment, she didn't move. He crossed to her and grabbed her wrist.

'Let me go!' She pushed him back, but he held on, his grip hard as iron.

'Get out, I tell you!' His face contorted, his breathing was ragged. 'You ken what happened to that man. Do you want to go the same way?'

Her blood chilled. Was he warning her against himself? She could smell whisky on his breath. Was he drunk, imagining things?

Still clutching the poker, he pulled her towards the door. Shaking, but determined not to show fear, she allowed herself to go with him outside the cottage and into the shelter of the trees. Then she snatched her wrist from his grasp.

'He's onto me,' he whispered urgently, darting nervous glances around them. 'For God's sake, lassie, go back to Edinburgh or wherever it is you're from.'

'Who is onto you?' Poppy's voice was a croak.

'*Wheesht!*' He was listening intently, his head a little bent.

She said steadily, 'You can find me at Balfour House. I shall stay until the murder is solved.'

He gave a low, mirthless laugh. 'You think those policemen will be able to do that? Find out who did it?'

Actually, I am intending to solve the murder by myself, she thought, fighting down hysteria.

'Listen!' he breathed in her ear.

A twig cracked, a sound that might have been a rabbit stirring in the undergrowth. He turned, his eyes searching through the trees. Quickly, he turned back and gave her a little push. 'Go!'

He moved away softly, back into the cottage, where the collie waited. The door closed.

For a moment Poppy stood there, dizzy, her legs weak. Then she took a step forward onto the path and stumbled away, her breath painful.

She was brought up short by the unmistakable snap of a twig. He had been right, there *was* someone else in the wood; someone coming in her direction. She darted for the cover of a thick clump of trees. The toe of her shoe caught in a tree root and she fell forward. Heart pounding in her chest, she scrambled to her feet and ran.

Breathless, Poppy crouched down behind a clump of blaeberry bushes. The rustling was louder now, coming closer. She was vaguely aware of a large shape but daren't raise her head to see who it was. To her horror, the tick of her wristwatch sounded loud to her ears.

The footsteps drew closer, cracking twigs as they advanced towards where she hid. Then they stopped. Whoever it was, was listening. She stayed still, waiting, terrified. A rustle on the other side of the bush almost made her scream, then she heard the person moving away. She stayed where she was, listening, praying. Silence.

Whoever it was had gone.

It was minutes before Poppy dared to move. She got to her feet and bent low, creeping on wobbly legs through the trees in the direction of the track. She stopped every few paces to look back and listen, but she could see and hear nothing.

At last she stumbled out of the woods, onto the track and broke into a run, glancing behind her too often to notice a large man step out of the undergrowth and into her path.

'*Ouff.*'

Poppy landed on her backside at the feet of Inspector MacKenzie.

'My lady! Are you all right?'

'It's you!' she gasped, and drew a long, relieved breath.

His dark brows drew together, as he offered his hand and helped her to her feet. 'You seem to be in a hurry.'

'I thought someone was following me.' Poppy brushed down the seat of her green tweed skirt, feeling rather foolish. It must have been the inspector in the woods, although she had no idea why he had been skulking about.

'You are shaken. Please, allow me to take you back to Lady Balfour's house,' Inspector MacKenzie said.

Poppy didn't move. 'What are you doing here,' she asked sharply, 'frightening poor Mr Finnie?' *And me.*

'You're getting back to your normal truculent self, I see.' MacKenzie smirked. 'What I should like to know is what are *you* doing here?'

'I shan't tell you a thing,' she said crossly. 'Not until you've answered my question first.'

He raised an eyebrow. 'Let me remind you, my lady, that I am the police officer here, which means I ask the questions.' He looked at her and gave a small sigh. 'But I suppose there is no harm in telling you that I wished to question Finnie as to his whereabouts on the night Harvey was murdered.'

'Well, I wanted to do the same thing,' Poppy admitted.

'How many times,' he began, clearly trying to maintain his patience, 'how many times do I have to ask you to leave policing to the professionals?'

Poppy didn't deem that a real question, but she answered him, nonetheless. 'I was simply trying to be of use. I would have thought you'd be pleased to have all the help you can get.'

'And you thought Finnie would confide in you, rather than in me?'

'Well, yes, as a matter of fact, I did,' she retorted. 'I went as a sort of *envoy* of Lady Balfour.' Which, in the scheme of things, was partially true.

'An envoy of Lady Balfour, is it? When I understand that

her husband sat on the Bench and had threatened Finnie with prison next time he was caught.'

'Ah, but Lady Balfour is not of the same frame of mind as her late husband. She believes that Jack Finnie takes only for his own pot.'

'And she's happy with that?' Inspector MacKenzie raised an eyebrow.

'So she says,' Poppy stated firmly. 'It helps to keep the rabbit population down and it doesn't cost her a penny.'

Inspector MacKenzie considered her for a moment. 'Come with me. I have my friend's motor car and it's parked at the village end of the track.'

She hesitated. 'Have you questioned the poacher yet? If not, you are going the wrong way, Inspector. Mr Finnie lives in the cottage behind us.'

'I ken that, my lady. I'll come back after I've escorted you to Balfour House.'

'I don't need an escort.' She was indignant. 'I came here alone, and I can return alone.'

He smiled. 'You seemed relieved enough to see me just now.'

Curse the man! That was a most unfair comment. 'That was when I thought someone was following me.' She glared at him. As he'd been the one, *he'd* been the source of her uneasiness. Poppy looked at her watch; it was getting on for half past five. They were closer to the village than to the house and it was almost time to dress for dinner. She might as well go with him in the car.

She set off in the direction he indicated. The inspector matched his normally long stride to keep pace beside her.

They walked in silence around the edge of the field. The sheep stared, chewing with their amused smiles.

'It's not that funny,' Poppy muttered.

'What isn't funny?' Inspector MacKenzie asked, surprised.

'The sheep. Cheviots always look as if they're being pleasantly entertained.'

'And why should they no' be?'

He was right. How ridiculous the pair of them must appear, striding along in silence at the edge of a field.

They approached the stile. Thank goodness her tweed skirt had a pleat at the back, she thought, readying herself to climb over. Inspector MacKenzie moved forward, put one foot on the wooden plank, stepped over and jumped down the either side.

Really! To push in front of her like that! She put out her hand towards the wooden post. Then MacKenzie reached out for her. Chastened, Poppy allowed her hand to rest in his as she steadied herself and climbed up and over the stile.

As they walked down the road to the village, towards where the Austin Seven was parked, he asked, 'Did you learn anything from Finnie?'

'Only that he's afraid and thinks whoever killed that man is going to kill him.'

'And why do you think he believes that?'

'Perhaps because he saw the person who killed Henry Harvey?' Poppy suggested.

'You are quite remarkable, my lady.' They reached the two-seater and he held open the door for her. 'I don't suppose he gave you a description and you could dash off a sketch for me?'

'And you, Inspector MacKenzie, are quite the most annoying man I have ever met!' she said as she slid into the car.

Poppy hurriedly bathed and changed into a cream dress in crêpe with a V-neck, short sleeves and a sash around the hips. She was only slightly late down to the drawing room and found that Dahlia was still to arrive.

Poppy was enjoying a cocktail before dinner with the rest of the party, when raised voices were heard in the hall. The door to the drawing room swung open and there stood Inspector MacKenzie. Ollie barked in protest.

'Not the police again!' groaned Nick, from his position by the fireplace. 'This is too much.'

'I'm sorry, your ladyship,' the butler said to Constance as he emerged from behind the inspector, 'but the policeman pushed his way in.'

'Thank you, Baird.' Constance dismissed her butler and sank onto a settee. Her little dachshund immediately jumped up onto her lap and settled himself.

'I had no time to wait and be introduced,' Inspector MacKenzie stated. 'I'd like a quiet word with yon lassie.' He nodded at Poppy.

'It's Lady Persephone, if you please,' Constance said sharply.

'Aye.'

'Martini, Inspector?' Beth asked, holding up her glass. Seeing his puzzled look, she added, 'Gin and vermouth, garnished with an olive.' She smiled, showing the neat, white teeth like a hunter to its prey.

That was an uncharitable thought, Poppy told herself, but was pleased that it *was* rather apt.

Poppy stepped forward. 'What is it you wish to see me about, Inspector?'

He fixed his eyes on her. 'It's a wee chat with you, alone, I'm after, my lady.'

'I'm sure you needn't be so anxious to keep me in the dark,' Constance said. 'Who has a better right to know what's going on? The murder took place in my grounds.'

'I am at your service, Inspector,' Poppy said, 'but I have no objection to the others hearing what you have to say.'

He inclined his head. 'As you wish. I have just been to the cottage of Jack Finnie...'

'Yes?'

'You told me you went there to ask him a question.'

She nodded. 'To ask if he'd seen or heard anything by the loch when Henry Harvey was murdered.'

Inspector MacKenzie took a deep breath before he continued. 'What did Finnie tell you?'

'He told me nothing. He was too frightened.'

'But you did go in?'

'Yes.'

'How long were you there?'

'Not long. A matter of minutes. Inspector,' Poppy asked, suddenly uneasy, 'what is this all about?'

'When I returned and went inside the cottage to question Finnie, I found him bludgeoned to death.'

The guests gasped, and Beth let out a little shriek, one hand on the long rope of pearls hanging down her chest.

'Gosh,' said Gregor from the window seat, his glass of lemonade halfway to his mouth. For once, he had little else to say.

'Doesn't that take the biscuit?' Beth said. 'That's *two* murders now inside a week.'

Constance shuddered. 'Miss Cornett, please. That makes it sound like... well, there might be more.'

'She's right, though, Lady B,' put in Eddie, rubbing his manly jaw. 'There might be more murders to come.'

'Two murders and an attempted murder,' Poppy announced, dropping into an armchair and looking round the drawing room. The faces of everyone in the room – bar that of Constance – creased with frowns.

Nick was the first to recover. 'What do you mean?' he demanded, putting down his empty cocktail glass on the mantelpiece. 'I've not heard of any attempted murder.'

'That's because it happened in Edinburgh, when I was there yesterday.'

He frowned. 'You seem to be the common factor.'

Poppy blinked. *And it seems you can be as impolite as your wife.*

'Nick, dear,' protested Constance, 'that is most unfair.'

Inspector MacKenzie interrupted the conversation. 'It appears to have been an attempt on her ladyship's life.'

Now Constance's face dropped.

Oh dear, Poppy realised she hadn't told Constance that part.

The little party broke into a babble of questions. Inspector MacKenzie held up his hand for silence. 'I can say no more at this stage.'

Poppy turned to Inspector MacKenzie. 'Thank you for taking the trouble to come and tell us about poor Mr Finnie, Inspector.'

'I'm sorry to say I've come for more than that, my lady.'

'Oh.' Poppy had a strong suspicion she knew what the inspector would say next.

'As I said, I'm here to see you specifically. First, though,' he went on, looking round the room, 'I would like to know where you all were this afternoon between four o'clock and the present time.'

'That's quite precise, Inspector,' said Constance sharply.

'The doctor has been to the cottage and seen Mr Finnie. His body is still warm, which means it is less than three hours since he was killed. It is now almost seven o'clock.'

'We were all here for tea at four,' Constance told him.

Inspector MacKenzie nodded. 'And after that?'

'I was in the library, looking for something to read,' said Morag, looking up from her knitting of some garment in lime green.

'Did you find anything interesting, Mother?' Innes asked with an amused look on his face.

'Not really.' Morag's pale eyes were without emotion.

'I do think reading is the most ghastly bore,' Rosie remarked, searching in her little beaded bag. She pulled out a cigarette case engraved with the initial R.

'Well, that's settled that topic,' Poppy murmured.

'I would like to remind you all that this is a murder investigation, not a social gathering,' Inspector MacKenzie admonished.

'I was in my room,' Constance informed him. 'As is usual after tea.'

'I think you'll find we were all in our respective rooms, as is usual at that time,' said Nick.

'Not quite.' Innes, seated on the arm of Rosie's chair, leaned forward and lit the cigarette his fiancée had placed between her lips. 'I was in Rosie's room, with Rosie.' He winked and sent her a rakish grin.

'How can...?' began Gregor with a frown.

Rosie exhaled a breath of smoke and laughed.

'Never mind,' his mother said sharply. 'There now, Inspector. The servants have from three to four o'clock to themselves, but from that time onwards they are occupied with their various tasks. Supper downstairs is at six and after that they are busy preparing our dinner. So it could not have been any of them, or any of us.'

'The inspector met me coming away from Jack Finnie's cottage around half past five,' Poppy felt obliged to point out.

Inspector MacKenzie turned to her. 'Which brings me to my second point.' Oh dear, she thought, here it comes. 'It appears that you were the last person to see Finnie alive, my lady.'

'The last but one, surely?' she said. 'Whoever killed Mr Finnie was the last.'

'That is correct.' The inspector's black eyes stayed on her face.

She fought back the temptation to laugh. Did he suspect she was the killer? It was too ridiculous! He must surely know that

Jack Finnie's murderer and that of Honest Harry must be one and the same? And that she couldn't have killed Harry because... Why could she not? Of course *she* knew she hadn't killed the bookie's runner, but Inspector MacKenzie couldn't be certain of that. The realisation hit Poppy with a shock; she was now a prime suspect.

'Is there anyone who can corroborate what took place between the two of you at Finnie's cottage?' the inspector asked.

'Only his dog,' she said, before realising how flippant that sounded.

The inspector frowned, his dark eyes boring into her. 'The evidence of a dog would not be acceptable in court, my lady.'

'In court!' Gregor exclaimed. 'Are you going to arrest Lady Poppy?'

'Of course he is not, foolish boy,' Constance scolded him affectionately.

Encouraged, Gregor went on, 'I've read lots of books where things happen just like that. Only now I come to think of it,' he added, 'it isn't ever the dame who actually did the murder. She's just the murderer's moll.'

'It's a pity for us you're not in the police force, young man,' said Inspector MacKenzie dryly.

'I ken. And when I'm old enough, I'm going to spend my time uncovering the truth and saving people. The country needs good detectives, doesn't it? I mean, you'd have to be awfa glaikit to think the killer is Lady Poppy!'

'Gregor!' Constance glared at her offspring.

He spread his arms wide as if appealing for everyone to see reason. 'It canna be, because you would have seen blood on her clothes, wouldn't you, Inspector?'

'Gregor.' Constance's voice was now deeper and contained an edge of threat.

'No, but really,' he protested, 'don't you think there is something in what I said?'

'That's enough from you!' said Nick. 'Leave this room, now!'

'I'm going to be a top-class detective one day, Uncle Nick, just you wait and see,' muttered Gregor, dragging his heels as he made his way to the door.

'Hey, kid,' Mr Emmett called to him, 'you can help me write the script for my new picture.'

Gregor turned back. 'Oh, I say, thanks!' He beamed at Mr Emmett and swaggered towards the door.

The inspector cleared his throat. 'If I can continue with my questions to her ladyship?'

'Of course, Inspector,' Poppy said.

'When you were at Finnie's cottage, did you see or hear anything unusual?'

She looked narrowly at him. 'Apart from the poor man being convinced someone was going to kill him and then you following me in the woods, you mean?'

There was a pause.

'I did not follow you in the woods,' he said.

'You did!' She glared at him. 'Creeping about among the trees and then jumping out in front of me on the path.'

Constance stared at him. 'Goodness, is that what the inspector did?' She turned to Poppy. 'Poppy, dear, you know all about the law. There must be something in Scotland against such behaviour.'

Inspector MacKenzie raised an eyebrow. 'What's all this about the law?'

'I gained a degree in law some years ago,' Poppy explained modestly.

'But you're no' a solicitor?'

She flushed. 'Well, no, but only because such a thing as a female solicitor was not permitted then.'

'Aye.' He nodded. Was that a nod in sympathy with her

plight, or in agreement with the law that had until recently forbidden female law agents?

'To get back to this evening,' the inspector went on. 'I was on my way to Finnie's cottage, when you appeared on the footpath in front of me.'

'*I* appeared on the footpath in front of *you?*' She rose and stared at him as his words sank in. 'I think, Inspector, you'll find it was the other way round. I was running along the footpath and you appeared. If it wasn't you creeping about in the woods, then who was it I'd been hiding from?'

In the shocked silence, Poppy was suddenly aware that she had been much closer to the murderer than she realised.

NINETEEN

Breaking into the silence, Mr Emmett said, 'This is going to be swell copy for my new movie. I can see it now' – he raised a hand in a sweeping gesture to indicate the imagined scene in front of him – 'there's this bird in his stately home—'

'What caused you to think there was someone in the woods?' Inspector MacKenzie asked Poppy.

'When I came out of the cottage, I heard rustling, then footsteps,' she told him. 'And I saw a figure, close to the trees.'

'A man or a woman?'

'I don't know, but after I'd run into you, I assumed it had been you. So I suppose it must have been a man.' Poppy felt shaken.

'And you say Finnie was under the impression that his life was in danger?' Inspector MacKenzie continued.

'I did tell you that at the time, Inspector,' Poppy said reproachfully.

'And now you come here, suspecting Lady Poppy of having killed Finnie?' exclaimed Constance. 'I've never heard of such a thing! Next you'll be accusing her of murdering the man by the loch.'

Inspector MacKenzie turned his dark, steady gaze on Constance. 'That's not what I was saying, your ladyship. But it's likely that whoever killed him also murdered the poacher.'

So he *had* worked that out. Poppy's face flushed. 'And you really think I am that person?'

There was a beat of silence.

'Some people think a person gets only what he or she deserves,' Morag suddenly remarked. She sat still, her knitting needles poised, her pale eyes gazing at Inspector MacKenzie.

'Not necessarily,' he said dryly.

Poppy wondered if he was replying to Morag or to her.

'Surely you can't think I'd bludgeon a man... no, *two* men... to death?' she asked, incredulous.

'Poppy, dear, no one who knows you could possibly think you'd do such a thing,' put in Constance.

'Certainly not in front of his dog,' added Inspector MacKenzie.

Poppy looked at him sharply, but let his comment pass. 'I wonder why the collie didn't bark when I entered the cottage? I suppose that means she also didn't bark when the killer came in. Although,' she went on, 'the nearest house was probably too far away to hear even if she did.'

'She's a poacher's dog, my lady – trained to remain silent,' said Inspector MacKenzie.

'Oh yes, of course.' *Dash it! I should have thought of that.*

'The method looks to be similar in both cases,' Inspector MacKenzie continued.

'Jack Finnie must have known who murdered Harry,' Poppy said. 'That would have given him a hold on the killer and therefore—'

'He had to be bumped off.' Gregor, loitering outside the open door, concluded the sentence with satisfaction.

'Why are you still here?' Nick demanded.

'You told me to *leave the room*,' he protested, 'so I've been standing in the hall.'

Poppy suppressed a smile. The boy needed taking in hand, but she had to admit there was much to commend in his reasoning. He was also, she thought, good at not being noticed.

'The boy's right about Finnie,' said Inspector MacKenzie, to Gregor's obvious delight. 'It's evident that the fellow had seen someone on the evening of the first murder, either committing the crime or in the area at the time, and perhaps he decided to do a bit of blackmailing.'

'But got more than he bargained for,' Poppy added.

'You're bound to find money in dirty notes in his cottage when you search it,' Gregor put in with confidence.

'We have already searched the premises, young man, and found no money.'

'Then you've not looked in the right place. I can give you a hand, if you like.' Gregor's eyes shone at the thought.

Inspector MacKenzie cleared his throat. 'I'll bear that in mind.'

'Perhaps Mr Finnie hadn't received his first payment yet,' Poppy said. 'He must have already told the killer what he'd seen and that he wanted money to keep quiet. Then he waited for the person to arrive with the money and instead he got me,' she went on, warming to her theme. 'He was certainly edgy when I turned up. He had a poker ready in his hand.'

'I knew it!' Gregor bounced back over the threshold in his enthusiasm.

'Well, I'm very sorry for the man,' said Constance sternly as she cast a withering glance towards her son, 'for both murdered men, of course, but if there's nothing further, Inspector, you really must excuse us now.' She lifted the little dog off her lap and got to her feet. 'It is almost time for dinner. I don't want to upset Andre by asking for the meal to be held back. French chefs can be rather temperamental, you know.'

Inspector MacKenzie, momentarily taken aback, was silent.

'Oh, Inspector MacKenzie,' Poppy said. 'Mr Finnie's dog. Is she all right?'

'Aye, my lady, have no fear. The dog is unharmed. She's at the police office and a home will be found for her.'

Poppy nodded. That, at least, was good news. But as to who had killed the two men...

Inspector MacKenzie was addressing her again. 'I must ask, my lady, that you remain here until further notice.'

'You mean I am under house arrest?'

'No, only that you don't go further than the village. Can you manage that, this time?'

'I should probably tell you that we are having a garden party on Saturday,' Nick said, 'which means that there will be a large number of people staying in the house.'

Inspector MacKenzie eyed him severely. 'You will have to cancel that, sir.'

'Sorry, old man' – Nick shook his head – 'can't be done. It's an annual event and everyone looks forward to it.'

Inspector MacKenzie sent him a dark look. 'I'm afraid I must insist.'

'Insist as much as you like, Inspector. It's impossible to cancel at such late notice. Besides, dash it all, it's going to be enormous fun.'

Before Inspector MacKenzie could speak again, Poppy said brightly, 'I'm sure you and I will have the case solved by then, Inspector.'

He raised an eyebrow. 'I don't—'

At that moment Dahlia Dalrymple marched into the drawing room, almost bumping into Gregor.

'Sorry I'm late,' she boomed. 'I dropped cigar ash on my evening dress, burned a beastly hole in it and had to change.' She indicated the dress she wore, wine-coloured with leopard-skin collar, cuffs and buttons, her ample figure all but bursting out of it.

Gazing round the room at the frozen tableau, she added, 'I say, have I missed something?'

'I'll *say!*'

'Gregor, hold your tongue!' Constance hissed.

In the ensuing distraction of Gregor supplying the details of Finnie's demise, Poppy took the inspector's arm and led him out of the drawing room, closing the door softly behind her.

She let go of his arm and turned towards him. 'Would you like me to describe the person I saw in the woods?'

'You did actually see someone?'

'I did.'

'Then go ahead, my lady.'

She glanced about them. The hall was empty and quiet, but she lowered her voice. 'As far as I could tell, he was tall and broad.'

He waited for more. When nothing further came, he raised an eyebrow. 'That's it? It's not much to go on.'

'It's more than you had before you arrived here this evening.'

Inspector MacKenzie hesitated.

There was something in the look he gave her, Poppy was sure, that suggested he was about to reveal certain information. She waited, and he came to a decision. He slid his hand into his jacket pocket and pulled out a small, cloth-bound notebook. 'Have you seen this before?'

Poppy looked at it. 'That's not a police pocketbook.'

'I ken it isn't.'

She peered closer at the slim book in MacKenzie's hand. 'It isn't a post office savings book either.'

He looked surprised. 'What makes you say that?'

Ah. The professional *police inspector doesn't know about Honest Harry paying in money at the Culross post office.*

Inspector MacKenzie was still looking at her.

She smiled. 'I will tell you what I know if you let me help you with the investigation.'

'That is not how it works, my lady,' he retorted. 'You will tell me what you know, or I will charge you with defeating the ends of justice.'

'I'm not attempting to bribe a witness, telling a lie or covering up a criminal offence,' she pointed out.

'You are trying to stop the police from doing their duty.'

The charge of defeating the ends of justice really was an annoying catch-all. She sighed. 'I just happened to visit the village post office two days ago—'

'Was that when I met you on the track?' At her nod, he continued, 'I can see I need to ask you much more often what you are up to.'

'You might learn a lot more that way,' she agreed.

He suppressed a smile. 'And what, my lady, did you learn in the post office?'

'That Honest Harry—'

'Sorry, who?'

Dear me; something else the inspector didn't know. 'Honest Harry, the name of the bookie's runner.'

'What do you mean?'

Poppy realised that not only had Inspector MacKenzie not heard of the name, he also hadn't known the man's occupation. 'I should have told you sooner, shouldn't I?'

'Indeed you should.' MacKenzie's black eyes appeared to grow even darker as he stared at her.

'Then perhaps I should tell you everything I have discovered.'

'Perhaps you should.'

'Well, Honest Harry, or rather Henry Harvey – only I didn't know his name then, of course—'

'Really? There was something you didn't ken? *Mo chreach 'sa thàinig!*'

Poppy frowned. 'What does that mean?'

'Would you like the English equivalent or the literal Gaelic translation?'

'The English equivalent, I think.'

'It's *goodness me!*'

'That's a very long *goodness me.*'

'You must know that the Gael has a poetic turn of phrase.'

She smiled. 'Then tell me the literal translation.'

He held her eye. '*My destruction has come!*'

Poppy laughed. 'Poetic indeed! I must learn some Gaelic.'

He smiled. 'I will teach you one day. But not until these murder investigations are concluded.' He became serious again.

'Absolutely, Inspector. Now where were we?'

'You were telling me about Harvey and the post office.'

She told Inspector MacKenzie of how she had seen Freddy and Harvey exchange words before going into the Red Lion Inn, of the footman's admission of having met the bookie's runner there to place his and Lord Balfour's bets, and of Harvey's decision to have no more dealings with Freddy. And of the postmistress's account of Harvey regularly coming into the post office to deposit money.

'Is there anything else you need to tell me?' he asked sternly, when Poppy had finished.

She decided against mentioning the case of the missing bracelet, as that didn't seem relevant. 'Oh no. That's absolutely everything,' she said, almost believing her words.

Seeing Poppy flush, he softened. 'And you have nothing to say on the matter of yesterday in Edinburgh, when a young lady was attacked in Princes Street Gardens, probably mistaken for you?'

Poppy's flush deepened. 'I'm sorry, but I can't discuss that with you.'

'Why not?'

'Because it's a separate investigation, one I am carrying out on behalf of Lady Balfour.'

He lifted a dark eyebrow. 'And yet you wish me to discuss the murder cases with you?'

'I think we can both agree it would be better if you did,' she said, holding his gaze. 'You'd get so much further.'

After a moment's pause, he laughed. Poppy was surprised, and rather thrilled, to see a dimple appear in his left cheek.

'Your information is verra useful,' he said. '*Tapadh leibh.* Thank you.'

She beamed. 'Apparently, Henry Harvey had been paying in a large sum of money on a regular basis, until about six months ago when the amounts became much smaller.'

'Had he now?' Inspector MacKenzie considered this. 'And what do you conclude from this discovery of yours?'

'I conclude,' Poppy began, being reminded of her legal studies and liking the sound of the expression, 'I conclude that Mr Harvey was receiving large sums from Lord Balfour to bet on horse races until his lordship's death six months ago, and that thereafter another person, one who had considerably less money, used the bookie's runner to place his own bets.'

'This other person being Freddy the footman?'

'Yes.'

'I haven't found Harvey's post office paying-in book.'

Poppy gestured to the notebook still in Inspector MacKenzie's hand. 'In reply to your earlier question, no I haven't seen that before. What is it?'

He glanced down at the object, as if surprised to find it there. 'It was found on Henry Harvey.'

'I thought there had to be a notebook! It was the presence of the pencil, you see.' She wrinkled her brow. 'But I thought there was nothing like that in his pockets. When you went through them by the loch,' she added quickly. Heaven forbid that MacKenzie should think she'd checked the dead man's pockets.

'No, it was discovered once we had him at the mortuary. The book was found in a concealed pocket in the lining of his jacket under the armpit.'

'Good Lord. He clearly didn't want it to be found. And it wasn't discovered by the murderer, assuming he was looking for it. He must have been disturbed in his search.'

'Just so.' Inspector MacKenzie indicated the book. 'It's written in some sort of code. And now you're telling me that Harvey was a bookie's runner, it makes sense. I intend to show this to the footman and interview him again.'

'May I see it?'

'I don't think I should be seen doing that, my lady,' he said softly. 'It's against the rules to share information with a civilian.'

Poppy understood. She drew herself up to her full five feet two inches. 'But you cannot prevent me going below stairs with you.'

'I cannot,' he agreed with a smile.

'Very well. Then let's go.'

He slipped the notebook back into his pocket, and with a dipped head and a wave of one hand, he gestured for her to proceed. Feeling his eyes on her, she walked ahead of him, across the tiled hall, through the green baize door and down the stone stairs to the semi-basement. She stopped before the door to the servants' hall and with an expansive gesture of her own, stood aside for him to enter first. He grinned and opened the door into the bustling kitchens.

As they entered, the servants fell silent and ceased their preparations for upstairs' dinner. Only Andre continued working, stirring something in a pan over the stove.

'*Mon Dieu!*' he muttered, 'I am making *pâte à choux* and I cannot be stopped in the middle of such a creation.'

'My lady,' the butler said, 'I trust there is no problem?'

'Not at all, Baird. It is simply that Inspector MacKenzie wishes to talk to Freddy.'

'Freddy,' said the butler in a low voice without looking round. 'Step forward.'

Looking uneasy, the footman did so.

'I need to talk to him in private,' Inspector MacKenzie told Baird.

'You can use my pantry, Inspector. Kindly follow me.' The butler led the way out of the kitchens, Inspector MacKenzie and Freddy close on his heels, with Poppy following. He took them along the flagstone corridor and ushered them into a comfortable-looking room with a large hearth, two upholstered chairs and a desk for doing the family's accounts. Cupboards for the family plate lined one wall and in another wall a door was set, which Poppy guessed led to the butler's bedroom.

'I will ensure you are not disturbed, but please be swift. He has to serve at table shortly,' said Baird as he went out, closing the door quietly behind him.

'Well, now, Freddy,' began the inspector.

'Yes, sir?' His voice was sullen.

Inspector MacKenzie took the book from his pocket. 'Do you recognise this?'

Freddy glanced at it and shook his head. 'I can't say I do.'

'Look again.' Inspector MacKenzie held it out to him.

Reluctantly, Freddy took it.

'Open it,' said the inspector, when Freddy made no move to do so.

He opened the book. 'What is it?' he asked, with an unconvincing nonchalance.

'It was found on Harvey.'

Freddy shrugged his shoulders. 'That means nothing to me.'

'Freddy,' Poppy cautioned gently, 'the inspector knows about your placing Lord Balfour's bets with Honest Harry. If the contents mean anything to you, it would be best if you said so.'

The footman's face flushed scarlet and he sent her an embarrassed look, before slowly turning the pages. Poppy moved to stand beside him. Each page consisted of a list of letters and numbers.

'His lordship did use Harry, it's true,' Freddy said, 'and when I handed over the money, he wrote in this book, but I don't know what all these are.'

'The letters must be the initials of Harry's customers and the numbers relate to money,' Poppy said, reading over Freddy's arm. 'LBB, MS, EPH, FS...'

'That last one is me,' Freddy put in. 'You can see I've only bet small amounts.'

'And won even less,' add the inspector wryly, coming to stand the other side of Freddy.

Freddy nodded miserably.

'And LBB is Lord Bruce Balfour?'

'Aye, it must be.'

'Quite a lot more lost by his lordship, it would seem. Do you recognise any of the other initials?' Inspector MacKenzie asked.

Freddy again considered the list, turning the pages. 'No, they could be anyone.'

'MS, EPH, there are quite a number of different initials,' the inspector noted.

'But the amounts are small and not frequent, so I think we can ignore them,' Poppy suggested. 'We should look for the largest sums of money, assuming that's what the figures represent.'

'I'm certain they do,' Inspector MacKenzie said.

'This one is unusual.' Poppy pointed to an entry for a large amount and against it a string of initials she hadn't noticed on any of the other pages.

She tapped on the letters. 'CCTLCB. Whoever this person

is, it was the only bet he or she made, and it was placed the day before Harry was murdered.'

Poppy smiled at Inspector MacKenzie. 'These initials could be the clue to solving the case!'

TWENTY

'CCTLCB.' Poppy repeated. 'We need to identify this person. As you see, Inspector, their bet is high. Three hundred pounds!'

'No, my lady,' Freddy said. 'It's not the bet that is high, but the payment.'

Poppy stared, first at the entry, then at Freddy and finally at Inspector MacKenzie. 'He is right, Inspector,' she said, crestfallen. 'It's in the paying-out column.'

Inspector MacKenzie quickly took the book back from Freddy. 'I'd been too busy concentrating on the various initials.'

'Can you check CCTLCB doesn't appear anywhere else in the book?' Poppy asked.

The inspector slowly turned the pages back, with Poppy and Freddy looking closely on.

'There,' she said, 'the same letters with the amount of their bet. A win of three hundred pounds for a three-pound bet.' That was a lucky win for a first-time punter.

'See here, the date for the bet itself is the same as for a separate entry for the footman,' said Inspector MacKenzie.

'So it is, sir,' Freddy said, surprised.

Poppy glanced at the date. 'The two bets were placed last Friday. When were the races, Freddy?'

'On Saturday, my lady.'

'So Harry came here on Sunday to pay out the winnings, and the following day he was murdered,' Poppy concluded. 'But that doesn't make sense. Why would the recipient of the money then kill him?'

'Nonetheless,' said Inspector MacKenzie, 'we might be onto something here.'

We! What a joyous word to Poppy's ear. And hopefully that meant she was off the inspector's suspect list.

'CCTLCB must reside somewhere in this area,' she went on eagerly.

'If LBB is Lord Bruce Balfour, then five letters must be someone with a long title.'

'Not necessarily.' Poppy frowned. 'There is something familiar about the arrangement, but as to what it is...'

The two men waited, looking at her.

'Oh, who is this CCTLCB?' Poppy said impatiently. 'I feel I should know it.'

'Countess somebody?' suggested Inspector MacKenzie.

Poppy shook her head.

'Commander...?'

'*Shh!* I am almost there...' She sighed. 'No, it's not coming at present.'

'I'm no' convinced it is our killer, my lady, now I come to think on it. It makes no sense for a man to kill the person who the day before gave him a considerable sum of money.'

Poppy had no answer.

Inspector MacKenzie turned to Freddy. 'That's all for now. You can return to your duties.'

'Yes, sir.' The footman looked relieved and hastened away.

'You know, I do think we could profitably work together, Inspector,' Poppy said.

'Perhaps one day, when female detectives are employed.'

She eyed him coolly. 'They already are, as I'm sure you very well know.'

'If you're referring to the M. McIntyre Agency, then yes, I am aware of those ladies. But they are employed in a private capacity. I meant when females are employed by the police detective service.'

Poppy glared at him. When would women be taken seriously? Since the Sex Disqualification (Removal) Act in 1919, there were now women working in medicine, engineering and the law, and the first policewomen, although without the same powers as policemen, had been appointed. But still by far the largest employer of women was as domestic servants.

'I will continue to investigate,' she said firmly.

Inspector MacKenzie spoke in a warning voice. 'My lady—'

'It's on my family crest, you know. *Leave no detective to struggle on his own.*'

'*Mo chreach 'sa thàinig!*' He gave a slow smile.

There was that delightful dimple again. 'Be warned,' she said, 'at a word from me, my feudal subjects will come out against you by divine right of my ladyshipness.'

He laughed.

Carpe diem. Seize the day. Poppy smiled. 'A truce?'

'Aye.' He nodded. 'I am thinking that we got off on the wrong foot. I'd like to start again.' He held out his hand. 'James MacKenzie, Inspector with the Edinburgh Detective Branch. How do you do.'

She took his large, cool hand and felt how comfortably her own small hand fitted into it. 'Persephone Proudfoot, daughter of the Earl of Crieff. How do you do.'

'Persephone, goddess of the earth and the harvest,' he said. 'One day she was out picking flowers when Hades, god of the underworld, on one of his rare trips to the upper world, saw her.

He was so entranced by Persephone that he took her down to his underground kingdom to become his bride.'

Poppy gazed at him, impressed. 'You know your Greek mythology, Inspector.'

'I studied various belief systems when I read theology.'

'You have a degree in theology?'

He nodded. 'I had thought of following my father and serving the community in a church in the Western Isles, but... well, as a young man I had no idea of city life. I thought the whole world was full of God-fearing folk. Then, when studying at Glasgow, I witnessed a serious crime and realised I'd had a sheltered upbringing. I decided I could do more good in the police than in the kirk.'

'Commendable, Inspector. That is why I studied the law – to be of help to others.'

'Also commendable, my lady.'

'And you attended the University of Glasgow, my own alma mater.'

They smiled at one another, realised their hands were still clasped and released them.

'I must go now,' she told him, 'but I'll let you know when I discover anything else of interest.'

'Take care not to be carried off by Hades.'

'I will.'

Poppy left the room and walked back up the stairs, a smile on her face.

She reached the drawing room just as the butler announced dinner.

'Where did you disappear to just now, Poppy, dear?' murmured Constance, rising to organise the procession into the dining room.

'I will tell you later,' she replied in a low voice.

'This evening we have an uneven number,' Constance said,

addressing everyone in the room. 'Gregor, you must eat in the school room—'

His face fell.

'Dash it all,' cried Dahlia, 'don't disappoint the little chap. Let him eat with us at table. Never mind about me. I'm not in the least bothered about the usual boy–girl arrangement.'

Gregor sent her a grateful look, while Mr Emmett stared at her, wide-eyed. 'Say, Mrs Dalrymple, I hope you will do me the honour of sitting next to me.'

She turned to gaze at him, equally fascinated. 'Wherever did you come from?'

'California – in the United States,' he clarified.

'I meant, where did Connie find you? No matter, I agree with your suggestion. Connie, old thing, put this gentleman—'

'J. Franklyn Emmett,' he volunteered.

She smiled. 'Put J. Franklyn Emmett next to me.'

'Certainly,' Constance said a little faintly. 'Innes, would you take me in this evening?'

Innes, looking amused at the proceedings, stepped forward. 'I'd be delighted to, Aunt.'

'Jolly good. That's that settled, then.' Dahlia took hold of Mr Emmett's arm. He started, recovered and was clearly set on enjoying himself.

Poppy suppressed a smile. Dahlia Dalrymple would no doubt be immortalised in one of the director's moving films.

They all made their way into the dining room and Gregor held out Poppy's seat for her. As she thanked him and sat down, he'd clearly had the same thought, for he leaned forward and whispered, 'I reckon a character like Mrs Dalrymple will appear in Mr Emmett's next picture, don't you?'

'I sure do,' she agreed with a smile.

Gregor, taking his seat between her and Beth, shot her a delighted grin.

Now that they were all seated, Poppy took note of everyone at the table. Mr Emmett and Dahlia Dalrymple were to the right of Constance seated at the head of the table, and engaged in intense conversation. Nick, in contrast, was almost as quiet as his wife this evening. To the side of Morag was an equally silent Eddie, his gaze focused across the table at Beth. Poor thing, Poppy thought, to be that smitten with someone and to have those feelings not returned.

As Baird and Freddy served the soup, Poppy noticed that Beth, sporting her new rope of pearls, kept her attention devotedly on Innes. Before long, at Dahlia's and Gregor's insistence, Mr Emmett was regaling the table with stories of Hollywood.

'What about Fatty Arbuckle, Mr Emmett? Did he really kill that actress?' asked Gregor, wide-eyed.

'Well, my boy, he *was* acquitted—'

'At the third trial,' snorted Dahlia. 'The first two trials resulted in hung juries.'

'Which couldn't happen in Scotland,' Poppy pointed out. 'A simple majority is required for a verdict, which means eight out of the fifteen jurors.'

'Is that so?' Mr Emmett raised his eyebrows. 'That sure makes the criminal justice system easier.'

'But not necessarily better,' Constance murmured, raising a spoonful of her mushroom soup to her mouth.

Poppy glanced around the table. She seemed to be the only one who'd heard the bitter edge to Constance's comment. Was she thinking about the law relating to infanticide? Poppy didn't want to believe so, but still... A mother could plead not guilty to the charge of murder on the ground of temporary insanity. The law changed three years ago to allow women, provided they met an age and property qualification, to be jury members. Were women more likely than men to acquit in a case where a mother killed her child? Poppy thought it possible – but even if the woman was found not guilty, she could immediately be detained in Perth Criminal Lunatic Department.

'About a year before Arbuckle was charged with the manslaughter of Virginia Rappe,' Mr Emmett was saying, 'he signed a contract with Paramount Pictures for one million dollars a year.'

'One million dollars,' Gregor breathed.

'But get this, after the trials his films were banned. Okay, that's been lifted now, but he's had no luck finding work these days.'

'Sheesh! I should think not. The big goon.' Beth knocked back her glass of wine.

They had reached the fish course, when Ollie, sitting under the table by Gregor's chair, started to cough.

'Gregor!' His mother dropped her fork. 'Are you feeding Ollie with fish?'

'Only a wee bit,' he admitted, looking anxious.

She got quickly to her feet. 'There must be a bone in it!'

'I'm sorry, Mother. I'll see if he's all right.' Gregor jumped up from his seat. 'Excuse me, everyone,' he said, disappearing under the table and emerging clutching the dachshund. 'He's fine, Mother, look.' He held Ollie out towards Constance.

'Not over the table, Gregor,' she admonished. 'Bring him round here.'

Gregor carried the little dog to Constance. 'Ollie, my sweet, what was my naughty son doing to you?' She kissed the top of Ollie's head and he gave a small bark of happiness. 'Take him up to my room, Gregor. My maid will look after him.'

'Yes, Mother,' he said, tucking Ollie under his arm and stroking the little dog's ears as he left.

Conversation resumed around the table. With Gregor's temporary absence, Poppy could now talk across the empty seat to Beth.

'I've been admiring your pearls, Miss Cornett. They really are beautiful.'

'Gee, thanks.' Beth fingered them. 'They are something, aren't they?'

'Did you have to visit many jewellers to find them?'

'No, they were in the first store I went in.'

'You were fortunate.'

'But it wasn't good luck, you know,' Beth said. 'Charlie, Connie's chauffeur, recommended the place.'

'Her chauffeur?' Poppy managed to hide her astonishment.

'That's the feller. He told me Lord Balfour used them, and I figured what was good enough for Bruce was good enough for me.' Beth beamed. 'Charlie said Bruce used to chat about this and that when he drove his lordship about.'

Before Poppy could ask more about the conversation, Beth added, 'First I had to dispose of some ice—'

'Ice?'

'Sell a diamond and emerald bracelet given to me by Buster.'

Buster? Was she actually referring to Buster Keaton, the star of *Sherlock Jr.*? *Mo chreach 'sa thàinig!* as the inspector would say. More importantly, assuming Beth was telling the truth about the actor, it cleared her of being involved in the case of the missing Balfour bracelet.

'But I think it was worth it to buy the pearls.' Beth turned to reply to a question from Innes, and Dahlia dropped heavily into the empty chair by Poppy's side.

'Just until the boy comes back,' she said, pausing to take a gulp from the wine glass she'd moved with her. 'What a to-do about these beastly murders, eh? Do the police have any idea who did them? You seem to be getting along well with that inspector fellow, so I thought I'd ask.'

Poppy bristled. 'I don't know about getting on with him. I'm asking him questions—'

Dahlia patted Poppy's hand. 'I was just teasing, my dear.

I've taken perhaps a little too much wine this evening.' She smiled.

Poppy returned the smile. 'In answer to your question, the police have no idea.' That wasn't strictly true, as she was sure the inspector had his eye on Freddy, but she had no wish to sully the footman's name. 'Everyone in this room is on the suspect list, with the exception of Innes, Rosie and yourself as none of you were here at the time of the first murder. The inspector is certain both were carried out by the same person.'

'I should jolly well hope I'm not a suspect.' Dahlia lowered her voice and studied Poppy. 'But tell me, how do you think poor Connie is taking it all?'

'As well as can be expected,' Poppy murmured.

'Not that long after old Bruce's death too.' Dahlia shook her head. 'It's ghastly enough, dealing with a husband's demise, without a couple of murders thrown in. When my hubby met his maker, I came across all sorts of paperwork: tailor's account, hat maker's, one for whisky, and a bill for a pair of gold and blue sapphire cufflinks which I can't even remember seeing him wear.'

Poppy pulse jumped. 'You received an unexpected jeweller's bill?'

'The cufflinks were probably a present for one of his many relatives.' Dahlia gave a fond sigh.

'I suppose,' Poppy said tentatively, 'you paid the jeweller's bill?'

'My dear girl, of course I did! One must honour one's accounts, you know.' Dahlia drank the last of her wine and signalled to the butler standing in attendance by the sideboard to refill her glass.

Gregor could return at any moment; Poppy had to speak without delay. 'Miss Cornett was in Edinburgh recently,' she said. 'She tells me she bought her exquisite pearls in Campbell's on George Street.'

'That's the very shop; what a coincidence,' Dahlia exclaimed. 'Some awfully nice stuff in there. Frightfully expensive, mind, but you get what you pay for.'

Oh, but do you? It looked very much as if Campbell's were sending out invoices to the widows of former customers for items of jewellery that didn't exist. How very clever of them. How very dishonest...

The dining room door opened and Gregor bounced back in.

'That's my cue,' Dahlia said, holding her refilled wine glass carefully aloft. 'We can have another chat later.' She moved back to her own seat.

Gregor sent a reassuring smile in his mother's direction and took his chair again. 'I say, I didn't mean to spoil your conversation with Mrs Dalrymple.'

'I think we had almost finished,' Poppy told him.

And it was about time the jeweller's fraudulent game was also brought to an end, she thought. All she had to do now was to gather some evidence, if she was to have a hope of convincing Inspector MacKenzie to arrest the jeweller and his assistant.

As Poppy lifted her glass to her mouth and sipped the excellent Soave, a thought came into her head.

Was there a connection between the jeweller, the runner and the strange attack on Isla?

TWENTY-ONE

A light tap on the bedroom door woke Poppy the following morning. And a piece of the puzzle that had been on her mind as she'd drifted off to sleep the previous night fell into place.

'*The bicycle!*' she exclaimed, sitting bolt upright in bed as her maid entered with the morning tea.

'Bicycle, my lady?' Elspeth enquired. 'Would you like me to ascertain if there is one you can use?' She placed the tray on the nightstand and drew back the chintz curtains. 'It looks like a pleasant day for a cycle ride.' Through the open window came the sound of birdsong.

'No, that wasn't what I meant at all, Elspeth.' Poppy jumped out of bed and hastened into the bathroom adjoining her room.

'Shall I draw a bath for you, my lady?' Elspeth asked through the closed door.

'No time today. I'm in a hurry.' She ran hot water into the basin. 'I'll wear the pale green cotton blouse, pleated skirt and tennis shoes,' she called.

Poppy couldn't quite hear her maid's sniff of disapproval,

but was sure it was there. 'I thought the cream dress with the Alençon lace hem for today, your ladyship.'

'Then think again, Elspeth,' she retorted. 'The green cotton is more practical.'

'*Practical*? Why does your ladyship want *practical*?'

'One never knows what opportunities the day will present,' Poppy replied cheerfully, quickly washing. 'Tennis, or... who knows?' Much as she enjoyed a game of tennis, it wasn't on her agenda for today. First, she would telephone the inspector at the Red Lion Inn and ask him to call at Balfour House. Then she would tell him how she had concluded her very first case – that of the missing bracelet – thanks to the bicycle!

She heard the wardrobe door opening and then drawers in the dresser, all with some force, as she dried herself. It was clear that Elspeth wasn't happy with her answer.

'And my straw hat,' Poppy added, coming out of the bathroom.

Slightly mollified, Elspeth removed the wide-brimmed straw hat from the top shelf of the wardrobe. 'At least your ladyship can't get up to too much trouble wearing a straw hat,' she muttered.

Poppy smiled, made no comment and dressed hurriedly.

Elspeth frowned at the silk stockings and suspender garment she had set out on the bed and which still lay there on the bedcover. 'You have forgotten part of your undergarments, my lady.'

'I've not forgotten them. It's simply too hot to wear stockings. And such a bother to be forever checking that the seams at the back are straight.'

'When I was personal maid to Lady MacCorkindale...'

'She never went without stockings,' Poppy finished the rest of her maid's sentence.

'Are you...' said Elspeth, 'are you intending to do investigative work?'

'If I possibly can.' Standing by the bed, Poppy drank the fast-cooling cup of tea.

Elspeth drew in a sharp breath through her nose. 'Very well, my lady.'

Poppy sat at the dressing table and suffered Elspeth to brush her hair, which she did with more force than was necessary. Finally, Poppy clipped on small jade earrings, applied a coat of coral lipstick and made her way downstairs.

The telephone was situated in an alcove in the hall of Balfour House, giving if not complete privacy, then at least an element of it. Poppy wound the handle, asked the operator to connect her to the Red Lion and waited for Inspector MacKenzie to answer.

A male voice came onto the line, his deep tones rather thrilling. 'My lady?'

'Inspector MacKenzie,' Poppy said briskly. 'I wonder if you could come up to the house as soon as you are able?'

'Has something happened?' His tone was urgent. 'Are you safe? No' another murder?'

'No, nothing like that, Inspector. It's just that I have a theory I'd like to discuss with you.'

'You'll have solved the killings, then?' Now he sounded amused.

Gregor was making his way through the hall from the dining room. 'Is that the inspector on the telephone?' he asked eagerly.

'Yes,' she replied to the boy.

'You have?' replied the inspector on the other end of the telephone line. The amusement in his voice had gone.

'Is he coming back?' went on Gregor.

'I think so,' she told him.

'Gosh!' He went off with a grin.

There was a pause on the other end of the line. 'Was that young Gregor I could hear in the background?'

'Yes, it was.'

'And we were having a three-way conversation?'

'Well, yes,' Poppy admitted. 'But I do have something I want to discuss with you.'

'You are not an easy lady to say no to, are you?'

She smiled. 'I do hope not.'

'I'll be finishing my breakfast and will be with you in half an hour.'

'Thank you, Inspector.' Poppy put down the telephone. She had time for a very quick cup of tea and a slice of toast and honey, before starting to make a list of suspects, their possible motivations and anything else that occurred to her.

She entered the dining room and bid everyone a good morning.

Only Constance looked up. 'Good morning, my dear.' She returned to the letter she was reading.

Nick continued to read his newspaper. There was no sign of Morag or the three Americans. Innes and Rosie sat stifling yawns and picking without enthusiasm at scrambled eggs and kidneys.

Poppy walked over to the sideboard where the breakfast dishes were set out. She helped herself to a piece of toast from the rack and took an empty seat at the table.

'If you were thinking of a game of tennis this morning,' Constance said to Poppy, looking up again having noticed her clothes, 'I'm afraid that Mr Emmett and his friends have already eaten and gone into Culross. They're hoping to visit the palace, if the caretaker will agree to show them round. It's owned by the Earl of Dundonald, but he doesn't stay there. Gregor is about somewhere and he might be persuaded to play,' she went on doubtfully, 'and there's Nick, Innes and Rosie.' They appeared not to hear. 'Goodness knows where Dahlia has gone. And I have to visit a friend this morning. Oh dear, I'm a poor hostess today, aren't I?'

'Not at all, Constance.' Poppy was delighted; she could use her notebook without feeling obliged to account to anyone for her time. She spread her toast with honey. 'I intend to have a lazy morning reading in the garden, if that is all right with you.' She nodded her thanks to Freddy, who set down a cup of tea.

'Of course,' Constance replied. 'You'll find the hammock already up on the lawn and I'll make sure one of the footmen sets out lemonade on the terrace.'

Poppy thanked her, and Constance returned once more to her letter. Nick turned a page in the newspaper. Innes and Rosie continued to push the food around on their plates and sip coffee. As Poppy ate, her brain buzzed – with answers in the case of the Balfour bracelet, and with questions relating to the killing of the runner and the poacher.

But chief among her thoughts, although she desperately didn't want it to be, was that her hostess, seated so calmly at the breakfast table, might be a murderer.

Balfour House dozed in the morning heat.

Constance had gone out in the landaulette to visit her friend, and the other adults were nowhere in sight. Gregor seemed to have disappeared too, which was a relief, Poppy thought, as the boy had a knack of intruding in such an earnest way that she felt guilty when she tried to turn his attention elsewhere.

The hammock had been slung in the shade of two great elms on the lawn. She sat on the canvas, swung her legs round and into it. The finest place to be was the Scottish countryside on a summer's day, she thought, and gave a soft sigh.

Comfortably propped up, she took hold of her pencil and opened her notebook at the first page. Her sketch of Isla's attacker stared back at her. The inspector was right: it lacked any defining features to be of use. How could she have thought otherwise? But it didn't matter now, for she had solved the case. She turned the page.

At the top of the fresh sheet, she wrote: *The Missing Bracelet.*

As she'd drifted off to sleep last night, a series of images had played in her head. The shop assistant in Edinburgh telling her of Lord Balfour's telephone call; his secretary informing Poppy that his lordship was profoundly deaf. The shop assistant's look of fear when Poppy told her she was close to solving the mystery; the attack on Isla in the gardens. And, finally, Dahlia telling her over dinner last night of the unexpected bill for an expensive pair of cufflinks.

There was no Balfour bracelet, she was sure of that now. Or Dalrymple cufflinks. Or any other pieces of jewellery that had no doubt been stated on other bills sent out to the wealthy bereaved.

It was a clever – and *cruel* – hoax, perpetrated by the jeweller, or his shop assistant, or both. Poppy favoured the shop assistant as the guilty party; the young woman would have been able to conceal her deception given that the jeweller himself was often absent.

No doubt too, Miss Strachan's unwillingness to sell the bracelet to Poppy had been an attempt to divert her from any further investigation of the crime. Well, that hadn't worked!

She moved on to consider the attack in Princes Street Gardens. The drawing she'd made using the young man's direction showed a face that could have been male or female. Mr Fraser, Isla's rescuer, had said the assailant was clean-shaven, but it could have been someone who didn't need to shave at all. A female.

Perhaps it was the savagery of the attack that had made everyone assume a male was the perpetrator. Poppy had got no further last night with her thoughts on the matter. How was she to satisfy herself, not to mention the inspector, that Miss Strachan had been the person wielding the knife?

And then the explanation of the bicycle came to her when she woke this morning. Delighted with her deductions, Poppy scribbled a series of cryptic notes.

> *Invoice received by Constance + no sign of bracelet + jeweller's shop assistant says Lord B telephoned his order +Lord B's secretary says impossible as he was deaf + Dalrymple cufflinks = assistant committing fraud. Assistant fears exposure + follows Isla*

Of course, she realised, the shop assistant hadn't needed to visit the library to consult *Who's Who*, because Poppy herself had given the young woman her card when she visited the shop. How could she have forgotten that? She scribbled on.

> *+ dons cloak carried in a parcel + attacks + escapes on bike*

The attacker's clumsy attempt to mount the stolen bicycle had been because she was a *woman* unused to the central bar of a *man's* cycle!

Poppy smiled as she concluded her notes.

> *+ female = assistant the attacker.*

Satisfied, she moved on to the more mystifying case of the two murders. Turning to a new page, she prepared to write in more detail. Later she could add the sheet of paper with timings which lay in the drawer in her room.

> *The Murder of Honest Harry. Committed on Monday between 5.30 p.m. and 7.30 p.m.*

And under it, a sub-heading: *Suspects*.

From across the lawn, she heard the distant sound of a table being set up on the terrace by two footmen. She frowned and returned her attention to her new heading. Who to start with?

Poppy gave a soft sigh. She didn't believe he was the killer, but there was no doubt he was the obvious person to place at the top of the list.

1. Freddy.

Next, she should add the reason why he was a suspect.

Found the body.

The ladies at the M. McIntyre Agency had noted that the person first on the scene could well be the murderer, but that this wasn't necessarily true.

Motive: Had dealings with the bookie's runner, who was threatening to end the arrangement against Freddy's wishes.

Would that be enough for the footman to commit murder? It didn't seem very likely, but it was not impossible. *Owed the runner something in the region of £100.* That might tip the balance.

Opportunity: Seen by the chauffeur returning from the loch around 6 p.m. Honest Harry's watch had stopped at 6 p.m. On the other hand, only the chauffeur's word he saw Freddy and he admits to disliking the footman. Freddy had Ollie with him and unlikely a murderer would take a dog with him.

At least, Poppy liked to think so. *On the third hand, Freddy was reluctant to admit he'd used the shortcut from the village and the timings fit.*

Poppy paused, suddenly remembering she'd told Inspector MacKenzie that it was a tall, broad man who'd followed her in the woods by the cottage. If Honest Harry and Jack Finnie were murdered by the same person, it followed that Harry's killer was of the same build. Freddy was tall, but his leanness could have been disguised by a coat with broad shoulders.

Poppy hesitated before she added the next suspect. Then she wrote:

2. *Constance.*

After all, she'd been wrong about the sex of Isla's attacker, so she could also have been mistaken here. Constance was tall for a woman and of a stately, Edwardian build.

All she had on her new friend was an anonymous letter with an allegation that was surely nothing more than gossip. But if she was going to be a detective, she had to be impartial.

May have killed before, she wrote. A reply was needed to her letter to Mrs Abbott.

> *Motive: Fiercely anti-gambling. May have learned that her husband had been secretly betting and he had lost a considerable sum on the horses. Was Harry for some reason threatening to reveal this? Could blackmail be a good enough reason to kill?*

Maybe!

> *Opportunity: Says she was dressing for dinner at the relevant time.*

The person who could confirm this would be Constance's personal maid. Assuming Poppy could persuade her, this was a job for Elspeth. *On the other hand, Constance was a respectable woman of middle age and most unlikely to slip down to the loch and batter someone to death.* Could she seriously enter that as evidence? *Of previous good character, My Lord,* she thought, as if addressing a judge in the High Court of Justiciary. But that would only be true if the claim in the anonymous letter was a lie.

3. Gregor.

Poppy tapped her pencil against her teeth. He seemed such a likeable boy, but who could be sure?

Capable of sudden bouts of animosity and has the build of a sturdy young man.

Gregor couldn't be considered tall – but she *had* been crouching behind a bush at the time, which could have made her stalker appear taller than he actually was.

Motive: Had he found out about his father's gambling and wanted to protect his mother from a threat of disclosure by Harry? (See above).

Opportunity: Admits to hanging about the loch about four o'clock some afternoons, in the hope of seeing Beth Cornett. Says he was dressing for dinner at the relevant time. On the other hand, how long does it take a fourteen-year-old boy to wash and dress for dinner, for goodness' sake? And he would have no alibi in this respect.

Poppy considered adding Beth Cornett's name to the list of suspects, but four o'clock was outside the doctor's estimated time of death. Admittedly, it was an *estimated* time, but the time the watch had broken must be important.

What about Nick Balfour? Poppy quickly decided he wasn't a suspect. The only thing against the man was the possibly suspicious behaviour she'd noted when the inspector first came to the house. It had very likely been due to the shock of having a murdered man in the grounds.

A thought came into Poppy's head: could Mr Emmett have killed Harry as *local colour* for his moving picture? She hadn't considered this before. He'd told them it featured a murder. Poppy shook her head. No, the idea was preposterous. Besides, Mr Emmett was short and thin, completely the wrong build to be the fellow in the woods; and wouldn't there have been a glint from his spectacles?

She pulled her thoughts together and ploughed on, with the feeling that the names on the list and their possible motives were growing increasingly tenuous.

4. *Charlie.*

She paused. The chauffeur was heavily built, but was he tall enough? And why would he be considered a suspect? *He and Freddy dislike each other.* Was dislike a strong enough word or would *loathe* be better?

Motive: He implicates Freddy in the murder. Is this to cause trouble for Freddy who could take his job, or to distract attention from himself as the killer?

Although that begged the question as to what motive Charlie might have for disposing of Harry.

Opportunity: Outside the house washing Constance's car around 6 p.m.

But there was nothing to suggest he'd been down to the loch.

5. *Jack Finnie.*

That the poacher was involved in some way was clear. *Did he murder Harry, or had he witnessed the murder and in turn been killed to keep him quiet?* The latter seemed more likely.

Motive:

Poppy could think of nothing to write here. A poacher's work was of necessity carried out alone and he might well have been working in the area at the time. But as to a conceivable motive to dispose of Harry? She crossed out his name.

Was there anyone else who should be on the list? Morag Balfour and Eddie Peavey had been at the house at the relevant time, but should she add them? For that matter, should she include all the servants at the house? No, she had to keep the list of suspects to those who it seemed might have committed the murder. If these came to nothing, then she would need to widen the net further.

She felt a little thrill at the phrase *widen the net*. It sounded like the sort of expression a detective would use.

The murder of Harry could have been committed by any of the four above. They all had a motive, or possible motive, and a degree of opportunity.

Poppy glanced at her watch. Inspector MacKenzie should be here shortly, and she wanted to get as much down on paper as possible before he arrived. Next, she would start a new list for the killing of the poacher.

She turned to a fresh page and at the top wrote:

The Murder of Jack Finnie. Committed on Thursday between 4 p.m. and 7 p.m.

Suspects followed underneath.

She had put Freddy at number one for the murder of Harry because he had found the body. If she followed the same pattern, then there could be no doubt whose name should be at the top of this list.

1. Inspector MacKenzie.

Found the body.

Poppy smiled. She didn't really believe the inspector had killed Jack, but for some reason it amused her to write his name there.

Motive. As far as she was aware, the inspector had no reason to kill Jack.

Less amusing was the name she had in all fairness to put at number two.

2. Poppy.

Last person to see Jack alive.

NO.

Someone else had visited Jack during the short period of time between her leaving his cottage and Inspector MacKenzie's finding of the body, but who? Once again everyone said they were in their rooms dressing for dinner, but, as with Harry's murder, it wouldn't be difficult for one of them to nip out and do the deed. Although, now she thought about it, nipping down to the loch would be easier than hiking to the poacher's cottage. But what might be an arduous trek for Constance would present no difficulty for Gregor.

Motive:

She most certainly did not have a motive to murder Jack Finnie.

Poppy moved on. 3.

Nick Balfour didn't like Finnie's poaching, but that seemed a flimsy motive. She could think of no other names. It seemed certain that both murders were committed by the same person. What about the three new arrivals at Balfour House: Innes, Rosie and Dahlia? None of the three had been at the house for the first murder, but did that mean they should be discounted regarding the second murder? Was this a leap of sharp detection on her part or a desperate attempt to solve the case before MacKenzie did?

Innes, Rosie and Dahlia? she wondered...

Willow warblers sang lazily, bees droned and the sun beat down.

Innes, Rosie, Dahlia...

The repetition of the names and the relative peace of the morning began to have a soporific effect on Poppy. Despite her best intentions, her eyes kept closing. She removed her straw hat and slid down in the hammock, rearranging her pleated skirt to cover her knees. Thank goodness for the invention of the soft girdle, she thought drowsily, her head resting on the sun-warmed canvas. How hot and uncomfortable those poor Edwardian ladies must have been in their corsets...

She tucked her pencil into the notebook, the notebook into her hat and lay it on her stomach. Putting her hands behind her head, she closed her eyes. Just for a few moments.

Poppy woke with a start when a shadow crossed her eyelids.

TWENTY-TWO

Poppy's senses came flooding back. She tried to sit up, her arms flailing to grasp the sides of the hammock.

A tall, broad figure stood there, outlined in the rays of the sun. Her heart lurched with fear, she struggled with the canvas and the hammock began to sway dangerously. Her hat with its contents slipped to the grass.

A large hand shot out and held the canvas fabric steady. 'Take your time, your ladyship,' said Inspector MacKenzie, a trace of amusement in his voice.

She had been caught napping – literally! – by the policeman. How very annoying.

'What do you mean by sneaking up on me like this?' she said, unnecessarily sharp.

'I did not sneak up on you, my lady.' He sounded offended. 'I addressed you twice, from a wee distance, but you were no' hearing me.'

With Inspector MacKenzie holding the hammock, Poppy managed to extricate herself from its folds and slip out of it to stand on the lawn. That was better; now she could see something of his face, still a little in shadow under his fedora.

He bent down and picked up her straw hat. The notebook had tumbled out, falling open at the page marked by the pencil.

'Ah, the famous notebook.'

Before she could stop him, he stooped to gather up the book and pencil, and his glance lit on what she had written. '*The Murder of Jack Finnie. Suspects... Inspector MacKenzie,*' he murmured, raising a sardonic eyebrow, before handing the items to her.

She felt some explanation was needed. 'I asked you to call, Inspector, to discuss the case. I've been making a list of suspects, as you see.'

'I do see. And I'm the main suspect for the murder of Jack Finnie?'

'Well, not really, of course. I was merely being fair. If you'd turned to the earlier page, you would have seen I have Freddy as the number one suspect for the murder of Henry Harvey. Because he found the body, as did you with Jack Finnie.'

He gave a nod. 'I can't deny that is a professional approach.'

'It's gratifying to hear you say that.' Poppy sent him an impish grin.

He gave a rueful smile. 'I walked into that, didn't I?'

'It's too hot to stand here, Inspector. There's lemonade on the terrace. Come with me.' Clutching the notebook and pencil, she replaced the straw hat on her head.

He followed her across the grass, up the stone steps and onto the terrace. It was very quiet, with just the sound of pigeons cooing on the roof. Under a parasol, a table had been laid with a white cloth and set with a jug of fresh lemonade and a bucket of ice cubes which were fast melting.

She poured them a glass each, and they settled themselves on two deckchairs set nearby.

'A pleasant view,' he observed, removing his hat and placing it on his knees.

She took a sip of lemonade. 'Yes,' she agreed.

'With a grand view of the loch,' he went on.

'Yes, but too far away to have a clear picture of any person who might be there.'

Still gazing at the sparkling blue water, he took a long draught of the lemonade. 'Most refreshing.'

'Can we talk about the case now?' she asked a little impatiently.

'You will no' make a good detective if you cannot be patient.'

Stifling a sigh, Poppy opened her notebook. 'I've made observations on the two murders, but there is another matter I really need to speak to you about first.'

He raised an eyebrow. 'Aye?'

'The matter of a missing bracelet.' She beamed. 'I believe I have solved my first case, and I can't help but wonder if it is in some way connected to the murders.'

'I'm all ears,' he told her, taking his pipe from his pocket. 'Do you mind if I smoke?'

'Go ahead.'

He began to fill it.

'Now, where to begin...'

'At the beginning is generally best.' He smiled.

Poppy took another sip of lemonade as she marshalled her thoughts, then began. 'Lady Balfour told me that after her husband's death she received a bill for a diamond and emerald bracelet bought a month before he passed away. She was surprised, having not seen the bracelet, and when her investigations failed to find it, she asked me to look into the matter.' Seeing the inspector about to comment, Poppy went on, 'I confess I also thought at first that Lord Balfour had purchased it for a lady friend. But I am now certain I know the answer.'

She looked at Inspector MacKenzie. He struck a match and lit his pipe, and inclined his head for her to continue. There was something about a man with a pipe, she thought. Her husband,

Stuart, had smoked cigarettes and... What was she thinking? This wasn't relevant.

'The answer is: there was no bracelet!' she said, triumphant.

'I need a little more than that, my lady.' Inspector MacKenzie deposited the spent match in an ashtray on the table.

'Yes, of course.' He was so maddeningly calm! 'When I visited Edinburgh two days ago...'

He frowned and cleared his throat.

'I went to the jeweller's shop that had issued the invoice,' she hurried on, 'and the assistant informed me that his lordship had telephoned her with his choice of bracelet. At Lord Balfour's office, I learned from his secretary that he was profoundly deaf and could not have made that phone call.'

Inspector MacKenzie puffed on his pipe as he watched Poppy carefully.

'Since then, I have discovered that another wealthy widow, Mrs Dalrymple, also at present staying at Balfour House, received an invoice from the same Edinburgh jeweller's in the days after her husband's passing. Despite not having seen the gold and sapphire cufflinks the invoice referred to, in all the upheaval of her husband's death, she paid the substantial bill without question.'

He removed his pipe. 'That's verra interesting, my lady. If you're right, that would be quite a lucrative system this jeweller has. I will get an officer to look into it at once.'

'I've not actually seen the jeweller,' Poppy added hastily, 'only the assistant, and I think it's more likely to be her scheme, rather than Mr Campbell's.'

Inspector MacKenzie drained his lemonade glass and waited for her to continue.

'The young lady who was stabbed in Princes Street Gardens,' she said.

'Miss Isla Macgregor?'

'Yes. I think there's a connection between the attack on her and the jewellery fraud.'

'Go on.' He tamped down with his finger the tobacco in his pipe and held a match to it once more.

'When I returned to the jeweller's shop to ask further questions, the assistant looked awfully uncomfortable. She asked me how my investigation was getting on and I told her what might be considered a wee white lie...'

'Which was?' he prompted and put the stem of the pipe in his mouth.

'That I was close to finding out the truth. And then Isla went out that evening in my coat and a hat very similar to mine, both of which I was wearing when I visited the jeweller's. I think she *was* mistaken for me. And this is the piece of deduction I'm most proud of.' Poppy smiled. 'I'm certain the attacker was not a man, but a woman. In fact, the jeweller's shop assistant.' Poppy's smile widened.

Inspector MacKenzie nodded thoughtfully. 'It's possible a woman could inflict such cuts with a knife. But what makes you think it was this woman?'

'I can't be certain it was the assistant,' Poppy added in fairness, 'but I'm sure it was a woman because she fumbled as she climbed on the bike she stole to escape. You see, it was a man's bike with a central bar.'

'You don't think the same thing might happen to a man in his haste to get away?'

Poppy pursued her lips. 'It's possible, of course. But I think it was the shop assistant – and that she did this because she realised I was on her trail!'

He frowned, deep in thought. 'It's a good theory. I will telephone my police office in Edinburgh and get an officer to question the woman on suspicion of fraud and attempted murder.' He rose.

'*Wait!* There's more.'

Resigned, he resumed his seat.

'We haven't yet discussed the two murders,' Poppy pointed out.

'I don't intend to,' he replied.

'And yet I have solved one case already, in a matter of days.'

'So it would seem.'

'The shop assistant will be interviewed and...' Poppy waved a hand airily, 'and so on?'

'Aye, she will be interviewed...' Inspector MacKenzie mimicked her hand gesture with a smile, 'and so on.'

'What exactly is the *so on*?' Poppy had a sudden, dreadful thought of the young woman being subject to the third degree. That sounded like an expression young Gregor would use. 'She won't be subject to any unnecessary force?'

'What sort of a monster do you take me for, my lady? She won't be subject to any force to make a confession, necessary or otherwise.'

Reassured, Poppy returned to the murder cases. She tapped the notebook in her lap. 'I've made notes on possible suspects, as you saw.'

'Certainly, I saw. By some miracle, my eyesight is still functioning.'

'Well, then...'

'Show me your book,' he said.

'Absolutely, Inspector!' Poppy opened it at the page headed *The Murder of Honest Harry* and handed it to him.

Inspector MacKenzie went through her list of suspects, giving nothing away. When he had finished reading, he looked up. 'There may be something in what you say here,' he conceded.

Poppy smiled. 'You see how profitable it is for us to work together.'

'Let us see how matters progress.'

'Oh, come, Inspector, you are being churlish!'

Inspector MacKenzie flushed.

Oh, I have touched on a nerve. She softened her voice. 'I could speak to Freddy again. Just in passing, as it were,' she added.

'In passing? Do you often have conversation with those below stairs?'

'Certainly I do.' She raised her eyebrows. 'This is nineteen twenty-four. What sort of a monster do you take me for, Inspector?'

His lips twitched in a smile. 'I cannot stop you having a chat with the footman, and if you learn anything of interest from him, I would like to know. I'll get nothing more from the fellow unless I beat it out of him.'

Poppy sucked in a sharp breath.

'I'm joking, your ladyship.' He gave a smile of genuine amusement.

Poppy nodded. That was the best response she could expect from Inspector MacKenzie for the time being.

He got to his feet, replaced his hat and wished her good day. He walked down the steps and took hold of the handlebars of a bicycle that she now noticed propped against the banister at the bottom. She called after him.

'Inspector, where is your Austin Seven?'

He turned. 'I have no car, my lady. Police officers, even detectives, are no' provided with one.'

'But the car you arrived in on Tuesday?'

'The Chummy was lent to me by my friend. Alas, he needs it today for his own use.'

'If you give me a moment, I'll get—'

'I've borrowed this bike from the police office. The exercise will do me good and will give me time to think on what you've told me. Good day, your ladyship.'

Inspector MacKenzie drew the bike away from the bottom of the steps and threw one long, muscular leg over the seat.

He lifted his hand in farewell, and she watched him pedal away.

Poppy looked at her watch. Half past ten. The servants would be about their various tasks, which meant that Freddy would be in the butler's pantry polishing the silver. She would go down now, ostensibly to ask Freddy a question about her dog, and take the opportunity to quiz the footman.

She made her way down the stairs to the semi-basement. She passed the kitchens, a hive of activity with the chef shouting orders, the housekeeper storing the day's deliveries in the tiled larders and a small girl bent over a vast sink in the scullery, washing up pots and pans in a cloud of steam. Poppy reached the open door of the butler's pantry and walked in.

Freddy was dipping a cloth into the mixture in a small bowl and rubbing it onto a knife. He looked up as she entered. A row of knives lay neatly on the table in front of him, awaiting his attention.

'Your ladyship,' he said in surprise, putting down the knife and getting to his feet. He wiped his hands on his green apron.

'Freddy, I wonder if I might ask if you have noticed anything unusual about Major the last couple of days.' *Forgive me, Major, for impugning your robust constitution.*

'Unusual, my lady? In what way?' Freddy asked, a frown creasing his brow.

'Oh, just not quite as...' she hesitated. Not quite as what? The dog was always so bouncy. 'As *bouncy*,' she said.

Freddy frowned. 'Major seems very bouncy, but I'm afraid I don't know him well enough to say whether he is more or less bouncy than usual.'

Why on earth did she choose the word bouncy? It sounded faintly ridiculous.

'Well, that is good to hear,' she said in a genuinely relieved tone.

There was a silence. Freddy looked at the line of unpolished knives on the table.

'I do hope the inspector has solved the murders before the midsummer party,' Poppy said, striving for a casual tone.

Another silence, and then Freddy blurted, 'I need to get on with my work, my lady. I'm already behind with the inspector asking me questions and going over the same things. I can't afford to lose my job. Not when I want to have a garage business one day.'

'It's good to have an ambition,' she told him. And hers at present was to solve the murders.

'Aye, but the other servants don't like me having aspirations above my station, especially Charlie.'

'I suppose that's not surprising. He thinks you're after his job.'

Freddy shrugged. 'Her ladyship is good to me, there's no doubt, but it's only because Ollie took a shine to me. She's told Charlie to teach me how to drive – but of course he hasn't. And now he's trying to get me into Lady Balfour's bad books by blaming me for Harry's murder.' Freddy sent her a sideways glance. 'Sorry, my lady, I shouldn't have told you all that.'

'Not at all,' Poppy said. 'It's good to get things off your chest.'

'Harry looked down on those of us below stairs, you know. As if a bookie's runner was better than us! After his lordship's death, he didn't want to come here any longer. Not until I paid back the money I owed him. The only way I could get him to come was to pay off a bit a week and to place larger bets.'

'Money you could ill afford?' Poppy asked gently.

'I had the occasional win,' he muttered.

'But, still...?'

'Aye, I admit that I lost my temper with him on the day he was killed!' Freddy burst out. 'But I didn't do it!'

He reached for the paste-covered knife lying on the table.

She took a silent breath. He repositioned the knife by a fraction of an inch. She breathed out.

'Can you tell me what happened that day?'

'The paste needs cleaning off,' he remarked dully. 'Thirty seconds for lightly soiled items and ten minutes for heavily tarnished silver.'

'Go ahead.' He might feel more comfortable talking if he could carry out a routine task, she reasoned.

Freddy turned to the sink behind him and rinsed the knife in clean water, before turning back to the table. As he dried and buffed it with a soft cloth, he said, 'There's not really much else to say. I wasn't pleased when Harry told me in Culross that he wasn't going to come here again because it wasn't worth his while. But I was to send the money I owed him, in regular instalments, or else.' Freddy grimaced.

What an unpleasant man, she thought. 'Or else what?'

'He didn't say and I wasn't keen to find out. I asked him to meet me by the loch as soon as I'd got back from the village and I'd bring him more money.'

'Oh, Freddy,' said Poppy, disappointment in her voice, 'so you *did* meet Harry by the loch that afternoon?'

The footman looked down, a flush of shame on his features. 'Yes, my lady,' he said quietly.

'Why the loch?' she asked.

Freddy began polishing another knife. 'I knew I'd be missed if I tried to walk back into the village. There's not much time between serving tea above stairs, and the servants' supper at six o'clock. And after that, we're all at work preparing for upstairs' dinner.'

'So you returned with Ollie to the house – using the overgrown track?'

Freddy glanced up at her and nodded unhappily.

'You got the money Harry wanted, met him at the loch and

handed it over, in addition to the cash you'd given him in the Red Lion?'

'I gave him money in the Red Lion for another bet, but instead he said he'd take if off my debt. He wanted more and I didn't have any, and when I got back here, Baird wouldn't let me have next week's wages on account. So I went to the loch to plead with Harry. Much good it did me,' Freddy said bitterly. 'And whoever killed him stole my money!'

'There was no money on him when the police searched his body,' Poppy agreed. Of course, Harry could have paid the cash into the post office before leaving the village. The man's savings book was missing, so the killer must have taken that. But had the footman really intended to give him more money, or had he asked for the meeting by the loch with the sole purpose of killing Harry? She looked at Freddy thoughtfully.

'We had an argument by the loch, but he was alive when I left him. Although that doesn't seem to matter if the number of times the inspector has questioned me is anything to go by. It doesn't look good for me, does it?' Freddy said anxiously.

Poppy had to admit that it didn't. 'For what it is worth,' she said truthfully, 'I believe you didn't kill him.'

He gave a grateful smile. 'Thank you, my lady.'

'One other thing, Freddy. Where were you yesterday around the time of Jack Finnie's death, between four and seven o'clock?'

'Here, my lady, with the rest of the servants,' he said bitterly. 'Where I'll always be – if I'm lucky.' She thought she knew what he was thinking. That he'd spend the rest of his life in service – if he wasn't first found guilty of murder.

As there didn't seem to be anything more to say, Poppy wished him luck and left him to his task.

Walking past the servants' hall, she saw the kitchen maid setting the long table in the centre of the room with teacups and saucers, milk jug and sugar bowl. The servants, her own maid among them, would soon be gathering for their morning tea. This would be a good time to catch Elspeth before she joined them and explain to her maid what she wanted to learn.

When Poppy returned to her room, she found Elspeth hanging the repaired white blouse in the wardrobe.

'Thank you, Elspeth. How efficient you are!' she said gaily.

Elspeth sent her a look that managed to convey both pride and suspicion.

'I was wondering if,' Poppy went on, 'while you are downstairs taking tea, you could find out—'

'I don't think so, my lady,' Elspeth said stiffly.

'You haven't let me finish...'

'I don't need to, your ladyship. I'm not a detective,' she said pointedly as she closed the wardrobe door. 'I'm a trained lady's maid.'

'But you would make an excellent detective. For one thing, you look... so honest.' It was true, Poppy, thought, if one ignored the disapproving glances her maid did so well.

Elspeth seemed momentarily bemused, so Poppy took advantage and pushed on. 'I'm sure you could persuade people to tell you anything.'

Elspeth stood a little straighter at the compliment. Poppy smiled inwardly and went on. 'It's merely a case of finding out if Lady Balfour's personal maid helped her dress on Monday evening.'

Elspeth wrinkled her brow. 'I suppose I *might* be able to do that...'

'Oh, and find out if on Monday afternoon Freddy asked Baird for next week's wages on account.' Poppy sat on the dressing table stool and assumed a guileless expression.

'Ask Mr Baird!' Elspeth looked horrified. 'That wouldn't be seemly, my lady.'

'Let me hear no such thing, Elspeth. He is a mere mortal, like the rest of us.'

'Mr Baird can be...' Elspeth sought for the phrase she wanted, 'a wee bit grand.'

'Pompous, you mean?' Poppy raised an eyebrow. 'Really, Elspeth, I never thought you would be bested by a butler.'

Elspeth drew herself up, her long nose quivering with emotion. 'You are right, my lady. I will do as you ask and not be scunnered by the likes of him.' She marched towards the door.

'That's the spirit, Elspeth!' Poppy called as her maid disappeared out of the room.

Elspeth would be gone for a while and Poppy had no time to waste. Who should she interview next?

The Americans were probably still enjoying Culross Palace, and it was unlikely that Constance had yet returned from the visit to her friend. Poppy wasn't interested in seeking out Innes or Rosie, no matter how tempting the thought of widening the net might be. They had arrived after Harry's murder, and she could see no possible connection between them and the dead man.

Dahlia Dalrymple, however, was a different matter. Not as a suspect herself in either murder case, but regarding Constance. She'd told Poppy that she had known Constance for many years. Dahlia knew something distressing about Constance's past, that was clear from the brief conversation they'd had at Viscountess Shand's charity event on Wednesday evening. But how much did she know, and would she be likely to tell Poppy? Nonetheless, Poppy was certain she had to try. She set off down the stairs.

As she passed through the hall, she spotted a number of envelopes lying on the silver tray on the table. The morning's post had arrived.

Poppy hastened over and searched quickly through the little pile of letters on the hall table.

Yes, there was a letter addressed to her, in an unfamiliar, flowing script, sent on from Ann Street.

Surely this was the reply she had been waiting for.

TWENTY-THREE

Poppy snatched up the letter and bore it quickly back up to her room.

Closing the bedroom door firmly behind her, she dropped into the armchair. With shaky hands, she tore open the envelope and drew out two sheets of headed notepaper.

My dear Lady Persephone,

I am unsure as to how best I may answer your letter.

Poppy's heart thumped.

Mary Murray was employed at Achavarasdal House as a nursery maid. She came to us aged fifteen and stayed for three years.

Poppy read on, her mouth dry.

In that time, I formed a favourable opinion of Mary. So favourable, in fact, that I had told her the position of lady's maid to my daughter, when she came of an age to have one, would be Mary's if she so wished. My daughter was delighted and Mary gave the impression that she was equally happy. It therefore came as something of a surprise when one day...

She hastily turned to the second page.

Mary informed me that she would be leaving us with immediate effect. I could have insisted that she worked out her notice, but the poor girl was distraught about something and I saw no purpose in doing so. The other servants were close-lipped and I never discovered the reason for her sudden departure.

I'm afraid this is not a very helpful reply,

On the contrary, she thought sadly.

but I can say with all honesty that I was perfectly satisfied with her work.

Sincerely yours,

The letter was signed Mrs George Abbott. Underneath she had written a postscript.

PS. I do not know if this is of any interest to your friend,

What friend? thought Poppy, startled. Oh yes, the one overseas she had invented.

but although she was known in the household as Mary, her full name was Constance Mary Murray.

Oh, Mrs George Abbott, that was indeed of interest. Although it wasn't the information Poppy wanted to hear.

This didn't mean the allegations made in the anonymous letter were true, of course, but it did lend them a credibility. She sighed.

Poppy folded the letter back into the envelope. What should she do with it? If she threw it away, the housemaid would find it in the wastepaper bin; if she hid it in a drawer, Elspeth was bound to come across it. The weather was too warm for a fire in the hearth, and if she set light to the letter, the ashes in the grate would look suspicious. And she had no intention of eating the paper, as spies supposedly did.

She chewed her lip instead. If he knew about it, the inspector would want to see the letter. She didn't want to withhold important evidence, but she needed first to be certain there was some truth in the allegation that Constance had given birth and the baby had disappeared; was presumed dead, possibly by Constance's hand. *Audi alteram partem.* She reminded herself of the legal maxim. *Hear the other side.*

Easier said than done in this case. Poppy was wondering how on earth she could broach such a subject with Constance, when the perfect place to conceal the letter came to her. Underneath the purple-blue silk scarf she wore as a bandeau that her maid so disapproved of. Hastily she pulled open the top drawer of the chest and slipped the envelope under the offending item.

She had just closed the drawer and taken a step away from the chest when Elspeth entered the bedroom.

'What news from below stairs?' Poppy asked briskly, to conceal a guilty look.

Elspeth was quite pink with pleasure. 'I did as you asked, my lady – and the answers are yes.'

'Yes to both questions?'

Elspeth nodded. 'Emily, Lady Balfour's maid, has been with her lady for the whole hour of dressing every day we have been here; she was quite shocked to think it might be otherwise. And on Monday the footman asked Baird for wages on account. I didn't pose the questions directly, of course, but I was a wee bit sleekit,' she added, relishing her moment of glory.

'I'm sure a police officer can be just as sly,' Poppy told her. Not Inspector MacKenzie, though; she was certain he was trustworthy if nothing else. 'Thank you, Elspeth. You have done well.'

Poppy was relieved to hear that Constance had an alibi and Freddy had been telling the truth about his conversation with the butler, but she was stumped as to where to go from here in her investigation. And today was Friday, meaning that tomorrow was the day of the garden party, and she *so* wanted to have the case solved by then.

'Any other news from downstairs?' Poppy asked.

Elspeth bristled, clearly uncomfortable in her newly acquired role as assistant detective. 'If you insist...

'I do.' Poppy sat on the edge of the bed. Was she at last to learn something relevant?

'It concerns Lady Balfour's chauffeur, although I can't think it has anything to do with the deaths of those men.' Elspeth paused.

'The chauffeur – Charlie?'

'Aye, my lady.'

If her ears could have pricked up like her Labrador's, they would have done so. 'What about him?'

'It's more about his wife, really.' Elspeth opened the wardrobe and took out Poppy's black and white coat.

'You see, my lady, how well the blood stain has come out.'

Poppy glanced at the coat her maid held out to show her. 'Excellent, Elspeth, thank you,' she said, controlling her impatience.

'And here,' went on Elspeth, 'I've done some embroidery on

both shoulders to disguise the repair on the one damaged by the knife.'

Poppy took the coat and gazed at the intricate vine leaves, her fingers tracing the white stitching. 'You really have made a beautiful job, Elspeth.'

Her maid gave a gratified sniff, before going on in a stern voice. 'I feel I should warn your ladyship against loaning any garment in future, lest the item be returned in a worse state.'

'You are right again, Elspeth,' Poppy said meekly, handing back the coat. She smiled and said, 'You were telling me about the chauffeur's wife?'

Elspeth sighed and returned the coat to the wardrobe. 'The housekeeper mentioned that the poor lady, Mrs Lamont, is in a nursing home.'

A nursing home! That would explain why she hadn't appeared yesterday when Poppy had visited the flat. No wonder Charlie was concerned about losing his job to Freddy. His accommodation above the stables came with the chauffeur position. No work meant no home – and no money to pay for his wife's care. So that's what Charlie had been alluding to when he mentioned his wife. He feared what would happen to her if he could no longer afford the nursing home. She remembered the lace cushions on the armchairs, the little jugs and the glass snowstorm globe on the mantelpiece; objects that presumably belonged to his wife and reminded him of her.

Elspeth had closed the wardrobe door and was now turning to the chest of drawers. 'Is there anything in here that needs to be mended?'

'No, thank you,' Poppy said hastily, thinking of the hurriedly concealed letter. 'Did the housekeeper say why Mrs Lamont was in the nursing home?'

'A nervous ailment, Mrs Oakley understands it to be.'

Poppy felt her head begin to spin, with Charlie desperate to keep his post, Freddy in serious debt, Constance's missing baby and Gregor's volatile temper. And Nick fancied himself in love with Beth, she was sure of it, but wouldn't he have disposed of Eddie rather than Harry? Had Harry started a blackmailing scheme as a sideline? Was Morag's drug addiction relevant? Poppy had barely given that much thought. But now, as she considered the matter, she realised although Morag was... abstracted, she was consistently so. If she were addicted, her behaviour would veer between highs and lows, depending on when the drug was administered. It was much more likely that Morag was simply away with the fairies...

But Poppy was still left with the bookie's runner and the poacher dead, Isla attacked in mistake for her, the jeweller's assistant up to no good...

What if she was wrong and it wasn't the shop assistant who'd tried to kill her, but the same person who murdered Honest Harry and Jack Finnie?

'You're looking a bit peely-wally, my lady, if you don't mind my saying so. It's all this dashing hither and yon, trying to be a detective.' Elspeth plumped up the pillow on the bed and guided Poppy to lie down. 'There now, have a nice wee rest and you'll feel better by lunch time.'

Trying to be a detective! She was a dashed good one, some of the time... But Poppy submitted to her maid's ministrations and, when Elspeth had let herself quietly out of the room, lay there wondering if anyone was free of suspicious behaviour.

At lunch time, Poppy was surprised to see Baird assisted in serving the *consommé polonaise* by an under-footman.

'Where is Freddy, Baird?' Constance asked her butler.

'I regret to say, my lady, that he cannot be found,' Baird murmured.

'Cannot be found?' asked Poppy sharply. A heavy feeling threatened to settle in her stomach.

'He was last seen cleaning the silver.'

'The silver!' cried Constance.

'He's done a bunk with it,' Gregor pronounced with relish.

'He had not made off with the silver, my lady,' Baird reassured her. 'I have checked and all is present.'

'Then what the devil is he up to?' demanded Nick. 'It's not his half-day, is it?'

'Indeed not, sir.'

'What time was he last seen, Baird?' Poppy asked, fearing she knew the answer.

'About an hour ago, my lady.'

Shortly after she had left him, Poppy thought. As she lifted her soup spoon, she ran through in her head the conversation they'd had. The salient point was that Freddy had admitted he'd lost his temper with Harry by the loch on the day the man was murdered.

'He can't have gone far in such a short time,' put in Innes. 'He's probably having forty winks in the laundry cupboard.' He stroked his fair moustache and Rosie laughed.

'Have you sent anyone to look for him, Baird?' asked Constance, setting down her soup spoon.

'I sent one of the other footmen to conduct a search, but your ladyship will appreciate that I cannot spare any more servants at this time of day.'

'It is most extraordinary,' Constance apologised to her guests. 'He has never done this before.'

Morag's placid countenance clouded over a little. 'I do hope he hasn't also been murdered.'

There was a shocked silence.

'Morag, my dear!' exclaimed Constance. 'How can you even think such a thing?'

'Too bad Mr Emmett stayed to eat his lunch in Culross,' put in Beth. 'He's missing another slice of excitement. Say, maybe Morag is right and you should ask that honey of an inspector to look for Freddy.'

Honey of an inspector? Poppy thought, bristling. She could think of a few less complimentary terms. And even if he was a honey, she went on to herself, relenting a little, it wasn't for Beth to call him that...

Nick laughed. 'You can't take up the inspector's time with such a trivial matter as a missing servant. You must remember that MacKenzie is engaged on more important work. Although I must say, it's high time he solved the murders. I begin to wonder if he is doing anything at all,' he grumbled. 'I expect the footman will return in his own time.'

The filleted sole was served and with that, the matter was dropped. Poppy was distracted by the news of Freddy's disappearance and listened with only half an ear to Beth telling them all about Culross Palace's history.

'It was built in 1597. Can you imagine anything so *old*?' she said, her eyes wide. 'And the caretaker told us that the owner, the Earl of Dundonald, is descended from Sir George Bruce who built the place. To think of the same family being around for all that time...'

After lunch, Innes and Gregor disappeared outside to demonstrate to Beth and Eddie the rudiments of cricket, with Major Lewis acting as fielder. Nick declined to play and he and Morag went upstairs for a rest, while Rosie set off to walk Ollie in Freddy's absence.

Poppy, Constance and Dahlia were taking their coffee in the drawing room, when Baird announced Inspector MacKenzie. Constance rose from the settee and immediately claimed his attention.

'Inspector, one of my footmen has gone missing. It's

completely out of character and I'm concerned that something may have happened to him.'

Inspector MacKenzie shot Poppy a questioning look.

'Yes, Inspector,' she confirmed, 'it's Freddy.'

Inspector MacKenzie turned back to Constance. 'When was he last seen, my lady?'

'An hour or so before lunch. Would you organise a search for him? After all, it is a detective's business to look for things, and considering the circumstances...'

'Innes suggests in the laundry cupboard,' Dahlia's voice reverberated around the room.

The inspector looked startled, whether by Dahlia's voice or her offering, Poppy didn't know. No sooner had her boom died away than Mr Emmett entered the room.

'My sincere apologies for missing one of your excellent lunches, Constance,' he said, 'but I was taking in the conversations of the rustics at the Red Lion.'

'The rustics?' murmured Constance. 'I believe our minister and the doctor take their lunches there.'

'And who should I meet at the inn but your footman, Freddy?' Mr Emmett went blithely on.

'The footman was there?' demanded Inspector MacKenzie.

'Yes, sir. He was having what I believe is called a wee dram. Then I heard him say he couldn't waste time hanging around and something about having to shoot off to Edinburgh to see a dame.'

'Freddy said that?' Constance asked in a faint voice.

'Well, they weren't his exact words, you understand, Constance, but you get the meaning.'

'We do,' said Inspector MacKenzie, his voice taut.

Through the open window came the traditional thwack of leather on willow and a cheer went up from the players on the lawn.

Mr Emmett looked towards the window with interest. 'Say, is that a game of cricket? I'd sure like to watch that, if I may.'

'Of course.' Constance waved one hand limply in the direction of the garden. 'Please do.'

Mr Emmett nodded to the three ladies and left the drawing room.

'We need to go after Freddy.' Poppy looked at Constance and the inspector. 'He ran away shortly after he admitted to me that he'd lost his temper with Honest Harry by the loch on Monday afternoon. But I still don't believe he's the murderer,' she added hastily, seeing the dark look on Inspector MacKenzie's face.

'The footman admitted that? Why did you no' tell me?' he demanded.

'Because you've only just walked into the room!' she retorted.

'You're both wasting time arguing,' Constance exclaimed. 'Go after Freddy.'

'We'll take the Bentley!' Poppy cried. 'Follow me, Inspector.'

She dashed out of the room, Inspector MacKenzie on her heels.

Fergusson was in his shirt sleeves and giving a final polish to the motor car when Poppy, followed by the inspector, then Major who'd heard the excitement and appeared from the direction of the lawn, came running round the side of the house.

'Thank you, Fergusson,' she called to her bemused chauffeur. 'I'll take it from here!'

The chauffeur stepped back, in his surprise touching his cap with the hand holding the flannel cloth, and Major leaped at once into the driving seat.

'No, Major!' Poppy exclaimed. '*Out!*'

The Labrador continued to sit there, gazing happily ahead

of him. Poppy took a firm hold of his collar and managed to tug him out of the car. He immediately jumped into the back seat.

'Let him be,' Inspector MacKenzie said, 'or we'll be here all afternoon.'

Major sat up, looking pleased with himself, as Poppy jumped into the driving seat. The inspector climbed in beside her. The key was in the ignition; she turned it and pressed her foot hard on the accelerator.

'If he's making for Edinburgh, then we can take a shortcut and head him off,' Inspector MacKenzie said as Poppy hurtled down the drive, out between the tall stone pillars and onto the main road. 'Once we're past the village, take the left turn.'

Following his directions, she drove through Culross and then plunged into a narrow lane, the banks crowded with clumps of rosebay willowherb.

'Very pretty,' Poppy observed.

'Aye,' said Inspector MacKenzie, holding on to the passenger door handle as she swerved to avoid a dog of uncertain heritage sunbathing in the middle of the road. 'You are knowing how to drive, aren't you?'

'Absolutely, Inspector!' The needle was almost over to the right-hand side of the dial. 'Is Major still in position?'

Inspector MacKenzie turned to look. 'Aye, he's doing grand.'

She could imagine the Labrador happily ricocheting about on the back seat, his ears flapping in the breeze. 'We can't have far to go now.'

They passed fields of pale golden wheat, grazing sheep and a row of men and women harvesting an early potato crop. The farm workers paused to stand and stare as Poppy, MacKenzie and Major dashed past to the roar of the Bentley.

'Turn right here!' Inspector MacKenzie called.

Poppy spun the Bentley back onto the main road and the glittering ribbon of the river Forth reappeared. She reduced speed and drove slowly along, both of them looking for any sign of the footman. A farm cart plodded towards them loaded with neeps, the driver slouched at the reins of his horse.

'Stop the car and I'll ask the fellow if he's seen our young man.' Inspector MacKenzie was already opening the door before she had time to bring the car to a stop.

'There he is!' Poppy screamed, pointing at the figure visible now the cart had moved forward, and walking briskly away from them along the road.

TWENTY-FOUR

'There is no need to shout, my lady,' said Inspector MacKenzie. 'I am seated immediately next to you.'

Freddy turned at the sound of the Bentley. Poppy sent him a friendly wave, hoping not to scare him off, and drew the car to a halt. With a look of weary resignation, Freddy waited as the three of them climbed out.

Major scampered across the road, reaching him first. Freddy crouched down to stroke the dog's broad head. Major licked his face. He couldn't possibly be the murderer if he and Major were such good friends, Poppy thought, knowing that conclusion was simply illogical. She slowly got out of the car, feeling deflated and sure that Freddy wasn't their man, as Inspector MacKenzie strode purposively towards the footman. She hastened forward, determined to speak to Freddy before the inspector did.

'Lady Balfour has been very worried about you, Freddy,' Poppy said as she reached him.

Freddy straightened. 'I'm sorry to let you both down, my lady. I just... wanted to get away.'

'Major, sit,' Poppy said to the dog, nudging his way into the little reunion. 'Are you not treated well at Balfour House?' she asked Freddy. 'I am sure you told me you got on well with her ladyship.'

'Yes, my lady,' Freddy said, his eyes downcast. 'I couldn't ask for a better employer.'

'Then why did you run away?'

'To see my sister,' he muttered.

'Come, lad,' said the inspector. 'I think we all know, even the dog, that it was more than that.'

Freddy stared at him. 'I was afraid you were going to arrest me for the murder of Honest Harry!'

'Of course you didn't murder that man,' Poppy said gently.

'I regret I do not share your ladyship's opinion of the footman.' Inspector MacKenzie turned back to Freddy. 'Frederick Strachan, you are under arrest for the murder of Henry Harvey.'

'Are you sure of this, Inspector?' Poppy asked, her eyes wide.

He fixed her with his dark look. 'I do know my job, my lady.'

'Of course you do,' she said. 'It's just that I think—'

Inspector MacKenzie continued addressing Freddy. 'You will be held in custody at the local police office until such time as I am able to escort you to Edinburgh pending enquiries.'

You are making a mistake, Inspector MacKenzie, Poppy thought as she watched him take a firm hold of the young man's arm and walk him to the car. Something stirred suddenly in the back of her mind, but whatever it was refused to move forward. One thing that didn't evade her, however, was the almost certain knowledge that the footman was not the murderer.

Poppy dropped the inspector and Freddy at the police office in Culross and drove back to Balfour House in a sober mood.

'By Jove, you look as if you've lost a shilling and found a

penny,' remarked Dahlia as Poppy, having returned Major to the kennels and the car to Fergusson's care, met the older woman mounting the steps to the house.

Poppy managed a small smile. 'Not quite, but close.'

Dahlia gazed at her. 'I say, are you all right?' she asked kindly.

Poppy wanted to speak to Dahlia about Constance's past and here was the opportunity.

'I have rather a sensitive question I would like to ask you,' Poppy said, coming to a halt on the steps.

'Ask away, my dear girl.'

'We should go somewhere more private.' Poppy looked around for a suitable place.

'There's a sort of folly in the orchard. Ridiculous place to build a folly, if you ask me, when there's a loch on the estate which would have set it off nicely, but that's where it is. Follow me.' Dahlia strode off.

Poppy hastened after her, heading west across the lawn. She had not visited this part of the grounds and found there was, as she'd spotted from her bedroom window on the day she arrived, just beyond the tennis court a pretty little orchard of apple trees.

As they drew near, a small mock temple in white marble came into view. It had ornate pillars holding up the roof and no door. The only furniture it contained was a marble bench, if a marble bench could be considered furniture. Dahlia marched in and sat down.

'Jolly cold on the posterior, but I've got enough padding.' She laughed heartily.

The sweet scent of the apple trees drifted into the folly as Poppy gingerly took her seat on the chilly bench.

'Ask away,' repeated Dahlia.

'It concerns Constance,' Poppy began tentatively.

'What has the old girl been up to now?'

'Not so much now, as some years ago.'

In the pause that followed, Poppy could hear the distant whirr of a mowing machine, preparing the lawn for the party the next day. Dahlia gazed out of the open temple towards the apple trees, their green foliage dotted with the gradually ripening fruit. 'What is it you wish to ask me?'

'I believe that Constance lived in a house in Thurso from the age of fifteen to eighteen.'

Dahlia turned to face Poppy.

Poppy held her gaze. 'Is it true?'

'It is.'

'And that she worked there as a nursery maid.'

'Why are you asking me this?'

'It is important, or I wouldn't ask.'

'Important in what way?'

How to say to Dahlia that her reply could either point a finger at Constance in the two murder cases or it could point the finger away?

'Something happened to her there and it may have a bearing on the current police investigation.'

Dahlia breathed in so deeply that her nostrils flared. 'What happened to Connie in Thurso was a long time ago. I can't see what it can possibly have to do with the present-day murders of a bookie's runner and a poacher.'

Poppy felt her way carefully. 'I've received an anonymous letter alleging something rather... unpleasant about Constance.'

'Have you indeed?' Dahlia said sharply. 'I think I can guess what it said.'

Poppy's eyebrows rose in surprise at this response. 'It must have been very difficult for her, a young, unmarried girl in that situation,' she went on cautiously.

'It was – and much use the young man!' Dahlia retorted.

'What happened to...?'

'The poor wee mite?'

Dear Lord, so there *had* been a baby. Poppy held her breath as she waited for Dahlia to continue.

'A local couple, a tenant farmer and his wife who Connie had got to know on the far side of the Abbott's estate, took the bairn in,' Dahlia said. 'And very glad they were, having none of their own. It broke poor Connie's heart to have to part with the wee girl. But there was no question of returning to the house with the babe, and she couldn't manage on her own with a child.'

Poppy breathed a sigh of relief. The baby had not been harmed. 'What did Constance do after that?' she asked gently.

'What could she do? After giving birth in the couple's cottage, she returned to Achavarasdal House the same day and tried to carry on as usual. But it was too hard.' Dahlia shook her head. 'The child's father was a footman there – the foolish creature had believed herself in love with him – and he started to treat her very badly. She left soon after.'

Thank the Lord, Poppy thought. At least poor Constance had been able to make provision for the baby and the accusation had been just spiteful, wagging tongues.

'I can guess who sent that malicious letter,' Dahlia said, as if reading Poppy's mind. 'Moira Begbie.'

'Who is Moira Begbie?' Poppy asked.

'The kitchen maid at Achavarasdal, that's who. She wanted Connie's job and her man, and didn't get either.' Dahlia snorted.

'But that was some twenty years ago...'

'Aye, and some people bear grudges for a lifetime.' Dahlia paused, and then continued. 'Have you noticed the gold locket Connie always wears?'

Poppy nodded.

'It contains a tiny lock of the bairn's hair.' Dahlia gave a sad sigh.

'Bruce knew of the baby?' Poppy asked, surprised.

'Heavens, no! She put the locket away as soon as the wedding was announced. She didn't start to wear it again until after his death.'

'Do you know what happened to Constance after she left her post with Mrs Abbott?' Poppy asked.

'She returned home, although it was the last thing she wanted. After all, she'd taken the nursery maid's position to get away from her gambling-addicted father. I lost contact with her during the next couple of years. And then out of the blue I received a letter from her, saying she was about to marry Bruce Balfour and inviting me to the wedding.

'Later, after they'd married, Connie told me how Bruce – he wasn't a peer then, of course, but was already doing well for himself – had been to her father's house a few times. They mixed in the same sort of circles. He spotted her and, well, you now know the rest.'

'I wonder, though, why she agreed to marry Bruce? It must have been humiliating for her, at the very least.'

'Not as humiliating as being abandoned by the man she thought loved her and believing no other chap would ever want her,' Dahlia said briskly. 'And Bruce's deafness made him unattractive to the ladies. Two lonely souls. Bruce did love her, you know, and no doubt in the first few years of their marriage he managed to keep to his promise not to gamble. But it's like a drug.' Dahlia shrugged. 'So there you have it, my dear girl. Does it exonerate Connie from the murders?'

'Yes, I believe it does.'

'Then I'm glad I told you. But what I've said must go no further. Connie has suffered enough.'

'It won't. You have my word,' Poppy promised.

There was no need to tell the inspector what she had learned, she decided. And Constance could be crossed off her list of suspects, leaving only three names. Unless there was another name she should add, someone with a motive which hadn't yet come to light.

Midsummer's day dawned bright and fair. Perfect for a garden party, thought Poppy, singing as she bathed.

'Elspeth!' she called through the bathroom door, ceasing in her song for the moment, 'please lay out my new flapper dress.'

'Is that the tasselled, gold-coloured item of knee-length, my lady?'

'Unless you know of any other flapper dress I have recently bought?'

A lull in the conversation, then her maid's disapproving voice. 'You are not really intending to wear that garment, my lady?'

'Certainly I am. What did you think I was going to do with it?'

Poppy couldn't hear Elspeth's muttered response and decided it was probably just as well. She sang the popular song more loudly as she splashed about in the bath. '*Ja-da, ja-da, jing...* Oh and Elspeth?'

'Yes, my lady?'

'There's no need to reply in that voice of doom. It is only a dress,' Poppy scolded.

'Yes, my lady.' Clearly, her maid was not of the same opinion.

'Please also put out the matching headband I bought in Edinburgh.' Poppy didn't wait for a response. '*Ja-da, ja-da, jing,*' she carolled.

A simple breakfast had been sent up to the bedrooms with this morning's tea, as the servants were too busy preparing for the garden party to set out the usual array of dishes in the dining room. Poppy didn't mind; she was too excited to have eaten anything beyond the boiled egg and toast she'd consumed.

She had a very good feeling about today. Midsummer. The summer solstice. The longest day of the year. Call it what you will, it was a time of good fortune. Somehow all would come together on such a magical day. *'Ja-da, ja-DAAA...'*

As to her exciting new dress, how fortunate she'd been to find it in *Magasin de Vêtements de Lux* where she had an account...

Poppy stopped singing.

Suddenly, when she hadn't been thinking about murders or bracelets, another piece of a puzzle had fallen into place. She was getting good at this! She had the solution to what had been hovering on the edge of her brain two days earlier, when the inspector had shown Freddy the code book and she'd read over the footman's shoulder the initials CCTLCB.

MacKenzie must be telephoned immediately!

Poppy stepped out of the bath and hurriedly towelled herself dry. She hastened into her bedroom, threw off the towel, drew on her peach silk camisole and French knickers, and began to pull the flapper dress over her head.

'Here, let me help, your ladyship.' Elspeth reached up to smooth the dress into position. 'You'll spoil your beautiful dress if you are not careful.'

'Thank you, Elspeth,' Poppy spluttered, coming up for air. 'It *is* beautiful, isn't it? But I must speak to the inspector as a matter of urgency.' As she slipped her bare feet into her strappy shoes with their high heels, Elspeth was on her knees securing the button on each strap.

'What would I do without you, Elspeth,' Poppy said fondly.

'I dread to imagine, my lady.'

There was no time to arrange the headband, so Poppy plucked it from the dressing table and suddenly the damning letter about Constance was forefront in her mind. She should destroy it, but how? She glanced at the fireplace. Could it wait until after dark? She should have done the deed already, but

Elspeth hadn't found it and no one else would be looking in the drawer. She'd leave it where it was for now and deal with it later. In a moment, she was out of the bedroom and flying down the stairs.

In the hall the main door stood wide open and from the lawn she heard the sounds of the band tuning up. The garden party would soon begin, but now there was something more pressing on Poppy's mind.

Snatching up the telephone receiver, she asked the operator to put her through to the Red Lion Inn and waited impatiently.

'Inspector MacKenzie?' came a voice down the line. 'I'm sorry, madam, but he is no longer with us.'

'No longer with us? What do you mean?' Had the inspector been murdered? Her pulse jumped, and hung there, at the mental image of him lying dead.

Her breath caught in her throat.

'The policeman has settled his account and checked out.'

She let out her breath. *Thank goodness!* Although, of course, her momentary concern had been for the progress of the investigation. But Inspector MacKenzie's checking out of the hotel meant she was too late. He had gone back to Edinburgh, taking Freddy with him, intent on charging the wrong man with murder – and leaving the real killer at large.

Wait, he might yet be at the local police office.

She tapped the connection to get the operator again. 'Try the police office in Culross. Do hurry!'

'One moment, please.'

A voice answered the telephone in a leisurely manner. 'Constable Watt, Culross police office.'

'Inspector MacKenzie! Quickly!' she cried.

'I'm sorry, miss, but he's not here.'

'He's already left for Edinburgh!' she groaned. 'Has he taken Freddy with him?'

'Who is this, miss?'

She could hear the frown in the constable's voice.

'It's Lady Persephone from Balfour House.'

'Ah.' The frown cleared. 'Aye, your ladyship, the inspector has taken the footman to the police headquarters in Parliament Square.'

'He's got the wrong man! You must get hold of the inspector and tell him he must return to Balfour House *urgently*.'

'Get hold of him?' the constable stammered. 'It's too late, my lady. They are on the train. The ten o'clock, so it will have already left.'

'Well, then, you will have to, I don't know – get the train to turn round and come back!'

'I can't do that, my lady—'

Of course a train couldn't simply be turned round. What was she thinking?

'There must be something you can do,' she cried. 'Yes! Contact all the police offices on the route and tell the officer at the one closest to the approaching train to wait on the platform and to inform the inspector he must return straightaway with his prisoner as I have solved the case.' Breathlessly, Poppy slammed down the receiver.

What to do now? She could hardly arrest the man herself. He believed he'd got away with the murders, so it was surely safe to wait until Inspector MacKenzie arrived. She glanced at her watch. Ten minutes past ten. How far would the train have travelled? It must be halfway to Dunfermline by now, perhaps somewhere between Cairneyhill and Charlestown Junction.

In the gardens, the music was becoming more tuneful. Finding the headband in her hand, she secured it in position looking into the mirror above the hall table. She turned her head this way and that, smiling at the slim gold band with a large white feather at the side, then her gaze went to her mouth. Lipstick! She ran back up the stairs and burst into her room. Her maid dropped the clothes hanger she was holding.

'Sorry to startle you, Elspeth. I shan't be a moment.' Poppy sank onto the dressing table stool, plucked a lipstick from a small selection neatly lined up and leaned towards the mirror to apply a coat of rose-pink. 'There.'

Before she could rise from the stool, Elspeth silently drew a double row of pearls around her neck and secured the clasp at the back.

'There!' said Elspeth.

'Thank you.' Poppy smiled and got to her feet.

'Don't run around like a wild thing, your ladyship,' Elspeth protested as Poppy hastened towards the door. 'Remember you're—'

'I know. A *Lady*.' The door banged shut behind her.

She went lightly down the staircase, out of the open main door and stood at the top of the steps. The sun shone out of a sapphire sky, the distant loch glittered and on the broad, close-clipped lawn, dotted with the occasional tall, shady elm, the servants were bustling around setting up a long trestle table with a white tablecloth, china and cutlery.

Constance, dressed in a splendid taffeta tea gown of jade green and with a charming hat to match, turned from where she was supervising the servants and saw Poppy. She hurried over the lawn as Poppy walked down the steps towards her.

'My dear,' Constance called, 'You look wonderful and fresh, but I am already quite exhausted!'

Poppy smiled. 'You look magnificent, Constance, but I'm certain the servants can manage without you for a while. It's very hot, so why not sit in the shade until the guests arrive?'

'I do so want this party to be a success...'

'It will be!'

'I'm sure you're right. Your idea is an excellent one, but you must sit with me and bring me up to date with everything.' Constance took her arm and led her back up the steps and onto the terrace. 'I'm afraid that I have been too busy with all the preparations to have heard how you have been getting on with the search for the bracelet.'

'Oh, I have solved the case!'

'Good heavens.' Constance plopped down into one of the deckchairs under the huge sunshade on the terrace. 'Tell me everything,' she said as Poppy took the deckchair next to her.

'The bracelet,' Poppy began, 'does not exist – it never did.'

'Whatever do you mean? You saw the invoice.'

'Yes, I saw the invoice, but there was no jewellery.'

Seeing Constance's astonished look, Poppy knew she really did have to tell her friend everything from the start. She settled herself into the deckchair and they each accepted a glass of lemonade from a footman. Poppy began her story with the visit to the jeweller's and the shop assistant's claim that Lord Balfour had bought the bracelet for his niece, moved on to his secretary's statement that his lordship was deaf and then back at the jeweller's, Miss Strachan...

Then she stopped.

'*Miss Strachan!*' Poppy gasped.

TWENTY-FIVE

'Who is Miss Strachan?' Constance asked, confused.

Could it really be the same family? Edinburgh was a big place and Strachan was a common name. But she was suddenly certain the two were related. It had been staring her in the face.

'Miss Strachan is the final link in the puzzle!' Poppy took a gulp of her lemonade and a tiny sliver of the zest tickled her nose.

'What you are saying is a puzzle to me.' Constance frowned.

'I will come to it in just a moment, I promise. Because of something I said to Miss Strachan, the shop assistant, she believed I was on her trail.' Poppy's mind was racing. 'Then at dinner the evening before last, Dahlia told me a similar story to yours. After her husband died, she received an invoice for a pair of gold and blue sapphire cufflinks she had not seen. Dahlia paid without question. The invoice came from Campbell's.'

'The same jeweller's shop as the bracelet.' Constance's face turned pale.

'I'm afraid so. I doubt that you and Dahlia are the only two victims in this clever deception. Yesterday morning, the inspector telephoned Edinburgh's Detective Branch to take Miss Strachan into custody in connection with the fraud and attempted murder.'

'Attempted murder? But whom did she try to kill?' Constance turned a shade paler. 'Not your young friend?'

Poppy nodded. 'Yes, mistakenly thinking Isla was me. Inspector MacKenzie will be interviewing Miss Strachan today.'

'And what did you mean by the final link in the puzzle?' Constance asked slowly.

'Your footman.'

'Freddy?'

'Yes, Freddy... *Strachan*.'

'I still don't see... Oh.' Constance paused. 'Freddy and this Miss Strachan are related?'

'I believe they are. When the inspector and I found him on the road yesterday, he said he was going to Edinburgh to see his sister.'

'That would explain the comment he made, according to Mr Emmett... what was it he said? Something about Freddy shooting off to see a dame. So he and this woman are siblings?'

'It certainly looks that way. Whether Freddy was involved in the fraud, I don't yet know. We'll learn more when the inspector returns.' *Oh, do hurry, Inspector MacKenzie.*

Constance gazed at her in admiration. 'My goodness, how clever of you to have uncovered all this.'

That was only part of it, Poppy thought. There was still the matter of the resident murderer...

Constance lowered her voice. 'Poppy, dear, I'm well aware that my husband had not led a blameless life...'

Poppy sent her a startled look. What was Constance about to confess at this late stage?

'But his vices stretched only to gambling and nothing more

than he could afford to lose,' Constance went on. 'I want to thank you for your discretion in this matter.'

Poppy reached out and pressed her friend's hand.

The sound of car engines and the tooting of horns drew their attention.

'Oh dear.' Constance sighed. 'The first guests have arrived.'

Excited passengers were alighting from a stream of cars drawn up along the side of the house. Poppy noticed the long trestle tables on the lawn were now laden with plates of food, silver tea urns and ice buckets, presided over by Baird and two under-footmen. On a platform at the side of the lawn, the band started up, the strains of jazz floating over the garden.

'The hostess must circulate at these things.' Constance extracted herself from the deckchair. 'I can't thank you enough for what you have done, my dear. We'll talk later.' She sailed down the steps and onto the grass, towards her guests.

Before long, groups of guests were standing around on the grass smoking, chatting and drinking. Footmen in livery and housemaids in blue checked dresses, aprons and white caps wandered about with trays of sandwiches, cakes and champagne. At the long table, the younger of the two under-footmen was busy mixing cocktails. Constance stood chatting to a group of guests. The ladies were in colourful, extravagant dresses and jewels, the men in white tie and coat-tails, all dressed to carry on partying throughout the night. Ollie was in a flower bed, eating purple African daisies with a thoughtful air, while Major, his nose to the grass for any dropped food, followed Gregor around.

Poppy rose and descended the steps onto the lawn. She must do *something*; the wait for Inspector MacKenzie to return was almost unbearable. Surely, he and Freddy didn't have to catch another train back, but would have found a car somewhere? If only they would get a move on! More cars were arriving, but not one of them contained the inspector and his prisoner.

She helped herself to a glass of champagne from a passing footman. Near the band she could see Beth teaching a large group of guests how to dance the Charleston. Eddie, his jacket discarded and his white shirtsleeves rolled up over his tanned forearms, was proving popular, judging by the number of young ladies surrounding him. Mr Emmett and Dahlia Dalrymple were getting on famously with each other. Innes and Rosie seemed to have disappeared. Poppy strolled around the garden, hearing snippets of conversation from the mingled groups as she passed.

'The British Empire Exhibition at Wembley is absolutely thrilling!' said a woman with an English accent and wearing a red velvet dress with a beaded fringe.

'The Palace of Machinery is too grim for words,' her friend, wearing a dress in pale green silk and net with sequins, responded. 'But Sir Roderick was *determined* to see it.' She took a gulp of her blue cocktail.

'Bertie and I simply dived into the Planters' Bar in the West Indian section,' went on the first woman. 'Their Green Swizzles are divine!' Her beaded cap jingled as she laughed.

Nick Balfour's friends from London, Poppy supposed, as her gaze travelled around the gardens.

A tall, slim, elegant woman with fair hair caught her eye. She wore a sleeveless dress in silver grey chiffon with a tiered skirt, short lace gloves and pale grey strapped shoes. Her hair was pinned into a French twist under the straw hat. Next to her stood a tall and exceptionally good-looking gentleman with dark hair. The couple, who looked to be in their thirties, were engaged in conversation with a man scribbling in a notebook.

Intrigued, Poppy wandered over and discreetly eavesdropped.

'And do you find married life a little quiet,' the journalist was asking the woman, 'after all the excitement of running Edinburgh's first female detective agency, Lady Urquhart?'

Poppy started. *Female detective agency? Lady Urquhart?* Surely this wasn't Maud McIntyre? And yet it had to be. How many other first female detective agencies have there been, for goodness' sake?

'There is nothing quiet about married life, sir,' Lady Urquhart responded with a smile.

'Indeed not,' added her husband, 'especially not with three children about the place. And another on the way.' He placed his hand lovingly on his wife's gently rounded stomach. 'Although my wife *has* managed to fit in solving another case or two with Miss Daisy Cameron.'

Seeing the journalist's eager look, Lady Urquhart said quickly, 'Now then, you know I can tell you nothing, as we lady detectives pride ourselves on being discreet.'

The journalist laughed. 'Can we at least have a photo of the two of you for our readers?'

At Lord Urquhart's nod, the journalist called forward the photographer who had been standing a little further back.

'Say cheese,' called the photographer, holding up his folding camera.

'Cheese.' The couple lifted their champagne glasses and the camera clicked.

The two men thanked Lord and Lady Urquhart and set off in search of other guests to feature in whichever society magazine they worked for.

Lady Urquhart caught Poppy's eye and smiled. 'A delightful party,' she said.

'Am I right in thinking you used to be Miss Maud McIntyre?' Poppy asked, stepping closer.

She laughed. 'I still am, in essence.'

'I have bought your *Casebook* and I wanted to say what an inspiration it is to me.'

Maud gave a theatrical sigh. 'Oh, I was irresponsible and carefree in those days.'

Lord Urquhart laughed. 'You were never irresponsible, my love.'

'But you say an inspiration?' Maud raised an eyebrow at Poppy. 'An interesting choice of word. Tell me, are you a budding detective yourself?'

'I am! I have very recently solved my first case and I'm on the brink of solving another.'

'Hamish, darling,' Maud said, glancing at her husband, 'would you mind finding a friend to talk to for a while? I want to have a chat with...' She turned back to Poppy.

'Poppy Proudfoot.'

'Proudfoot? I know a little of your people. I believe your parents are now in Australia?'

'They are.'

'Pleased to meet you, Poppy.' Hamish smiled and shook her hand. 'I'll take myself off and let you two ladies have what our friend Daisy calls a blether.' He set his empty glass on a passing waiter's tray and moved away.

Maud drew Poppy into the shade of a leafy elm, a little way from the other guests who were continuing to grow in number. She gestured to the small group of cane chairs set up under the tree. 'Do sit down and tell me about your cases – only as much as you can, of course.' Maud lowered herself into a seat and set her champagne glass by her side. 'Lemonade,' she told Poppy, indicating the glass, 'on account of the budding Urquhart.'

Poppy smiled and took a chair next to her. 'First let me say that I met Miss Cameron earlier this week at the agency in Edinburgh.'

'You did? How delightful!' Maud's eyes shone. 'How is dear Daisy?'

'Very well, I believe, and she and Kirsty seemed busy.'

'Daisy tells me that they are not short of cases. But you say you met her at the agency. Was this in connection with your investigation?'

Poppy smiled. 'I called in to ask Miss Cameron if she had any advice for a new detective.'

'It sounds as though you are managing quite well by yourself.' Maud returned her smile.

'I do have some help from another,' Poppy conceded, wondering again where Inspector MacKenzie was.

'Does one of the cases concern the man found murdered by the loch? I read about it in the newspapers.'

Poppy nodded. 'There's been another one since.'

Maud's large grey eyes widened. 'Another murder? Goodness, you have got off to a busy start.'

'I'm waiting for the police inspector to arrive and arrest the person I'm sure is responsible for them. But what were the other cases your husband mentioned to the journalist?'

'I will tell you one day, I promise. Here comes our hostess.'

Constance reached them, beamed at the two women and sat in an empty chair. 'I didn't realise you knew each other.'

'We don't – or didn't,' Maud said with a smile, 'but we're about to correct that oversight.'

Poppy remembered the conversation she'd had with Constance, when they had first discussed the missing bracelet. 'And Constance, I didn't realise you knew Maud McIntyre of the M. McIntyre Agency.'

Constance frowned. 'Lady Urquhart is Maud McIntyre?'

'The very same,' Maud admitted.

'I had no idea. Good heavens!' Constance smiled. 'How fortunate I am to have two lady detectives on my lawn.'

They chatted for a while about the party, and Constance told them how even more delightful it would be in the evening when yet more guests would arrive, with coloured lanterns strung in the branches of the trees and all the doors open with guests flowing in and out of the reception rooms and the gardens. And after a suitable rest, of course, the band would move into the ballroom, where chandeliers and candelabra would cast a warm glow...

Poppy began to feel restless. She took a quick peek at her wristwatch. It was almost half an hour since she had spoken to Constable Watt. Where was Inspector MacKenzie? What if the killer had got wind of the inspector's imminent return with the exonerated footman?

It was no good; she was going to have to confront him before it was too late.

Maud caught her eye and gave an almost imperceptible nod. She understood, Poppy realised.

Poppy got to her feet. 'If you will both excuse me, I have something to attend to.'

'Of course, my dear,' Constance said.

'We will speak again before the day is out. And Poppy,' Maud said, 'keep up the good work.'

Poppy smiled, then made her way round the house and towards the garage. She reached the door that led to the chauffeur's flat and knocked. Footsteps sounded on the stairs and the door was flung open.

'What now, my lady?' Charlie said, his voice gruff. 'I've told you and that police inspector all I ken about the murder of that bookie's runner.'

'There are still one or two questions, Mr Lamont.'

'Oh aye?'

'Yes. I think you know more about the murder than you've said.'

'Even if I do, I dinna ken what it's got to do with you, *your ladyship*.' His face flushed with anger as he looked her up and down in her shimmering gold flapper dress. 'You're nae a police officer. And anyway why would I want to kill the runner?'

'I've seen his notebook, Mr Lamont, and you are listed as one of his customers.'

'That's nae possible.'

'I've worked out the code,' she told him. 'CCTLCB is you.'

'Rubbish,' he said, but she saw him blanch.

'And what about Jack Finnie?' she went on.

'Who?' he blustered.

'Come now, Mr Lamont, you must surely know the poacher.'

'Och, him.' He shrugged. 'Aye, I ken of him, but I've had nae dealings with the fellow.'

'Do you know a young woman named Miss Strachan?'

'Nae another murder you're trying to pin on me?' he said grimly.

'She's not been murdered...'

'There's a mercy.'

'She's an assistant in a jeweller's shop in Edinburgh.'

'This is ridiculous. I've nae idea who you're talking about!'

To this last suggestion, his response appeared to be genuine. 'The young woman has claimed money from Lady Balfour for a non-existent item of jewellery.'

'Murderer; fraudster. What will you try to pin on me next?' He paused and his expression changed. 'I want to show you something I've found that will confirm Freddy's guilt.'

He stepped away from his door and closed it behind him. 'This way. It's in the garage.'

Warily, Poppy followed him round to the front of the old coach house. He opened the small door set into one of the huge double doors and walked in. She followed, leaving the door open behind her.

It was gloomy inside, with the only light coming from the door. The sounds of the band playing a lively piece and the hum of animated conversation and laughter faded into the distance. Constance's motor car stood to one side and a workbench stretched the length of the opposite wall.

Poppy's heart picked up speed. She should have told the

constable to inform Inspector MacKenzie that the murderer was Charlie Lamont. She could hear Inspector MacKenzie's lilting voice; he would warn her that confronting the man would be a foolhardy thing to do. And, looking at Charlie's scowling face as he beckoned her further inside the garage, she was afraid he was right...

'I think what you're looking for might be here,' said the chauffeur as he searched along the row of tools hanging from hooks on the wall. 'The murder weapon hidden in plain sight. You have to admit any of these tools could stove in a man's heid.'

On the workbench amid spare parts for the motor car lay a starter handle. The doctor, or was it the inspector, had said the weapon could be iron bar... Quietly, she lifted the long, cast-iron rod, felt its weight and gripped it tight. She would whack Charlie with it if he came too close. She couldn't afford to get hurt, with two murder cases to wrap up! Her professional standing would be in tatters before she even got started. Next time, she must think ahead; if there was a next time. Poppy straightened and addressed the back of the chauffeur.

'Is this what you're looking for, Mr Lamont?'

He spun round, staring at the heavy bar in her hand. 'What are you doing with that?'

'I think this is what was used to kill Henry Harvey and Jack Finnie.' She steadied herself.

He laughed. 'Well, whatever will you think of next?'

'I think you saw Freddy arguing with the runner by the loch and you took the opportunity to do something about the footman once and for all. You couldn't bring yourself to kill him. But a bookie's runner – well, that would be different. Who would miss a man like that? A common villain?'

'How could I see an argument going on at that distance? The whole thing is nonsense...'

'If you could point the finger of blame at Freddy,' she

continued, securing her grip on the crank handle, 'then he would be out of your way for good.'

'I canna stand here any longer. I'm busy. I've got to check the oil level on Lady Balfour's car.' He stepped forward and in an instant snatched the starter handle from her hand. He lifted the heavy tool above his head, his intention clear. 'Why couldna you just leave things well alone?'

Poppy screamed.

TWENTY-SIX

The door slammed open against the wall and in flew Major.

'*Major!*' she cried, backing away from the chauffeur. '*Get him, Major!*'

The dog gave a joyous yelp, bounded over to Charlie and jumped up at him.

'Get off me, you muckle beast!' Charlie tried to shake the dog off. Major, enjoying the game, became more excited, barking and running round the man. Charlie turned to lunge at the him, the starter handle gripped firmly in his hand.

Poppy felt suddenly, sickeningly, icily cold as the handle missed her dog's head by a hair's breadth.

'*Run, Major!*' she shrieked, jumping forward and jerking Lamont's arm holding the weapon. He swore violently at her and the metal tool swung down as the dog jumped up at him again. She heard Major give a sharp howl as he caught a glancing blow on his nose.

Poppy's blood boiled and, for a second or two, she and Charlie struggled together in some form of hideous *danse macabre*. Just as she felt her strength ebbing, a large shape at the door blocked the light.

Inspector MacKenzie pushed in through the small door and daylight returned. Barrelling into Charlie, he caught hold of him, pinioned the chauffeur's arms to his side and kicked the heavy starter handle away. It dropped with a thud to the floor.

'Now, Mr Lamont, that'll do.' He forced Charlie to the floor and knelt on the man's back as he addressed Poppy. 'Are you all right, your ladyship? You have blood on your bottom lip.' He pulled a set of handcuffs from his pocket and drew Charlie's hands together.

Poppy pulled the handkerchief out from under the strap of her wristwatch and dabbed at her lip with a shaking hand. 'I couldn't be better.' It was true – she *did* feel good. Shaky, but good.

She looked at Major. He sneezed a few times, but otherwise appeared well and exceedingly pleased with himself.

Inspector MacKenzie clipped the cuffs onto Charlie's wrists, then lifted himself off the man's back and helped him to sit. 'Mr Lamont, we know you killed the runner and the poacher.'

Charlie glared up at him. 'I dinna ken what the devil you're on about. I'll have you up for libel and assault.'

'I think you mean defamation, Mr Lamont.' Her pulse was still beating fast, and she was surprised to find her voice almost steady. 'In Scotland there is no distinction between libel and slander. Given that the inspector's statement is true, there can be no case. As to assault—'

'Thank you, my lady,' said Inspector MacKenzie. He turned to the chauffeur. 'Charles Lamont, you are under arrest for the murders of Henry Harvey and Jack Finnie. You are not obliged to say anything—'

'Bit late for that.' Charlie slumped, his back against the work bench.

'But anything you do say will be noted and may be given as evidence in a court of law.'

'What's the use?' Charlie groaned.

Constable Watt rushed in through the door, out of breath, and hastened to pull out his pocketbook.

'You're a bit late, lad,' Inspector MacKenzie observed.

'Sorry, sir,' said the flustered constable. 'I had to find the money to pay the taxi driver.'

Inspector MacKenzie shook his head. 'You should have told him to collect it from the police office.'

Charlie ignored Constable Watt. He glanced up at Poppy and then back to Inspector MacKenzie. 'You may as well ken it all. Honest Harry – that name's a joke – accepted a bet from me. The only time in my life I've gambled. And I won three hundred pounds on a double bet.'

'What is a double bet?' Poppy asked, curious.

Charlie shook his head. 'I didna ken either. Harry recommended it to me. Don't ask me how it works, but he said if two horses win in two different races, and are put together as one bet, I would get a greater payout than if I'd placed two separate bets. So on the Friday I gave him three pounds, an entire week's wages, to put on two horses on Saturday at nine to one – and I was lucky. I could hardly believe it. Enough money to pay for my wife's care without all the worry about the cost.'

'But why kill the man who the day before had paid you such a large sum of money?' Poppy asked.

'He didna pay me!' Charlie gave a bitter laugh. 'He couldna pay me. It turned out he hadna even placed my bet because he thought those nags had nae chance. I was already angry at that footman after my job. It's difficult enough anyway on a chauffeur's wages to pay the nursing home bills for Una...'

'How did you know that he and Freddy would be there?' Poppy realised she might be overstepping the mark and glanced at the inspector. Inspector MacKenzie's face showed no sign of annoyance, so she carried on. 'By the loch, I mean.'

Charlie drew a shaky breath. 'I keep a pair of binoculars in the sideboard. I like watching the birds. But I get lonely sometimes and the binoculars allow me to look from the window at what others are doing.' He glanced at Poppy. 'You guessed right, your ladyship. It was pure chance I saw Freddy and Harry by the loch that afternoon. The next step was easy. I determined to have it out with that boastful wee gowk of a footman and the runner. I went into the garage and took the crank handle. I wanted to show the pair of them that I meant business. But when I came out and saw Freddy walking back towards the house, I realised I was too late.'

Charlie paused to catch his breath. 'So I threw a bucket of soapy water over the landaulette to make it look as though I'd been busy washing her ladyship's motor car for a while, and when Freddy had disappeared, I went down to the loch. Harry was sitting there smoking, as if he had nought to do in life but enjoy the view. I told him I wanted a word with him and he told me to—'

The chauffeur glanced at Poppy. 'It's nae the sort of language I'd repeat in front of a woman and especially not a lady. He walked away laughing. I've never felt such rage. Before I ken it, I'd caught up with him and dunted him on the back of his heid. When he fell to the ground, I told him to get up and fight like a man. He didna, of course; he was already gone.' Charlie choked back a sob.

'Then I thought about my Una and what would happen to her if I were arrested for murder. I ken she couldna survive on her own and no one else would pay the nursing home fees. I sat on the ground beside the man's deid body. I hadna made anything better, but much worse. And then I realised I would swing for what I'd done and that I had to think of how to get out of it.'

Charlie blinked to try to clear his tears. 'Freddy has no one to support, no one to think of but himself, but he delighted in telling me, boasting of it, that one day soon *he'd* be the person driving Lady Balfour around. It was then I came up with the idea of putting the blame on him.' He looked at Poppy and said nothing for a few seconds, as though trying to work out how his plan had gone so wrong.

When Charlie failed to continue with the confession, she flashed a warning look at Inspector MacKenzie as he opened his mouth to speak, and gently prompted Charlie. 'Please go on, Mr Lamont.'

Charlie looked up at her from where he sat on the floor. 'That's about it. The following morning Freddy raised the alarm. No one thought the death of the runner was anything to do with me, until you came snooping, my lady.' He looked away from her.

'Where is Harry's post office savings book?' Poppy wanted to tie up the loose ends.

'You'll find it in the sideboard drawer, next to the binoculars. I thought if I could hide the fact he was collecting money, there was a chance of his death being written off as some sort of a mindless killing. My temper had cooled and I'd already decided I wouldna point the finger at Freddy. Well, not unless I had to.'

'And Jack Finnie?' asked Inspector MacKenzie.

Charlie grimaced. 'The poacher came here the next evening, said he'd seen me kill Harry. I thought I'd heard something when I was searching the fellow for the book I'd seen him write the bets in, so I took off. Finnie wanted to be paid for his silence. As if I had any money to give him! He wanted a sum down in cash – a ridiculous amount – and so much every month after. I couldna have that over my heid. So I told him I didna have that sort of money in the house, but I would get it and take it to his cottage the following day. You ken what happened next.'

'We do.' Poppy glanced at Inspector MacKenzie, who had stepped closer to the chauffeur. She raised a hand to tell him to wait. She wanted to hear Charlie's full confession for herself, here in the old coach house. Would he really have killed her? Once he was inside the police office, she would not be allowed in. 'Go on.'

Charlie shrugged. 'I thought nobody could possibly see me at Finnie's place. Just my luck that your ladyship chose that moment to arrive on the scene.' Charlie turned his head towards Inspector MacKenzie. 'I kent I'd have to silence her, sooner or later... I didn't like the idea, but I had to save my own neck. You understand that, don't you?' He passed a trembling hand over his forehead and swallowed. 'I couldna bear to think about what would happen to my wife without me here, paying the fees, but that's going to happen now, anyway. What a mess I've made of everything.'

'If that's all, Mr Lamont.' Inspector MacKenzie bent to help Charlie to his feet. 'You'd better accompany me to the police office, where you can sign a statement.'

As the chauffeur gained his feet, he suddenly twisted heavily to one side. Inspector MacKenzie's hat went flying as he jerked his head back and away from Charlie's forehead set on a course with his own nose. Constable Watt stepped forward to assist, caught the crack on his nose and went down like a sack of potatoes.

Poppy heard Charlie's rough exclamations as his forehead missed its intended target. Inspector MacKenzie shouted out something in Gaelic, which certainly sounded stronger than *goodness me*, as the two men wrestled. Major danced about on the outside, keen to join in but unsure how. Poppy stood, equally uncertain, for a moment or two.

Her eyes fell on the starter handle, lying on the floor where Inspector MacKenzie had kicked it. She picked it up. Advancing on the confused mass of arms and legs, she carefully selected the head of Charlie Lamont and raised the iron bar high.

As if he'd read her mind and keen to save her from arrest, Major Lewis jumped into action. His mouth wrapped around Charlie's leg, sending the chauffeur once more face first onto the concrete floor.

'What happened to Freddy?' Poppy asked, when Inspector MacKenzie joined her later on the terrace. Below them, the garden party was in full swing.

Constable Watt had recovered and discreetly taken Charlie away to the police cell in Culross. Major lay sleeping on the ground next to Poppy, having been praised, cuddled and rewarded with a sausage from the kitchens.

'The footman has been released from custody and is back at his duties,' said Inspector MacKenzie. 'Why do you ask?'

Oh dear, she thought, hoping that Freddy wouldn't soon have to be re-arrested, this time for an art and part role in his sister's crime. 'First, tell me what happened in Edinburgh when your colleague detained the jeweller's shop assistant.'

'It was as you suggested. Miss Strachan had mistakenly thought you were onto her little scheme—'

'But I *was!*'

'Aye, but not at that point. Not when you told her you were close to finding out the truth.'

'That's true.' She would concede that.

'She attacked your friend, Miss Macgregor, mistaking her for you, and when Mr Fraser came to Miss Macgregor's aid, in a panic she stabbed him too. Miss Strachan has been arrested for the attempted murder of both, and for fraud.' Inspector MacKenzie gave her a tired smile.

'Are you all right, Inspector?' Poppy asked, concerned. 'You weren't hurt in the fight with Charlie Lamont?'

'I couldn't be better.' The smile reached his eyes fringed

with their dark lashes. 'Now, tell me why the concern for Freddy Strachan? He is a free man again.'

'Prepare yourself, Inspector. Freddy Strachan and Miss Strachan are *brother and sister.*'

He raised an eyebrow 'Just so, my lady.'

She stared at him. 'What do you mean, *just so, my lady?*'

'I ken they are brother and sister.'

'Oh. Well then, I thought it was possible that Freddy might be involved in the jewellery fraud with his sister.'

'I am satisfied that he had nothing to do with it, and that the jeweller, Mr Campbell, also had no knowledge of her little game.'

'That is a relief. But how can you be certain that Freddy wasn't involved?'

'Apart from your insisting on his innocence all the way through this murder case?'

She smiled. 'Yes.'

'Miss Strachan promptly admitted everything. That it was her idea and she alone carried it out. There was no need at all for the third degree.'

Poppy became aware that curious glances from the lawn were being sent their way. The inspector was not dressed as were the other men, but it seemed more than that. Perhaps something was amiss with her own appearance.

'Is my feather still there?' she asked, putting up a hand to check the side of her headband.

'It's there,' Inspector MacKenzie confirmed, 'but not necessarily as it was when you dressed earlier.'

He was right. She could feel it was a poor, broken thing of a feather, bent at a right angle over her head.

'Oh well,' she said, plucking it from the headband, 'easy come, easy go.' She released it from her fingers. The feather floated down and tickled Major's nose. His nose twitched, but he slept on.

Inspector MacKenzie laughed, exposing that delightful dimple. And talk of her dressing earlier made Poppy realise that in her gold, tasselled flapper dress her bare knees were on show. She tugged at the hem, but it would go no further. Worse, she could now see that her thigh was exposed through a cunningly disguised slit at the side of the garment. What had she been thinking to buy such a dress and to wear it in broad daylight?

And worse again, her pulling at the hem had drawn Inspector MacKenzie's gaze to her knees and thigh. He looked up, their eyes met and he flushed.

'If you'll excuse me, my lady,' he said, picking up his hat and getting to his feet, 'I should go. I have a prisoner to take back to Edinburgh.'

'Of course.' Poppy rose. 'You know, Inspector, if Charlie will allow me, I will pay for his wife's nursing fees.'

Inspector MacKenzie looked surprised. 'Even though he was going to kill you?'

'Even though. His Una can't be held responsible for that.'

'That's verra kind of you. I will let the man know.'

She nodded. 'There is one final mystery to clear up, you know. The initials CCTLCB in Harry's code book.'

'Aye,' said Inspector MacKenzie. 'It was as well for me that the chauffeur confessed. Kindly explain to me how it was you worked out that the mystery initials referred to Charlie Lamont.'

'ELMTLPP!'

Inspector MacKenzie blinked. 'ELMTLPP is your answer to CCTLCB?'

'Yes. No.' She took a breath. 'That is, it's the code system used in the places where I shop. When my lady's maid, Elspeth, places an order for me, the entry in the order book reads ELMTLPP. Now do you see?'

'Not quite...'

'Poppy, dear!' Constance was approaching them. 'Word has

got around about your clever detective work and everyone is longing to speak to you. You simply must come down.'

'The inspector did a pretty good job too,' she said to Constance, with a smile at him.

'Oh, but of course he must also come and speak to everyone.' Constance smiled and nodded at Inspector MacKenzie, turned and walked back down the steps.

'Will you join us?' Poppy asked Inspector MacKenzie. 'No one will really mind about your lack of proper dress.'

'I'm no' so sure about that, your ladyship. But I have a job to do.'

'So I can't tempt you to stay and dance until that soft light in our midsummer night when sunset and sunlight fuse?' she asked teasingly.

He smiled back at her, but shook his head. 'I'm afraid not. But before I go, you were about to explain your reasoning.'

'ELMTLPP stands for Elspeth Lady's Maid to Lady Persephone Proudfoot.' She beamed at MacKenzie. 'So CCTLCB was Charlie Chauffeur to Lady Constance Balfour.'

'*Mo chreach 'sa thàinig!*'

They smiled at each other and fell silent for a moment. She couldn't let Inspector MacKenzie go just yet.

'Thank you, Inspector,' Poppy said, 'for all your work on this case, despite the annoying interventions from me you've had to suffer. You have been fairly patient, all things considered, and now I expect you're keen to return home to Edinburgh and your wife and children.' *I can be just as sleekit as Elspeth*, Poppy thought.

'I have no wife or children, my lady.'

That's good to know.

He hesitated, then said, 'I find it hard to believe that you have remained unmarried.'

'What can you mean by that?' Poppy's body grew suddenly very warm.

'I beg your pardon, my lady.' Inspector MacKenzie ran his fingers through his thick dark curls. 'I meant only that the gentlemen in your circle cannot be aware of what is in front of them.'

'I don't know if I should be flattered by that statement or not,' she said, taken aback.

Wordlessly, Inspector MacKenzie turned and descended the stone steps. At the bottom, he looked up to where she stood. A sudden smile lit his face and his dimples danced.

'I'm certain you'll have worked it out in no time.' He placed the fedora on his head. 'Until the next murder!' He strode away down the drive.

'Oh, absolutely, Inspector!' Poppy murmured with a smile.

A LETTER FROM LYDIA

Dear reader,

I want to say a huge thank you for choosing to read *Death at the Highland Loch*. If you did enjoy it, and want to keep up to date with all my latest releases, just sign up at the following link. Your email address will never be shared and you can unsubscribe at any time.

www.bookouture.com/lydia-travers

If you have enjoyed this first book in my new series, I'd be really grateful if you would leave a review on Amazon and Goodreads. I love to hear from readers, so please keep in touch through Facebook, X or Instagram.

Thank you!

Love,

Lydia x

facebook.com/LindaTylerAuthorScotland
x.com/LindaTyler100
instagram.com/lindatylerauthorScotland

ACKNOWLEDGEMENTS

My thanks go foremost to Julie Perkins, who is my first reader, sharpest critic and greatest support. I am also, as always, grateful to Joan Cameron, who has been with me all the way on my writing journey.

Special thanks go to retired detective Iain Souter for his cheerful and enthusiastic advice.

I am also grateful to the following friends for their help and suggestions on various matters: Sheila Gray, Deb Goodman, Margaret Owen, Rachel Stewart, Jon Tyler, Mark Wright, Vicki Singleton and Lynda Leslie.

My thanks, too, to the team at Bookouture.

Other influences on my writing include the work of comic genius, PG Wodehouse.

A small liberty has been taken with the date of midsummer. In 1924, 21st June was a Wednesday; I have changed it to a Saturday, as that is the day Lady Balfour wished to host her garden party.

Any mistakes are my own.

PUBLISHING TEAM

Turning a manuscript into a book requires the efforts of many people. The publishing team at Bookouture would like to acknowledge everyone who contributed to this publication.

Audio
Alba Proko
Melissa Tran
Sinead O'Connor

Commercial
Lauren Morrissette
Hannah Richmond
Imogen Allport

Cover design
Debbie Clement

Data and analysis
Mark Alder
Mohamed Bussuri

Editorial
Jess Whitlum-Cooper
Imogen Allport

Copyeditor
Angela Snowden

Proofreader
Catherine Lenderi

Marketing
Alex Crow
Melanie Price
Occy Carr
Cíara Rosney
Martyna Młynarska

Operations and distribution
Marina Valles
Stephanie Straub
Joe Morris

Production
Hannah Snetsinger
Mandy Kullar
Jen Shannon
Ria Clare

Publicity
Kim Nash
Noelle Holten
Jess Readett
Sarah Hardy

Rights and contracts
Peta Nightingale
Richard King
Saidah Graham